The Shadow of Polaris

D. L. Houpt

Edited by Ashley Chapman
Book Cover by D. L. Houpt
Illustrations by D. L. Houpt

To my mother, my daughter,
and the women who choose me.
This has always been for you.

Ursae

Canissae

Venia

Aquilae

The Narrows

The Mortal Realm

.

Chapter 1

The portrait mounted against the otherwise bare wall stared at me in pitiful silence. Jagged features of the late Queen Adria, so cold and hateful, pricked my skin with ice. How many nights did I stare into those menacing blue eyes and feel nothing? Now, as I awaited the verdict that could ultimately destroy my already feeble existence, I studied the canvas with such disdain. Her subtle cruelty was nauseating.

That resentful gaze held me captive. With her pointed chin tipped slightly up, her last words were a gut-wrenching echo. You're as much of a coward as our father. Sleek black hair, pulled tightly into a neat braid, followed the unending length of her slender neck. Cheeks, the shade of moonlight, hollowed just below the bone. I hated how much I resembled her. My hair was not nearly as pin straight, but just as raven black.

We shared the same forbidding eyes as our mother and the sharp, almost geometric cheek bones of our father. Beads of amethyst and pearl draped across the neckline of

1

her crystalline black gown. Two pale, delicate hands with long skeletal fingers clasped the gleaming hilt of a gun-metal dagger whose point was almost as piercing as the distaste stretched around her thin, white lips.

Part of me was glad she was gone, although I'd never speak those words into existence. I'd surely face the consequences. When that sudden illness consumed my sister, the realm grieved publicly, but rejoiced privately. Her reign of paranoia and destruction had finally, and most abruptly, ended. The future of Ursae now lay in the hands of Adria's successor- her twelve-year-old son, Vikar.

Although still only a boy, I truly believed his reign would far surpass that of his mother's. Vikar had inherited Adria's wisdom without her haunted cruelty and suspicion. Even as a toddler, faint ripples appeared beneath the surface of his small, rounded blue eyes. Vikar was a gentle boy, always curious about the world, always smiling shyly behind his mother's skirts.

When he was three, he fell incredibly ill. I spent many nights praying to the Gods that he'd not cross into their realm. Our family sent for healers from all four realms to find a cure for his ailments. When none were successful, Adria pleaded to our city's goddess, Polaris, to save her young son. She spent countless hours kneeling at the base of the temple, whimpering in the cloak of night. When she finally returned with stiff knees and swollen eyes, all the essence of hope was gone.

Against all odds, Vikar regained his strength and overcame the illness. Adria vowed to never allow him to fall ill again. Her love for her son, entwined with the deep fear of loss, grew so fierce it nearly destroyed her. She locked him away in an isolated wing of the castle so he'd never risk exposure to another illness. Little did she know resentment and hate for her spread through his heart like an infection, far greater than that he contracted as a babe. As each day passed, locked away in that castle wing, Vikar slowly retreated into himself, his blood stream infected with growing frustration and loathing for his overbearing mother.

The late queen's constant paranoia left our kingdom in crumbles. Hated by the other realms, isolated in a wasteland of snow and ice, we survived on meager scraps. Before taking the throne only five years prior, our people had thrived. The deeply rooted treaties our father, King Herald, had spent his entire reign working to establish, snapped in a manner of seconds.

Only minutes after Adria's coronation, she declared our allies to the east, Venia, and west, Canissa, fruitless and disloyal. She turned her back on vital trade agreements and, in doing so, sentenced our realm to a reign of hunger and hardship. With each passing year, as my sister's fears deepened, Ursae sank more and more into its snowy fjord until only the ghost of a great kingdom remained. The winters were harsher, the crops dwindled, and the livestock grew barren. The snowfall eventually became permanent, burying Ursae's resilience until it was snuffed out entirely.

"Lady Elpis. He's ready for you," a voice behind announced, breaking the chains my sister's portrait had seized me in. Breathing deeply, I turned my back on the once mighty queen and entered through the intricately carved oak double doors. A servant closed the doors behind me. Creaking wood broke the thick silence the way a scream hits packed snow, abruptly diffusing into the air. The throne room was brutally cold. Cobwebs and ash engulfed a fireplace on the left wall, lonely from years of neglect. The last time a fire roared beneath that mantle, Vikar had still been in diapers. Dilapidated bookshelves lined the right wall with forgotten ledgers, musty from years of decay. Wolf pelts, sprawled on the slate floor, led to a dais framed by two withered oak columns. A single gunmetal throne sat vacant and bitter atop the dais.

The remnants of my sister's reign still suffocated the room. Even with shallow breaths, my lungs struggled to filter out her very memory.

Vikar stood at the windows overlooking the castle's garden, now blooming only with crystalline ice. His hands crossed behind his back. The weight of the steel crown rested awkwardly atop his small head. His short black hair crimped at sharp, unnatural points. His compact frame drowned in a purple tunic with intricate silver beading along the hem. A boy pretending to be a man. Vikar sighed, his shoulders tense. A lifetime of trepidation already muted those small eyes, like jade tarnished with imperfections.

"I'm sorry Elpis, the Elders have made their decision," he stated firmly. His voice shook slightly, as if he battled to force the words from his tongue.

The four Elders served as the line between each city and its namesake immortal. They held council only in extreme circumstances, and when they came to their verdict, not even a king himself could oppose it.

They lived in a large temple with stark white towers penetrating into the endless sky on an island hundreds of miles from any coastline. The island itself was one cliff-line jutting from the sea, its jagged-edged precipice molded from thousands of years of erosion. At the entrance of the temple, four cloaked stone figures stood at least a hundred feet high with palms outstretched towards the immortal realm above. No mortal had ever entered the Temple of the Elders and returned. Only those who had committed catastrophic crimes passed beneath the outstretched arms of the cloaked, marbled giants. Just the thought of the furious waves crashing against the rocky bluff turned my blood to ice.

"The evidence against you is just too great. I tried to tell them, but they wouldn't listen. Their minds were made up before I could even try to convince them otherwise. It's their judgment that you murdered my mother. There is no alternative explanation." He turned to me, grief streaking down his narrow cheeks in little drops.

I sighed and dropped my gaze to the wolf pelt beneath my bare feet. The grey and white fur was coarse with age as it scratched between each of my toes. I couldn't imagine that this ancient, ratty thing had once had a soul. A life within those round, predatory eyes. When Adria and I were children, we would beg our father to tell us the story of how he'd taken down the mighty wolven king sent from the immortal realm with a single dagger. How he'd skinned the gigantic black wolf and its soldiers alive.

He'd sit us down in front of the roaring fireplace and I'd imagine the wolf pelts coming to life, dancing around the room, stalking their prey, howling at the moon. It was as if our father returned their stolen lives with each word he spoke.

Although the younger of the two, I never grew afraid of the violence and death my father spoke of in his stories. Adria would often burst into tears, begging him to tell us a better story- one with a happy fairytale ending. Who would have thought that now, nearly twenty years later, I would be the one shaking in fear?

Of course the Elders blamed me for the Queen's untimely death. Evil, conniving Elpis. The jealous younger sister who, even as a child, held death and darkness at her fingertips. I could hear Adria's voice again, echoing in my thoughts. It's pathetic, truly. All you've ever wanted was my throne and my title.

"Elpis, I'm so sorry. I tried, I really did." Vikar dropped to his knees, burying his head in his hands. With each heart wrenching sob his small body shook, and I found it more and more difficult to breathe.

"I know. I know you did what you could. I don't blame you, Vikar. It's okay." Reaching for him, I swallowed the realization of what my life would become- what awaited me outside of this throne room. I couldn't afford to crack right now, not for the sake of my nephew.

Vikar cried into his hands as I knelt beside him and placed my hand on his back. The crown atop his head gleamed in the cool moonlight shining through the arched windows behind us. Vikar was fated to live a life worse than mine. The stifling responsibility his mother left him shattered any hope of a normal upbringing, a normal childhood. He would never again get to be that carefree boy who loved imaginary adventures through the castle garden and crafting trinkets from twigs or old pieces of twine.

All he could be now was an empty king in an empty castle, illuminated only by an empty winter sky.

Whatever piece of my heart that had survived the cruelty of my sister shattered instantly as I watched this young boy struggle to withstand the force of his new title.

"The guards are waiting for you outside this room. They'll take you to the tower north of the city where you're meant to live out the rest of your days." He spoke in a low voice.

I gazed out the window at the new flurries of snow drifting down from the sky. The pines, just past the castle gardens, shivered as the nightly winter breeze caressed through their frosted needles. If not for the gaping hole forming in the pit of my stomach, I may have found the sight beautiful. Instead, it filled me with dread.

"I will never forget your kindness, dear Aunt. You were more of a mother to me than my own. You saved me," he said, finally regaining his composure and lifting his head high, the pain only narrowly hidden beneath the surface.

"You will be a great king, Vikar. Don't let anyone convince you otherwise. You're not your mother," I said, kissing him on the forehead just below that wretched crown.

He gave me a sad smile, tears pooling on his lower lashes. A knock on the door announced it was my time to go. I let my hand slip away from the newly crowned king and prepared to take my leave.

Tucking a stray strand of hair behind my ear, I wiped the few tears I had allowed myself to shed and tipped my chin up, mimicking my sister's portrait. If she taught me anything, it was to never let my enemies see weakness. I stopped in front of the tall wooden doors, not ready to face whatever awaited me. Placing my hand on the cold cast iron handles, I exhaled and glanced back at Vikar, trying to ingrain his likeness into my memories.

"The people of Ursae will thrive under your reign if you promise me one thing." My eyes sharpened, and a tinge of disgust hit my tongue. "Promise me you'll destroy every single remnant of that bitch from this realm."

The new king's mouth dropped to the floor. Not once had anyone spoken a word against Queen Adria. His gaping mouth curled slightly upward and a faint sparkle blinked from his eye.

"I promise."

With that, I swung the oak doors open and stepped into the fate decided for me.

Chapter 2

Habitually, for the last five years, I'd wake up and scan about the room. It seems like only yesterday that I had wiped the tears from my nephew's eyes and left my home for the last time. The circular room was bare and a terrible draft snuck through the hairline cracks of its dull grey stone. When I first arrived, only a large canopy bed with carved teak posters and matching armoire occupied the room. To lessen the severity of my perpetual isolation, I did all I could to create a home in the uninviting space.

Next to the neglected mantle sat an ornate wooden rocking chair with cushions that had lost their fluff years ago. Black velvet curtains draped over a window whose exterior glass was coated in a thick film of dust. Faded oriental rugs with pale grey and green hues provided some shield against the gritty stone flooring, but the frigid air still numbed my toes.

A large bookshelf, housing books with marbled front covers and faded leather bindings, leaned against the wall opposite the window. When I arrived at the tower, the shelves were bare. After my first night, however, when the existential dread of my confinement forced me to my knees in a melting heap, I awoke on the dusty, dark floor to find the case packed.

So many texts squeezed on each shelf that the knotted, varnished wood buckled slightly in the center. It was as if I had willed the books into existence simply from my tears. I never spoke of how the books miraculously appeared, and neither the guards nor my chambermaid seemed to notice.

A small knock on my door announced Hela's arrival. I groaned and slammed my pillow over my face. Another knock came, this time more forceful. Gods, she was relentless. She'd continue knocking until sheer annoyance and frustration alone drew me from the warmth of my bed.

"I'm awake." I tossed the thick down comforter aside and stepped on to the icy floor.

Brow wrinkled with irritation, I swung open the door to greet the small, bulbous woman in the corridor. I learned quite early in our acquaintance that Hela was an insufferable woman. Her small beady eyes drowned beneath swollen, crimson cheekbones. She possessed a beaklike nose, constantly running and red, and permanently puckered, chapped lips. She always wore her mousy hair in neat plaits coiled above her head. She wore a large grey shift and matching overcoat that buckled just above the waist. A wide leather belt was strapped around her midriff with such constraint that her broad belly looked as if it were about to burst through the iron buckle.

"Ah, Lady Elpis. It's a chilly one this morning. Best you bundle up, dear. How'd you sleep?" Her shrill voice resonated throughout the room with a sickening sweetness. Its tone never lowered from that high, piercing octave. She spat with each consonant she spoke, requiring her audience to take a handkerchief or tissue to their slightly damp face.

Every morning she'd enter as if a bright, gleaming

smile could melt the snow from the entire realm. She stepped to the window and threw the heavy black drapery open with a forceful whip of her thick arms, the skin sagging low and gelatinous beneath her biceps. Light bounced off scattered dust particles in radiant beams. Blinking, I forced my eyes to adjust to the winter morning sun and wiped the crusted sleep from between my lashes.

"Fine thanks, Hela."

She glanced over her shoulder and beamed a toothy, rotting grin my way.

Upon my arrival at the tower, Hela was the first and only person I'd seen. She had placed my hand in her sticky palms and relayed to me the strict rules and regulations of my sentencing. I remember vividly her crooked yellowing teeth as she recounted the number of lashings I'd earn myself if she caught me breaking even the slightest of rules.

"Coffee." Hela placed a cracked china saucer on the side table tucked between the rocking chair and the window. The bitter aromatics spread through the room in tendrils of steam as warm liquid poured from Hela's cracked carafe into the saucer. The scent of freshly brewed coffee was the only thing that made my sentence somewhat bearable.

She motioned for me to sit. I draped a thick woolen throw over my shoulders as I headed for the chair, clicking my tongue in irritation. Hela stepped behind me and began brushing through my hair. The pulls of the comb were rough and impatient. I sipped my coffee, trying not to shake the saucer with every wince as the wooden teeth of her comb snagged in my unkempt hair. Hela's sausage-like fingers scratched against my scalp and I hissed as she pulled the roots tightly into a plait mirroring her own.

When she finished, my eyelids stretched unnaturally high on my brow. She tucked the final loose hair behind my ear and asked, "Have you forgotten what today is, ma'am?"

The spray of verbiage was a warm, slimy mist against the nape of my neck. I jerked away from her breath and pushed myself up from the chair. Forcing a small smile, I shook my head and stepped into the bathing chamber to wash the film of sleep from my skin.

I, in fact, did not forget what day it was, having already started counting down the minutes until the final chime of midnight. Today marked my twenty-third year of existence. How I had managed to survive twenty-three years, I couldn't begin to know.

When I first arrived at the tower, I vowed I wouldn't see eighteen. I did everything in my power to assure that I fulfilled that promise: squeezing through the rusted metal bars mounted to the window to leap from the hundred story tower, scraping paint particles off the walls to brew into a deadly tonic, even shattering the small mirror into shards to slit my skin.

Each attempt was fruitless because of the enchantment bubbled around the tower. The wounds I inflicted healed immediately, the bars shrank around my abdomen, and the paint particles simply fizzled away in my brew. I received lashings from Hela's thick leather belt after every failed attempt. My sentence was forever. I'd remain in this tower until my hair turned white, my skin wrinkled into grey, and my soul eventually faded into nothing.

When I turned nineteen, I had given up on my promise, falling into a hopeless, never-ending cycle of mindless fury and inhibiting sadness. Sometimes fits of rage burned through me so fiercely, I smashed furniture and slammed my fists into the stone walls until my knuckles bled. At the sight of red splattered against stone, I'd begin pounding even harder until the mangled mess of bone and flesh no longer resembled my hands. As soon as the skin broke around white bone, the wounds miraculously closed and I'd begin again until my muscles cramped with exhaustion.

I'd slide down the wall and rock myself to sleep in a cold puddle of my blood.

Sometimes I'd feel sadness so deeply and become so paralyzed I had to look down at my limbs to reassure myself I hadn't turned to stone. Hours in bed turned into days that turned into weeks. Self loathing and pitiful grief consumed every part of me. Nausea washed over me at the thought of food, and my throat closed at the thought of drink. Just as I reached the point of withering into nothing, my sternum almost skeletal and my lips dried shut, the atrophied muscles would swell back to normal. The hollows around my eyes would grow shallower and shallower until they disappeared all together. When I finally willed my legs to move, I sat up and moved about the room as if I had just awoken from a restful sleep.

When I turned twenty, acceptance hit me so abruptly it felt as if a knife had plunged directly into my chest. My lungs contracted and pushed my breath out with a whoosh, refusing to expand again. The already too small chamber seemed to shrink around me until I crumpled. I folded myself into a tight ball, pulling my legs up to my chest and gripping my knees with white knuckles. Heaving and gulping for air, I begged my lungs to expand, pleading with the organs inside a body that had become so alien; the fleshy feel of it encasing my soul was unrecognizable.

Everything broke into pieces. Sheer panic took hold and didn't let go until everything that defined who I was fell away and I simply ceased to exist. My emotions froze over like the winter night air, leaving me a lifeless shell of my former self. Floating around the chamber like a spirit stuck in an endless haunting, with no peace in sight, I never did quite recover from the shock that had shoved itself down my throat.

Now, here I stood, one year older.

I turned the faucet all the way to the left and splashed a palm full of water across my face. A crisp numbness webbed over my cheeks from the harsh cold. With my eyes still closed, I blotted away adhered beads of water with a scratchy, faded towel. Not until slight tingles poked beneath the surface of my numbed brow did I open my eyes and look in the dirty mirror. The reflection staring back at me was a monstrosity. Dark circles were bruised under dull eyes that had once glinted like sunlight dancing atop a crashing wave. Cheeks bones, sharply geometric, but never entirely skeletal, reached high on my face.

"Lady Elpis," Hela scowled behind me. She stood in the door frame, hands on her hips, a dribble of saliva glistened on her chin. "You know the rules. Never walk away from me while I'm speaking to you."

I sighed, throwing the towel on the counter beside me. "Sorry Hela, I'm not really in the mood for conversation today."

"I simply don't care what you're in the mood for. Rules are to be followed no matter how we're feeling. Would you kill someone if you were simply feeling angry?" She unclasped the belt around her waist, letting the rolls of her rounded midsection free.

"I guess it depends on the person," I smirked, brushing by her. Sweaty fingers gripped around my biceps, pulling me back into the bathing chamber.

Hela's eyes lit up, fire blazing behind her pupils. "Did you just back talk to me?"

The moment she pulled the belt from its straps across her overcoat, I knew what was about to happen. It was so frequent these days. When you're constantly shrouded in self hate, inflicted pain grows tiresome. These daily lashings were more of a chore than they were a punishment now.

"I've grown bored with your constant nagging, Hela. If you're going to hurt me, just get on with it. I can assure you that nothing you do feels worse than what I've already

13

done to myself," I hissed.

She tsked and shook her head, motioning to kneel before her. "A rule breaker must always be reprimanded. How else will they learn?"

I stared at the wooden hair brush resting on a rickety table beside the bathtub. Hela moved as fast as a slug. I'd reach it before she could straighten the leather against my back. My palms itched at the thought of beating her bloody with its blunt wooden handle. I could kill her where she stood, bash her skull in and dispose of the evidence out the hundredth story window. She would be unrecognizable by the time I finished.

"No, Lady Elpis. You know the punishment." She snapped her fingers, sweat beading beneath her armpits.

If I killed her, the Elders would send another. Someone worse, I was sure. The hair brush called my name, beckoning me toward the violence it held. I sighed again and dropped to my knees. As horrible as Hela was, I couldn't kill her. As much as the voice in my head screamed her battle cries, I wouldn't follow through. Aside from the lashings, Hela was harmless. A broken woman with a taste of control. Given her appearance, I assumed she'd had a harsh upbringing. Dealing out punishments was her way of coping with whatever monsters appeared when she closed her eyes at night.

She'd answer for her cruelty one day. Today, I was tired. I was sick of existing. Sick of fighting to live. I'd long ago given up, and as pathetic as I felt, as disgusted as I was, I couldn't find the energy to perform the deliciously violent acts that played out in my mind. So, I knelt before her and let her expose the flesh of my back to the cruel morning air.

Her breathing was ragged as she stepped back, readying the leather belt in her right hand. I shut my eyes and pictured my home. Vikar's round jade eyes looked through thick ivy as he crouched around the castle's courtyard, searching for winter mice.

When the first crack of her whip seared across my back, I began counting down from fifty. Losing myself in Vikar's joyous laughter as he discovered a nest of young mice huddled and warm around their mother.

Forty-nine. Crack!

Vikar stroked the pelt of the mother mouse, her squeaking babies rolling and nuzzling into the warmth of her belly.

Forty-eight. Crack!

I knelt beside him, watching the toothless grin widen as the mice sniffed at his finger.

Forty-seven. Crack!

The memory shimmered, throwing me back into a glimpse of reality.

Forty-six. Crack!

My body jerked forward on impact, skin howling against the cool air. I bit my lower lip, refusing to expel the agonizing pain from my body. I wouldn't let her hear me cry. Hela could feel powerful, inflicting pain across my back, but I wouldn't allow her satisfaction along with it.

Forty-five. Crack!

A tear rolled down my cheek, across my lips, and dripped from my chin. I watched it splatter against the tile, the water dispersing. What once was a perfect, spherical bead in the corner of my eye now scattered across the floor. I lost count as the whizz of the whip struck my back, then retreated and struck, then retreated over and over again. My flesh was moist as blood oozed from the open wounds and mixed with the salty tears now pooling at my knees.

"Have you learned your lesson?" Hela asked through shallow gasps. I imagined movement was hard with a body like a globe. It always surprised me how forceful her lashings were.

"Yes," I said, my voice a mere whisper.

Hela's heels clicked across the tile as she stopped before me and knelt to meet my lowered gaze. "It pains me to have to do that, dear. I wish you'd simply just follow the rules. It would make our lives much easier."

I looked up at the monstrosity disguised as a woman and nodded, unsure how to respond. Nothing would make it easier, because I didn't live. I existed. I floated through time in the palm of my jailers, helpless to their will.

"Now, your wounds will heal in a few minutes. I'll draw you a bath. You're soaked in sweat." She sprayed her words across my brow.

She stepped to the clawfoot tub in the middle of the room and turned the brass knob. The roaring sound of streaming water filled the room. Plumbing in the tower never produced entirely hot water. Its piping traveled up a hundred stories until it reached my bathing chamber. Losing most of the heat as it traveled upwards, the water would exit the faucet lukewarm.

Relative to the frigid temperatures outside, though, a soak still eased some of the shiver beneath my skin. Hela uncorked a small glass bottle of lavender oil and let a few drops hit the surface of the bath. Immediately, the bite of the oil pinched my nose and coiled around the room in lustrous tendrils. Waiting for the bath to draw, she re-looped her belt and smoothed her overcoat back in place. Smiling at me, as if we'd just finished a friendly conversation, she turned the knob back in place and started for the door.

"Lady Elpis, dear, happy birthday," she gleamed at me one last time before disappearing into my bedchamber.

I undressed my remaining clothes as swiftly as I could, gingerly rolling the dull ache from my shoulders. With a soft click of the door, I heard Hela quietly exit my chambers. Pulling the tight plait atop my head undone, I let my brittle black hair fall around me. I needed to cleanse myself of her essence completely. All reminders of the pain she so casually imposed. Happy birthday. The words were sour on my tongue as I sank into the water and stared at the ceiling, counting the stone tiles as if there'd be fewer than yesterday morning. Aside from the small brown spider who had spun her web in the fold where the ceiling met the wall, I was entirely alone again. I reached for the ragged sea sponge resting in a ceramic dish next to the tub and scrubbed time off my skin.

Chapter 3

After I dressed into an ankle-length grey shift, I twisted my hair into a neat low bun at the base of my neck and pinned it in place with a black pearl comb. It was the one piece of my old self I held on to. My mother, Queen Signe, wore her hair in the same manner with the same comb. When she died, I snuck into her chambers and took the comb before my older sister could steal it away. I didn't get the chance to really know my mother. Adria and I weren't old enough yet to understand the concept of death when she was taken from us.

Her travel party was attacked, returning from a council meeting with our allies in Aquilae. Although the attacks outside our walls were few and infrequent back then, monsters from the north ambushed the party only a few miles from the city gates. The lone survivor returned, my mother in pieces trailing behind him on a rickety wooden cart.

The black pearl comb was the only piece of jewelry I ever wore, and all the shifts hanging in my armoire were various shades of grey. Color was forbidden for prisoners of Ursae. They deemed us unworthy of the rich violets and blues of the realm. When I first came to the tower, I clung

18

to the memory of those colors. I forced myself to imagine the satins and tulle textures of the gowns I left behind. It grew too painful to hold on, though, and I eventually allowed the memories to vanish from my mind.

Now the only colors I saw were fading shades of grey, black, and blinding white reflecting off the fallen snow outside my window. I barely could remember the interior of the castle, save for the library and that hideous portrait of my sister. Occasionally, when my shields were down, a memory would boil up unexpectedly. Sometimes it was the scent of weathered, aging books. Other times, it was the flicker of a sconce mounted neatly to a row of shelves. Or it was as simple as the sound of a page turning, its sharp edge slicing against my fingertip. Total, unyielding grief would surge through me with a flash of one of these memories, and I'd take weeks to lock it back into its ugly cage within the depths of my stomach. I'd refuse to speak or eat until I transformed back into my comfortably numb armor.

There was a light knock on the door. I pulled the cast iron handle open, expecting Hela with a tray of tasteless porridge ready for another round of lashings. It wasn't Hela, however. The abrupt swing of the oak door startled the guard standing in front of me. He took a step back, the sharp muscle of his jaw contracting with unease. The tunic and matching trousers he wore fit a little too comfortably against his rigid body. Large silver buttons lined the quilted tunic and neat, tight seams ran snugly down each leg of his trousers.

A small leather holster with a sheathed silver dagger hung loosely at the hips. I imagined myself lunging for that dagger and slitting the guard's throat before he'd even make a sound. With a weapon like that, I could cause a lot of pain to a certain chambermaid. He shifted uncomfortably in his black leather boots as I realized I was staring, my eyes gone menacing with the darkness of my thoughts.

"Uh, sorry…" I lowered my gaze to the floor, trying to

suppress the violence now erupting within me. He peered around the hallway, his short blonde hair whipping side to side with the motion of his neck. Ensuring no one was within earshot, he said, "Erm.. Lady Elpis, this is for you."

His voice was practically a whisper in the silent hallway as he passed a small, lavender box to me. My eyes widened. The painted wooden box, only slightly bigger than my palm, was wrapped in a silk ribbon of the same shade.

"What is this?" I questioned, trailing off in suspicion. What if this was a trap? A test of obedience? If I accepted this gift, Hela would surely appear at the end of the corridor and punish me for breaking another of the rules in my sentencing.

"I.. um.. I was only told to deliver this package," the guard stuttered. I plucked the box from his hand as if it were searing hot. He took a shallow breath, gave me a rigid bow and hurried down the hall, disappearing through the entrance of the stone stairwell. My eyes trailed back down to the box that still rested on my outstretched palm.

Was I dreaming? Panic punched me in the gut and I frantically searched around the corridor, reassuring myself that no one had seen this strange interaction. I was alone for now; however, I expected Hela to return any minute with breakfast.

Slamming the door of my chamber, I clicked the lock behind me and set the box down on my bed. Wearily kneeling before it with delicate, shaking hands, I untied the smooth ribbon, letting it fall limply off the painted wooden box. The paint on its sides was slightly granular under my touch.

As I lifted the lid, I realized I hadn't exhaled since the guard had disappeared into the dark shadow of the stairwell. My lungs burned for release, and I forced myself to let go of the tension now building in my throat. Inside was a roll of parchment, only an inch long. I straightened the scroll and read the contents of the note. Its lettering was plain and each curve of the words was sharp and concise. It said:

Happy birthday Elpis.
I wish I could give you your freedom back,
but a breath of fresh air will have to suffice.

There was no signature at the bottom. I didn't need a signature to know who had sent me such a gift. How could I forget the lavender packaging? It had been over five years since I'd seen my nephew and I swallowed those feelings down the best I could. With each passing birthday, he'd leave a small wooden box outside my bedchamber with a trinket crafted from scavenged buttons, thread, and twigs. It had been two years since I'd thought of his gifts. How much had he grown? Did he outgrow those awkwardly monstrous feet? Had the features of his face deflated from that rounded juvenile shape? Did he ever get to smile and laugh and enjoy being a child? Or had he permanently become the grim and serious king the North demanded he be? No news of the realm ever reached within these tower walls. Everything could be entirely different or entirely the same. All I knew was that the snow still fell, and the ground stayed frozen beneath an endless sheet of thick ice.

Now, as I brushed a fingertip against his ink words, I hoped, for the first time in an incredibly long time, that he was well. I rolled the note back into its tiny scroll and slid it beneath my pillow. What could he have meant? A breath of fresh air will have to suffice. I tilted the box and peered inside. Beneath where the parchment scroll had been rested a small silver key atop a purple velvet cushion. Its bow webbed into an intricate, bulbous shape.

The rich color of the cushion brought back a rush of memories from my home: the heavy drapery in my old bedchambers, the stifling tunics that decorated the royal guards, even the velvet cushions of my father's study. I looked away, flushing the images before they broke me.

I took the key in both hands and examined its surface. The metal was cool to the touch as I rubbed it beneath my fingertips. What could this possibly unlock? Bringing it up to my face, its long stem nearly touching the tip of my nose, I inspected it as closely as physically possible. There was an almost microscopic word engraved into the bit of the key. Squinting, I struggled to sound out the letters: vincio.

Even more mystified, I sat back on my heels. I'm not sure how long I stared at the small silver key. However, the midmorning sun soon faded to a lazy afternoon. My mind raced with questions I likely could not answer. What was Vikar trying to tell me? Where did this key lead? The words of his note repeated over and over in my mind. Frantic, I stood from my knees. The bones of my kneecaps creaked as I stretched the joints upright.

I had expected Hela hours ago for breakfast; however, she didn't return. Placing an ear on the bedchamber door, I listened for the heavy clip of her slippers down the corridor. There was nothing but silence.

With a click from the lock, I pulled the door open. A dirty footprint in the hall was the only sign that the guard had been there earlier in the morning. Hela never missed a meal. Panic strung through me with the chime of the tower's bell. What if she somehow had discovered my gift and was heading straight to the Elders? Pacing the room, thoughts of Hela's conversations with the Elders and her suggested punishments raced through me. My heart pounded beneath my chest, banging against my bones with such force I had to place a hand there in order to keep it from breaking free. Minutes drew by at a snail's pace. With each tick of the clock mounted above the doorway, I grew more restless.

Outside my chamber, there was utter silence. Not even the footsteps of the guard on duty echoed through the corridor. Something strange was happening. Suddenly, the furthest sconce down the hallway extinguished. Then the next. Then the next. Each sconce down the narrow corridor extinguished one by one until a thick, dark fog consumed the space.

I slammed my door shut, locking it behind me. Leaning against the entryway for support, my legs quaked. I scrambled for the key and my nephew's note, tucking both away within the internal pocket of my shift. In attempts to hide from whatever invisible force blew out those torches, I shrouded my head beneath the throw and plopped into the rocking chair.

Sliding down the back of the chair, I looked out at the lazy afternoon light. The tower was tall enough to see the skyline of my city's uniform stone buildings encircling the snowy peak of our sacred mountain. Not a single cloud floated in the piercing blue sky and sunshine beamed down on the barren white flatlands that separated the tower from the city. A faint shiver ran through me. I inhaled and closed my eyes. I had to be dreaming. This wasn't real. I had to be dreaming. Clamping my eyes shut and focusing on my breath, I counted down from fifty. At some point, around thirty-eight, a restless, unforgiving sleep found me.

Chapter 4

A clock chimed from the floor below, jerking me awake. Sweat soaked through my shift, dampness clinging to my skin. A burnt orange glow illuminated the window. Dusk had arrived and still Hela had not returned. The air was too quiet, too thick.

Maybe this was the fresh air Vikar was talking about.

Maybe he had sent the guards away and somehow distracted Hela from her duties as my chambermaid.

Maybe this was my chance.

All I had to do was sneak down the stairwell, find the entrance of the tower, make it through the front courtyard undetected, and slip out of the gate. If this feeling I had was real, there'd be no one there to catch me.

If they caught me outside of my chamber, however, I'm not sure what the Elders would do. My sentence forbade them from ending my life and the ward around the tower prison healed any physical wounds I received fairly rapidly, but would I risk the wellbeing of my nephew? I swallowed hard at the thought of Hela beaming one of her sickening smiles as she cracked her leather belt against his exposed back.

Surely she wouldn't dare touch him. He was the King of Ursae, after all. Pushing myself up from the chair, I stepped to my armoire. I already had a cloak and a pair of leather boots. A few years ago when I was still plotting my escape, I persuaded a guard to find me a pair during one of his trips into the city. Of course, the pair he returned with were a size and a half too big and already discolored from years of wear. Until now they had sat in the back of my armoire, hidden beneath old scraps of fabric and pelts, waiting for their perfect moment.

This might be my only chance to steal back my freedom. What awaited me in the flatlands was worth the risk, and Vikar's title meant he was untouchable. Besides, with no evidence they couldn't pin my escape on him. This taste of freedom shrank the surrounding walls. Inhaling deeply, I felt the stifling air fill my lungs to their limit. I'd sneak into the flatlands and disappear. My entire life had been spent in the shadows. Slipping away unnoticed would be easy.

Maybe I'd return to my city, maybe I'd travel to the southern coast. The taste of salty, tropical air was sharp on my tongue. The crashing of waves against bleached white sands roared in my ears. I'd travel to my city, then when the time was right, I'd disappear to the south. For good.

I made my decision as I grabbed the cloak off of its hook. With quaking hands, I slipped on the old boots and laced them tightly up to my ankles. Checking once more that the key and scroll were safely tucked away within my shift, I wrapped the cloak tightly around myself and silently pulled the bedchamber door open.

The only sound in the dim hallway was the squeak of leather against the balls of my feet. I lit a sconce and unhooked the torch, extending it in front of me. My shadow, illuminated by the dim glow, flickered as I snuck down the

hallway to the winding stone steps the guard had frantically disappeared down earlier. Peering around the corner
into the bleak darkness, I confirmed I hadn't been seen.

As noiselessly as possible, I crept down the marble
stairway and plunged into its forbidden depths. The winding, cavernous staircase amplified the sound of my shallow
breathing as I descended, my destination below shrouded
in darkness. I plunged deeper and deeper into the heart of
the tower, the flame casting shadows with each winding
curve of the stairwell.

The last step led me to a pointed door. The aged wood-
en panels, fastened by sturdy cast iron bolts, were knotted
and withered. Warm light snuck through the cracks between each slat, projecting streams of crimson across my
face. The rusted iron handle and small keyhole glared at
me.

With shaking hands, I wrapped my fingers around the
metal, hesitating before turning the handle.

I could feel my knees buckling beneath me, as if they
were warning me of my stupidity. Maybe I should retreat to
the safety of my chamber. Maybe this was a mistake. The
warmth of seaside sunshine licked against my forehead. A
salty breeze draped around me. I was so close to my freedom. So close to a life beyond these foreboding walls.

I clenched my fists. There was no turning back. I made
it down the steps without being detected. I could do this.
Digging within the folds of my shift, I pulled the key out
and inserted it into the door.

Heavy footsteps from the top step echoed through the
chamber. My heart fluttered so fast I thought I may have
had a heart attack. Peering back up the winding steps, I
could see the faint glow of a lantern filling the hallway
with candle light. If I stayed here any longer I would be
seen, and then Gods know what would happen to me.

"Who's down there?" a female voice at the top of the
staircase called. Hela. Acting out of sheer terror alone, I

gulped down the bile that was now rising in my throat and turned the key. The lock clicked and the sound of metal grinding against itself echoed through the small chamber as I turned the handle and faintly pulled the door open.

"Answer me. Now! Who's down there?" the chambermaid repeated. Hurried footsteps descending the staircase broke the silence.

Without checking behind the door, I stepped inside and clicked the handle locked. Leaning against the rickety old door, my knees buckled as my back slid down the wooden frame. The air was warmer than in the stairwell. A fire blazed brightly to my left, filling what looked to be a kitchen with honey colored light. A wooden butcher's table took up most of the floor space, where pots and pans of all shapes and sizes dangled from iron hooks mounted on the low ceiling. Across from the hearth, crisp moonlight beamed through three dust covered windows made from honeycomb glass plates. Bunches of thyme, rosemary, and sage hung to dry above the windows, and baskets of garlic and onion bulbs sat next to the hearth.

I didn't dare move, let alone breathe, as Hela reached the bottom step. The scuff of her boots paused and the swing of a lantern scanned the stairwell. Time seemed to stop as the door handle rotated. This was it. Frozen with fear, the punishment for leaving my chamber flashed before my eyes. Searching the room frantically, I pleaded for somewhere to hide. The light from the hearth illuminated every crack and crevice of the kitchen. There was nowhere to go. I was stuck.

Just as I tiptoed to the butcher's block and swiped the small dinner knife from the surface, I heard the door handle click. Locked. Hela shoved against the door, assuring herself that the lock held in place, and continued back up the stairwell. The only sound was her ragged breathing as she struggled to push her large thighs up the hundreds of steps.

I pressed myself into the butcher's table as temporary relief fell over me. I was safe for now. The guards would be alerted and the tower would go on lockdown the second she discovered my absence upstairs. It was only a matter of time.

An ember popped in the hearth as I glanced out the moonlit windows. The kitchen overlooked a frozen courtyard flooded by pale moonlight below. Snow fell in silent flakes and gathered on the outer sill of the glass panes. A layer of ice covered the barren ground of the courtyard and whittled brown vines of clustered wisteria whipped against the brick outer walls. A single arched gate marked the exit of the tower yard.

Tucking the dinner knife into the fold of my cloak, I started towards my escape. The window slid open with a gentle push. Dead vines wrapped around the exterior just to the left of the sill. If I could reach the thickest one, I'd be able to propel down the wall to the ground below.

Pulling my cloak tighter around my body, I hooked a leg out the small window and shimmied my way onto the outer ledge. Outstretching my palm, my fingers brushed the frozen wisteria. I took a small, hesitant step further off the ledge until I could comfortably grasp the full width of the vine. Praying to the Gods, I gathered the hem of my shift and leapt, clinging to the wisteria in desperation.

The vines groaned under my weight and I squeezed my eyelids shut, preparing to be ripped from the wall and to fall to my death. Miraculously, I remained where I was. I counted to three, then kicked my boot into the next vine down and let gravity take my weight.

Again, the wisteria wailed in protest. Any second I'd be torn from my perch. Breathe Elpis. One foot after the other, I repeated to myself, lowering my other leg a little further. Repeating the motion again and again.

I was still about ten feet above the snow-covered

ground when the vines ended. My ungloved fingers now clenched around the icy dead growth. My knuckles shrieked with a numbness that spread up my hands. I'd have to jump to the ground from here, or I'd surely freeze to death.

Imagining what Hela would say when she found me frozen in the wisteria above the courtyard, I pictured her throwing me a dazzling smile, hoping the warmth of her expression would melt away the icicles drooping from my frozen lashes. She'd give everything in her power to unthaw and revive my lifeless body, only to whip me back into obedience herself.

I willed my fingers to uncurl themselves around the vines one by one, steadying my breathing as best I could between my chattering teeth. Counting to three, I jumped backward. My stomach rushed into my chest, slamming into my lungs and forcing the air out in a shallow gasp. One second I was in free fall; the next, my boots slammed into the snow bank below, sinking deep into the powder. Digging myself out of the mound, I rolled on my side and vomited. Somehow, I was alive.

For a moment, I laid on that cold dry ground. I'd survived. The starry night sky was a wonder above me. I inhaled the fresh winter scent. No longer confined to the stuffy, mildewed air within the tower chamber. With powdered snow in each fist, I let it slip through my fingers. This cold was familiar, like a distant childhood memory. Silence, insulated by compact snow, brought a peace I hadn't experienced before in my life. With overwhelming relief, I gripped the soles of my boots with my toes to ensure I wouldn't take flight.

An owl hooted somewhere in the distance. I hadn't heard such a somber tune in years. Tears welled in my eyes as I realized I'd forgotten the sounds I longed to hear when I felt trapped in my family's cruelty. Escaping to the forest to hunt or hike was my only remedy for the all too familiar loneliness of my life.

For the first time in a very long time, a weight lifted from my lungs and breathing felt natural. Felt effortless. I allowed myself a few more moments of bliss until the icy ground numbed my cheeks. Only then did reality snap back into place. I sat up, quickly scanning my surroundings for any guards. There were none.

Flipping up the large wool hood of my cloak to shield my face from the harsh night air, I started towards my freedom. Clear, crystalline ice dripped from the heavy iron gate at the courtyard's entrance. Using my entire body weight, I spun the wheel of the gate mechanism and watched the metal lattice rise. When it had risen just enough, I ducked my head under and slipped into the bleak night that led outside of the tower walls. As I strutted down the pathway lined with evergreen firs, not once did I glance back at that Gods-forsaken tower.

Chapter 5

It wasn't long before the panic set in. I snuck out of the tower with only a wool cloak and old leather boots to shield myself from the elements. I had no money and only a rusty dinner knife for protection. With each crunch of snow beneath me, regrets built thicker and thicker. It was far too late to go back. Once Hela had returned upstairs, she would've checked my bedchamber. Guards must already be searching the tower grounds for me.

The temperature continued to drop as I carried on, pausing every so often to listen behind me. Nothing but silence scattered through the flat barren land. Nothing but snow extended as far as my eye could see. Packed ice melted into the night horizon in streaks of purplish hues. I peered into the deep blackness of the sky above and located the four twinkling points of the Crux. If I continued to keep it straight ahead, I could reach Ursae by dawn.

The tower was due North of the city, constructed at the dead center of a vast flatland extending for miles. I wasn't sure how much distance I'd need to travel before reaching the forest out-skirting the city walls, but based on the journey when I first arrived, I'd guess it would take me most of the remaining night. If my pace slowed even the slightest, I'd risk having to travel in daylight. Aside from a few withered shrubs, there was nothing but a vast openness surrounding me. I would be exposed with the next morning's dawn. Pulling my cloak tighter around my torso, I trudged on, my boots sinking deeper into the packed snowy ground.

The wind howled in my ears as flurries fell heavier and heavier into the frozen darkness. Sharp numbness crawled up my toes and into my legs. With a clenched jaw, I swallowed down the alarm rapidly bubbling up the back of my throat and broadened my stride. I needed to get across this unending stretch and find somewhere to weather the encroaching blizzard.

I walked for what felt like hours, keeping my eyes on the blurry horizon. Coaxing my frozen limbs to propel me forward with the thought of shelter. A sudden crack in the ice behind me halted me in my tracks. Another. And another. With each crack of the ground, the air electrified with a tense current.

The footsteps paused only a few feet behind me. My pulse raced beneath my wrists. Reaching for the dinner knife sheathed beneath the folds of my cloak, I whirled around to find a nightmarish face piercing through the snowy darkness.

Grey, frozen flesh drooped from a pale, cracked skull. Lines of dagger-like teeth filled a swollen purple mouth. The smell of the creature percolated into the air. As it hit my nostrils, I had to pinch myself to keep from gagging. With a shaking palm, I outstretched the knife in the creature's direction just as its deep, crimson eyes locked on to me.

A quiet groan skimmed over its extended lips as it

crawled on four gangly limbs towards me. The hands and feet resembled human extremities far too closely. A cold sweat dripped from my brow as it lurched towards me, its limbs cracking unnaturally. I swiped at the creature as it grasped a sharp clawed hand towards me, the red glow emulating from those sunken eyes flickering like a flame.

It pounced for me with a deep, animalistic howl and I flung myself backwards, slipping on the ice. The back of my skull slammed against the packed frozen ground, knocking the air from my lungs. With blurred vision, I scrambled away as fast as I could.

I wasn't fast enough. It started towards me again, wrapping its long, skeletal fingers around my ankles. Its smile revealed rows of fang-like, yellowed teeth, and I could smell its putrid breath. A paralysis grew within me, extending to each of my limbs as it climbed over my feet, up my legs, across my torso, and on to my chest. Pain bubbled beneath my skin with each piercing grip of a claw.

Sobbing silently, I willed my hand, still clenching the knife, to move. Overcome with fear, I remained frozen. A rotten, grey tongue slid around its lips as it stroked my cheek with its claw. I begged my muscles to move. Still, I remained limp beneath the creature's weight. It leaned down and slid its frozen tongue across my cheek, licking up the salty tears that now streamed down my face. I needed to move. Gripping my fingers around the dinner knife, the sharp pinch of broken skin beneath its blade pulled me from my paralysis.

With all of my might, I jerked away from the creature's touch and plunged the dagger into its temple. A thick, black ooze dripped from the wound and splattered across my cheeks. The creature went limp instantly and fell to the side, its shriveled mouth only inches from my face. I suppressed the scream now roaring through my body and pushed its dead limbs away from me.

Its carcass rolled off with a squelch, and that same

black substance pooled beneath it. I jerked upright, pulled the knife from its skull, and sprinted away as fast as I could. What the hell was that?

The soulless red eyes smoldered beneath my eyelids with each blink. I ran until my lungs pleaded for air, and my calves cramped with exhaustion. Finally, my muscles gave out, and I stumbled to my knees, sobbing and vomiting with sheer primal terror. Stories of dark, undead creatures lurking through the flatlands were told in the shadows of the city as ghost stories not for the faint of heart. However, I had thought them just that. Stories. Until tonight. I spat out the remnants of bile and forced myself up. I couldn't risk staying in one place any longer. Locating the Crux once more, I continued running.

The sky had transitioned to a deep shade of periwinkle when I finally stopped to catch breath. Placing my hands on my knees in support, I wheezed. The frigid air burned in my lungs as I struggled to take in enough oxygen. Between the loud heaves of my chest, a faint yelp echoed through the air. Grasping for the dinner knife again, I scanned the surrounding snowpack.

A slight flurry of black caught my eye as I squinted through the blizzard, praying to the Gods it wasn't another of those creatures for me to fight off. The yelping continued as I took a few steps towards the wriggling mass in the distance, stretching the knife out as far as I could in front of me.

As I got closer, the mass appeared soft with spikes of dark fur. A short tail slapped at the frozen ground from one end. It cried in fear as I approached. Dropping the knife, I fell to my knees, stroking my fingers delicately down its little furry spine.

A sharpness erupted at the tip of my index finger as two little fangs pierced my skin, drawing a bead of blood. Yellow eyes and a snout, no longer than my thumb, snarled up at me. I jerked my fingers away as the tiny creature nipped at me again. The little mass of fur and fluff was a wolf pup. Judging by her size, only a few months in age.

"What are you doing out here, little one?" I said, again reaching towards the jet black pup. She rolled on to her stomach and pawed at my hands. A soft warning to keep my distance. She growled weakly, deep in her belly.

"It's okay, I won't hurt you. Let me help you, little one. Where's your mother?" I said, keeping my voice calm. After another attempt warily reaching my index finger towards her fur, the pup nudged at my palm with a cold, wet nose. A matted, bloody mound of fur lay limp in the near distance. The pup smelled of the black ooze that seeped from my previous attacker. The poor creature was alone in this world, orphaned and lost. That made two of us.

"It's okay. You're safe."

She tilted her snout, sniffing the scent of blood stained on my hands.

"I won't hurt you. I promise. It's okay."

I stroked down her fragile spine as she wriggled toward me, the yellow of her eyes bouncing moonlight across the frozen land. Craving my warmth, she crawled into my outstretched arms. Slowly, I wrapped my hands around her belly and lifted her to my chest. Her delicate bones protruded from beneath a pelt of silky, thick fur.

As I nestled the little creature into my cloak, a jolt of electricity channeled through me, emulating from my feet to the crown of my head. The current sparked through my chest and I nearly dropped her from the shock. She poked her head out from beneath the thick woolen fabric and gazed up at me, her eyes gleaming in wonder.

"You felt that too, didn't you, little one?" She huffed in response and buried herself beneath my cloak again, curling into the warmth radiating from my chest. I chuckled and stroked her soft, juvenile fur until her breathing evened into a uniform rise and fall. Clasping my cloak further up my neck, I continued forward, keeping a watchful eye on my surroundings, hoping to catch sight of the pup's littermates. There was nothing but silence and snow.

By the time the tree line of Ursae came into view, a flame of crimson licked across the horizon and the indigo winter night had turned a shade of burnt sienna. I sped for the trees, heart pounding as the golden sun of dawn crept closer to the horizon. As the last shadow of night faded away, I dove for cover under a row of tall balsam firs. Panting, I curled up in a bed of dead, snowy pines and stroked the wolf pup who had stirred.

"We're safe, little one." She peeped from her wool cocoon and yawned widely. "For now." I chuckled and scratched behind her ear, my pulse normalizing. As we watched the sunrise together, it hit me suddenly that this was real. I wouldn't wake up in my tower bedchambers. Freedom tasted warm, like a sun ray across my cheeks.

The pup nestled into the crook of my neck, huffing deeply as she closed her eyes. I stroked her fur, welcoming the comfort of my new companion.

"I wonder if you have a name."

She leaned into my touch. Opening her eyes, the yellow amber glinted in the new dawn light. She had powerful eyes. Blazing eyes. Eyes that felt as old as time. They reminded me of a glimmering, golden star, orbiting across the northern sky.

"Arcturas. That's what I'll call you." I poked the tip of her wet, spongy nose.

Huffing lazily, she tucked her ears back and fit her head against mine. We stayed there for a little while, curled together beneath the shelter of thick firs. The branches were deep enough to block the snowfall and harsh whistling wind. Eventually I dozed into a shallow sleep, the image of those horrendous red eyes chased away by the warmth of the tiny creature nestled against my body.

Chapter 6

When I awoke, the sun breached high in the sky and the nighttime frost had melted in droplets from the branches above. Crawling out from our makeshift den, Arcturas and I stretched the sleep from our limbs and continued on our journey. A mourning dove cried in the distance as we trudged through the damp forest. The ache of my empty stomach and burn of my throat was a reminder that I hadn't had a meal since the morning before last.

Arcturas sniffed at my boot, urging me to follow, and trailed through the thick, misty morning. The wolf pup led me to a clearing full of deep brown undergrowth. She curled around trees and tucked under branches with heavy, fresh snowfall. A small stream meandered through a bramble covered embankment and fluorescent fish bubbled against its gentle current. Winter birds cooed and squawked from the bare, slender branches of colossal pines that lined the glade. Sunlight from the late morning sky beamed through the tree canopy in spurts of crisp, cool light.

I scrambled to the stream and dropped to my knees, frantically gulping down palmfuls. Desperation overpowered the frigid burn of the icy water sliding down my throat. Gasping for air and finally quenched of my thirst, I sat back on my heels and let the wintry sun radiate across my cheeks. I hadn't experienced the world like this in so long I'd nearly forgotten it. She was an old friend that'd lost touch. A chorus of winter finches sang a peaceful melody that ebbed and flowed around me, raising the hairs across my forearms.

I couldn't suppress the visions of my father on our frosty morning hunts. How he'd guide my bow to our prey with steady hands. Hands that swallowed up my little mittened fingers around the bowstring.

"Take a deep breath. Let the energy of the bow string connect through your fingertips. Feel it deep in your heart," he whispered.

My boots melted into the snow, rooting into the frozen earth below. When I was ready to let my arrow fly, it hit the mark straight on.

Narrow beams of sunlight washed over me as I lost myself in time. I was finding a version of myself I used to know. A version of my father I loved the most, whose patience and gentle strength could fill even the deepest of voids within me. I wanted to stay there forever, just him and me, in that peaceful time when my mind was whole and my head was filled with hopes and dreams.

Arcturas moved to sit next to me and lapped at the stream. I'm not sure how long I sat letting the sunlight bask against my brow, but when I finally opened my eyes, warm tears streaked my cheeks and my lips had curled into a peaceful grin. The chill of the night melted with each beam of light, taking the image of those demonic eyes with it. The earthy, sweet taste of freedom splashed across my tongue as a small piece of my old self ignited beneath my surface.

A patch of chokeberries poked through the freshly powdered snow of last night's storm. Wiping my knees, I plucked a handful of its black, beady berries and tossed them in my mouth. The tart plum-colored juice stained my fingers as I continued to feast until the entire bush was nearly bare. Berries alone wouldn't sustain me forever, but the ache in my stomach had dulled enough for me to think more clearly. Arcturas nipped at my heel as if reminding me that wolves can't live off of chokeberries either.

"You're probably hungry too, little one. I'll try to catch us some fish. Don't wander off too far," I said, bending over to unlace my boots. Sliding my feet out and pulling the hem of my shift above my knees, I waded into the glacial stream. My toes instantly numbed from the icy current whirling around my feet. I forced my shaking limbs still while I waited for the iridescent trout to slip between my ankles.

A lone fish paddled by my curled toes and I struck. Grasping for the fish with my outstretched hands, I snapped for its slithering body. The scaled creature slipped right through my fist. After three failed attempts and many loud curses, I finally caught one- only a few inches in length.

Tossing the fish to Arcturas, I began my hunt again while she tore into the scaly flesh. When I finally lost feeling below both of my knees, I had four small fish to roast. I cleaned and gutted them near the shore, then started off to find some kindling for a fire. Being in the wild like this felt natural. It brought ease to my broken mind. As a child, every once in a while my father and I would sneak through a hole in the city walls to spend the day together. He taught me everything I knew about survival.

When I was eight, he gave me my first dagger. When I was ten, he gave me a bow. I'd spend hours in the court-yard, practicing my aim at apples stolen from the castle stores. I was determined to be the best, hoping that he'd notice my skills. After months of practice, my arms exhausted and sore from long days of practice, I could hit every apple in the courtyard.

One day, my mother and sister were searching for winter mice when my aim struck true. Neither one cared to even glance my way, but my father clapped his hand on my shoulder with a big bushy grin as he applauded the hard work. His pride was all I ever needed. With him by my side, I couldn't care less about my sister and the Queen.

As I began throwing twigs and sticks I'd scavenged into a pile, Arcturas sprinted to the heap and pulled one out to play with. She shook the twig about as if it were the scruff of her prey, until the wood snapped beneath the pressure of her fangs. When it became too small for her to pick up, she moved on to another, leaving only wooden shards.

Dusk appeared, and I hastily built my fire. The moon not only brought blinding darkness, but it also brought a deathly cold. Clumping the kindling beneath a stack of twigs, I flicked my dinner knife against the piece of flint I'd found beneath a patch of thick brambles. Embers shot at the kindling and fizzled on impact. It took a few tries before the grass lit, but when it finally did, I tossed the rock to the side and leaned in close to feed oxygen into the weak flame. Once the fire radiated enough heat and light, I skewered the fish filets with the remaining twigs and roasted them above the flames. Mouth watering, I rotated the meat for an even cook.

The aroma of cooked fish wafted around us as I tossed Arcturas two of the skewers. With sharp, predatory teeth, she devoured the meat in seconds. Ripping pieces off my own skewers, I savored each warm bite. In the tower they had served me tasteless sludge and stale bread. Not a single southern spiced chicken or ale stewed beef compared to the delicate flavor now swirling around my tastebuds. The flakes of fish, spiced with fresh night air and smoky pine, melted on my tongue.

Arcturas tucked her oversized paws beneath her and peacefully dozed off, letting the heat from the fire warm her exposed, full belly. Wiping the grease from my fingertips on my stained, ratty shift, I pulled the flaps of my cloak tightly together and closed my eyes too. I kept the fire roaring. If the guards had searched this far for me, they'd assumed the smoke was a hunting camp. It wasn't uncommon for bands of hunters to spend a few nights in these woods.

The unease melted away with the chill of the night. Maybe it was the endless days I'd spent in the woods or the memories I'd made with my father, but the soft rustle of rabbits and the quiet tune of the night birds soothed my racing mind. I closed my eyes, letting the memories flow in again. I fell asleep to the deep chuckle of my father, reliving each fleeting second we'd shared.

Chapter 7

The scent of blood assaulted my nose. I cringed at the sounds of breaking bones and squelching flesh. Thick grey smoke swirled around me and I shielded my eyes from the glint of fiery flame in the distance. I struggled to breathe, the smoky air searing a trail of pain down my throat. Clenching the hilt of the tarnished longsword I held in my bloodstained hands, I ran. Tendrils of black hair escaped from the plait hanging down my spine and tickled my cheeks. Every muscle in my body throbbed in utter exhaustion.

With every crack of bone beneath my boot, I advanced closer and closer. Just as the pyre came into focus, the sky shifted abruptly to a deep, endless black. Darkness entrenched me. The great flames roared higher, but no light radiated across my face.

I fell to my knees.

It had begun.

Suddenly, cold, rough hands wrapped themselves around my ankles and pulled me back. My skin screamed as the hands dragged me against dead flesh and bone. The earth of the battlefield rushed past me. Claws pierced the tops of my feet with a pain so excruciating my vision blurred in crackles of black.

Sobbing, I raked at its grip. I begged it to let go; the words poured from my mouth in waves of frantic gargles. The unseen force stopped short and I skidded to a halt. I couldn't breathe through the pain of my raw skin and mutilated feet.

The temperature dropped around me and a pair of menacing red eyes glared at me from the surrounding blackness. A silent sob escaped my lips as I tried to pull my limp body away. With an inhuman speed, the beast leapt at me. Squeezing my eyes shut, I shielded my face with my forearms from the impending death racing towards me.

Chapter 8

Engulfed in darkness, I jerked awake and reached for the dinner knife that rested beside me and swung at that unseen beast. Arcturas stirred from her sleep and sniffed the air. Sensing my terror, she threw her tiny body towards me. Her little claws scraped against my thighs as she jumped to my lap and began licking my cheeks, the scratch of her tongue wiping away salty tears that fell.

Short, shallow breaths escaped my lungs as I struggled to regain control of my body. The black, starless sky was caving down on top of me and I thrashed and wailed beneath its weight. A piercing nip at my fingers brought me back to reality. Arcturas whimpered through fangs latched onto my skin. The pain of her bite pulled me up from beneath the depths of a stifling panic and I heaved full, gasping breaths.

She licked the now blotched red skin of my palm and nuzzled into the fold of my elbow. A dream. It had just been a dream. There was no monster waiting in the horizon's darkness. The snapping bones beneath my feet transformed into twigs. Stars rekindled in the stretch of unforgiving black overhead. I wiped the tears from my eyes and gazed into the cooling embers of our fire.

Smoothing back the stray hairs falling around my face, I apologized to my little companion. Arcturas nudged me until I stroked down the length of her spine. Wiry black fur was poking through her adolescent coat. Curling into the warmth of my lap, she settled back into sleep. Clasping my still shaking hands together, I looked up at the night sky. The countless stars speckled across the stretch of blackness glinted with a fluidity that seemed to ebb and flow with the soft caress of a silent wind. I wondered if this same sky beamed down on the immortal realm. Or did they have another galaxy of stars to wonder up at in the late hours of the night?

There was a time, thousands of years ago, when mortals and gods walked the Earth hand in hand. Stories of love and mortal consorts solidified the peace between the two races and all existed harmoniously. The bond we had with our gods, however, disintegrated when the goddess Tethys discovered her husband's plan to run away with a mortal chambermaid.

In a fit of rage and deeply rooted jealousy, Tethys slaughtered her entire mortal court, including her faithless husband, splaying their bodies from the outer fortress walls. It is said that the affair caused her undoing, and she spiraled into a mania that has since imprisoned her mind. When the immortal leaders of the other realms caught wind of Tethys's murderous spree, they broke our partnership.

Leaving a council of four, nearly immortal, elders to act as their emissaries, the Gods retreated to their separate realm. Despised by the other immortals, Tethys stole away into her fortress, plotting the downfall of the mortal realm with vigorous revenge. Without the protection of our namesake gods, the monster attacks increased. More and more mortals disappeared outside of city walls. Before my sentencing, it was not uncommon for men, women, and even children to vanish.

Shuddering at the thought of Tethys's army of beasts and the monsters that lurked in the shadows of our realm, I forced my mind to silence and shut my eyes.

Hours crept by and finally, the quiet dawn appeared. Splashing a handful of spring water across my face, I extinguished the remaining coals and buried them. Arcturas, with newfound energy, zoomed through the clearing, chasing snow mice back into their burrows.

We traveled for miles through the forest, stopping to sip from the stream or pluck a handful of berries. Grey wisps of clouds gathered overhead, marking the approach of another snowfall. The pines thinned and eventually cleared away altogether. In their place, a weathered stone wall towered over us.

The wall, constructed of huge bricks molded together with a thick layer of mortar, extended into the sky hundreds of feet. Crippled turrets scattered across its length with tattered, faded flags carrying the signet of the northern goddess- a single pointed star. We'd finally reached Ursae. Arcturas let out a growl of excitement and took off down the pathway lining the edge of the wall, her tail bouncing with each kick of her hind legs.

"Wait!" The hem of my cloak trailed behind me as I sprinted after her. She leapt down the trail faster and faster until blurring into the horizon. The bricks continued on as I followed the prints of her tiny pads. The city wall finally gave way to a cavernous, dark tunnel. Arcturas sat before the entrance, her pink tongue hanging loosely out the side of her open mouth and tail swiftly brushing fallen flurries from side to side.

"You couldn't have walked with me?" I panted, wiping my clammy brow. Sweat pooled in the creases of my armpits as I fought the urge to collapse.

Arcturas simply glanced at me, then took off down the tunnel. Grumbling with aching calves, I started into the darkness after her. The tunnel stretched through the width of the city's outer walls, at least a mile in thickness. City folk spread fables of the giants who'd carved the wall from a mountain top thousands of years ago. In reality, the first people of the north devoted generations upon generations to its construction. Only a small, glowing speck of light marked the entrance on the horizon. Water droplets gathered on either wall and slowly trailed to the paved stone floor. Fortified metal gates at each quarter mile of the tunnel were raised, allowing free passage into the city. Never in my life had those gates closed. Never in my life had they needed to be. It would take a sea of monsters or men to penetrate the tunnel into the city. And even then, they'd have to face our people. City folks- men, women, and children alike, we're all trained as warriors from their first steps to their last. The Northern Realm was infamous for our fighting ability. Rugged and harsh from the cold, the other realms kept cautious allies.

A chill whipped through the darkness as Arcturas and I traveled deeper and deeper. A rat, giving a startled squeak, scurried across the tip of my boot as I took a step. Jumping back, I watched it scamper into the shadows behind us. We continued on. With each step, the daylight of the city's entrance grew brighter.

Approaching the tunnel's exit, I shielded my eyes from the searing contrast of the white, late afternoon sky. We stepped out of the darkness. Flipping my hood over my eyes, we wandered down a rickety cobblestone street towards the heart of the city. Ursae had once been a glorious, northern fortress with marvelous stone carved towers jutting over lively city squares. Guards stood watch along gilded turrets, embellished with massive amethyst flags floating permanently beneath the inexhaustible winter

wind. Scents of various roast meats and vegetables filled
the air at the merchant's market, with spices from every
corner of the realms for sale. The air was electric with the
buzz of a flourishing kingdom.

The Temple of Polaris was the beating heart of the
realm, its walls carved out of the mountainside that lived
at the city's very core. A statue of our patron goddess
stood hundreds of feet tall. Her long, trailing robes delicately wrapped around her curved frame. Outstretched
in graceful arms was a broadsword- its hilt carved with
an intricate crystalline pattern. Atop her head rested an
iron crown, its apex as sharp as a dagger, with a single,
four-pointed star carved delicately at its center. The star
was the symbol of the North, representing the celestial
body that guides us to it- the vertex of the night sky in
which all other stars rotate around. The marble goddess
stood guard over thousands of jagged steps snaking up the
mountainside to the summit temple. A large pyre with a
constant flame overlooked the city at the temple's highest
point. The flame blazed as long as the bond between our
realm and our namesake goddess remained intact.

Although the flame still burned brightly, a beacon in
the wintry haze, the city had begun to crumble and die.
The gilded turrets- now tarnished. The markets- now
feeble and cold. And the temple- now sinking back into the
earth. It had been five years since I'd walked these cobblestone streets, and all that was recognizable had vanished
entirely.

Arcturas and I started towards the center of the city,
passing crumbling stone homes with deteriorating wooden
rooftops. I wasn't entirely sure where we were going, but
we needed to find shelter from the approaching storm, and
soon. Judging by the darkness of the clouds lurking in the
distance, we wouldn't just see a light snowfall. Temperatures would reach dangerous lows, and we'd be subjected

to harsh blizzard conditions.

The cold had already set in; I could feel it down to my bones. Exhaustion from my trek across the Flatlands and the cruel reminder from my stomach made me desperate. The logical side of my brain told me to stay away from city folk or local inns; however, the animal side told me I needed to take the risk. I would die out there. Then, this grand escape would've been for nothing. I'd practically be doing the city guards' job for them.

Warm light of a hearth radiated from weathered glass windows of a tavern across the street. Further investigation proved the bar to be fairly empty and quiet. With its old, rickety wooden door and dusty window panes, the city guards steered clear of this type of place. I guess this'd have to do.

Securing my hood below my eyes, I pulled on the heavy front door, and we stepped inside. Gods, please keep me from being recognized. Shaking the snow from her pelt, Arcturas scampered to the hearth and curled by the warmth.

"Hey! No animals allowed in my establishment." With her bloodshot protruding eyes, the barkeep glared at me and pointed a long skeletal finger towards the wolf pup.

"I'm sorry," I said, pulling my arms from the cloak and draping it over my arm, "we just need to warm up, then we'll be on our way."

The tavern was empty, aside from a fat, red-faced man who teetered on his barstool. Sipping from his pint, he glanced at me and belched loudly. Ale dripped from his mouth as he grinned. I grimaced and he returned to his pint. At least I didn't have to worry about him recognizing me.

The barkeep was an ancient-looking woman with deep wrinkles creasing her forehead. Her brows arched permanently and a long nose curved over her small, thin mouth.

"That thing better not cause any trouble." She scowled

and continued polishing a glass chalice. The final bit of cold leaving my skin, I pulled a rickety stool next to the now sleeping Arcturas, and settled into the warmth. The barkeep tucked her polishing rag into her flour stained apron and poured a chalice of spiced wine. Motioning for the drunk to finish his drink and leave, she limped over to the hearth.

"I can't pay for that." My gaze lowered to the floor. I let the loose strands of hair fall in front of my eyes, attempting to conceal my identity. The barkeep's eyes softened slightly.

"On the house," she croaked, pushing the wine into my hands.

Grasping for the chalice, I drank deeply. The nutty spice burned my throat.

"Thank you," I choked out between gulps.

"So...What's your story, girl? You got a name?" Her voice was as withered as the skin of her cheeks. I sank lower into my chair, hiding my face in the flickering shadows.

"It's Elpi- erm Ell, ma'am. I was hunting out in the woods and got caught up in a storm. I found her alone. Something had attacked her mother and littermates. She was the only survivor. I couldn't just leave her stranded," I said, pointing to Arcturas, who was now sprawled across the warm floor. The barkeep eyed us, silently scanning me from the too-big boots on my feet to the matted black hair of my bun and bruises forming.

"Alright...Ell..., where's your hunting gear then?"

"What?" Stuttering, I looked around the tavern, now empty. I hadn't noticed the drunk leave. Rickety wooden tables with broken, mismatched chairs tucked beneath them scattered about the room. A single candle flickered on each tabletop, casting shadows across the faded, cracked walls. At the archway leading into the back kitchen, a small, gangly rat chewed on a slice of stale bread, its cheeks puffed with crumbs.

"Well, if you were hunting like you say, where's your weapon? I don't know many hunters who'd go out in this weather unarmed and in merely a shift with boots three times too big." The barkeep raised a brow and tucked her withered hands into her apron pockets.

"Oh, um, I was rushing to get back to the city and I must have left it in the forest accidentally. And this is all I can afford, if you must know." My gaze lowered to the deep red liquid swirling in my chalice. I prayed to the Gods she didn't see right through me.

"I see." She scratched her long, jagged chin. "Well, finish your drink and get going. I'm closing up early to prepare for the storm and I 'spose you best be getting home to your family."

I nodded, gulping down the rest of the wine. Dreading the freezing cold awaiting me outside, I shivered and stood. At least I'd had a short bit of reprieve.

"Thank you for your hospitality," I said, trying my best to smile at the ancient woman. Something like pity flashed across her eyes as she inspected my ratty, grey clothes. Large, bloody gashes from the flatland creature's attack ran up my calves and a purple bruise had surfaced on my left cheek.

"Judging by those frail little arms of yours, you're probably hungry," she said, eyeing my wounds. I shook my head, but the grumble of an empty stomach gave me away.

"From the looks of you, I'll bet you have nowhere to go. I don't normally entertain beggars, but I 'spose you can stay in the spare room upstairs, girl. I don't want no trouble. There's some mutton stew in the kitchen on the stove and a jar of chicken livers for your little beast on the shelf in the pantry." She stood from her seat, decrepit knees cracking and straining as she straightened them. "Bathing chamber is upstairs, at the end of the hall. Wash all that mud off. I don't want you tracking anything into the spare room."

"Thank you, but I couldn't," I said, securing the laces of my boots.

"Don't be stupid, girl. If you don't stay here, without anywhere to go you wouldn't make it through the night with this storm," she said.

The barkeep had a point. I had no options. I'd have to trust in this total stranger or face the unrelenting elements.

"If you insist..." I trailed off, realizing I didn't catch her name.

"Frya." She grunted as she locked the front door, dimmed the oil sconces and began slowly ascending the dusty stairs in the far corner of the tavern. "I expect you to be up and ready to work in the morning. Oh, and next time you're trying to hide who you are, Lady Elpis, might I suggest coming up with your story beforehand, eh?" She chuckled and disappeared into the shadow of the second story.

My jaw dropped to the floor. She had recognized me. Should I take the risk or slit her throat while she slept? Under no circumstance would she report to the city guard. Was her hospitality a trick? I glanced out a dusty window, inspecting the street for any sign of the guards. Maybe she had sent the drunk to fetch them. If that were the case, they'd be here any second.

All was quiet and still outside as snow whipped across the glass. My stomach grumbled louder. I was out of options. Arcturas grumbled in her sleep at my feet, content in the warmth of shelter. If we left now, we wouldn't last long. Even if we stayed hidden from the guards, we'd freeze to death in this cold front. Glancing out the window once more, I scanned the sidewalks for any sign of commotion. Not even a lone guard patrolled the street. The smell of mutton stew simmering in the kitchen and the crackle of firewood held me captive. I couldn't bear the thought of going out again. Sighing, I rose to my feet. I'd stay for the night, but keep my cloak close and my knife even closer.

Trailing into the kitchen, I ladled a serving of thick brown stew into a chipped ceramic bowl and pulled a tarnished spoon from the drawer beneath the spice rack. Searching the pantry, I found the jar of chicken livers, scooped a few on to a cracked tea plate, and returned to my seat by the hearth.

Arcturas stirred from her peaceful sleep at the smell of the raw livers. Setting down the plate for her, I slurped up a spoonful of stew. The wolf pup devoured her meal instantaneously and returned to her peaceful slumber. I sat and savored mine, keeping my eye on the window. Each spoonful tasted better than the last. It had a rich flavor with hints of cardamom and clove. The velvety tenderness of cooked carrots and potatoes offset the tough texture of the mutton. Cherishing the warmth now settling into my stomach, I sat back and rubbed my eyes, a heavy sleepiness washing over me.

Licking the last remnants of the stew from my spoon, I set my bowl in the kitchen and began up the stairs, Arcturas nipping at my heels behind me. The second floor of the tavern was a long, drafty hallway lined with doors. Oil lamp sconces projected shadows in the crevices of the alcove. An open doorway a few doors down to my left marked the guest bedroom.

I crept to the bathing chamber at the end of the hall, and softly clicked the door shut. Frya had laid out a pair of faded brown trousers and a white tunic, worn with tears. Peeling the remnants of the grey shift from my aching body, I gazed in the mirror, taking inventory of the gashes and scrapes I'd accumulated throughout my journey. Large swells of bruising protruded from my abdomen. Wincing, I touched each tender spot. My body had taken more of a beating than I'd realized. No wonder the old barkeep took pity on me. Turning on the faucet of the stained tub, steam revolved around the hot stream until it clouded the entire room.

I stepped into the scorching water, embracing the sharpness of the heat against the bottoms of my feet. How long had it been since I'd soaked in a truly hot bath? Sinking up to my neck, I tipped my head back, half expecting to see the stone tiles of the tower's bathing chamber. Instead, beige ceramic tile lined the ceiling. I laughed and counted each one. There were more tonight than there were before.

A sudden rush of emotions escaped from that locked away piece of me, and I broke into hysterics. I had lost so much of myself during my imprisonment. I had become a stranger to my body. Now that I was free, I wanted to remember her. I hoped that one day the empty carcass of flesh I'd become would swell back to life with the woman I used to be. I prayed that one day it wouldn't be painful to think of her.

She was a woman who truly saw the beauty of the world in kaleidoscope shades of countless colors and hues. A woman who felt deeply and thoroughly with her entire soul and who fought, tirelessly and unyieldingly for those that she loved. Including herself. I wanted to know her, to feel her coursing through my veins once more.

Hushing my sobs beneath my now raisin fingers, I took a deep breath and tried to regain composure. Quiet freedom like this leant room to outbursts of feelings I'd worked so hard to suppress. I pulled the black comb from my hair, letting it untwist from its low knot, and began working through the snarls with my fingers. Focusing on one task after another kept my mind locked down and under control. I scrubbed my nail beds until not a speck of dried blood or dirt remained. I polished the grimy stains off of my skin.

When I was thoroughly clean, I dressed in the scratchy old clothing and tiptoed off to bed, floorboards creaking beneath each step. Greeted by Arcturas, who had slid beneath the yellow quilted covers of the small twin bed, I locked the door behind me. The room had a single window that overlooked the snowy, dark street below. Checking once more for guards, I peered out through its frozen pane. The only motion was that of the heavy, blanketed snow fall.

On the nightstand, a single candle flame quivered in the drafty night air. I laid my cloak and boots next to bed and slid the knife and my key beneath the flat, feather pillow. Climbing in, springs squealing beneath my weight, I let my exhausted limbs, now swollen from the heat of the bath, sink into the cotton mattress. A warm little body curled against me beneath the covers. The rise and fall of her delicate chest quieted my thoughts until our breath was in sync. The two of us drifted into a peaceful sleep. We were far from being safe, but I was far away from the tower. I had made it. Just as that key had unlocked my freedom, it had unlocked something within me. Truly, this was a breath of fresh air.

Chapter 9

Sun gleamed through the guest room window as I awoke with crusty lashes and aching muscles. I had slept so deeply it was as if I'd awoken from the dead. Rubbing my eyes and stretching limbs now speckled with dark purple bruises, I threw off the covers and started towards the window. The cobblestone of the street was now covered entirely with snow and a deep, frozen breeze whistled through the draft between the panes. Arcturas curled her spine and yawned widely.

"Good morning, little one. Looks like you slept as well as I did." She sniffed towards me, shaking her thick pelt. All was quiet in the house, save for the popping of grease in a skillet downstairs. Combing tendrils of hair into a bun atop my head, I stepped into the hallway with the looming aroma of pork belly and sausages. Arcturas zoomed down the flight of stairs, nearly losing her step and crashing to the bottom. A faint chuckle and the clank of a metal spatula echoed to the second floor.

"Ah, you're awake," Frya said, smudging grease on

her apron as I entered the tavern's main room. Each set of chairs was flipped onto their tables and the floor was swept. It was only an hour or two after sunrise. I wondered what time Frya had started her day. She flipped the slices of pork belly with a sizzle and began cracking eggs into a wooden bowl.

"I hope you're hungry. I went a little overboard with the cooking this morning. Your little companion is gonna love the extra servings I made for her." She smiled brightly, no trace of the cold, witchy woman from the night before. Arcturas stretched her neck, standing on hind legs against the kitchen counter. Her nose sniffed frantically at the cooking meat.

"You best get down and out of my kitchen, little wolf, or you'll be getting nothing this morning!" Frya swatted her spatula at Arcturas's tail, swinging droplets of oil across the room. With a yip, the pup scampered out, stopping to lick the bits of grease that had landed in her path.

"You seem...different this morning. Now that you know who I am," I pressed, my voice trailing off as Frya glanced up from her stove.

Her lips curved into a thin line and she returned to the eggs now bubbling in her iron skillet. I shuffled to the hearth, my eyes never leaving the ancient woman. Rubbing my hands in the radiating warmth, I watched as she transferred the eggs to a cracked serving bowl and placed them on the bar.

"I ain't gonna get the city guard if that's what you're suggesting," she snapped, sliding a plate down the bar towards me. I reached for a fork and poked at the steaming eggs.

"I also ain't gonna poison you, so you best eat up before those get cold." With creaking knees, the barkeep bent to place a small plate of pork belly and chicken livers on the floor. Arcturas trotted over to her, grabbed a slice of meat, and began flinging it from side to side. She leaped joyously as she toyed with her prey.

"Hey! This ain't the wild, you beast! Don't be dirtying up my nice clean floors!" Frya jutted her bony finger at the pup. Arcturas skidded to a halt and guiltily swallowed the slice whole. Burying her face in her plate, she began slopping up her breakfast.

"I guess I'm just a little suspicious. Why are you being so kind to me? I'm an escaped alleged murderer." The barstool creaked beneath my weight as I leaned in to pop a forkful of food into my mouth.

Scowling, Frya smoothed back her thinning, grey hair.

"If you don't want my hospitality, you know where the door is. And guilty or not, the late Queen's death was the best thing to happen to this city in a long time." She plopped a spoonful of rubbery egg on to her own plate and took a seat across from me.

"Aren't you afraid of my murderous tendencies sending me straight to your bed while you sleep?" I stabbed an egg with my fork.

"No, I'm not afraid of your violent streak, Lady Elpis. Not all city folk trust the Elders' judgements. I certainly don't."

My cheeks reddened as I bit into a crunchy slice of pork belly, the fat melting on my tongue. We finished our breakfasts in silence, avoiding the barkeep's penetrating gaze as she crunched on the remaining sausages straight from the skillet. Arcturas scampered to the tavern's entrance, her ears back in a defensive stance, and growled deeply towards the door. Alarm stitched through me.

"Quick, down to the wine cellar. You two stay quiet until I give the okay. The city guard's doing their rounds collecting up all the drunks and thieves this morning. That's probably them now, wanting the late-night crowd who overstay their welcome." Frya led us hastily into the kitchen and whipped the reed utility mat aside to reveal a small trap shoot in the floor. Pulling together on the ring handle, we lifted the square door, disturbing a thick layer of spider webs as it swung open. Ushering Arcturas down the stone cellar stairs, I trailed behind her.

"Not a peep," Frya said, shutting the door behind me. Dust fell from the creases in the wooden flooring as she pulled the utility mat back into place.

The cellar itself was pitch dark. Heart pounding, I didn't dare move as I silently inhaled the stale air. Arcturas sniffed at the corners of the room, her nails scraping against the rough stone. Scooping her into my arms, I stroked her little head to keep her from whining. Above us, two muffled male voices conversed with Frya's familiar croak. I held my breath, praying to the Gods that Arcturas would remain silent in my arms as footsteps entered the kitchen above.

"I told you, the storm scared the usual suspects away last night. There's no one here. And I haven't seen or heard of Lady Elpis since they sent her to that tower," Frya scowled.

My blood turned to ice. So the search party had made it to the city. It didn't come as a surprise that word would've made it back to the city guard; however, it still sent a boulder down my throat to think of the Elders' reaction to my escape. And what of Vikar? Would they reprimand him? Surely they couldn't. I thought of the guard who'd delivered my birthday gift. He'd been in a royal uniform, meaning a royal guard. He was sworn to the king and to use discretion when carrying out assigned tasks. A royal guard would rather be sent to death than betray the trust of his commander. Vikar was untouchable, and hopefully free from the suspicion of the Elders.

"I know it's a pain, ma'am, but we're checking every establishment for her. She's dangerous and unpredictable. We're just trying to keep the city safe," one voice said as footsteps paused directly above the trapdoor.

"Well, she ain't here. Just me and the drunks," Frya

snapped as her limping step followed behind the second voice.

Groans of cupboards opening and closing echoed through the floorboards as I continued holding my breath. Don't look under the mat. Don't look under the mat. I begged, desperately stroking Arcturas's pelt beneath shaking hands. She stared with an intense ferocity at the cellar's ceiling, but continued to stay silent. I promised that if she stayed quiet, and we avoided being caught, I'd buy her a steak bigger than her whole body.

"Who's the second breakfast for if you're here by yourself?" the other voice questioned.

Frya seemed to stop dead in her tracks. There was a desperate hesitation and finally, with a convincing sharpness Frya replied, "A tenant had just stepped out before you arrived. I was about to clean this mess until I was rudely interrupted by the likes of you two."

There was silence then. Dear Gods, I hope they bought it. Frya had managed enough irritation in her tone to mask the quiver in her throat. Seconds dripped by like a leak to a faucet, my heart pumping in overdrive. The blood rushed to my face and I felt a deep roaring in my ears. More shuffling footsteps. The click of Frya's small feet stopped directly above the trap chute.

"Alright then, Ma'am. We won't take up any more of your morning," the first voice said.

Hearing the footsteps recede and the sound of the front door swing open then closed, I finally exhaled. Relief washed over me. I let Arcturas wriggle out of my grasp as light poured into the shadowy cellar from Frya struggling to lift the grainy wooden door.

"Alright, come on out," she said, offering me a small, leathery hand.

Grasping for it, I climbed up the steps and into the kitchen, Arcturas sprinting by me.

"Thanks for not giving me up." I smiled towards the

barkeep, now flicking a speck of dust off her crudely stained apron.

"At least now you can stop eyeballin' me every move I make." Turning the spout, Frya began scrubbing away at the breakfast dishes in her basin sink.

"I appreciate it," I said, handing her a plate. "I'm sorry for not trusting you. It's just been... a rough few years. I'm not used to such kindness." Speckles of sympathy flashed in Frya's eyes as I choked back the knot now forming in my throat. A silent pause thickened the air between us.

"Well," she cleared her throat and continued scrubbing, "I expect you to earn your keep around here. I ain't no charity. There's a bag of potatoes and carrots in the stores that need peeling." She nodded to the door opposite the stove.

"Right, of course," I said, crossing the room and swinging the door open. Glancing back towards the old barkeep, I thanked her once more. I swear a glimmer of a smile swiped across those ancient lips as I stepped into the stores and worked.

The deep blue bruises faded to green, then to yellow as I began my quiet life in the backrooms of the tavern. Calluses formed on my palms from the days of sweeping, cleaning, and peeling vegetables. When I wasn't in the kitchen stores, I was at the sink- scrubbing a sticky, wine stained chalice.

Frya wasn't joking when she said I'd earn my keep. Most nights were dreamless. I'd instantly drift to sleep when my cheek hit the pillow. Some nights, I dreamt only of the tower- waking in a dazed fit, thinking the tavern was just my imagination and I was still imprisoned in that lifeless place.

Those nights I'd throw off the covers and pace beside the window, staring at the cobblestone street below until finally my breathing evened and the shivers of the lingering nightmare subsided. With every paralyzing nightmare, a piece I'd fought so hard to rebuild crumbled again.

My wolf companion was there to guide me back when I'd lost my way too deep into myself. If my thoughts carried me away, she'd lick my toes and nip at my heels until I returned to steady ground. And when I crumpled to the floor like a piece of parchment, she was there, licking away the tears and snuggling into me, her warmth chasing away the frigid defeat spreading through my abdomen.

She had nearly doubled in size after only two weeks at the tavern, her little body beginning to fill into a muscular frame under wiry, jet black fur. Her fangs grew sharper and longer. Her eyes were more piercing and predatory. As she grew, our bedchamber shrank. I knew she yearned to stretch her legs. I'd watch her gaze longingly out the windows, her nose pressed so close to the glass it scrunched an inch up her snout. No matter how much scolding the wolf received from our hostess, she still left runny smudges against the glass.

I, too, craved the crisp air of the glade. The crunch of snow beneath boots and the white, gleaming sun flickering between the pines sang to me. If I closed my eyes and truly concentrated, I convinced myself that those mourning doves and winter finches faintly chirped their melodies in my ear. A secret song, just for me.

Chapter 10

It was easy to lose sight of my goal for freedom when the days were swept away with the crumbs and dirt from the tavern floor. I grew comfortable in the storeroom's stillness. The strict monotony of daily life pushed me into autopilot until three months' time had passed in a blink.

Occasionally, the city guards did their rounds, reminding shopkeepers and city folk that a murderess was still at large. However, after failed search parties, they focused their efforts on the other realms. The rumors and initial fear that spread through our people of my escape had long since faded away, replaced with uneasiness around the increase in attacks. The creatures of the flatlands were growing bold, attacking hunting parties only a couple of miles from the city's outer wall. Whispers of panic kindled like a spark in a drought until the entire Northern Realm burned with fear.

Tavern customers became infrequent after nightfall, save from the usual drunkards. The streets fell silent.

Those that did pass by were heavily armed with spears, knives and various makeshift weapons. So far, the creatures had maintained some distance from the wall; however, with each new attack, they grew closer. It was only a matter of time.

Four months since we'd arrived at Frya's marked the eve of our city's most honored tradition- Festival. The energy of the city changed entirely on winter solstice. The northerners needed relief from the suffocating fear of the recent attacks.

Leaning against the bar with Arcturas curled at my feet, I could hear the echoes of bright, euphoric music and boisterous laughter through the cracked tavern window.

The longest night of the year, filled with spiced berry cider and buttery, flaky moon cakes, was the peak of Polaris's power. Drawing from the burning, bright stars speckled across the midnight sky, she'd summon the wards shrouding our realm, shielding us from the dangers roaming the far north. From the creatures with horrid red eyes and putrid flesh. As time went on and our people lost faith, her wards weakened- leaving cracks for the creatures to slip through. Now, more than ever, our people prayed for strength in her wards. With the increasing attacks, more and more northerners sought Polaris for her protection. The city folk turned to their faith, considering their fear. With this dramatic shift of faith, I prayed her wards would be impenetrable again.

The glass chalice I was polishing shattered in my hand with thoughts of the flatlands and the countless hunters that'd gone missing since my return. The youngest was 8, a boy who'd gone out with his father on his first hunt. They'd found his small body two weeks later, torn to pieces, drenched in that familiar black ooze.

It wasn't until warm, scarlet drops splattered on to the bar beneath me did I snap back into reality. Scowling, I reached for my cotton rag and wrapped my bleeding palm tightly; the gash throbbed under pressure.

I needed air. It was hard to keep track of what was reality and what wasn't these days. Endless hours hidden in the shadows left room for wandering thoughts. Pacing to the window, I unlatched the lock and slid it open, letting the cold front wrap its tendrils around me. Flurries whipped in from the night, melting against my feverish brow.

Would I wither away in the shadows of this tavern? How long could I remain hidden away until the bedroom upstairs became another prison? My throat tightened and I rubbed at my cloth covered hand, holding back short, quiet sobs. That key was my second chance. My new life. How could I live it sitting in fear, wasting away between sacks of potatoes? A fracture cracked up the old glass as I slammed it shut.

My cheeks cried for another kiss of crisp night air. My toes yearned for the exhaustion of an endless night of dancing. A couple pranced hand in hand down the street outside- their laughter rippled through the dim, dusk light. Frya had already retired to her bedroom upstairs, closing up early before any drunken festival goers made a mess of her bar.

Her claims of wanting some peace seemed to only scratch the surface of why she avoided the solstice and its celebrations like it was the deadliest of plagues. When I begged her to celebrate with me, even over just one glass of berry cider, she snapped- she pushed her barstool away and grumbled up the stairs about stumbling drunkards and fools.

Arcturas, now wrapped against my bare feet, kicked and grumbled in her sleep. I stroked behind her neck with my toes to settle her as I examined the wound and began picking particles of glass from the open gash, now brown with a clot. Reaching for the broom behind the bar, I cleaned up the shards of the chalice.

I returned to the window, shadows deepening beneath my eyes. Pressing my hand to the chilled glass, another couple passed by the tavern, their small son skipping and chasing snowflakes behind them. The old woman wouldn't notice if I were gone for an hour or two. She probably wouldn't leave her bedchamber for the rest of the night. A foolish thought pressed its way to the front of my mind.

"Arcturas, wake up." Bending down, I scratched the wolf behind her ear. One bright amber eye flicked open and peered up at me. She lifted her paw to expose her warm belly. A request for scratches. Complying, I stroked her underfur.

"So... You wanna go on an adventure?" Her ears perked, but still only a single eye blinked towards me.

"I was thinking about going to check out the festival.... There probably would be treats there." Her second eye snapped open.

"Well..?"

As if in response, she jumped to her feet, shaking her bushy tail rapidly. I chuckled and tiptoed to the coatroom. Silently creaking the closet door open, I lifted my cloak from its hanger and started towards the door. Being sure to tuck my hood over my brow, we stepped into the chilly night. The soft click of the door was the only sound behind us.

Arcturas padded along the cobblestone as we approached the city's center. With each step closer, the chatter of a crowd, laughing and giddy, grew louder and louder until it finally roared into the night. A sea of amethyst cloaks and robes ebbed around the mountainous city center, gathering most densely at the tall, now-polished statue of Polaris.

The aroma of roasting meat and baking pastries percolated into the air as street vendors jumped busily to work, serving customer after customer orders of salt lamb and cinnamon pies. Children bustled through the crowds in lines, their faces smudged with chocolate or hands holding a tin of solstice cakes.

Everyone smiled and laughed and danced.

Blues, purples, and greens of all shades bustled around me through the city's center. Colors I'd nearly forgotten pulsed and whirled through the space as city folk danced and twirled in the celebration. Clenching my chest, I nearly fell to my knees. Everything around me, so bright, so full of life, was overwhelming.

This was not the city I'd left five years ago, and a feeling of joy struck at my heartstring. No longer did the people of Ursae carry shadows on their backs, their frail bodies slowly fading into starvation. I stopped in my tracks, wide eyed at the vision of gaiety around me.

The city had healed while I was away, under Vikar's rule. Not a single trace of my sister's reign fluttered through passing expressions or conversations. My nephew had fulfilled the promise he'd made to me all those years ago. Grinning so wide a cramp settled into the creases of my lips, I leapt into the swirling crowd of dancers- jumping and moving to the rhythm of a nearby fiddle.

Interlacing fingers with the small blonde woman across from me, we giggled like children as we spun faster and faster; the world circled us in bright, warm colors of celebration. Arcturas bounced between us, her tongue flinging against an open mouth, drool pouring from both sides as she sniffed for scraps along the cobblestone. No one noticed the wolf with vicious fangs and flaming eyes sneaking beneath them, lapping up the treats their children spilled. She was even so bold as to sneak a bite of an unsuspecting turkey leg directly from the hand of a man immersed in jolly conversation.

The music slowed, bringing the crowd of dancers to a halt. I smiled at my partner. One too many glasses of solstice wine stained her lips a deep purple. Judging by the sway in her step and the beads of sweat dripping on her brow, even if she had recognized me, she surely wouldn't remember tomorrow morning.

"It's a shame the King couldn't see the festival his council threw," a round, red-nosed man nudged beside me.

"Why? Where is he?" I asked him, scanning the crowd for Vikar's royal guards or carriage.

"Hmm?" He turned to me, surprised by my interruption. "Haven't you heard? He's traveled to Aquilae, hoping to reestablish shipping routes. It's a real shame, y'know. I bet he'da loved seeing his people so happy."

A piece of me had hoped to see Vikar at the festival, but another piece was relieved that I wouldn't. I'm not sure I'd be ready to face that moment in time. To see how he's grown would be to see how much time had passed. How much I'd wasted away in that tower. I wondered if I'd ever see him again, or if he'd stayed the innocent twelve-year-old boy I'd left in that throne room. Maybe it was for the best. I'd simply slip away without stirring up the trauma of losing his makeshift mother for a second time. Clearly, the realm had healed most of its wounds during my exile; hopefully so had their King. The frantic melody of a fiddle picked up and, with it, the surrounding crowd. Tonight I shouldn't worry about the past. Or the future. I wanted to exist in the moment, to breathe in the night air and feel the joyous buzz of the city folk.

By the time the moon drew to its pinnacle, fatigue swelled my ankles. Arcturas had found a warm spot beneath a vendor's cart, stomach bulging in satiated bliss. A large bell rang from the temple above as the dancing slowed to a natural stop. Another bell struck, and the sky ignited with wisps of greens and blues so bright the shades reflected against the onlookers' wonder-struck faces. Flecks of silver and purple marked the stars of our galaxy above. The veil of color shimmered and whirled as if it was alive. A hush fell over the crowd as ringing bells erupted into the air, announcing our goddess's arrival.

There, stepping out from beneath the marble columns at the temple's entrance, was the most beautiful woman I'd ever laid eyes on. Her jet black hair seemed to float and wrap itself around her silvery frame as a satin cloak, the darkest shade of night, shimmered with each graceful step. She wore a dress that matched the color of the northern sky, with gauzy cerulean and magenta ribbons trailing behind her. An iron crown rested atop her head, its single point glinting in the moonlight. On each bicep she wore a matching iron cuff. Bewitched by our goddess, I fell to my knees, feeling the softness of Arcturas's tail curling against my thigh.

As she raised her hands into the air and looked to the sky with bright indigo eyes, a stillness thickened through-out the crowd. She whispered something I couldn't quite make out and an electricity blinked across the city, travel-ing to the outskirts just beyond the tower. Tingles spread from my toes to the crown of my head as the pulse washed over me.

Feeling as if someone had kicked me in the gut, a rush of air escaped my lungs and I reached for the grounding support of the street in front of me. Arcturas's fur straight-ened along her spine, her ears perked stiffly into the air and her eyes burned so deeply I thought they might burst into flames. The surrounding others were still smiling wide eyed from ear to ear, clasping their hands together in awe. The ward didn't have nearly as intense an effect on them.

Struggling to my feet, I stumbled forward, nearly shov-ing the small, ancient man in front of me to the ground. Apologizing profusely, I pulled the hood of my cloak lower over my face and wove through the city square littered with people. Arcturas trailed frantically behind me. My lungs needed air as the crowd began closing in tighter around me. Bile rose in my throat and I knew if I didn't shake away these tingles, now needle pricks against my skin, I'd be sick. I couldn't afford to draw that attention to myself- not with city guards posted at every corner of the square.

Finally, I darted through a break between bodies and gasped for the night air. The smell of meat and sticky wine, still low in the air, hit my nostrils and I lurched for a shadowy side street just in time to be sick. The roaring cheer of the crowd drowned the sound of my retching as Polaris returned to the temple and the festivities concluded. Arcturas nuzzled against my calves as I continued to be sick, heaving up the entirety of my stomach contents.

A couple, who I recognized as the pair I had seen crossing the tavern window, pointed their noses disgustedly away from my direction. To them, I probably just looked like a drunk who'd had one too many spiced wines. Wiping the bile from my lips and the sweat from my brow, I straightened and wobbled towards the street that'd lead me back to the tavern.

The lamplights had all burnt out hours ago as I struggled up the stone sidewalk. Dizzy with nausea and exhaustion, my legs were bags of cement beneath my weight. The brilliant borealis had faded until only a dim shade of purple remained in the sky. Concerned, Arcturas matched my step, never straying from my side. When the tavern stood only a few blocks away, three figures in deep purple uniforms marched towards me on the opposing sidewalk. Even with blurred vision, I recognized those horrendous velvet tunics anywhere.

City guards.

Scowling under my breath, I pulled my cloak tighter around myself and continued on, praying the boisterous group trailing behind me distracted them enough. As the guards grew nearer, they seemed to slow their pace. When we crossed each other's paths, they halted entirely. Shit.

"Hey! You there. Stop," one said, his voice rough with

intoxication.

I held my breath and continued on.

"I said stop, girl," he called, staggering across the street on imbalanced legs.

"I'm just trying to get home, Sir," I said in a voice that wasn't quite my own. Through clenched fangs, Arcturas let out a threatening growl, warning the guard not to come any closer.

"A little lady shouldn't be out at this hour all alone. Why don't I escort you home?" he suggested, his eyes trailing the outline of my figure beneath the baggy cloak. My skin burned against his wandering gaze and the nausea returned as he licked his lips.

"It's only a few blocks away. I wouldn't want to trouble you," I said, lowering my gaze to the ground.

His two companions crossed the street and flanked each side, surrounding me. With ears lowered and tail erect, Arcturas bared her teeth, eyes flashing with ferocity.

"Tell your dog we're no threat," the one to his right said, a slight slur of his words.

"She's just protective. Now please, I really should be on my way," I said, fists clenched tightly beneath the folds of woolen material. Even if I had my trusty dinner knife, they outnumbered me. Not only would I be overpowered, but I'd also make a scene.

My eyes darkened with a deep, nearly primal violence as I pictured Arcturas ripping the soft, fleshy crease of the middle guard's neck open, sending blood spraying bright droplets of red on the pure snow beneath us.

"Nonsense. A poor, young thing like you, all alone, un-protected. You don't know who could roam the streets at this hour." The middle guard stepped closer, his breath hot and pungent on my cheeks. His two companions chuckled and closed the gap between us. My blood curdled as the one to my right nodded towards an alleyway, empty and dark.

"My husband is expecting me home any minute," I said, voice shaking.

"I don't see a wedding band on your finger, miss. Does your husband know you left the house without it? I bet he'd be real upset to find out you've been flirting with a group of city guards." The middle guard's lip glistened in the moonlight.

"We'll walk you home. We insist." The guard on the right reached for my arm. Before his fingers could wrap around my bicep, Arcturas leapt up. Her fangs pierced pale flesh, shredding his purple tunic. The guard yelped and kicked at her as she clenched down and tore at his forearm, as if his skin and muscle tissue were paper thin.

Swinging my leg, I knocked the middle guard's feet out from under him with a swiftness I'd never been capable of before. As the guard to my left lunged for me, I ducked beneath his outstretched arms and punched him where I knew it'd hurt. He fell instantly to the ground, cupping himself and wrenching in agony. The middle guard had cracked his head against the cobblestone walkway, but not hard enough to knock him out. He staggered to his knees as I towered over him, flames of fury flickering in my eyes.

With all of my strength, I kicked directly towards the center of his brow, his neck snapping backwards as he slid across the street to the opposing sidewalk. Leaving all three barely conscious, my wolf and I continued home as if nothing out of the ordinary had just occurred.

Although the tingles had subsided, my head throbbed. I stopped in my tracks, nearly keeling over from the onset of a splitting headache.

"Miss, are you okay?" A breathy male voice said behind me. Arcturas stopped in her tracks, ready to pounce again. A brunette man hunched at the knees was breathing deeply to catch his breath.

"What? Yes, I'm fine, thanks," I said, my brow twitching.

"You don't look fine; please let me help you," he said, offering his hand. Arcturas growled deeply. Blotches of black painted my vision as I stumbled to straighten out.

"I'm fine. Thank you, though. Why are you breathing so heavy?" I asked him, rubbing the crease between my eyes to relieve some of the tension.

"Well, I sprinted up here to save you from those asshole guards, but clearly you're more than capable of saving yourself."

"If that wasn't proof enough that I can kick your ass if you try anything, she'll rip your throat out if given the chance," I said, nodding towards the now tense wolf standing between us.

"I heard what those guards were saying as they walked towards you. I just wanted to help, I swear." Begging, he threw up his hands. Eyeing him, I stroked the wiry fur of Arcturas's back to settle her. She grunted, relaxing slightly, but continuing to glare at the man. The pounding behind my skull subsided with each stroke down her back.

"I'm Rune," he said, the brown of his eyes warming in the reflection of candlelight peeking through the window of a nearby home. Extending his hand towards me again, he hesitated and backed it away as Arcturas took a step towards him.

"Okay, Rune. Have a nice night," I said, turning to take my leave.

"Wait!" He stepped after me, "I'm headed this direction too! Let's walk together. Gods know I could use your protection." He chuckled at himself, but trailed off as he caught sight of my furrowed brow.

"I'd prefer to walk alone," I said, my voice clipped.

"Well... I could just walk behind you?" He fell into step. Two sets of boots crunched in the frozen layer of snow on the street as we walked in silence. Every so often Arcturas turned to check behind us, keeping Rune a comfortable distance away.

"The festival really was something, don't you think?" he called up to me.

"Yes. It was quite nice."

"I think I may have had one too many cinnamon pies though." He chuckled again. Grumbling, I stopped walking to turn back at him.

"What do you think you're doing, Rune?" I snapped.

"Just making conversation?" He eyed me innocently, flashing a toothy grin. Dimples appeared at each corner of his mouth and I couldn't help but notice how perfectly straight his teeth were. The geometrics of his features, now more defined by the clear moonlight, were sharp and straight. He had high cheekbones and prominent eyebrows that wiggled as he grinned. Nearly a giant, the man towered over me with broad shoulders and arms muscular from years of manual labor. Something warmed beneath my cheeks and I tore my gaze away from him before the feeling grew.

"Well don't," I said, stomping back up the street. We were only two blocks from the tavern now.

"Alright then. Can I at least get your name?" he asked, continuing to trail behind me.

"Ell." One block away.

"How about your companion here?" He pointed towards Arcturas who, in reply, snapped at his index finger. Jerking his hand back, he tucked them into the pockets of his trousers and threw her a sheepish shrug.

"Arcturas." Nearly there. I could see the flickers of the candles in the tavern windows.

"Well, it's nice to meet you both! It's nice to have someone to chat with on the walk home, especially after a night such as this," he said, brushing back the golden brown hair that fell lazily above his brow. Finally, I reached

74

the tavern's knotted front door.

"This is me," I said, pulling open the door.

"You're staying at Frya's place? She's a lovely old woman... if you're on her good side, of course," Rune said, shoving his hands back into his pockets.

"Why do you say that?" With one foot over the threshold, I turned back towards the honey-brown haired man now leaning against the lamppost.

"Oh, um..," he trailed off thoughtfully, "I've heard she keeps a tight ship of that tavern of hers. I myself haven't been, but you know. City folk talk." He looked at his feet, scuffing a leather boot through the light dusting of snow now accumulating on the sidewalk.

Scanning his face, I noticed a faint glimmer bouncing off the sharp arches of his brow. Interesting. The way his skin seemed to shimmer in the coldness of the night was intriguing. The way his cheeks dimpled slightly as he smiled was somehow familiar. The way his eyes rounded as he spoke, depthless brown with flecks of amber scattering warmth in the paleness of the night, put me at ease. My chest softened. It felt easy to trust his gentle demeanor.

If I were thinking rationally, that'd make me nervous, but in the safety of the tavern's stores, I'd locked myself away. I secured my trust beneath thick, guarded layers. Frya, with her kindness and compassion, had slowly chipped it away, but at this moment I realized just how lonely a protected heart could be. If I were thinking rationally, I would tell him to fuck off and go to bed. But I wasn't thinking rationally. I was drunk from the night, the electric air of the festival, and the intoxicating beat of the fiddlers.

This Rune seemed innocent enough. And if he tried anything, I'd taken down animals nearly twice his size on my hunts. Something about his aura soothed the ache in my chest. Whether it be the strangeness of the night or the taste of frosted freedom, I yearned for connection. I craved

75

a normal conversation between companions. Just for the night, I'd allow myself this freedom.

"Alright well-" he said, starting to take his leave.

"Thanks for, um, walking me home. Would you like to come in for a drink? We just got a shipment of elderberry spiced ale in. It'll keep you warm for the rest of your walk home," I said, pointing a thumb behind my back into the warm, dim light.

Rune continued to shuffle his feet, looking uncomfortable.

"That's okay, you probably have someone waiting up for you at home, anyway," I backpedaled, stepping further into the tavern.

"Oh, no no! I'd- I'd love to come in for a drink," he stammered, stepping past me into the held-open door. Shaking the cold from his bones, he unbuttoned the navy cloak he wore and hung it beside mine in the coatroom. Smiling, I hastily reached for two glasses behind the bar and uncorked the dark purple bottle of wine. Like two teenagers sneaking through a sleeping home, we crept to a table by the hearth, smiling shyly at one another as we settled into our seats.

With a pop of the cork, hints of elderberry, clove, and cardamom tingled my nose. Handing Rune a smudged glass, I took a sip of my own, enjoying the sharpness against the back of my tongue. He sipped slowly, grinning widely. An uncomfortable silence floated between us as we both struggled to find something to say.

"You really meant it when you said it'd keep me warm the rest of my walk home," he chuckled, a rosy pink appearing on his cheeks.

"It's my favorite. I sneak a few bottles for myself anytime we get a shipment in. Frya pretends like she doesn't notice, but judging by how she keeps this place, I'm sure she turns a blind eye." I laughed, feeling the warmth of the alcohol deep in my belly.

"So," Rune said, resting his chalice on the table with a light tap, "where did you learn to fight like that?"

"Oh, I don't know," I said, not meeting his curious gaze. "I guess I grew up fighting. I never really had any protection, so I picked it up fairly quickly." He ran his fingers down the stem of his chalice, listening intently to my reply.

"How'd you end up at Frya's place? I've heard usually only people passing through stayed with her. She doesn't strike me as the type to keep a staff," he asked.

I took a sip of my wine, letting the dryness burn down my throat, leaving a trail of warmth in its path. Suddenly, it occurred to me that by inviting this man for a drink, I'd most likely have to talk about myself. What would I say? I was an escaped convicted lady of Ursae's court with the accusation of murdering her sister in cold blood weighing on my back? I nearly laughed out loud.

Clearing my throat, I said, "Oh.. um, I was just returning for a visit initially. I left the city a few years ago, but I've been here for about four months now. Frya keeps me busy with work, and Arcturas doesn't seem to mind it here." The wolf curled up on her down-stuffed burlap bed by the hearth and gnawed on a bone contently.

"What about you? I presume you live in the city," I asked him, deflecting the conversation off of me.

"I do now, but I wasn't born here. I grew up in Venia, believe it or not. My Uncle's a farmer on the west side of Ursae. I moved in to help him when the winters grew too harsh. Gods, that was probably about ten years ago now."

"Venia?" I'd met no one from the East before. The bloody history surrounding them kept the Easterners isolated from the other realms.

"Yeah, I know." He trailed off. "I left when I was only a boy. I remember little about it, just the scent of the plumerias that run rampant throughout the city. They're always blooming. Growing up there, you grow sick of their sweet smell. Sometimes, when I was a boy, I'd pray to the Gods for a frost to come and wipe out all of those little white flowers." His gaze looked distant, as if he had been pulled into a memory.

I cleared my throat and swirled the remaining wine around my chalice. He drained the rest of his glass and smiled up at me, a faint hint of sadness curling around his lips. Unsure what to say, I pulled the cork from the bottle and filled his glass again.

"You traded eternal spring for eternal winter. I wouldn't say that's a fair bargain." I chuckled, refreshing my glass.

"No, maybe not, but at least ice doesn't smell."

Arcturas grumbled in her sleep, rolling to her back, fully exposing the soft undercoat of her belly.

"Are you high born?" Rune asked, cautiously brushing a finger through Arcturas's fur. Raising an arm for better access, she welcomed the pets.

"What?" I choked on my wine.

"You're very well-spoken for city folk. Your dialect is quite rare around these parts."

"My father was a Lord of the court, but I wasn't close with my family. The black sheep, if you will. I spent more time in the forest just outside the city walls than I ever did in court. How about you? You don't sound like a farm-hand." I glanced at my hands, trying to suppress the flood of nerves as I confessed a hint of my truth.

"My parents were of status in Venia, but I never wanted that lifestyle. The courts, the politics, it was all so shallow. The lords and ladies were more concerned with the appearance of a thriving city than the wellbeing of their citizens." He trailed off, continuing to scratch Arcturas's belly.

"The courts of Ursae were cruel in their own way. Hardened from years of famine and snow, I think. It was difficult to trust even the closest of allies," I said, watching my wolf accept this stranger's affection, leaning into his pets. "She seems to trust you. Maybe you don't have ill intentions after all," I smirked.

Rune chuckled, looking up at me from his seat through thick, curled lashes. "What's the story with her? Not everyday does one come across a woman with a wolf as a pet."

"She isn't a pet," I snapped. "Erm, sorry. She's more than that. I was out on a hunt when I rescued her. She was so small I tucked her into the pockets of my cloak and carried her back into the city. One of the flatland creatures attacked her mother and littermates. She was the only survivor. We seem to understand each other, maybe because we're both alone." I smiled at the wolf, her right paw twitching in the air. Rune grew quiet. His mouth was a thin line. Most likely contemplating just how crazy I was.

"I sound insane..." I said, gulping down my wine, letting it sear down my throat.

"Maybe a little," he chuckled. I hope he'd take the deep crimson burning across my cheeks because of the wine and not my embarrassment.

"But," he said, looking at me earnestly, "I think I understand. Maybe you saved each other."

"Maybe." My eyes met his. The deep hazel glimmered gold in the candlelight between us. The wine had flushed his lips with a tinge of purple. Seconds ticked by, and we sat across from one another in silence, taking in the other's likeness. Finally, the scrape of my barstool broke the forming tension between us.

"Well, it's late. I'd best be getting to bed." I gulped down the rest of my wine and set the chalice down in the sink behind the bar before I could make any more poor decisions this evening. Rune cleared his throat, rising from his seat.

"Thank you for the wine, Ell," he said, handing his empty chalice to me. Our fingers brushed as I reached for it. The warmth of his skin opposed the ice of my own. An electric jolt coursed between us and we jerked our hands away simultaneously.

"Um. Well, I'll.. I'll be on my way." Stammering, he turned to go, nearly tripping over Arcturas's outstretched hind legs.

"Watch your step," I chuckled, "she might bite if you land on her tail." A soft warning growl rose in her throat as the wolf poked a single piercing eye up at him.

"Sorry, sorry!" Rune stepped over her apologetically, footing gingerly towards the front door. Pulling his cloak from the hanger, I handed it to him, making sure our fingers didn't touch again.

"It was nice meeting you, Rune," I said, handing him his cloak.

"You too, Ell. Thank you for a most unexpected evening. Maybe our paths will cross again." He threw his cloak over his broad shoulders and made for the door. Giving him a slight nod, I watched as he stepped into the night and disappeared down the sidewalk, glancing over his shoulder to shoot me one last tipsy smile. I returned to the candlelight of the tavern, clicking the lock. Arcturas peered over at me, her chin resting on her large, black paws.

"Oh, don't give me that look," I snapped, blowing out the nearly-melted candles on the bar with a huff. Washing the two chalices and replacing them softly on their shelf, the night replayed in my head. My skin still felt the warmth where our hands had met. Maybe the wine had gotten to me, but judging by his expression, I knew Rune felt that jolt of energy between us too. I crept up the stairs to my bedchamber with Arcturas padding behind me.

Tucked beneath scratchy sheets, the image of his soft, brown eyes flickered through my thoughts as I sank into a hazy sleep.

Chapter 11

I awoke to a sting of pain across my face. Jolting upright, there was Frya standing over me, one hand on her hip, the other now red from the violent slap she'd just sent across my right cheek. Her eyes burned like a furnace of rage and her lips were thin across her leathery mouth.

"What were you thinking?" She pointed a knotted finger towards me.

I sat up, rubbing the now-dull ache off my cheek. Suddenly I was transported back to the tower. To Hela's whip. Whether it be the jolt from awakening abruptly from a deep sleep or the trauma of memories suddenly rushing in, I couldn't move. Couldn't breathe.

"Someone could have seen you, you stupid girl!" she exclaimed. Her voice was like knives against my pounding head.

"I just needed to get out. Everything was fine. No one saw us."

"No one saw you? Tell that to the three guards who're running their mouths around the city this morning that a cloaked woman and her dog attacked them on the street only a few blocks from here!"

Sighing, I tossed the covers aside and swung my legs to the floor. Soreness was spreading from the peak of my neck up to my forehead.

"If they had seen your face! They would've taken you back to that tower immediately. Gods know what fate awaited your there! Then they would've come for me!" Frya said.

The soreness magnified until it was nearly unbearable.

The barkeep's words strung together in a continuous, shrill creak as a high-pitched tone rang through my ears. There was a brief pause in her words, waiting for a response. I remained quiet, leaning against the windowsill with my eyes low. The scolding resumed and with it, the pressure in my chest built higher and higher until I felt as if I'd burst. Finally, I snapped.

"You can't expect me to stay hidden away in here forever. I've traded one prison for another!" I cried.

Her jaw dropped open, and a pang of hurt welled beneath her sunken, wrinkled eyes. Snapping my mouth shut, I knew I'd gone too far. I went to speak, but Frya held up her pale hand.

"I have opened my home to you. Fed you. Given you work. Kept you safe. If my hospitality is nothing more than a jail cell to you, then you can go," she whispered, taking her leave.

The soft click of the door behind her left an airless silence. Back sliding down the rough brick wall, I threw my head in my hands. The throbbing continued to pound in my ears as Arcturas pawed her way over to me, her nails scraping across cold tile. I lifted my head towards her as she nuzzled into me. I needed to fix this, or else Arcturas and I would be back on the street.

When the pain subsided from my head, I found Frya downstairs furiously scrubbing a tabletop opposite the hearth. Grabbing a rag, I joined her, wiping sudsy water away from the withered wood. Without looking up, she placed a small bucket of warm soapy water next to me and we continued to clean. It wasn't until the space was immaculate did we acknowledge one another. I opened my mouth, starting the apology I rehearsed again and again in my mind as I cleaned.

"I know what you're going to say," the barkeep said, dumping the now murky bucket down the drain. "I'm sorry I raised my hand at you. I can understand why you snuck out last night. It's easy to forget about your demons when you've hidden them so well from me."

"I shouldn't have said what I did," I said, wringing out my dishrag.

"It's alright. I've been working you to the bone. It's the truth. I shouldn't have hit you."

Setting the bucket beside her, she looked across the bar at me. I swallowed, uncomfortable by her acknowledgement.

Opening my mouth to speak, I wasn't sure what to say.

"You don't have to say anything, Elpis, just hand me that rag. If you'd like to leave, I won't hold it against you. There are a few other taverns needing some extra hands. I can send word to one of 'em if you'd like." She looked down at her hands, still glistening with soap.

I paused for a minute, rubbing a finger across my chin. Somewhere outside, a clock chimed. She could have thrown me into the cold, forgetting the very memory of my stay at her tavern. I had risked not just my life sneaking off to Festival, but also hers. Had the city guards discovered I was staying here, they could have executed her for harboring a fugitive. I shuddered at the thought.

"I'd like to stay."

Frya stopped her rapid scrubbing and threw down her brush.

"Besides, who would peel your potatoes for you if I

left?" I said, smirking.

A small smile escaped her lips as I tossed her the dish rag.

Catching it between her frail hands, she said, "I had a daughter, you know."

Frya wiped the soapy scum off her hands across the stained apron she wore. "When her father found out I was pregnant, he took off- ran all the way to Canissa, claiming he'd find us a better life in the West. The minute he stepped out of this tavern, I knew, though. He wasn't coming back." She unclasped a tarnished silver locket from beneath her wool tunic and handed it to me.

"Her name was Astri. She was all I needed in this world, with her small green eyes and little hands. When she was a baby, I lost time because I'd just stare at her and her perfect button nose and toothless smile. I'd set her down to change her and get sidetracked by her laughter. It was us against the world. Raising her made me feel invincible."

I opened the locket to look at the painted little girl with flaming red hair and a wide-eyed grin.

"When she was four, I took her to Festival. She'd always beg me to see the lights and taste all the different treats. It's funny; when you become a mother, you want to protect your child- lock them away from all the horrible darkness in the world. But they grow up, and you can't keep them safe forever. They have to learn on their own."

There was a glint in Astri's eye, and I couldn't help but think just how full of life she looked and how much youthful wonder her portrait captured.

"After begging me all day, I caved. I remember thinking to myself, she deserved to see the borealis and celebrate along with the other children. So we went. We bought butter cakes until we were entirely stuffed and danced to the fiddler tunes until I thought my toes would fall off. When finally our Goddess appeared, Astri stared up at her in awe. It was so magical, getting to give her that experience. The whole city was watching Polaris except for me. I was watching my little girl."

"When the festival ended, we turned to head home. That's when I lost her. It was only a fleeting moment, but that's all it took. Her hand slipped from mine and she disappeared into the crowd. I panicked and searched through people, pushing past them, calling her name, even crawling on the street to see if I could catch sight of her little red slippers. But she was gone. The city guards took over the search, escorting me back to the tavern and telling me to get some rest and that they'd find her. How can you rest when your whole heart is missing?"

"That was the worst night of my life. There's no torture on this Earth worse than waiting for something, knowing you're powerless. It wasn't until the morning when a guard knocked on my door." She swallowed the lump rising in her throat.

"He was so pale and uncomfortable when he spoke. I knew then that I'd never get to hold her again. I guess she'd found her way through a crack in the city wall and gotten lost in the northern woods." Frya took a breath and placed her shaking hand atop mine.

"They found a red slipper by the wall and tracked a trail of footprints into the forest. The guard said maybe it was an animal attack. Those woods have never been safe, but with the attacks from the northern creatures, it was likely it wasn't just an animal." There was a length of silence before she continued, her eyes now damp with painful memories. "It shredded her tiny body to bits. Aside from a matching red slipper on her foot, she was otherwise unrecognizable."

"Frya... I'm so sorry." I whispered, lacing my fingers between hers. The feel of her skin was almost as cold as the sorrow in her voice.

"The attacks weren't nearly as bad back then as they

are now. I know you can handle yourself, but when I found your bed empty last night, I was terrified. Everything came back to me. I wasn't in control when I confronted you this morning. I'm sorry."

"No, I understand. I have moments where I lose myself in my pain, too. No mother should have to go through what you did."

She smiled sadly through wet lashes. The harsh exterior she so tirelessly built was a defense. The woman beneath those ancient scowls and sarcastic jabs was broken—she had lost everything.

"I think I need a minute. Talking about Astri is difficult, even after all these years." She pulled her hand away.

"I'll be right back. Why don't you start the stew for this evening?" she said, smoothing the wrinkles of her apron.

"Sure. Take as long as you need," I nodded.

She cleared her throat and disappeared upstairs, joints cracking as she stepped.

Frya didn't return until the stew was simmering and the morning light faded into a gloomy afternoon. The knocking of the tavern door pulled me back from the depth of my thoughts as I stirred our supper on the stove. The barkeep hobbled to the door, unlatched it, and peered at the unexpected visitor with shaggy brown hair.

"We don't open for another couple hours, boy," she snapped, slamming the door shut.

"I- I know! I'm actually not here for a drink," he stammered, his voice muffled through thick oak.

Frya reopened the door, glaring at him, "What do you want, then?"

"I um... I'm here to see Ell. A-and Arcturas, of course," he said. I shook my head, snorting at the awkward tone in his voice.

"Ell, there's a boy here to see you." Frya raised a brow toward me, her lip thinning into a pin straight line across her face. Opening the door just enough for Rune to slide through, she slammed it behind him, re-latching the lock, her eyes following his every movement.

"Hi Ell!" He smiled, the brown of his eyes brightening as he spoke. "I was on my way to the market, and I thought I'd stop by and say hello."

Arcturas padded toward her newfound friend, her tail wagging violently with each step. Rune knelt beside her, scratching behind her ear as she lapped at his cheek.

"I see it wasn't just a few guards you met last night." Leaning against the entryway threshold, Frya crossed her arms, eyeballing the wolf and her new companion.

"Frya, this is Rune. He helped me scare away those drunken guards last night. If it wasn't for him..." I shuddered, thoughts of that dark alleyway pricking the hair on the nape of my neck.

"I see... Well, thank you. The city guards these days think they're above the law- taking anything they want. Are you hungry? Stew's almost ready." Frya hobbled to the kitchen and stirred the thick simmer, maintaining a watchful eye through the open doorframe.

"Stew sounds wonderful. Thank you." Rune threw her a cautious smile before rising from his knees, now covered in short, black hair.

I motioned for us to sit, returning to our seats from the night before. A residual tingle tickled my fingertips as we faced each other, and a rosy shade of pink flushed across my cheeks. Rune shifted in his seat, frantically searching for something to say. "Did you sleep well?"

"Yes, I did," I said, glancing at his hands resting across from mine. "The wine put me right out."

Rune smiled quietly, uncomfortable beneath the hawk-like vision of our chaperone.

"I was wondering if you'd like to go for a walk this evening. It's going to be a clear one tonight. The borealis should be beautiful."

Arcturas's ears perked straighter than a nail at the

mention of a walk. I nodded, suppressing my eagerness as best I could. I could feel the fresh air on my face, the crack of snow beneath my boots. My legs yearned to stretch.

"I would love that, but..." I turned toward Frya, watching her expression curdle into suspicion, "Frya may need help here. The clear weather always brings in a swarm of patrons."

Ladling stew into three chipped bowls, the barkeep snorted and placed our supper on the table before taking her seat beside me.

"Oh, well, that's alright." Rune stroked the stubble on his chin, avoiding Frya's snarled lip.

I sighed, resigning into my seat. The clanking of spoons filled our thick silence. It wasn't smart to leave the tavern, especially walking through the city. I would risk my safety for a second taste of freedom, but was I willing to risk hers? After the tragedy she'd experienced with her own daughter, I couldn't threaten the sliver of comfort she'd built just for my selfishness. We continued eating, wandering eyes meeting between mouthfuls, then abruptly darting away. Placing my spoon in the empty bowl in front of me, I caught Frya's gaze. Her eyes softened as she glanced toward Rune.

Patting her lips with a cotton napkin, she said, "If you're careful, I 'spose Arcturas would like a hike up the mountainside tonight to see the borealis. With the cold, you'll likely not run into anyone and Gods know the poor creature probably needs to stretch her legs."

A grin, wider than I thought physically possible, cracked across my lips. Arcturas's eyes glittered as she trotted over to the barkeep.

"She'd love that," I said, not sure if I was talking about the wolf or myself. There was an unmistakable twinkle in Frya's eye as she witnessed my face light up. For the first time since we arrived, her eyes softened in indisputable compassion. I reveled in the airiness of her expression until it snapped abruptly back to her usual scowl.

"But you best behave yourself, boy. Any funny business and this one here'll make sure they can't recognize your body when you they find you frozen on the mountainside." She pointed her spoon at Rune. He gulped back his last bite of the meal.

"And you!" She swung it towards Arcturas, "If I find pieces of bone on my floor again, I'll cook you into supper and use your pelt for a new cloak!" Whimpering, the wolf lowered her ears and sulked back to her bed by the hearth.

"I just need to finish up my chores, if you don't mind waiting," I said, scurrying to the back storeroom.

The skin on my fingertips was raw and red by the time the shadow of night fell over the horizon. As I had rushed around the tavern- sweeping ash from the hearth, chopping bushels of wood outback, and peeling bag after bag of potatoes, Arcturas remained stretched on her bed- licking the remnants of bone off the floor, chasing a rabbit in the back courtyard, and curling into a warm nap by the hearth. Rune, seated at the bar, silently sipped on an ale. I felt his eyes follow me as I rushed back and forth, a taste of freedom fueling each step.

"Let me change, then we'll go," I called to him, tossing my apron across the bar. I couldn't decide which ached more, my back or my knees as I hobbled up the staircase to my bedchamber, Arcturas racing past me. My exhaustion didn't hinder the growing excitement deep in my belly at the thought of seeing the borealis once again. After five years surrounded by shades of grey, seeing the vibrant greens and violets felt like a drug. I craved the fluorescence like an addict craved the poppy.

It was nearly time to go, as the sun had fully set, and the city lampposts had been lit. Hastily, I washed the layer of grime and sweat from my body and changed into a fresh black tunic with matching trousers. Braiding my hair into a tight plait down my back and twisting it into a bun, I secured my mother's comb into place. Arcturas whined impatiently, scratching at the door as I finished dressing.

"Alright, alright, I'm ready!" I said, turning the knob of the chamber door. Just as I pulled it ajar, she shot past me, leaping over the last few steps and landing with a thunk on the wooden flooring below. I guess her ferocity made up for the grace she so clearly lacked when she was excited. Clicking the door shut behind me, Frya's scolding carried through the house and I couldn't help but chuckle as I bounced down the stairwell and met them in the tavern.

"I packed you an extra cloak and gloves in case you catch the cold," Frya said, handing me a brown leather pack. The strap, nearly worn entirely off, sagged as I thanked her and took it across my shoulder. Arcturas, now howling by the door, clawed at the wood. Frya shot her a glare and said, "Well, you best be going before that beast tears down the door. Remember what I said, boy."

The night air was crisp across my cheeks as we started towards the city center. Snow fell silently around us, slowly erasing our tracks as we made them. Arcturas, with her tongue bouncing from one side of her jaw, trotted happily beside me.

Frya had been right. Not even a rat passed by us as we crossed block after block down the street. Moonlight beamed through grey, wispy clouds, washing the world in shades of silver as we neared the city's heart. Standing erect and illuminated by the night, the giant marble Polaris gazed upon us with watchful eyes. Her arm was outstretched towards the North with a sharp metal dagger, glinting in starlight.

Arcturas sniffed at her large marble foot, and continued on, passing through the archway and starting up the slope of stairs to the summit.

It was known across the city that the temple had the best view of the borealis. With heavy, winded breaths, I climbed after my wolf as she leapt from step to step with incomparable ease. What seemed like a thousand steps later, we arrived at the peak. A brisk wind whipped through my bones as Arcturas sprinted around boulders shrouded in blue ice. Her thick black fur jolted with each powerful stride of her legs.

"She's loving every second of this," Rune chuckled. I realized we'd walked in silence up the mountainside. The beauty of a silent, snowy landscape had distracted me from my companion.

"Oh, I know." I smiled, letting the frost in the breeze caress my cheeks. "She was born of the wilderness. I know she loves Frya and her bed by the hearth, but it's cramped. There's nowhere for her to run or explore. Out here, she can do or be everything she needs."

"Why do I feel like you're not so much talking about your wolf?" he said, watching me with awestruck eyes. I smiled wildly. A playfulness sparked from somewhere I'd kept locked up. Shoving Rune into the snow, I took off up the mountainside, letting my legs reach the speed they'd yearned for over this last month. With lungs that felt as if they'd burst, I finally reached the top. Stopping to catch my breath, I leaned against a tree and gazed across the sleeping city.

Freedom was as crisp on my tongue as a freshly picked fall apple. Rows of lampposts flickered peacefully on the cobblestone streets below. The piercing whistle of wind faded away as I closed my eyes and let the mountainside consume me.

A whisper echoed through the air, and the ground beneath my boots vibrated with tension. Flurries fell from the surrounding sky, landing on my closed lashes. The blackness behind my eyelids brightened abruptly and I opened my eyes, shielding them with my fist from the harsh waves of green light now ebbing across the horizon.

"It's glorious tonight, isn't it?" Rune said through ragged breaths. His cloak, now powdered with snow, swirled around his broad shoulders as he joined me against my perch.

"It's breathtaking. I don't think the sight of it will ever get old," I said, watching the borealis writhe against the black night- now a deep shade of navy. Strings of magenta and amethyst threaded themselves through the gemstone greens. The breath in my throat vanished as I looked upon such beauty. Arcturas had made her way to my side, the light reflecting in her wide, round eyes like a kaleidoscope.

She was shaking beneath her pelt, but not in fear; it was something else. Suddenly, everything faded away but her. It was as if we'd been transported somewhere far beyond the mountainside. Far beyond the city. A vibration beneath us rose from the deepest core of the mountain and reverberated into our bodies.

The same tingles I felt at the festival washed over me and I fell to my knees- my body growing too heavy for my feet to support. Rune knelt beside me, his frantic voice muffled beneath a sharp ringing in my ears. Lifting my chin, concern etched across his face, he continued to speak, but his voice was gone away entirely. Black spots formed in my vision until they replaced him altogether.

The tingling swept through my body with such ferocity it was almost painful. I reached for Arcturas. She, too, was hunched to the ground, her fur pricking up her spine. Trembling, I stroked her pelt, but jerked away at the sight. Deep tendrils of shadow licked at my fingers and a flame of colors similar to the borealis above us emulated from my palm. Rune's jaw dropped, taking a step back as he saw the light expelling from beneath my skin.

Terror washed through me, penetrating the core of my being as I struggled to stand and stare at my hands. What was happening to me? With startled eyes that reflected that same vibrant light, Arcturas whined towards me. I wasn't the only one consumed in fear. She lurched toward me, needing the comfort of my warmth as much as

92

I needed hers. As our bodies met, a rush of energy pulsed through us with a force so great I flew backward, landing against the hard, frozen ground at least a hundred feet away. Rune fell to his knees, feeling the force of the pulse wash over him.

With blurred eyes and pounding heart, I wiped the snow from my face and sat up. Arcturas lay in a crumpled heap of fur a ways from where she had been sitting. Her face filled with panic, mimicking my own, I was sure. I coughed up the air that had been pressed out of me upon impact with the ground. The tingling subsided, and in its place, a wave of tranquility soaked through my bones.

"What the fuck was that?" I asked Arcturas, now shaking the snow from her fur. She stared at me with a deep expression of confusion in her eyes. The borealis had faded entirely. Its navy background returned to a deep shade of black.

With my vision finally returning to normal, I looked around the clearing. Rune lay beside me, knocked completely unconscious. A deep, black singe now marked the Earth where Arcturas and I had stood. All the snow and ice and cold within the radius of the scorned ground had melted. No, not melted. It had evaporated. Not a droplet remained on the surrounding branches. The ground was as dry as if it'd experienced a long, hot drought. The wind had stopped, leaving in its place a silence so heavy, it was deafening in my ears. Sickness washed through me, and I swallowed hard to keep it from rising in my throat.

Turning from the spot, I ran. I couldn't think of an explanation to give the man I'd abandoned. Sprinting away from the summit, away from whatever had just happened, away from the questions I couldn't answer. I didn't stop running until I had passed beneath the statue of our goddess and my lungs quaked beneath my chest.

With Arcturas in tow, we continued through the city square towards the safety and comfort of my tavern. Tears of panic blurred my vision as I continued to run, stride after stride crunching beneath the snow. The stars screamed in my direction as the sky flattened against the ground. Nothing made sense. My thoughts raced through me.

Panting too hard, I was forced to stop running. Arcturas wrapped herself around me. The empty midnight street brought me to my knees. What the hell was that? Placing my hands across my chest to keep my pounding heart from cracking through my sternum, I curled into my wolf, seeking her warmth.

"Oh my Gods! Are you okay?" Rune called, sprinting up the sidewalk towards us. I couldn't think, couldn't breathe, couldn't speak. Familiar brown eyes and auburn hair looked down at me with frantic concern.

"Ell?" he said, reaching a hand to help me back to my feet. Rubbing my aching skull, I reached for his hand, pulling myself up.

"What... what was that?" he questioned, brushing the snow from my cloak and stroking his hand across my frozen cheek.

"I...I..." I trailed off, realizing I wasn't really sure. Taking a few deep breaths, I begged my fluttering heart to be quiet.

"Well, are you okay?" he said, glancing towards my trembling fingers. "You were gone when I woke up. Thank the Gods I found you."

"I...I..." Again growing quiet, I was unsure what to say. There'd be too many questions, too much suspicion. How could I twist reality just enough to hide when I wasn't sure what was real anymore? Maybe an irreparable piece had snapped in my mind from all the time locked away. Maybe I'd lost my mind. Or maybe what'd happened tonight was real. I swallowed hard at the thought.

"Alright, let's get you back to Frya's," Rune said, holding his arm out for me to grasp. Leaning into him, we started up the street. I was like a moth drawn to a flame for his warmth. Clinging to his side, my shivering subsided. Wrapping his cloak tightly around my shoulders, Rune pulled me closer to his body. The strength from years of hard work were carved beneath a cotton tunic.

Notes of rosemary and citrus peppered the inside of my nose. His scent was fresh and bright, reminding me of sunshine bouncing off newly sprouted greenery. I closed my eyes and, for a moment, allowed myself to live in his scent. To be comforted by his warmth. It had been so long since I'd been held; I had forgotten the softness of another's body against mine. I had forgotten the tenderness of another's arm wrapped around me. For a moment, I allowed myself to enjoy his intoxicating touch supporting me beneath my arm.

Reaching the tavern, Rune dropped his embrace to pull open the front door. Frya, startled by our entrance, rose to her feet from behind the bar. Her mouth dropped as her eyes snapped from Rune to me. Helping to unclasp my cloak, he led me to a barstool and urged me to sit. The candlelight of the tavern was too bright. My eyes watered with each lick of the flames that flickered before me. Clenching my jaw, I looked to Frya, meeting her concerned eyes.

"What happened?" she asked, her words sharp in a whisper.

"I'm not sure, in all honesty. She hasn't said a word to me. I think she's in shock," Rune said, placing my hand on his. Frya dropped to her knees in front of me, grasping at my cold, ashen face, now blank from any expression. Rune smoothed back his disheveled hair, lines of concern wrinkled over his brow.

"What happened, girl?" Staring into my eyes, she shook at my shoulders, willing me to speak. I opened my mouth, but I still couldn't form words. Arcturas padded to my side, licking at my fingers.

How could I explain what happened at the summit when I was still unsure? I looked down at my hands, begging I wouldn't see those strange black shadows and orbs of light. They were the same as they always were, pale, slightly dry, and ridden with thick, spongy callous. Arcturas curled at my feet, wrapping her warmth around my toes. I looked at Frya, still eager for my response. Then to Rune.

"Something happened up there. I don't really know what, but if I tell you, you'll think I'm crazy."

"Maybe so, but regardless. Tell me, dear." Frya urged me to go on.

Swallowing the large knot that had tightened in my throat, I continued, "We reached the summit and were waiting for the borealis to appear. When it finally did, I... I don't know. The ground felt like it was shaking and my hands," I glanced down at my trembling fingers, "they were glowing. Arcturas was looking nervous, but when I went to comfort her, it was like there was an explosion between the two of us and we flew backward." I trailed off, tucking a strand of hair back behind my ear.

"What do you mean, you flew backward?" Frya's voice was low. She carried a bewildered wrinkle beneath her brow as she glanced from me to Rune.

"I was launched backward. Like someone threw me across the clearing." There was silence then. Words escaped them both as they tried to comprehend my absurd claims. I scratched Arcturas behind the ear with a toe. Apprehension electrified the air.

"I know it sounds insane or like I'd imagined it, but please, you must believe me." My eyes welled with a release of warm tears. "You must." Rune shot towards me, kneeling beside the barstool and placing his palms into mine.

"We believe you, Ell, don't worry. We do, I promise. I was there; I felt it too. One minute we were smiling, watching the horizon. The next minute I was on my ass, buried in snow." His voice was firm and reassuring.

Giving me a soft smile, he brushed his thumb against

my wrist, leaving only warmth on its trail. I stared down at his hands; the veins protruding like webs across his skin. Traces of citrine flickered across his eyes, now staring up at me through thick lashes. There was a profound kindness within them that buzzed through my aching mind. I wanted to curl up beneath their warmth and stay there for a while until the darkness within me settled back into the box. I locked it in.

Something struck at my chest as I lost what little breath I had taken in. In all of my life, I had never known such gentleness, such compassion. It was sweet on my tongue, cinnamon and spiced in flavor. My words had never been trusted with such conviction before.

"Thank you," I whispered, letting the tears roll to my chin and fall to my lap. A kettle whistled from the kitchen, interrupting the charge that now pulsed between us. Rune cleared his throat and stood, shaking the wrinkles from his white tunic. Frya appeared from the archway of the kitchen, a tray of three mugs and a teapot, now steaming with jasmine, in hand. Placing it on the table beside us with a clank, she poured us each a mug and settled into her seat across from me.

"I'm not sure what to make of all this," she sipped from her mug, both of her wrinkled hands wrapped around its base, "but one thing's for sure. Not a soul outside this room should hear about it. If the city guards were to catch wind of this, they'd think it was some sort of magic." She shot Rune a look through wisps of steam swirling from her mug.

A muscle in his sharp jaw clenched then relaxed, and his back straightened against his chair. He nodded coldly at the old woman and sipped from his mug, avoiding her watchful eye.

"Until we figure out what this means, don't give it your energy. We can't take the risk of another incident. Especially with eyes at every corner. The city folk around here talk," she said.

"I'd like to just forget this entire night," I said, stirring my tea, "but I'm not sure I can."

"Of course you can, girl. We just have to find some distraction. It's what's best." Smiling, Frya finished her tea and placed her now empty mug back on the tray resting between us.

She had a point. If I dwelled, maybe I would feed whatever it was my energy. Panicked that it would grow and solidify into something more, something dangerous, I tried to wipe it from my mind. The rise and fall of Arcturas's chest as it evened into a peaceful rhythm brought relief to my aching mind. The feel of her fur against my toes dulled the panic creeping up my throat.

"Alright..." I said, shaking the image of the blackened earth from my mind.

"Now, let's get you upstairs. I'll draw a bath for you, dear." She looked at Rune. "You best be getting home." Something changed in her eyes as she spoke to him. Was it a film of suspicion that I saw now peeled across her expression?

"Right, yes," he got to his feet, looking at me, "I won't tell anyone what happened, I promise. I have to help my uncle tomorrow with the potato harvest, but I'll come back as soon as I can."

I nodded, silently thanking him for his trust, and continued up to my bedchamber. Their brief goodbyes echoed up to my bedchamber as Rune took his leave.

After soaking away the cold, my fingers now withered and prune-y, I climbed into bed, laying in the darkness with Arcturas at my side. Images I tried to ignore scraped against me with their sharp talons. The feel of those shadows woven through my fingers hadn't felt menacing.

They almost felt familiar and natural, as if they were another limb extended from my body, like an arm or a leg.

I realized it wasn't pain or malice that had frightened me. It was the acute sense of calm and awareness. The events of the night continued to replay through my mind until exhaustion took over and they faded into black.

Chapter 12

Darkness burned my eyes as the familiar scent of smoke pinched my lungs. Coughing, I couldn't breathe. I couldn't move. My limbs were heavy against my body, muscles refusing to flex. Droplets of water echoed throughout the vastness of my surroundings. High caverns of night arched around me.

Panic traced its way through my veins as I tried again to move from where I lay. I had to get out; I had to run. She was coming. Scratching my nails against the cold floor beneath me, I continued to fight the paralysis. This couldn't be the end. It wouldn't be.

Somewhere beyond, a hum buzzed through the earth as pebbles of dirt loosened and shook from the walls above me. A faint glow radiated from my palms as licks of emerald wrapped themselves around each finger and up my wrist. I welcomed the electrifying comfort that now coursed through me in a rush of tingles.

As the light traveled outwards, it grew in intensity until my limbs themselves were nearly blinding. Its rays bounced off of a high marble ceiling. My body, now glowing with the borealis, cast away the shadows of the prison, illuminating huge white pillars and a dais beneath a pristine, white throne.

Seated upon the throne was a woman with golden hair trailing down her frame. Ringlets of curls bounced from the crown of her head down below her waist. Atop her head, a golden diadem dripping with topaz- both yellow and pink. She wore a gauzy golden gown that plunged to her hips, secured with a chain around her petite waist. Strips of apricot, lilac, and fuchsia draped down her thin, crossed legs. Her eyes burned brightly with orbs of morning sunlight as she rested her head on her arm and leaned against the side of the throne. A faint, yellow glow slithered through her veins.

"Elpis, my dear, how long I've waited to meet you." Opposite her warm and gentle likeness, her voice was bitter with a venom that trickled down the back of my neck. I swallowed hard, still unmoving.

"It seems your power has finally awakened. Good." She rose to her bare feet.

With silent, graceful steps, she seemed to float towards me, the swish of her gauzy train trailing behind her. Snapping her fingers, the chamber lit in a blaze of candles and sconces. The glow surrounding my body receded back through my fingertips, leaving a heaviness in its place. I flexed my fingers, relieved to feel the muscles contract to my will once again.

"Who are you? What do you want from me?" I asked, pushing off the floor to my feet. My knees creaked beneath my stance as I straightened them. There was something about this goddess I didn't quite trust. She was beautiful and bright, but the surrounding lightness was too intense, too harsh. It ignited only a chill down my spine as she glared at me, her eyes burning into my own with fiery hatred. I needed to get away. The goddess laughed- the sound sharp and clipped.

"My dear, you know who I am."

In that moment, I knew her. Mortals and gods alike trembled with fear in her presence. Hated across the realms, a scorned lover who had slaughtered an entire court of innocents. Tethys.

"What the hell do you want?" I hissed, taking a step away from the immortal. Her eyes lowered, and she closed the distance between us again. Her words were flames against my cheeks as she spoke.

"You." Her fingers wrapped around my throat and squeezed, cutting off my air supply. I clawed at her iron grip, gasping and wrenching for breath. She was too strong. Tears welled in my eyes as I continued struggling, the world vignetting around me. My skin burned as she squeezed tighter and tighter. The ground fell away and everything faded to black. I was dying.

Chapter 13

Gasping for air, I awoke beneath sweat drenched sheets. Dampness pooled on my brow and I scratched at my throat, trying to break free from those fierce, talon-like fingers. Throwing the covers from me, I rolled to the floor and took the musty air deeply into my lungs.

I laid there for a few minutes, not existing outside of my breath. Inhale, exhale. I wasn't dying. I was alive. Fighting away the image of those burning hands, I closed my eyes. Just a dream. I was alive.

The sun hadn't yet risen across the skyline and a tranquility hushed over the sleeping city. Hobbling to the window and pushing the pane open slightly, I embraced the chill of early morning against my skin. Had that really been Tethys I'd dreamt of? Dreams were visions of the future, forecasted across the mind. If that was true, then what could the goddess want with me? Placing my hand on my neck, I traced where her fingers had seared into my skin.

Something she said resonated within me. Your power has finally awoken. My power. Did she mean the shadows? The kernels of light that spread from my palms? They had felt so familiar, so natural- it had shaken me to my core. Maybe something within me had freed itself. Perhaps it was something that had always been there.

I needed to think. I needed to learn about my past, my history. Information kept from me as a child, knowledge hidden in shadow, anything that could pull these pieces together. The walls felt too tight, too cramped for these big thoughts. The air was too thick, too stifling. Leaving Arcturas, now curled in my residual heat, I crept down the hall to the bathing chamber, hoping a crisp splash of water across my face might clear my racing mind.

The reflection staring through me in the small, dirty mirror was unrecognizable. Beads of cold water rolled down my face as I inhaled deeply. My eyes no longer sunk into my cheekbones. My lips were no longer a dull grey. I hated to admit it, but freedom suited me. The shine of my obsidian hair had returned, and with it a delicate glimmer of content now danced along my flesh. The coldness of the water on my brow had soothed those burning thoughts, and I could think clearly.

Even if the dream had been truth, there were only two in this city, two in this realm that knew my secret. Both I trusted endlessly. For now, I was safe from Tethys. Drying the remaining beads from my face, I returned to my bedchambers to dress for the day.

Frya emerged from her chambers shortly after I began my work, fiercely sweeping, mopping, scrubbing- anything to keep my mind from reeling.

"Good morning," she said behind me, clearing her throat.

Surprised to hear her voice, I jumped, nicking my thumb with my peeling knife. Red dripped from the gash and splattered on the bowl of turnips I had been peeling. I swiveled around on the rickety wooden storeroom stool to glare.

"You scared me," I scowled, placing the wound in my mouth to keep from dripping blood.

"Aren't you supposed to be aware of your surroundings, Huntress?" Frya snickered. She pulled a stool beside me and held out the rag from her apron.

"I was lost in my thoughts," I said, wrapping it around my hand.

I plucked another turnip from its dirty burlap sack.

"I was thinking about my family line and I realized I know nothing of my ancestors. My grandparents had long since passed before either my sister or I were born. We descended from an ancient northern line, but that's the most I know."

The northern crown's familial line was veiled in secrecy. Whether a strategic decision to separate the royalty from city folk or for some other reason, maybe it was time I learned of my past.

"The temple archives might have what you're looking for. There's information on practically anything down there. I've heard it's left unguarded after dark. It'd be stupid to enter the temple chambers when Polaris is at her most powerful, but your sneaking skills seem... good enough."

"That could be our best shot," I said, looking at the barkeep. I considered telling her about my nightmare last night, but something in me thought it best to keep it to myself. If, in fact, it had been a vision, I couldn't involve Frya. It was too dangerous. I tossed the now naked turnip into my large wooden bowl and reached for another. Frya eyed me impatiently.

"Well? Think you're up for it?" she asked, rising from her stool. She shifted her weight from her cane and leaned on the doorframe.

"What did you mean my sneaking skills are good enough? Not only did I sneak out of exile, but I snuck past you during Festival! I'd say they're better than good enough."

Frya snorted, rubbing her chin thoughtfully. "You should go tonight, once the city guards blow the lamp posts out. I'll try to pull out a warmer cloak. It's supposed to be well below freezing. I'll check the spare closet."

"Thank you, Frya. Truly," I said, grabbing her leathery hand.

She smiled softly with a vacant expression flushed across her eyes. It wasn't uncommon for thoughts to consume her. What was she thinking about now? Maybe she'd found herself in a memory from long ago. I knew what it felt like to be overwhelmed by the past. I hoped, for her heart's sake, that she'd gone to a happier time. One filled with love and light, where the heartbreak of her lost child couldn't reach her.

Turning back into the kitchen, Frya began her own daily chores. We didn't speak for the rest of the day, both withdrawn into ourselves.

Just after the city bell chimed midnight, Arcturas and I departed for the temple. Creeping in shadow through the town square, we slipped up the mountainous steps, hidden from the guards finishing their watch at the temple's entrance. We were silent observers lurking in the shadow of a large boulder. The two men completed their last turn of the perimeter, yawning and swinging their lanterns lazily.

With their descent down the summit steps, Arcturas and I padded softly to the entrance marked by grand wooden doors stretching up the full length of the exterior marble walls. Glancing back toward the sloped path, I hesitated.

Was this stupid? The hilt of the silver dagger Frya gifted me just before I left now burned in my palm beneath my cloak. I knew what had to be done if anyone saw me. Was I ready to face that darkness? I had to be. This was too important, too critical. Pulling the double doors open just enough to slip through, I faded into the shadows of the temple's interior as if a terrible beast swallowed me whole.

All the sconces were blown out hours ago. Only the silver moonlight beaming through glass skylights overhead illuminated the strip of cedar beams and pillars that lined the walls of the vestibule. Obsidian sculptures of Polaris rose from matching stone floors, projecting speckles of light across the cavernous walls. Like a replica of twinkling stars across our northern sky. Each statuette posed with outstretched arms, as if beckoning me to plunge deeper into the temple's subterranean secrets.

At the back of the corridor was a dais, shrouded in gauzy drapes. On the dais, a glorious throne. I sucked in a breath, half expecting the Queen of Spring to await me there with her blonde ringlet curls and perfect little foot bouncing over her crossed leg. Only starlight and dust rested upon the throne. My footsteps echoed through the high, multi-story ceilings as I snuck behind the dais and slipped down dusty stone steps leading to the temple's archives.

The archives were vast, stretching for miles into the earth beneath the mountain. Symmetrical, unlit chandeliers, cast from iron, hung down the stretch of the corridor. Round oak desks with matching stools dispersed between row after row of leather-bound books and dusty ledgers.

Only the sound of my cautious footsteps filled the space, refracting off ornate black tiles, speckled with amethysts mapping the northern constellations. The crux stood opposite the northern star. Ursa Major and Cassiopeia beckoned to one another from their adjoining tiles.

What I was searching for, I wasn't sure exactly. I traced my hand across leather spine after spine along the shelves. Arcturas, having picked up a scent, sniffed frantically at a trail, winding her through sections and weaving between desks.

I paused at the stack of shelves labeled Immortal History. Scanning the titles on each shelf, I finally found something of promise. Pulling a thick, black leather-bound book, I started towards the closest desk. Arcturas was still furiously sniffing as I began flipping through the pages.

Tethys, goddess of Spring, Patron of Dawn, was once a benevolent and loving ruler over her people. Venia and its mortal citizens flourished beneath her reign. However, that all changed when she fell into a fit of fury, fueled by retribution.

Rumors circulated that a relationship between her mortal consort and a handmaiden had been uncovered. Heartbroken and enraged, Tethys slaughtered her husband and the entire mortal court beneath her. Although the account of this affair is not documented, historians have heavily investigated the aftermath of this massacre from across the realms.

The members of the court, in an incredibly gruesome sight, were strung from the outer city walls, warning all immortals and mortals alike not to cross the vengeful goddess. Thus started the Great War- an effort lead by Altair, God of Summer, Patron of Day and supported by Procyon, God of Autumn, Patron of Dusk.

Polaris, Goddess of Winter, Patron of Night, however, withheld her army's involvement in the bloodshed. Thousands of mortal lives were lost in the seventy-five years of battle. It wasn't until Aquilae nearly crumbled beneath Tethys's force did Polaris send her armies to support.

During the legendary Battle at Aquilae, Altair himself was seconds from forfeiting to his female enemy when the battle horns of the Northern army rang from outside the city walls. With these new reinforcements, Altair and Procyon pushed Tethys and her armies East- back to her territory.

Venia nearly burned to the ground on that historic day. Accounts from mortal citizens tell of violence and death across the flourishing Eastern Realm. A common legend spread throughout the modern city of Venia. It states that anywhere a plumeria blossomed, mortal blood was shed under their patron goddess's knife.

Once the realms were secured from war, the immortal council decreed that to prevent any more bloodshed of scorned lovers or vengeful gods, a realm isolated from the four mortal cities was to be constructed and the four patron gods would rule, invisible and separate from their mortal peoples.

They appointed four elders as conduits between the cities and their immortal namesakes. Hearts were left broken, and children were left with single parents as the immortals evacuated from their cities. Now, over a thousand years later, the bond between the two races has become seemingly nonexistent.

Venia, still isolated from the other realms, has rebuilt and grown into a prospering city. Without the active presence of their namesake goddess, mortal leadership has taken command of the city.

I smacked the thick book shut. Grumbling, I returned it to its shelf and continued to scan the aisles. The history of Tethys and the Great War was common knowledge. Everyone knew the stories. This was pointless. The archives were public record. There wouldn't be anything here I hadn't already learned in my history lessons.

I continued to hunt for an answer down the rows, however. I couldn't give up that easily. With each page after page I scanned, my frustration boiled. At my tipping point, I threw a leather text to the ground and stomped like a child, tears springing from my eyes.

I was an idiot. Nothing was here to help me. There was no explanation for what happened. The historical records of the royal lineage had told me nothing. We'd come from a pure northern line. Ancient, dating back to the first mortal settlers in the fjord. They'd been just like every other northern family. Nothing miraculous or mystical. We had descended from mere farmers. The only thing that'd set us apart from the city folk was sheer luck. They had selected the first northern king with a bone toss. A child's game.

I slid to my knees, letting the full force of my hysterics erupt out of me. Ripping pages from the books I'd pulled from their shelves, I wailed and sobbed until I expelled all the moisture from my body. When my cries faded into gulps of breath, I thought of my parents.

What would they say if they could see what I'd be-come- a shell of their daughter, consumed by her fear, cal-loused by years of cruelty and betrayal? I pictured myself as a child, running through the castle gardens, chasing butterflies, and collecting worms from the dirt.

Where was that girl?

It had been so long since I felt her presence within me. I longed for her light, for her carefree disposition, for her kindled warmth. Had she simply retreated too deep or had they murdered her the day I stepped foot into the tower? I wasn't sure anymore.

Wiping the snot now trailing down my upper lip, I inhaled deeply, chasing the sadness and anger away until only the usual numbness remained. Gathering the torn pages into my cloak pockets, I turned out of the aisle and stepped toward the exit. Something caused me to stop in my tracks, however. My heart dropped into my chest and my knees buckled beneath my weight.

At the end of the alcove, just beside the exit, stood a black-haired woman with dark indigo eyes.

Chapter 14

"What causes such pain within you that brings out those heartbreaking cries?" Polaris's voice was velvet in my ears, radiating goosebumps up my arms. I gaped at her, unable to form words, let alone conscious thought. Up close, the deep purple of her eyes swirled in rhythmic waves, seeming to glow with a buzzing power. Swallowing hard, I interlaced my trembling fingers, falling to my knees to bow before her.

"Although I appreciate your gesture of respect, there's no need for it, my dear." Suddenly, she was before me, tipping my chin up to meet her gaze with delicate, cool fingers.

The softness of her touch on my face brought a flush across my cheeks. She stood so close, if I leaned slightly forward, my nose would touch hers. Her sharp but sweet aroma wrapped around me. She smelled of apple and bergamot. She brought me to my feet, my knees still gelatinous and shaking. Smiling, the goddess tucked a loose strand of hair back behind my ear and brushed the dirt from my cloak.

"Child, why have you come here tonight?" The hem of her deep navy dress swished as she took a step back and encouraged me to speak, letting her hands fall gently to her sides. The material shimmered as if every star in the sky above had been collected and sewn into its folds. I noticed she wore no crown, just a carved amethyst clip collecting strands of hair neatly at the nape.

"I was looking for answers, Goddess," I said, my voice nearly a whisper. She raised a brow in my direction, and I could've sworn a slight smile curled at the corner of her plum colored lips.

"And did you find them?" she asked.

A trace of amusement floated just beneath the surface of her words. I sighed and shook my head, picking at a hangnail on my thumb nervously. Her eyes sparkled as she snapped her open fingers in front of her. The sconces mounted in each corner of the room erupted into flame, then faded into a dim crackle. Polaris placed her hands behind her back and began down the corridor, her steps so gentle she seemed to float above the floor.

"I would disagree, my dear. I think you've found everything you needed tonight." Smiling, she pulled a book from a shelf, opening it and perusing its contents until deciding it wasn't what she sought and returned it to its place.

"I have found no clarity here. Just a history lesson on the Great War and the fact that I descended from farmers," I grumbled, my brow wrinkling with frustration. Polaris reached for another book and flipped to its first page, rubbing her chin as she scanned each line.

Without looking up from the text, she said, "Elpis, dear, how can you expect to find clarity when you aren't truly looking for it?" she asked, without looking up from the text.

I hesitated, unsure what she meant.

"When you're ready for the truth, it will appear," she whispered.

What was it with immortals and riddles?

"But I am ready for the truth! I need to know what I'm up against. I... I'm frightened." My voice trailed off.

It was the first time I'd truly acknowledged my fear out loud. Speaking those words, it made everything solid. Polaris closed her book gently and looked up at me, her glittering eyes now soft and loving.

"It is you, my dear, that you are frightened of. Just remember that."

I sighed and slumped onto the oak stool next to me. Holding my head in my hands, I begged the goddess to tell me what she meant. I needed her to explain what was happening and why.

"Goddess, please, I don't know what that means." I looked up, wiping the new tears from my eyes.

The sconces, once lit, were cold and dark. I was utterly alone. Had I just imagined that? I rubbed at my eyes, making sure I wasn't hallucinating. The shadows of these archives must have caused me to see things that weren't truly there.

I shuddered, wrapping my cloak tightly around myself to warm the deep chill that now dripped down my bones. Scanning the room once more, I noticed a book resting on the desk in the center of the space where the imaginary Polaris had stood. The book hadn't been there when I entered, and I definitely didn't place it there.

Something struck within me that maybe what I'd just experienced was real, and I truly did just converse with our namesake goddess. With shaky fingers, I lifted the text from the marble tabletop. A dictionary? What was so special about a Gods damned dictionary? Maybe the Goddess was mocking me. Maybe that's what immortals did, simply toyed with their mortal people. I slammed the dictionary shut, gripped the leather bound and flung it across the room.

The heavy text hit the opposing wall with a thud, smashing the glass mirror mounted there upon impact. I sucked in a gasp, praying the guards above hadn't returned yet to hear the sudden disturbance of glass shatter. Save for the blood now roaring in my ears, all was quiet.

Gathering the glass shards, my mouth thinned with growing frustration. I needed to clean this mess to avoid igniting suspicion when the morning guards did their rounds. The last thing I needed was to spark up my search party in the city again. I'd heard they'd scoured the western realm with no success and were making their way down the southern trade routes, hunting for a lead.

When I bent down to pick up the final shard, however, something struck my eye. In the crease where the tile flooring met the wall, a sliver of vibrant magenta peeked from beneath the aging wallpaper. Placing the shards in a pile beside me, I scratched at the wall. The adhesive was aged enough that the wallpaper panel peeled cleanly off.

Hidden beneath was a mural so vibrant, so masterfully painted, it stole every breath in my lungs. Fluorescent greens, blues, and violets washed across the wall. A symbol of our northern goddess and her power.

The borealis bent and curled around a black mountain peak. Something about the landscape felt familiar. The colorful swirls in the painted sky seemed to call to me, inviting me to come closer with its beauty.

As if in a trance, I traced my finger along the mountain range, feeling the raised ridges of the brushstrokes. The landscape extended further beneath the wallpaper. With each panel of wallpaper I tore, the mural grew in size and splendor. A fjord in front of snowy mountain tops. A frozen lake, the reflection of the starry sky bouncing off its surface. A small cottage with smoke meandering out its stone chimney.

What was this place? The area resembled the Northern Realm, with slight variations. Where I expected a dip in the mountainous background, there would be a peak. A crystalline lake where there should have been flatland. I needed to know what this beautiful world was.

Finally, I ripped the final panel of wallpaper from its paste,revealing the last section of the mural. Inscribed within a small box was a sentence or two written in the ancient northern folk's language. Most of our realm's written history hadn't yet been transcribed in the modern tongue. With the hardships of winter and the depression that swallowed our city, transcription was lost to the wayside. And so, my sister and I were required to learn the ancient dialect. Academics and chroniclers maintained primarily, but as royals, it was equally important that we'd read it proficiently.

"When winter and spring coincide, darkness's heir brings the light of truth and the fall of vanity. Only embers of life can destroy visions of death." What did that mean? Someone had clearly covered this up. It must be of significance. I had a lot to report to Frya and Rune. Maybe they'd make some sense of this cryptic message. I had come to the archives seeking clarity, but would leave with something far from it.

A shuffle on the level above caused my heart to plummet into my stomach. Shit. How much time had I spent down here? And where the hell was Arcturas? She'd caught on a scent trail and disappeared down some shadowy alcove.

Hastily, I rolled the shreds of wallpaper into a dark corner row, tossing the mirror shards into a pile beside them. The dictionary, I tucked into my cloak. Not that I expected it to unlock the hidden mysteries of the realm, but Polaris had left it for a reason. I needed time to figure out why.

As I hastily made my way up the steps to the upper

foyer of the temple, I couldn't shake the sinking feeling of dread. Something was coming for me, and if I didn't figure out what or why... I cast out the thought before it could bubble to the surface. Sitting at the top step was Arcturas, happily wagging her bushy tail, tongue hanging to the side of her mouth.

"Where have you been?" I hissed, reaching the top level, and tiptoeing toward the temple's entrance. She whined quietly and fell in step behind me. There was no sign of the guards returning for shift. All was quiet. Still, I had already risked too much time here. With each passing second, city guards could be returning to their post. We swiftly exited the temple, leaving the unlit sconces and shadows with their secrets.

The late night air stung in my throat as we made our frosty descent. I barely noticed it though, as thoughts and questions whizzed around my mind. Polaris and her riddles echoed through me until her words were exhaustively carved into my memories. The landscaped mural and its ancient message. Something had been so familiar about that place. Like I'd been there in a daydream, or a distant memory. I needed to think, to reflect on what I'd seen and experienced tonight. I needed to get out of this damned cold.

By the time we reached the tavern, a thin, dewy glaze of delirium had filmed over my eyes and my body ached in every muscle. Greeted by candlelight and bombarded by questions from a frantic Frya as we entered, all I could do was hold up my hand, mutter a few words, and climb the stairs to bed.

Throughout the next morning, Frya swarmed me like a fly to decay, asking question after question about the temple and what I'd found out. I'd chosen not to mention the part where I'd come face to face with our patron goddess, and instead focused on the mural and its mysterious inscription.

She devoured every piece of information I fed her and exploded with dozens more questions I didn't have the answer to. By the time the morning sun reached its pinnacle, I wanted to rip all of my hair out and scream at her until my cheeks were blue. I held my tongue, of course, throwing myself into my chores.

An hour or two before the tavern's opening, a knock on the locked front door interrupted Frya's relentless interrogation, however, and we looked at each other with startled expressions. Hiding in the kitchen, ready to slip into the cellar at a moment's notice, I watched the barkeep hobble to the front of the tavern. She slowly unlocked the door and cracked it open, just enough to peek through at the unannounced visitor. A familiar male voice, cheery with energy, spoke from outside as Frya said, "Oh, it's you."

Scowling, she stepped aside. Rune wore a thick fur-lined cloak, his espresso hair speckled with flurries. His eyes lit up as they met mine. Shedding the heavy layer, he trotted towards me, hands hidden beneath the pockets of black wool trousers.

"Ell! I wanted to make sure you were okay after the other night. I'm sorry I couldn't come sooner. The harvest held me up. Here, I brought you something I thought might cheer you up." Pulling a mason jar of what appeared to be some sort of jam littered with minuscule black seeds from his left pocket, he said, "Plum! Freshly made this morning."

He held the jar out, grinning widely. The deep red color of its contents reminded me more of congealed blood than a sweet topping for toast. Plucking the jar from his open palm, I faked a smile and thanked him, praying silently that he didn't insist I try it.

"It's delicious on fresh bread. I thought about bringing a loaf from my uncle's stores, but it would've been a cube of ice after traveling through this storm," he chuckled.

"Oh, that's alright, I'll try it with breakfast tomorrow morning." The lie slipped through my teeth, maybe too sweetly, and I cleared my throat, hoping he hadn't noticed.

"So," I began, changing the subject as abruptly as I could, "I did some...research... last night." Frya's intense stare burned holes in the back of my head as I crossed the tavern and pulled three chairs in front of the hearth.

"Anyone want some tea?" she interrupted. The bluntness in her tone screamed at me to keep the events of last night from him.

"No, thank you though Frya," I said, turning back to Rune who's golden eyes now burned with fierce curiosity.

If I held out now, the poor man might explode. I started the retelling of my experience in the archives, still leaving out Polaris and her speech of riddles. Rune's brow furrowed deeper across his face. With each passing question, another wrinkle creased itself between his eyes.

The white cotton tunic he wore hung loosely down his chest, revealing a peak of tanned, muscular flesh. Catching my traitorous eyes as they trailed to the exposed, smooth skin, I blinked towards my feet, stroking the sleeping wolf beneath me, my cheeks now the color of his plum jam.

"I can't believe you snuck into the temple! The guards could have seen you! Or worse, I've heard Polaris frequents the archives at night. Disappointing there wasn't much insight to find, though. The mural sounds promising. If we knew what it meant." He leaned forward, elbows resting on his knees, chin cupped in the palm of his hands. Frya joined us, carrying a tarnished glass and her polishing rag.

"So, this inscription. Tell me again exactly what it said." She sat behind Rune.

"When winter and spring coincide, darkness's heir brings the light of truth and the fall of vanity. Only embers of life can destroy visions of death," I recited.

"I'm not sure about the first bit, but darkness's heir... that reminds me of a story I'd been told as a girl." Frya placed the glass gently. "My grandmother loved ancient folk fables. There was one she'd tell me occasionally about the old gods. The predecessors of our namesakes today. There was Night, Day, Dawn, and Dusk. The points of the circadian cycle. Night, the ancestral god of our Polaris, was sometimes also referred to as simply darkness. Maybe that's what the ancients were referring to?"

"If that's the case, that mural must be hundreds of thousands of years old. I knew the temple was old, but damn, not that old," I said, stroking Arcturas's ear beneath the table.

"The ancient folk built around the mountain. Maybe the archives had already been there? darkness's heir could be simply suggesting our goddess. She was his descendent," Frya said.

"Maybe. I don't know what this all means or even if it has anything to do with me, but what I know is that someone covered it up. Someone wanted to keep this a secret. Maybe we shouldn't go poking our noses into this. Gods only know what it'll stir up." I tapped my fingers on the rough wooden table. The heat from the hearth turned stifling. I was treading into something I wasn't sure I should be. Something ancient. Something big.

My brow beaded with sweat. All I'd wanted was my freedom from this world. To live a quiet life far away, without the constant breath of fear tickling down my neck. That tower had taken everything from me, and yet I'd risked it all twice over to escape. Wasn't that enough? I was sinking into quicksand, unable to pull myself free from whatever shadows lurked beneath my skin.

Pulling the neck of my tunic from my sticky flesh, I stood from my seat.

"Rune, would you like to walk with me through the

courtyard? I think I need some air."

He nodded and rose to his feet.

"I need to get dinner started. Don't worry, dear. We'll figure this out. Everything will be fine." Tucking the tray under her arm, Frya smiled sadly and limped to the kitchen. Arcturas trailed behind her, hoping to catch a rogue scrap or two fallen from the counter.

The courtyard, although small, was peaceful at night. Torches mounted on the exterior walls of the tavern and the adjoining brick townhomes flickered quietly, throwing shadows across the small stone fountain babbling at the yard's center. Our steps sunk into the snow as we passed firs that speckled the bleached ground with emeralds and olives. The air of the evening left my cheeks riddled with a harsh chill, but I welcomed it, trying to cool the heat of the hearth from my face.

Rune was quieter than I'd expected. A distance had glazed over him, as if he'd been carried somewhere far from here. Just like Frya, whose mind often tangled with memory and reality, I'd notice that same vacancy blink across Rune's eye. It was subtle and fleeting, but I recognized it. Demons of something, or someone, or somewhere, haunted him. Just as I was. Just as Frya was. Maybe the three of us had found each other for a reason. Maybe he needed this friendship just as much as I needed it.

"I love coming out here at night. Everything's so peaceful. It's one of the few places I truly feel at ease," I said, plucking a needle from a juvenile tree.

Rune gazed at the sky. Thousands of stars twinkled at us in a milky wave of ancient light.

"It's a clear one tonight," he said, silver moonlight reflecting off his sharp jawline. "I haven't seen the stars quite like this in a long time."

Not a grey cloud was visible above us. We stopped to admire the infinite stretch of galaxies and constellations extending from horizon to horizon. I took a long breath, letting the calmness of the night wash through me.

"My mother used to tell me the myths and legends of the sky when I was a child. There was a time when I could recite any of the constellations and their fables." Rune's expression grew dim.

"I don't think I remember a single one now, though."

A nighthawk screeched from above, its raven-colored wingspan nearly invisible against the blackness of the sky as it soared across the courtyard.

"How did you lose her?" I asked, hoping I hadn't overstepped.

He was quiet for a while, contemplating a response.

With a voice, nearly a whisper, he said, "She was sick."

We circled the courtyard once more.

"Flatland creatures killed my mother when I was young. I know what it's like to have someone you loved taken from you."

Faces of everyone I'd lost throughout my life blurred together. My mother. My father. Vikar. Even my sister. I hadn't realized I'd grown so quiet until Rune took my hand in his. That familiar spark pricked at the skin beneath his touch and it took everything in me not to jerk away from it.

"You have the look," he said, eyes burning into mine.

"What look?"

"The look of someone who's far too familiar with loss. I can see it behind those eyes of yours, no matter how hard you try to hide it. It's there."

The warmth of his hand against mine rose through my arm and into my chest, causing my heart to thud rapidly.

I scanned his expression, looking for something, anything, that'd give away his thoughts right now. There was nothing but kindness. Kindness and a trace of heartbreak.

"You have the look too, then."

I couldn't break the line of energy that buzzed between

us.

He nodded, rubbing his thumb across the back of my hand.

Draped in curtains of moonlight, we stood there, reflecting on the demons of grief and trauma from our pasts.

I hadn't realized I was crying until Rune lifted a finger to my cheek. He wiped a salty bead of memories from my skin.

I'd been isolated, beaten, humiliated, destroyed.

My life, my future, had all been stripped from me in a matter of seconds.

My fate was decided for me.

I was losing control. My choices in life were stolen away with each passing day.

Maybe it was time I stole them back.

I was free from that tower and all the horrors it brought, but fear had been my true jailer. Fear of those shadows that dripped from my palms, fear of the Spring Queen and her vicious words. Most of all, I realized, fear of what might happen if I let myself out of that place I'd run to when everything fell apart.

What would happen if I unlocked the door? Even for a moment.

I wouldn't be afraid anymore. I leaned into Rune and brushed my lips against his. Everything inside me erupted with life. His lips burned against mine, stunned into stillness for a split second, then moving fiercely, matching the rhythm of my own. Draping my arms around his neck, I stepped into him, letting the ember of his body against mine send shockwaves throughout me.

I didn't care if this was foolish. I didn't care if he did not know who I really was. I wanted this- maybe even needed this. It was just me and him, beneath a washing of stars. It wasn't just a glimpse I'd set free, but my complete self. The brightness of who I'd been cast out those demons that had taken control. Even if only for a moment. There was nothing beyond where our lips met. Tears swelled and streaked my face. Here and now, I was truly and utterly free.

Someone cleared their throat behind me, causing Rune to rip away. Breathing with an unsteady rise and fall of my chest, I turned towards the light of the now open back door. It was Frya, wild with panic. Behind her, in atrocious purple uniforms, stood two city guards.

Chapter 15

Every muscle in my body clenched and an immediate, frantic sweat flushed itself through me. Frya stared, silently apologizing, as the two guards pushed her aside and marched towards me, the hems of violet cloaks dragging flurries of snow behind them. My eyes darted to each corner of the courtyard, looking for something- anything to help me out of this situation.

Rune's head jerked toward the two men, then back to me, confusion pouring from his gaping mouth. My lips still tingled from where his had been as the guards continued to march forward, their motion slowing with every approaching step. I had only seconds to make my move, or I'd be captured. I couldn't go back to that fucking tower.

Everything became much, much worse, however, when a plump old woman with auburn hair stepped out from behind Frya.

"My, my," her voice was like venom, "Lady Elpis. You've got a lot of explaining to do, my dear."

Hela knocked the handle of a brown leather whip

across her open palm as she hobbled towards me. The guards, now circling my position, nodded at her as she waved them to take a step back.

"L-Lady Elpis…" Rune stammered, "as in the Queen Slayer?" His eyes were wide and bright with uncertainty as he processed the situation at hand.

I looked at him, mouthing an apology as I backed away from the approaching handmaiden.

"Don't even think about going anywhere. We've got the yard circled, dear. Might as well accept that you're coming with us. Do you know exactly how many rules you've broken?" Hela grinned, her chin doubling over in layers of swollen flesh beneath her neck.

I scanned the yard again. There had to be something. Anything.

"I think I'd like to deliver your punishment before we return to the tower." The whip glowed in her fat hands. Glaring at me, yearning to be cracked against my bare flesh.

My feet, frozen beneath me, refused to move as I tried to run. If I could reach the wall on the opposite side of the courtyard, scale it and escape through the neighbor's flat, I'd be free. I'd need my legs to work, though.

Frya sobbed, falling to her knees in the tavern's threshold, the deep navy skirts she wore pooling around her fragile frame. I couldn't leave her to face the punishment alone. What was I thinking? They'd arrest her for helping me, and after everything she'd done, how could I possibly abandon her?

Then there was Rune, the innocent, charming man whose lips I'd just attacked. Thousands of thoughts probably zipped through his head in this moment. Queen Slayer he had called me. Regardless of the innocence he'd try to claim, the guards would accuse him of aiding me. They'd most likely arrest him, too. My throat was dry as everything around me collapsed. This couldn't be happening.

I just gained my freedom back, tasted a future without fear.

"Guards, hold her down for me, please," Hela snarled.

The men grabbed my arms and threw me to the ground, ripping away my cloak and slicing down the fabric of my cotton tunic, exposing bare flesh to the frigid night air.

With a mouthful of snow, I struggled beneath their firm grip, trying to tear myself free. Cold, clammy hands traced each of my shoulder blades as Rune's screams of protest echoed across the yard. Frya's sobs grew into wails as the two guards pulled at the sleeves of my tunic, exposing more of my back to the pale wash of moonlight.

I took in a breath, no longer struggling to escape, and preparing for what was about to come. I'd been through this before. This time, I'd remain still. Emotionless.

I would not show her my pain.

I would not show her my tears.

There would be no begging or pleading.

No cries or sobs.

Just silence.

Biting my bottom lip until the metal taste of blood soaked into my tongue, I flexed every muscle beneath my skin, building up my fortress walls.

Crack! Pain erupted across my flesh as the whip whistled and retracted back to its handler. Clenching harder, I fought against the automatic jerk of my body. Thinking only of Rune's lips against mine. Igniting flames at the pit of my stomach. Only of Frya's stews and peeling potatoes until my fingers cramped and grew numb. Only of Arcturas and the feel of her thick fur beneath my hand as I stroked her to sleep.

Crack! Another lash sent me spiralling into torturous ash as the welts across my back rose like mountain ridges of red, stinging flesh. Crack! Crack! Crack! With each swing of her whip, Frya's breath deepened until she heaved for air like a fish out of water.

My entire being was trembling fiercely now, so much so I struggled to stay on my knees. Drops of red sprayed across the snow beneath me as the lashings oozed and dripped down my spine.

Crack! Rune, hoarse from roaring at the guards, had sunken to his knees- tears pooling from his lower lids. I prayed to the gods for strength as a tear escaped from my scrunched eyes.

Fight, Elpis. You must fight. A whisper licked at the back of my neck. I recognized the silkiness of her voice.

The Northern Goddess was guiding me, urging me to carry on when I teetered on the precipice.

Fight, Elpis! Fight back!

Biting harder against my lower lip, I struggled to pull free once more from the two unmoving men holding me down.

The whip flung through the air, and I shut myself down preparing for its impact.

It never came.

Screams of agony and shredding flesh rang out. The guards, flanking each side of me, rushed back towards where Frya had stood, leaving my wrists bruised and swollen. Rune ran to my side and pulled me up by my elbow, careful not to touch the tender, bleeding skin of my back.

The scene behind me was bloody and brutal- nearly as nightmarish as the vivid dreams I'd been having. A hand, missing its adjoining arm. A body mangled in the snow. Sprays of blood and shreds of fabric stained the bleached white snowpack.

Hela, squirming beneath a jet black beast, flailed and screamed as sharp fangs penetrated the gushing stump where her left hand used to be. The handle of the whip rolled to my feet.

"Arcturas, enough," I commanded, straightening

against the pain of my wounds.

The wolf stopped immediately, rushing to my side and sitting eagerly for her next order. The guards, now paralyzed by fear, simply stared at the horror. Their faces were spattered with crimson. The violet of their uniforms was stained an unsettling shade of brown. I uncurled my spine, neck cracking on each side.

Shadows slithered around me, extinguishing the starlight until the air was heavy with a deep, unending blackness. I closed my eyes, breathing in the rush of pain from the wounds across my back.

"Oh Lady Elpis, please, please help me. That.. that.. thing came out of nowhere. My hand! It's gone. My hand." The round woman rolled in the snow like a sausage, cradling her stump as she begged.

I continued forward until I towered over her, a violent glint refracting beneath the surface of my eyes. A rush of tingles bolted through me, and darkness leaked from every pore of my skin. Flames of jade and magenta licked between my fingers, wrapping themselves down the hilt of the whip until the entire length of it glowed like the northern borealis.

This time I welcomed the charge, the power. I didn't run from it. I didn't fear it. This electricity coursing through me had always been there. It was as much a part of me as my lungs or my stomach. Smiling with deadly sweetness, I lowered my gaze to the handmaiden and knelt before her. I tipped her chin up, forcing her eyes to meet mine. They were full of terror.

"Oh, my dear," I spat, "you've broken a rule. Are you ready for your punishment?"

My voice, laced with shadows and smoke, interrupted her pleading sobs and forced her into silence.

I raised the whip and watched as the power emulating from my fingertips connected with its cold metal handle. The leather glimmered as I jerked my hand down and split it across Hela's open jaw.

The glow spread to her skin as she dissolved like acid. In seconds, nothing but bones and burnt flesh remained.

Arcturas howled deeply towards the sky.

"They're all yours, my friend." As the words exited my mouth, she shot across the yard, lunging at the guards. The gleam of power fading from my palms, and the shadows receding back into my flesh, I reached for Rune. With wide eyes and shaking hands, he interlaced his fingers through mine and rose from the hedge he now hid behind.

Frya sat against the brick of the tavern's exterior, her fingers white knuckled around the hem of her skirts.

"It's okay," I assured her, my voice my own again, "I won't hurt you."

She stammered, trying to find a response, but I hushed her and placed her hands in mine. The deafening sounds of two men being shredded apart consumed the night as I led her back into the tavern's warmth.

Chapter 16

"I think we all could use a drink," I said, wiping away the speckles of blood scattered across my brow.

Frya nodded, her complexion still ghostly. Glasses clinked beneath her quaking hands as she poured three bourbons. Draining hers, then refilling, she returned to where we sat, passing each of us our drinks. It wasn't until we had finished two rounds did Arcturas trot inside, unrecognizable under scraps of sickly, grayish skin and dried blood.

Looking upon her, Frya gasped, her glass shattering across the floor. I jumped to collect the shards. Rune grabbed my wrist and pulled me back to my feet.

"Ell...Your back. It's... it's healed. There's nothing but scars there." He traced the patterns of raised, purple scar tissue across my skin.

Before I could lean into his touch, he jerked away, suddenly remembering who I truly was. I continued picking up the final shards of glass, hoping to distract myself from the feel of his fingers against my skin and the ripped tunic that now partially exposed my undergarments.

"I'm not really sure the extent of this power yet. It was enough to heal my wounds, I guess." Beckoning Arcturas over, I started picking the flesh from her fur. Her blood-soaked paws left prints across the hardwood and Frya, scowling about her floors, hobbled to the kitchen for a bucket of warm water.

"I guess you're probably wondering what the hell that was about." I glanced cautiously at Rune after discarding a bit of muscle tissue on to the hearth. He locked eyes with the flesh charring against hot coals.

"Maybe a little." He took the final swig of his drink, grimacing as it washed down his throat, and reached for the bottle Frya had brought over for a refill.

Continuing to groom Arcturas, who now lay contently on her side with legs fully stretched, I recounted my story to Rune. The key from Vikar, the creature in the flatlands, even my nightmares and what actually happened in the temple.

Once I began, I couldn't stop. Words escaped from my mouth like a landslide gaining momentum with each sentence. Everything poured from me until there was nothing left. I leaned my head into my hands, barely breathing, awaiting Rune's response.

"I see." He crossed his legs, tapping his empty glass with a slender index finger. "That explains a lot."

"I'm sorry I lied to you. I shouldn't have brought you into this. It was selfish of me." My voice trembled as I spoke. "I put you and Frya in danger."

"The bloodshed tonight was… shocking, but you don't scare me. I'm here. Frya's here. Regardless of who you are." Rune leaned across the table and kissed me softly. His touch was all the comfort I needed. I wanted to melt into him, leave the night behind, and float away in his scent.

So, what are we going to do now?" Frya cleared her

throat from the kitchenette window.

Rune's lips parted from mine, leaving me yearning to fill the space they'd taken up.

"I'm assuming that others will come looking when those three," she nodded towards the courtyard, "don't return. It breaks my heart to say this, but you can't stay here, let alone in the city."

"I'll leave now, get out of the North. The sooner I'm away from here, the sooner you're safe," I said, sucking in a breath.

"You don't think I'll let you go alone, do you?" Rune's eyes ignited a molten gold as the corner of his mouth curled slightly into a mischievous smile.

"You're not coming. I can't ask that of you. You'd never be able to return. If they didn't think you were guilty of helping me now, they would if they caught both of us." Before I could continue to protest, he reached across the table and placed his hands on top of mine.

Staring at me with a burning intensity, his words were low, but unwavering as he spoke, "My life in Ursae was over the second I met you, Elpis. I'm coming with you."

It took a moment to comprehend the depth of his words. My full name whispered across his lips like an intoxicating melody. It took all of my strength to keep my jaw from dropping to the stained, rough tabletop beneath me.

"I don't have a plan, Rune. I don't know where I'm going or how I'll get there. How could I ask that of you? It's too dangerous."

"All the more reason for me to come with you. Plus, I have an idea, but it might be a little crazy." He squeezed my hand in reassurance.

Raising my gaze from our interlaced fingers, I noticed something about his features I hadn't recognized before. There was a shimmer, almost like the blur of heat rising off a concrete surface on a torched summer's day, drifting across his eyes. It was strange, but maybe it was the bourbon or the flicker of candlelight playing tricks.

"Venia," he said, and my back straightened against my chair. "No one goes in or out. You'd be safe there. No one would recognize you; you could start anew. Create the life you've always wanted. I have a distant family member remaining there. She wouldn't ask questions."

"I don't know..." I trailed off, lowering my eyes to my feet. I thought of the blonde goddess wrapping her long, burning fingers around my throat, the tips of her nails digging into my skin.

Rune was a genius or a complete madman for suggesting we willfully travel into her realm. I realized either way, we'd likely be killed. If we stayed, more city guards would come sniffing. If we went, we risked a fate against the Queen of Spring herself.

"Look, I'd say Canissa, but the North has pull there. Some loyalist would recognize you and report back to the Elders. I'm telling you, we could hide in plain sight in Venia. City folk are so focused on themselves, they would never notice us. I promise, this could work."

Rune's argument was convincing, but I was still hesitant. Something inside told me to find another route.

"He's right. They'll find you in Canissa and Aquilae is too far to travel. It's at least a two week long ride." Frya returned with warmed cinnamon biscuits and jam, plopping a sudsy bucket and rag beside me. "Plus, those roads are treacherous, especially for those wishing to remain unseen. The only safe passage is the main trade line and you can be sure it'll be flooded with guards. Venia is the unexpected plan."

"Yeah, because no one in their right mind would willingly visit the Eastern Realm." I countered, "Unfortunately, all other plans end in imprisonment or death so... I hope we don't regret this."

Rune stood from his seat and knelt before me and

rested his hands on both of my knees. He looked up at me through brown, unkempt locks. "I promise you, Lady Elpis, I won't let anything happen to you. You're safe with me."

He smiled, then erupted into laughter, his shoulders shaking with each escaping snicker.

"Who am I kidding?" he snorted. "You'll be the one protecting my ass. Tell me, did you actually melt the skin from that horrible woman, or was I imagining that?"

I couldn't help but chuckle along with him, feeling the weight of my lungs lessen. It should have been concerning how lightheartedly we spoke of melting flesh and gruesome bloodshed, but I embraced the easiness of the room around us and allowed myself a smile.

"I'm not sure, but that definitely was real." The laughter faded as we looked at each other. Entirely aware that his hands still rested gently on my kneecaps, I adjusted uncomfortably and cleared my throat.

"You are such a strange creature," he said, and a shimmer around his face flickered. Rune must have caught my expression as I watched the blur shift across his nose, because he rose to his feet abruptly, collected the glasses and empty bourbon bottle, and returned them to the bar.

"Are you going to be okay here?" I asked the barkeep I cherished so deeply.

"Dear, I've been okay here longer than you've even been alive. I'll be fine. The guards'll come asking questions, but nothing I can't handle."

"I wish you could come with us, but I can't ask you to take any more risks than you already have. You've done so much already."

She smiled sadly and stroked Arcturas behind the ear.

"Hand me that rag," Frya said, washing away the remaining grime from her pelt. "Stay until dawn. I'll pack you some rations for the travel and there's some old clothes upstairs you can take."

There was a forcefulness in her tone, as if she were

holding back tears. I stared into the soapy bucket, afraid that if I looked at the barkeep, I, too, would lose control.

"Frya, I..." my voice cracked, and I swallowed the sob now rising in my throat, "I don't know if I could ever thank you enough."

She took my hand. The wrinkled skin was rough and colder than the snow falling outside, but I didn't jerk away. I squeezed her fingers between mine and risked a glance up at her, feeling a tear roll down my cheek.

"You'll always have a home here," she said, her eyes glistening. With a sad goodnight, Frya retired upstairs. Only the embers popping from the hearth filled the quiet.

"I should dash home, say my goodbyes to my uncle, and pack a bag. I'll be back before dawn," Rune said, interrupting the thoughts racing through my mind. Leaning next to me, he tipped my chin up towards him so our noses nearly touched.

"It'll be okay," he whispered, the sound like velvet in my ear. He lowered his lips and brushed a gentle kiss across mine, causing a flutter to push the heartache away.

"I know," I lied. The weight of the night pressed the walls in on me, and I knew in my bones that nothing would be okay again. Not for Rune, not for Frya, and most certainly not for me.

Later, laying beneath my scratchy quilt, sleep didn't find me. The worry of what tomorrow would yield tightened its grip around my neck, and the inexplicable events of tonight clawed at my throat. I unleashed something within me, let it rise to the surface and take control. Something filled with darkness, so violently all-consuming.

Images of Hela's boiling skin flashed every time my eyes drifted shut- another nightmare to add to my collection, I supposed. I let my hatred towards the old chambermaid take hold.

Polaris had told me this unmeasurable power had always been there, but that unsettled me more. There was something, once locked away, that was now coursing through me. How long until it devoured anything and everything that remained of me?

Arcturas, feeling my body trembling, nuzzled against my chest and tucked her snout into the crease of my neck. Her slow, steady heartbeat calmed my own as I focused on the feel of her fur against my cheek and the cold wetness of her nose by my ear. Collecting my thoughts with each gentle stroke down her muscular back, I couldn't help but feel our connection pulsating between us. Like an electric current, jolting from wolf to mortal.

From monster to monster.

We were the same, the two of us. She didn't hesitate to pounce when I needed her, just as I didn't hesitate to pluck her tiny body up from the barren, frozen ground.

Heartbeats syncing into one monotonous rhythm, we both finally drifted to sleep, with only a few hours remaining before dawn's approach.

Chapter 17

Blood. There was so much blood. The stench was ripe in my nose as it rushed down my face by the bucket load. The rancid taste of iron flooded my mouth. I clawed at my eyes. There was too much streaming down to wipe away. I couldn't see, couldn't hear, couldn't breathe. I was drowning in it. It continued flowing down my neck, my chest, my legs.

"Look at what you've done," a voice hissed from the darkness behind me, like a serpent of the shadows. Still wiping away the sickeningly hot fluid gushing down my brow, I turned to face it.

"Open your eyes Elpis. Look at the destruction you've caused." Its words slithered around me in tendrils of ice.

Finally, the flow slowed enough for me to wipe the remaining drops from my face. My blurred vision, stained in crimson hues, finally focused on the bodies below me.

Hundreds of them.

No.

Thousands.

Twisted and mangled in unnatural positions. Two feet folded against the forehead of a crumpled dark haired man. Hands, broken at the wrists, coiled backwards across a woman with the same jet black hair. These had been city folk. The entire northern city was dead and rotting beneath my feet.

Sobs escaped me. Bones cracked and popped under my weight as I fell to my knees, entirely overwhelmed by the horror.

"You did this," the voice, now licking the back of my neck, whispered. I jerked my head around and stared at the lips that had produced those words.

All the air was sucked out of the darkness. My chest burned until I thought my sternum might collapse in on itself. I shook my head and stifled the desperate breaths now escaping my lips. The geometric features and pale complexion of my sister glared back at me.

Gaping black voids remained where her ice-blue eyes once were. Her complexion, once white and pure as snowfall, was a leathery, rotten grey.

"Look at all the innocence lost, Elpis. Look at them all. Look at what you've taken from them," she said, pointing her long, perfectly shaped fingernail at the bodies of our people.

"Look at what you've done to me," she hissed through a putrid breath.

This wasn't real. She couldn't be here. I couldn't have killed these people. I pressed against a broken skull to support myself from the shock. The hands beneath me were not my own. Instead of the usual short nails, claws protruded from my fingertips.

"You did this," she hissed again, rage seething through

her clenched, rotten teeth.

My heart flamed against the inside of my chest. Clutching for it, I fell across the pile of bodies, my face squelching against the innards of an eviscerated city guard. The scream of horror building pressure at the top of my throat finally unleashed and echoed through the chamber.

"Look at them. Look at me. Look at what you did. What you took." Adria's voice grew into screams until it overpowered the chamber, echoing against every corner and curve of the walls. Repeating those words over and over again, she reached for a mangled body and threw it on top of me. Then another, and another, and another until I was buried beneath the still warm carcasses. I clawed and pounded at the body. My cries, muffled through dead flesh, became nothing but a murmur. Everything faded into red as the pile of innocent, slaughtered lives devoured me.

Chapter 18

I awoke with a terror unlike any I'd ever felt. Arcturas, seemingly just as shaken by something as I was, scratched at the door and whined. Pacing the bedchamber until the first trace of dawn touched the sky, we waited to head downstairs to meet our fate. I pulled Vikar's key from its hiding place beneath a loose floorboard and looped it through a silver chain I'd borrowed from Frya, securing it in place beneath my tunic.

Finally, after dressing in an olive green tunic and thick leather trousers, I slipped on the new pair of fur-lined boots and crept down the stairs. Leaving before the barkeep awoke would be easiest. I wasn't sure I could look her in the eyes and walk away. Rune sat at the bar, a thermos of coffee in one hand, a slice of toast in the other- smothered in plum jam. Pots clanked from the kitchen, illuminated only by candlelight.

"I guess she's awake then," I sighed. We'd have to do this the hard way.

Rune shrugged and took a long sip of his coffee. His

hair was ragged, as if he hadn't bathed since the night before. Somehow, the shaggy mess above his brow curled and twisted in all the right directions. He really was effortlessly handsome.

I crumpled the note I had written Frya last night and shoved it into the pocket of my trousers as she appeared from the kitchen carrying plates of sausage and potatoes in both hands.

"Figured you best have a hot breakfast before heading out. It'll be a long day of traveling. You'll need something to keep your strength up." She set the steaming food in front of us.

The smell, any other morning I'd find delightful, only nauseated me as I thought of those torn up bodies from my dream. Rune dove right in, taking sausage links and scoops of eggs, until the plate was nearly empty.

Reaching for his next serving, Frya smacked his hand away. "Boy. Save some for Lady Elpis."

Her nostrils flared as he gulped down the bite of potato and folded his hands in his lap.

"I haven't eaten since last night. I'm sorry, My Lady. The rest is all yours." He smiled, pushing the plates toward me. My stomach knotted, and I swallowed back the bile now rising in up to my throat.

"I don't think I'm up for eating yet. But we can take it for the road."

"I packed you a bag with some loaves, cheese, and the dried meats from our stores. But I'll wrap this for you. Maybe once you get going, you'll feel better." Frya took the plates back into the kitchen and wrapped the leftover breakfast.

"It'll be okay. I promise." Rune glanced nervously at me as he took my hand.

Faking a smile, I let him think his reassurance gave me the comfort I needed. Nothing could distract me from the smell of that blood, or the feel of dead flesh pressing against my chest. Arcturas pawed at my ankle, pulling me back from the brink of spiraling again, and sniffed towards the window. The sky was a light periwinkle, marking the day's arrival.

"You best be going now. Take to the eastern wall; the roads are better protected from the creatures of the North. Stay in the shadows, and if anyone recognizes you..." Frya trailed off, placing a black leather sheath into my hands. The hilt of her silver dagger protruding from the leather was cold against my palms. I nodded, strapping the sheath around my thigh.

"Keep this with you always," she said, her voice quivering.

"Thank you." I choked back my tears and reached for the barkeep's hand. She took it, lacing her fingers through mine. Looking at me fiercely, with damp cheeks, she smiled and pulled my forehead to her lips.

"Be safe. I hope we meet again." Dabbing her eyes with the kitchen rag tucked in her apron, she motioned for the door.

"You have shown me such kindness I don't deserve. I'm endlessly in your debt, Frya. Truly." I squeezed her hand one last time and stepped into the faint morning light.

The empty streets were silent as we snuck through the shadows to the eastern wall. Neither of us spoke as Arcturas led the way, always keeping a few yards ahead.

It was a change of watch, leaving the gates unguarded for only a few minutes. The sun crept just below the horizon as we charged towards the passageway, stepping silently through the darkness. When finally, I felt the bright orange light of the sunrise against my face, we were beyond the wall. I could breathe again, drawing in long pulls for my neglected lungs.

"You ready for this?" Rune asked, taking my hand in his.

I nodded towards Arcturas, who had shot ahead down

the dirt road.

"I don't think I have a choice, even if I'm not."

"You're probably right." He smirked as we followed the wolf's trail.

We walked for most of the day, following our shadows as they stretched further and further in front of us. As we traveled East, the snowpack began to thin and green buds perked on the tips of branches. I had shed my thick cloak and my skin glistened across my brow by the time the evening arrived.

"We should set up camp here before it gets dark. I don't want to know what roams these woods after dark." Rune dropped his pack and stretched his arms. The skin of his hips peeked from beneath the hem of his white cotton tunic.

My face burned. I focused on unrolling my sleeping pad, catching my wandering eyes follow the sliver of exposed skin.

"I'll go find us some firewood." Rune trailed into the shadows of the surrounding woods, twigs cracking beneath each step.

The fading day's light cast shadows across the clearing. Pockets of young greenery poked through cracks in the forest floor. I closed my eyes, letting the gentle breeze brush against my brow. The air was vibrant and new, as if it too was a fresh bud of spring, nearing its bloom. Evening birds cooed in the distance, letting their melody bounce across the branches above.

The harsh frigidity of the northern climate was far behind us, and I couldn't help but smile. The mild, setting sun beams warmed the nape of my neck. Piling my locks in a messy knot at the top of my head, I let the cool air dry the beads of sweat that accumulated during our travel. When Rune returned, staggering against his arm full of kindling and fallen branches, we built a fire and unpacked the rations Frya had sent us with. Nibbling on a wedge of dry cheese, I tossed Arcturas a strip of dried lamb.

"Look what else that crazy barkeep packed for us." Rune's eyes grew mischievous as he pulled an amber bottle of spiced wine from his sack. I raised a brow in his direction.

"Are you sure she packed that? Or did you slip that from behind the bar when she wasn't looking?"

He shrugged and pulled the cork with his teeth. The bottleneck popped loudly, and he drank deeply before passing it across the firelight. Wiping the remnants of cheese from my hands, reaching for it, I took a sip, the familiar warmth of cinnamon and clove pooling in my stomach.

"So the woman you um...melted, who was she?" The amber flames flickering across Rune's face reflected in the golden flecks of his unsure eyes. I paused for a moment. Hela's dissolving skin flashed through my mind.

"She was my chambermaid in the tower. A cruel, insufferable woman. She'd look for any chance she got to crack that whip across my back." I took a large swig of the wine and passed it back to him. "It was rare if I didn't receive a lashing for not answering a question the right way or leaving too much of my breakfast untouched."

Rune's gaze drifted to the flames between us.

"I'm so sorry." His voice was low, struggling to find the proper response. "I can't imagine the strength it took to survive so many years around such cruelty."

"It wasn't strength or resilience that got me through it." I took a breath, hesitating before admitting to him what I hadn't yet accepted myself, "Anger. That's how I survived. I'd lay in bed at night, sore from the healing wounds on my back, and imagine all the slow and painful ways I'd murder that bitch." Rune was quiet, a look of fear, and maybe wonder passed across his face as he handed the wine over once more.

"I'm the Queen Slayer, as you said. A monster. That

tower stripped everything from me. All that's left is violence and this horrible, unwavering rage." I swallowed the rest of my words. I'd said too much. The wine numbed the feelings bubbling up, so I continued to drink deeply.

"I'm sorry I called you that. It's not true." Rune slid around the fire until he sat next to me, the heat of his body radiating against me. "I should've stopped those guards the second they held you down. I'm so sorry Elpis. She should've never even gotten close to you in that courtyard. I should have done something. Anything."

His eyes were intense, and he took my hand in his. "You're not a monster. Anyone who'd been through even a fraction of what you have would feel the same way."

The shadows lurking just beneath the surface of my skin said otherwise, but I smiled anyway. Maybe he'd truly believed what he said, but death and darkness gravitated around me, haunting my thoughts and flooding my veins with icy violence and this barbaric rage.

The embers dimmed softly as the last lick of flame fizzled away, leaving us in a quiet darkness. I wrapped the scratchy wool blanket tighter around me, attempting to push out the chill spreading through my chest.

Rune leaned into me. That familiar pulse of electricity jumped between us, jolting across my chest and settling in the pit of my stomach. Running his thumb against my cheek, he lowered his lips, only inches from my mine. The scratch of shadow lurking beneath the surface faded until it was merely a tickle. His warmth against mine chased the darkness away. He wrapped himself around me, holding me fiercely against his solid chest. The heat of his touch melted my blood until I felt human again.

The Queen Slayer, the Monster, the Demon.

It didn't matter what they called me, so long as I was safely tucked away in him.

His kiss stole the remaining breath in my lungs, and I pulled away, lips swollen and cheeks burning. Those eyes didn't belong to the goofy, pestering man who'd followed me into the tavern after Festival, cracking jokes and making himself laugh.

No, they were the eyes of a man who'd experienced just as much hurt and despair as I had in his life. They were eyes that glimmered in the starlight and sent shivers throughout my entire body. Tracing the length of his jaw, I was the one to close the gap between us this time.

Curling my fingers through his soft, brown hair, something unlocked. A faint groan escaped his lips as I lowered the two of us to my sleeping mat and laced myself against him. Something ancient and powerful pulsated through me, taking hold of my body as I explored each curve of his chest.

Rune slid the back of my tunic over my head, letting it fall beside us, exposing the bareness of my skin. He followed the raised rows of scars across my back with his fingers, as if his touch alone could heal the damage those ridges of flesh caused. Pulling away to catch his breath, he soaked in the moonlight, reflecting off my skin in beams of silver. Following the arch of my neck, down across my breast, to the curve of my hips, his eyes now ignited with golden flecks of desire.

"You're not a monster," he whispered, sliding his hand down my waist.

I wasn't sure if it was his touch that raised goosebumps across my arms or the chill of the night. His hand stopped just above my knee, digging his fingers into the muscle of my thigh. He pulled me closer, wrapping my leg around his torso.

My skin, electrified and aware of every point of contact between us. His lips found mine again, their warmth melting down my throat with each frenzied kiss. Everything within me was alive with his scent, with the feel of his calloused hands against my waist, moving my hips against his.

I could sense I was slipping away. The power between us consumed me entirely, and a deep, frantic need blossomed in my chest. It'd been so long since I'd exposed this part of myself to another. My intimate self, my most feminine, most divine self. It all washed through me as if my skin glowed brilliantly and beautifully with magic.

This yearning that coursed through my veins wasn't a desire for the man that lay beneath me. Not really. It was a desire for myself. My old self. A suffocating need for her to emerge from that self-confined prison and step into the moonlight. To join me once again in this life. To bring her pallet of colors and paint each back into the world around me.

I clung to Rune, almost savagely, as I willed her to show herself. When our bodies finally molded together, flesh against flesh, she surfaced, bringing with her an upwelling of joy that sent me spiraling and spiraling into sheer, encompassing bliss.

We laid next to one another for a while in silence, as he traced the outline of my collarbone with his fingertip. The pale, bleached moonlight illuminated our bodies as we watched the stars above. Millions of glinting orbs dusted across the sky in hues of blue and violet.

"Did you do it?" Rune turned to face me, silver constellations reflected in his eyes.

I sucked in a breath, curling fistfuls of gravels in my fists.

"Did you kill your sister?" Those deep voids and rotten teeth flashed through my mind.

You did this.

Look what you did.

I squeezed my eyes shut, pushing her decrepit voice out of my head. Rune stroked my cheek, his thumb smoothing away a strand of hair.

"No. I didn't. She fell ill unexpectedly, and the Elders

blamed me. No one believes that, though, and they have punished me for it my entire adult life." Fiddling with a pebble between my fingers, I turned back to the stars, seeking their comforting light across my face.

Midnight birds cooed at one another as they flittered above us- sporadic little shadows against the infinite chasm overhead.

"I believe you, Elpis," he whispered.

My chest tightened. Not a single person had ever said those words to me, not even Vikar. Deep down, I think even he suspected me. Hearing those sounds and syllables strung together, I couldn't help but cry.

"You don't know how much that means to me," I said between hushed sobs.

Rune squeezed my hand and I relaxed my fist, letting the gravel scatter back across the ground. He pulled me into his chest, letting me cry.

I sobbed until all the pain and hurt and anguish of my past was stained across his tunic in damp patches of tears. Brushing away the hair stuck to my wet cheeks, he placed a gentle kiss across my brow and squeezed me tighter. I wanted to stay wrapped in his heat forever, safe from my uncertain future and my unforgiving past. I'm not sure when I dozed off, but what felt like only minutes later, ringlets of dawn coiled across our faces.

Chapter 19

At dawn, Rune and I packed and continued our journey east. Arcturas, having slept soundly through the night, now zoomed up and down the road as we trudged on, every once in a while returning with a stick for Rune to toss.

"She's so happy out here." Rune smiled, watching my wolf sprint back and forth across the trail.

"She'd been cooped up in the tavern for far too long. She can finally stretch her legs and feel the fresh breeze on her face," I said, feeling tendrils of cool, morning air lick across my cheeks.

"Being out here suits you, too." He gazed at me with those sparkling, cherry wood eyes.

I found myself lost in those eyes, swimming in them, warm and cool at the same time. Dreaming, but awake. Images of last night rushed through me, pooling in my stomach. My cheeks burned as I remembered the feel of his hands against my skin.

"I feel more myself when I'm not confined in one

place," I said, clearing my throat.

"You and I are similar in that way," Rune said, trailing off as he drifted away, into his thoughts. I wondered where his day dreams took him, what shadows lurked in his mind, what light banished them away. His brow softened with a hint of sadness as we carried on down the road.

With each passing mile, the landscape became more overgrown, more unkempt. Underbrush crept into the roadway, thickening into dense patches of thistles.

We struggled through the nearly impenetrable clusters of thorny growth where small magenta blooms poked between razor-edged spikes, sharp enough to pierce skin with the lightest of touch. It was as if the wild greenery of eternal spring swallowed up the cobblestone road, its weeds invading the cracks between laid rock.

Arcturas stayed close, uneasy and wary of the shadows that loomed beneath the brush. A deep dread fell over us as the high afternoon sun beamed down upon the feral vegetation obstructing our path.

Wide, bulbous tendrils of roots coiled into a blockade towering before us almost 20 feet in height. Arcturas, sniffing at the slithering vines, yipped when a thick branch gave out and slammed to the ground just in front of her nose.

"Well, this makes things difficult," Rune said, running his hand across a vine.

The root system extended in either direction, fading into the blackness of the forest.

"We could climb it," I suggested, tugging on a loosened vine. It snapped beneath my weight, flopping limply to the ground. "Or maybe we don't climb."

Rune scanned the massive wall, looking for an opening to crawl our way through. The sun beat down harshly on our backs as I wiped a bead of anxious sweat from the nape of my neck. My skin crawled as if there were thousands of eyes searing through my flesh.

The air was thick with the perfume of malice. We needed to keep moving and find a solution to this impasse as quickly as possible. I didn't want to stick around too long to find out what lurked in these woods.

"I think if we squeezed and cut a few of these smaller vines away, we might get through here." Rune motioned towards a narrow burrow. "There's light on the other side. It looks like it goes all the way through."

Growing antsy and impatient to press on, I unclasped my pack. Unsheathing the dagger from my thigh, I began clearing away the jagged vines. The edge of the blade was sharp enough to slash the smaller vines in one clean slice, but some with armor-like bark, I had to saw back and forth until the incision was deep enough to snap the root entirely.

Arcturas scurried through behind me withRune gingerly crawling after her, careful not to pinch her tail. The burrow felt like it extended for miles, and after what felt like hours of writhing through vines, the opening of the tunnel came into view. Reaching my hand in front of me, I shifted my weight and slid my knees forward. Something groaned above us as soil and dust particles sprinkled from above us.

"What was that?" Rune whispered.

Arcturas growled deeply in her throat and bared her teeth. I stretched my neck to see behind us as best I could.

The tunnel was too narrow to turn around. We exposed our backs to any threat that snuck in after us. Another groan came from above. More debris fell from the tangle of vines. Rotating my shoulder up, I unsheathed my dagger, knuckles white against my grip around its hilt.

"I don't know, but let's keep moving."

We squirmed towards the tunnel's exit, picking up our pace to close the distance as fast as possible. Another groan, this time louder. The vines above us seemed to wriggle and writhe like a knot of snakes.

We needed to get out of here.

Now.

I crawled faster, Arcturas restlessly nipping at my an-kles behind me. The sound of Rune's breathing quickened as he kept my pace and raced for the exit. My blood cur-dled when a shadow passed across the light of the tunnel's exit. I held up my hand for us to stop.

"There's something out there," I whispered. "We need to be careful."

A vine snapped behind us and my heart stopped.

"Elpis," Rune's whisper was now only a tremor, "there's something in here, too."

We took off down the tunnel, crawling frantically toward the exit. Panting and sweating, I struggled through the narrow opening into harsh sunlight. My eyes watered from the contrast of the burrow's darkness.

Arcturas shimmied through and shook the dust off her pelt. Seconds passed. Then a minute. Rune hadn't yet appeared. There was a crack from within. Then a low, men-acing groan.

Rune's scream was a blow that nearly knocked me to my knees. Fuck.

Without a second thought, I dove back into the dark-ness, darting through the narrow passage. Thorns pierced my skin and nicked scrapes across my arms. Rune con-tinued screaming, his voice echoing through the tunnel, drowning out all the other sounds.

Blood pumped through my ears and I grasped at the earth in front of me, flinging mud and gravel everywhere as I continued to crawl. Time seemed to stop when his screams cut off, a deafening silence rushing between the serpentine vines. I picked up my pace, throwing myself forward with bleeding arms and tangles of thorns trapped in escaped strands of hair.

Finally, his limp body came into view and I scrambled

toward him, only to stop dead in my tracks when a pair of crimson eyes blinked out of the shadows in front of us. I'd seen those eyes before. Meeting their gaze, I felt as if every organ inside my body froze. I gripped my dagger tighter as I slowly crawled closer to Rune.

Relief spread through me with the reassuring rise and fall of his chest. With the tip of the dagger pointed toward the invisible beast, I curled my fingers around his limp wrist and began pulling him backwards down the tunnel. Never breaking contact with those ruby eyes glowing through darkness. At any hint of an attack, I was ready to throw myself over Rune and slit the throat attached to those deadly eyes.

The creature, however, blinked and receded into the shadows. I dragged Rune, still unconscious, through mud and dirt as we finally made it to the exit.

Stepping into the sunlight, mud caked on both of my knees and elbows, I breathed deeply. Rune stirred softly, wiping the dirt from his eyes. Arcturas's fur straightened down her spine, sensing that we weren't alone.

"Rune, I need you to roll behind those rocks and stay quiet," I said through gritted teeth.

My hands shook and I forced them still as I scanned our surroundings. Trees, flourishing and green, whispered with a gentle breeze. It was too quiet. Not a single chickadee chirped. Not a single field mouse squeaked across the forest floor. My toes curled in my boot, ready for an ambush.

Rune struggled to the boulder, gasping and wheezing as he tucked himself into its shadow. A blood stain across his tunic grew. I needed to tend to his wounds. A twig cracked to our left and a flock of birds flurried into the sky. I couldn't do that, however, if we were both dead.

Without hesitation, Arcturas shot into the trees, darting between roots and boulders. I sprung forward, following behind her. The muscles in my calves strained as I pushed faster to keep the wolf in sight.

Blood pounded in my ears and my vision tunneled. Arcturas growled and roared as she tore through the flesh of our unseen enemy. I skidded to a halt, watching the creature howl in agony as Arcturas ripped at its neck, thick black ooze spewing from the open artery. My skin pricked behind me. Just as another leapt for my back I ducked to the ground, rolling away from its yellow claws.

The creature landed inches from my face and straightened its spine to stand on two hairless, dirty feet. Its toenails, vile with green fungus, curled around the front of each toe. The creature hunched down to face me, cracking its skeletal fingers. Its leathery body, humanoid and hairless, wrinkled beneath the movement. Instead of eyelids, the creature's four emerald eyes protruded from its face like an arachnid. There were two small slits where its nose should be.

It pounced once more, and I raised my forearms to block the rows of needle-like teeth snapping at my skin. Hot, floral scented breath licked across my cheeks. With all of my strength, I pushed the creature away. It flung backward, as if weightless, and slammed into a large tree across from us. I jumped to my feet. Before it could lurch for me once again, I flung the hilt of my dagger toward it.

The blade spun and hurtled through the air. Seconds drew by until my aim struck true, plunging through the creature's eye, pinning it against a tree trunk. It shrieked in fury, frantically clawing at its now gushing face.

Arcturas, having torn the other creature to shreds, pounced and tore the sagging flesh from its chest. With her muzzle soaked in black sludge, she ripped at its insides, letting its organs hang limply from its frame as the life faded from its gelatinous eyes.

My head spun and a cold sweat washed over me as I watched blood spurt from the carcass now splayed across the forest floor. In its cold, white knuckles, was a strand of long black hair and a scrap of dirty grey cotton. They had been tracking us, using my scent to follow our route. Blood sprayed across the undergrowth, and a foul sweet scent burned my nostrils like wilting flowers. Falling to my knees I released the contents of my stomach, heaving violently and spitting up bile profusely. Arcturas nuzzled against my face, smudging blood across my cheek.

Staggering back to my feet, we made our way back to Rune who had straightened himself against the boulder.

"What happened?" His eyes grew wide at the muddy flesh caked up my arms.

"There were trackers, some sort of hairless creatures with buggy green eyes. They had a scrap of my clothes and a few strands of my hair." I kneeled next to him, wiping the sweat from his brow. "Are you okay?"

I pulled off his bloodied tunic, but there were no gashes or wounds. Only smooth, tanned skin.

"Yeah, I'm alright. I must've passed out when that thing dragged me back through that burrow," he said, rubbing a hand through his hair.

"Who's blood is that?" I asked, pointing to the discarded tunic.

"It all happened so fast, but I must've wounded whatever had grabbed me. Those creatures you're describing, they sound like Arachnae. They're beasts of the Eastern Realm. Once they're summoned and introduced to a smell, they'll relentlessly stalk their prey. Do you think someone in Venia summoned them to find you?"

"Maybe. By now, I'm sure the Elders have gotten wind of my escape." My stomach knotted at the thought of those ancient men in their high thrones.

"Well, they normally travel in pairs. So, I think we're safe. Let's just pray to the Gods that they don't send more after you." I helped Rune to his feet, using my shoulder for support.

"The thing that pulled you into the burrow," I said,

kicking a pebble across the path, "I think I've seen it before."

"What do you mean? It's attacked you before?" Rune asked, watching the round, grey stone scatter down the sloping trail.

"Well, not in real life," I said. "I've seen it in my dreams, I think. At first, I thought they were just nightmares, but now I'm thinking they're premonitions."

"With everything else going on, that wouldn't surprise me," he said.

"I know. That's what worries me. These dreams, they..." I trailed off, my stomach lurching at the stench of rotten flesh. "They terrify me. At the end of each one, I end up dead."

"Well, that thing didn't kill you." Rune reached for my hand. His skin was warm against the cold sweat of my palms. "It went after me and it sounds like it let you go."

"I guess you're right. Still, something about those red eyes. I can't shake them." I shuddered. A gentle breeze rustled the leaves overhead, scattering gems of afternoon sunlight across the cobblestone.

"We're safe for now. Let's focus on getting to the city. Once we're there, nothing can touch us. Not even your dreams." Rune smiled and continued down the road.

At every snapping twig or rustle of leaves, my fingers, still wrapped tightly around my weapon, twitched. He was right, we were safe for now. Dwelling on nightmares wouldn't do me any good, I thought, but the feeling of unease only grew as we carried on.

Chapter 20

It wasn't until we reached the city gates did I loosen my grip on the dagger. Sheathing it back against my thigh, I uncorked my water pouch and drank deeply. The afternoon's journey left my mouth parched.

A double lane stone bridge with guard towers erected on either side marked Venia's entrance. A crystal river below roared over rapids and glittering fish breached its iridescent waves. The reflection of the city lights flickered with the setting sun.

Wildflowers of every color bloomed brilliantly along the river bank and blades of grass rustled in a warm breeze. Even the city walls felt alive with greenery. Honeysuckle and ivy vines crept along the marble bricks, releasing their sweetness into the air. As the final beams of daylight faded away, we scurried past the white marble turrets, every so often glancing up at the guards who swung their bows and leaned lazily against their posts. With Tethys's reputation, it wasn't likely they'd suspect travelers sneaking through the gates.

Unlike Ursae, the streets of Venia brightened the nighttime air. Candles burned from every window and sconces roared at every street corner as if the city itself tried to wash out the stars overhead.

Rune, having regained his strength, grasped my hand and pulled me silently behind him. I glanced at the starless sky above us, shrouded in clouds. My connection to the sky, and the northern goddess who ruled overhead, was snipped as we snuck through the open gates. Without her watchful eye in the presence of moonlight, I felt a void growing deep in my chest. Every fiber of my being was on high alert.

"It's alright. You're safe here." Rune squeezed my hand.

"I know... I just don't feel right." I whispered.

Arcturas brushed against my leg, her brilliant eyes illuminating the shadows of the city's entrance. Rune's brow glistened with a nervous sweat, and the familiar sheen across his features now glimmered brightly and rapidly. A suspicion flowered at the back of my throat. Something was wrong. Had I made a grave mistake in trusting this man to lead me here? Was I walking straight into my enemy's hands? I inspected his face, my eyes narrowing with the bloom of hesitation.

"You trust me, right?" he asked, leading us down the gravel street. He smoothed back my disheveled hair and brushed his lips softly against mine. When I pulled away, the glimmer was gone and only honey-brown eyes looked back at me. The growing uncertainty faded with the touch of his lips, replaced only with a warmth that spread across my cheeks. I trusted Rune with my whole heart. He'd pulled me from the depths of myself. He'd awakened my old self, my best self, despite all the rage that surrounded me. Even in this strange city, with lights that outshined the moon, I was safe. Settling into the soles of my boots, I took his hand and swallowed the rising lump in my throat.

"Yes, of course," I said, and we continued deeper into the heart of the city.

Picketed gardens of endless floral blooms spilling from their neatly trimmed hedges rustled in the springtime air as we traveled further away from the city's entrance. Pale pink and yellow flags, masted on marble pillars, billowed in the night time. Two interlaced swans, crested between ornate golden vines, the sigils of Tethys, were painted on every pristine white wall we passed. Babbling fountains and man made brooks whispered peaceful lullabies to a sleeping city. The quiet was eerie. We were two sneaking souls, disrupting the stillness as if we were the only two left in the realms.

"I know somewhere we can stay the night," Rune said, leading us down a side street. Hedges, speckled with white blooms, lined row after row of stone townhomes. At the end of the sidewalk, a crystalline woman stood tall, her delicately carved fingers plucking from a harp. Amber candlelight reflected on each geometric surface of the statue with beads of topaz lining the flowing crystal robes that draped against her delicately carved frame. Even in moonlight I recognized that divine face, causing my blood to flare.

"I thought Venians hated their patron goddess," I said, tracing the delicate curves of the statue's curly, long hair. Even in the crystal, malice filled her eyes.

"Most do. There are some still loyal to her, waiting for her return. Queen Magdalaine and her mortal court have tried to remove these shrines, but it's pointless. The high born who insist on maintaining them have too much influence. Too much wealth." Rune bit his lip in disgust as he, too, looked upon the crystal goddess. Her hands, neatly clasped at the base of her dress, were slender. The essence of femininity. Also, the essence of death. The base of my neck burned at the vision of her fiery smile as she wrung the breath from my lungs.

"Are you cold? Let's keep moving and get you by a fire-side." Rune brushed his thumb across my cheek. I didn't notice I was shaking until his touch pulled me from the statue's hypnotic gaze.

"Oh, um, yes. Let's go," I said, taking his hand in mine.

We continued to sneak through the sleeping streets. Rune led me deeper into the city, passing lush courtyards and tidy chateaus. As we twisted and turned through rows of flowers and uniform trees, my pulse quickened. Every fiber of my being screamed to turn and run, but even if I wanted to, I couldn't.

Fully trusting Rune's guidance, I had lost my footing in the seemingly endless maze of white and yellow town-homes. Finally, the narrow streets opened to a three story manor. Arched windows lined the faded blue siding and fields of plumeria trees bordered the gravel roadway at the manor's front gate. Torches cast flickering shadows across a labyrinth of clipped, blooming hedges that stretched infinitely in front of us.

"It's my family home. No one's lived here for years. We'll be safe here," Rune said, gripping my hand and lead-ing us to the main gate. "Only the city gardeners who tend to the courtyards walk the grounds, but they're only day workers."

I remained silent, lost in the estate's grandeur.

"You said your family holds court in the city. They must have high status. This place is... impressive."

Rune grimaced at the mention of his family, kicking up gravel with his gaze lowered to the ground.

"We did once. When we lost my mother, though, things sort of fell apart for us. Now all that's left is this house." His voice was strained as he swung the wrought-iron gate open, letting Arcturas and I pass through first.

The sweet perfume of plumeria was overwhelming. Its stifling stench crept into my lungs. Rune's demeanor

darkened with each step as we continued past a peacefully bubbling fountain and reached the manor's entrance.
Wiping away a film of dust coating the amber glass panes,
Rune pulled on the door's golden handle. With a heavy
groan, it croaked open.

Cobwebs lurked in every corner of the dark foyer. A
golden bannister coiled around a grand marble staircase
that centered the room. Ornate sconces, cold and forgotten, hung between massive portraits of men and women
draped with gems and silken fabrics. Overhead, a golden
chandelier with crystal-carved candelabras swung lightly
from our intrusion. The dust settled in thick layers across
the checkerboard tile floor. It seemed only the outer
grounds were maintained. The interior was left to rot
away, isolated in time.

"I'll see if I can find some candles for these sconces.
The house should be empty, but be careful if you decide
to look around. I'm not sure the condition of the floors
upstairs. It's been years since I've been here." Rune smiled
sadly, then disappeared into a dark hallway to our left,
which I assumed led to the kitchen.

A soft draft licked through the foyer, raising the flesh
of my arms. Arcturas, rubbing between my legs, leapt up
the stairway. Lost in the fresh smells of springtime and
abandoned wealth, she climbed the steps. Her nose collected dust as she sniffed a trail to the second floor and out
of sight.

I sighed, not wanting to be alone with the lurking gaze
of Rune's ancestors scattered across the walls, and followed the wolf. The steps creaked in protest beneath my
weight. They most likely hadn't been disturbed in years.
My family's palace was incomparable to the opulence of
this home. If all the lords and ladies of Venia lived in man-
ors like this, I couldn't imagine the royal palace.

A match flick echoed through the foyer below as Rune
lit each sconce, casting out the abandoned darkness with

blazing candles. The light kindled across each portrait, illuminating tanned complexions and golden blonde hair. Each painting was rich with color- gold, pinks, and deep oranges, reminding me of the most glorious of sunrises. Every lady's neck was extravagant with diamonds, topaz, and delicate laced gold. All the lords held finely carved swords embedded with hundreds of gems.

At the top of the stairs, a portrait far larger than the others hung proudly. I stopped at the last step, fingers curled around the cold, metal bannister. The portrait hung so high only the rim of the ornately detailed frame was at eye level.

My lungs collapsed as I followed the canvas up the wall. Staring down at me was a woman with cruel eyes and a delicate frame. Blonde hair flowed in ringlet curls down her bare shoulders. A circlet of topaz sat atop her slender head. I slowly reached for the dagger against my leg. Expecting to wrap my hand around the heavy metal hilt, my fingers only hit the stitching of an empty leather sheath.

My muscles froze as the realization sank its teeth into my chest.

A pained yip echoed from the darkness down the second story hallway, and without thought, I slammed into the shadows. The yipping turned into agonized whines as I threw myself into an open doorway.

There, with her claws wrapped around my wolf's neck, stood the goddess, an exact duplicate of the oil portrait I'd just laid my eyes on. Arcturas screeched and scratched at the goddess who was, without effort, holding her in mid-air as if she weighed only a feather. My nostrils flared and with clenched fists, I lunged at the Spring Queen. Flicking her open hand, a wave of invisible force sent me flying back and I landed on my tailbone, the remnants of breath pushed out of my throat.

"Get your fucking hands off my wolf," I hissed, rubbing

my aching back.

"Oh, Lady Elpis, I couldn't possibly do that. This beast would tear me to shreds the minute I released her." Tethys's voice was just as velvety as it was in my dreams. She tucked a loose curl behind her ear and smiled sweetly at me as she tightened her grip.

Arcturas, now squealing frantically, nipped at her fingers, choking as Tethys cut off her airway.

"Let her go. Now," I screeched, jumping to my feet and lunging again.

Vines pierced through the deep crimson carpet beneath us, binding my ankles to the floor and trailing up my body, paralyzing me with their venomous thorns.

"I think it's time I tamed this beast." One second Arcturas flailed in her outstretched arm, the next she cracked against the floor, limp and unmoving.

Something within me snapped and the tether between my wolf and me faded until I could barely feel the thread of her life against mine. My blood turned to flames. Rage ignited across my skin as the hair on my arms pricked up. The scream that poured out of me was more than agony. It was a primal, animalistic roar of sheer anguish.

"Oh, don't be dramatic." Tethys stepped towards me, floating across the dusty floor until her bright eyes were mere inches from mine.

She smelled of honeysuckle and the dewy air of early morning.

With a click of her tongue, she brushed the back of her hand against my cheek. "It's not dead, just subdued."

I trembled against her touch. If I could wriggle out of these vines, I'd rip her throat out with my teeth and watch her blood spill onto the dirty carpet.

"What do you want from me, Tethys?" I spat. "Let us go and I'll give you whatever you want."

"Well, Lady Elpis, you're the only thing standing in the way of what I want." She turned, lacing her fingers behind her back, and stepped to the large oval window that over-looked the manor's gardens.

Strings of pearly shrubs and blooming flowers swayed in the gentle breeze. The only light illuminating their pink and yellow petals was from the flicker of torches lining the gravel paths.

"I don't know what you're planning, but it has nothing to do with me. So let us go, please."

I glanced at Arcturas. She was too still. Too limp. The fur of her pelt brushed down her spine as if it were melting into the floor.

"You truly don't know who you are?" Tethys glanced over her shoulder at me, sincere shock stretched across her perfect lips. "Oh, you poor thing. Well, let me enlighten you. Twenty-three years ago, your saintly goddess fell in love with a mortal king. She whisked him away to the immortal realm and, while his kingdom starved and withered away, they had a child. Polaris realized that her infant daughter was prophesied to bring war to the mortal realms, so she sent her loving king and their child away. Did you ever wonder why your sister hated you so much? Or why your mortal mother treated you differently?"

"No. That's not true," I hissed, struggling beneath my tightening binds. Lies. She was just trying to get under my skin.

"Elpis, come now. You may be pathetic, but you're not stupid. Those shadows lurking beneath your skin had to have come from somewhere. No mortal holds power like you," she said.

I shook my head, tears streaming down my cheeks as thorns pierced the flesh of my arms.

"You are the daughter of Polaris. You're to bring utter destruction to the mortal realm. Thousands of lives will be lost because of you. I'm protecting not just my people, but the people of Ursae, Aquilae and Canissa alike. From you." She emphasized her words, enunciating each syllable with her full lips.

"That's why I sent my son after you. Although, I didn't think it'd be that easy to get you here. You really are too trusting. Aryx, come in here." With a flick of her wrist, the chamber door swung open, and a broad-shouldered figure stepped in from the shadows.

Dangerous power dripped from the man's entire being as he towered over his mother, making the immortal beside him look as weak as a mouse. Shoulder length, golden hair peeked from beneath a tinted black helmet that shielded all of his features. Amber pupils glowed from beneath his helmet, sending shivers down my spine as he scanned me from head to toe. Every hair on my body pricked at his energy. Never in my life had I experienced someone so deadly. Someone who commanded the attention of every molecule in their presence.

"Aryx, my love, take off your helmet. Let her see your face," Tethys grinned widely as he pulled the bronze off his face. My knees gave out and suddenly, there was no air left in the room for me to breathe.

Standing before me was Rune.

Chapter 21

His dark brown hair now gleamed with streaks of golden blonde. His eyes, once a warm, compassionate chestnut, now glowed a cold, piercing amber. The only feature I recognized were his lips, the lips that had whispered such sweetness. The lips that had comforted me time and time again.

On the left side of his face, black ink wrapped around his high, angular cheekbone, the mark of a battled warrior. He was glorious, with deadly beauty. Every inch of him oozed predatory prowess. A fitted black leather breastplate replaced the fur-lined cloak, highlighting every curve of his muscle.

"I trusted you." My voice was low, barely a whisper, as this betrayal shattered me into a thousand pieces. He spoke, but Tethys raised her hand to his lips, cutting off the words before they rolled from his tongue.

"Elpis, darling, I think it's time I take my leave. The filth in this godsforsaken house is making me sick." The goddess plucked a piece of lint from her flowing gossamer gown. "Aryx, take care of this for me, will you?"

He nodded silently as his mother, smiling with a deep satisfaction, exited the chamber. The vines loosened their grip around me and snaked back into the floor, leaving broken tile and shredded carpet in their absence.

Without hesitation, I threw myself at the man I once trusted, fully intending to slaughter him where he stood. He grasped my clenched fists and held them at my sides, staring with those piercing, deadly eyes. Tears dripped from my chin as the heartbreak flowed freely from my ducts. With shallow breaths, I tried shaking free, but he overpowered me with the strength of his grip.

"Listen to me," he whispered.

I kicked at his legs, hoping to steal his balance and bring him to the floor.

"Listen to me!" he whispered again, wrapping an arm around my waist.

I slammed my head into his shoulder and bit into the sensitive flesh of his neck. Scowling, he dropped his hold for only a split second. It was just enough time for me to rip the dagger sheathed at his side from its holster and press it against his throat.

"You betrayed me." I pushed the blade further into his skin, drawing a slow drip of blood.

"Please, just listen." His voice was hoarse, with cold iron pressed at his throat. "Let me explain."

"You don't deserve my ear," I hissed, the tip of my blade now pointed at his carotid artery. The muscle in his jaw clenched as he swallowed.

"Elpis, please. Keep the knife at my neck, kill me if you want, but just listen first."

"You have five seconds to say what you want, then I slit your throat."

"I had no choice. She has my father. She threatened to kill him if I didn't follow her orders. You have to understand that. I'd do anything, even something as despicable as this." His eyes glittered frantically, begging me to understand.

My instincts told me this was just another manipulation, but my heart told me to believe him. There was a flash of familiarity across his eyes, and a sliver of the Rune I had grown to care for surfaced. Maybe it was a mistake, but I lowered the dagger, leaving a droplet of blood rolling down his long neck. His demeanor relaxed slightly. Rubbing his neck, the wound stitched itself together, leaving only a bead of blood trailing down towards his collarbone.

"You have a choice now. Either I kill you where you stand, or you let us go." I took a step back. The hilt of my weapon still burned the inside of my palm.

Arcturas stirred in the corner, her snout wrinkling in pain as she came to.

"She'll just keep searching for you. She'll send more arachnae like the ones in the woods. There's another part of the prophecy. You don't just bring war to the realms. You also bring her demise. She won't let you live. No matter where you hide or how much you fight, she'll find you and she'll kill you."

"So you knew what that inscription written in the archives was? This so-called prophecy about darkness's Heir and the light of truth? That's about me? How do I know you aren't lying through your teeth? Clearly, it comes so naturally to you." I sat in front of Arcturas, stroking her pelt as she whined softly.

"Yes, like my mother said. Polaris knew her heir would be the harbinger of destruction. That's why she distanced herself from not only you, but also all of Ursae. The other gods still hold council with their mortal leaders. Polaris doesn't. Didn't you ever find that strange? Listen, I know you won't trust me ever again. I'm sorry I had to trick you, but I didn't have any other choice. You'd never agree to come here, to help me free my father." He knelt beside me, eyeing the blade in my hand. "Help me kill her. We take her out together and prevent the war she plans to wage against the mortals."

"I don't want any part of this. Please, just let us go," I said, cradling Arcturas's head in my lap.

"Elpis, please. You're the daughter of Polaris. She's the most powerful goddess of the realms. I can't do this without you. I need to save my father." He reached his hand toward mine.

Before his skin could make contact, my dagger was raised and back at his throat.

"Touch me and you die," I threatened through clenched teeth.

Arcturas, lifting her head weakly, snarled at Aryx as he backed away slightly.

"Fine. Slit my throat now and spend the rest of your life hiding from my mother. Or help me kill her and live freely. I promise you'll get the freedom you deserve when it's all over. Besides, how will you find peace in a continent at war?" His voice was frigid, entirely unrecognizable. He sucked in a breath and leaned against his heels. "Isn't that ultimately what you want? Your freedom? A quiet life? It's your choice."

It was true. All I'd ever wanted was to choose my fate. I stared at the beautiful half-god who now sat on his knees. I wondered if he'd kneeled before anyone else like this. The impending war he spoke of frightened me. It was true. My immortal bloodline explained the power that'd surfaced in me, but I didn't want to believe I was a harbinger of destruction.

Visions of a scorched, polluted battlefield, then the piles and piles of northern city folk flashed before my eyes. The nightmares, the shadows, the ancient inscription. It was all connected, leading me on an inescapable journey here. To this moment. This choice.

"I didn't ask for any of this. I can't help you." I looked

at Arcturas and stroked her snout. She looked so fragile with the slow rise and fall of her ribs.

"Elpis. Please. I need you," he said, crouching beside me.

"I needed you, Rune. You betrayed me." A tear escaped down my cheek and splattered on the crimson rug.

"I'm so sorry," he whispered.

"It's a bit too late for an apology. Now, let us go." I wiped the dampness from my eyes and pulled Arcturas into my chest, seeking her warmth.

"Elpis. I can't do that. I can't let you go."

"So, if I don't agree with your plan, you'll force me?" A fire lit up my chest as tingles ignited in my toes and rushed through my veins with voracious force.

"If I have to. I will." His eyes darkened. The amber turned a deep shade of ruby, like a powerful sunrise as it crossed over the horizon.

Tendrils of shadows licked at my fingertips, begging to be unleashed. "You can't force me to do anything."

"We'll see about that," he hissed.

I lunged for him. Throwing my shoulder into his abdomen, the breath rushed from my lungs, knocking me to the floor. In the split second he hit the carpet, I wrapped myself around his back, gripping my elbow to block his airway. Aryx coughed and sputtered, clawing at my death hold. As the tendrils of shadow curled tighter around his neck, I felt the muscles in his back flex beneath me.

Suddenly, he shifted his weight and jerked forward. My grip slipped and I flew through the air, landing on my spine with a crack. Aryx leapt for me. His hands tightened around my wrists. I was pinned. Kicking and flailing against his sheer weight, I screamed until my throat burned.

"Elpis. Stop. Please," Aryx pleaded.

"Get off me!" I cried, cracking my forehead into his. Blood dripped from the crown of my head as Aryx fell backward. He grunted, holding his head in his hands. I rose to my feet, grabbing my dagger from the floor. Pointing it at his heart, I spat the taste of iron from my mouth.

"Goodbye, Aryx," I hissed.

"Wait. Please," he pleaded. "Help me free my father."

His eyes faded into a faint glimmer of golden as I watched the man kneeling before me break apart.

"I need him. He's the only family I have left," he whispered.

The grip around my weapon softened as I knelt beside him. Prophecy aside, here was a man with nothing left in this world, utterly alone. Would I have done the same if it was Vikar's life at risk? What about Arcturas? Or Frya? I sighed and sat beside him. He looked at me with an expression I realized was all too familiar. It'd been staring back at me from within every mirror for the last five years. There had been a glimmer in Arcturas's eye when I found her as a pup. My brain told me to run from the chamber, leave the prophecy, Tethys, hell, the entire continent behind. But my heart? Like attracts like, and here we sat, nearly identical in our brokenness.

"If you betray me again, I won't hesitate next time." The strength of my voice was a surprise as I questioned my choice over and over in my mind.

"I promise you I'm not going to," he said, standing to his feet and offering me his hand. I pushed it away and stood on my own. The embers of torchlight in the gardens poured in across my face. Arcturas, regaining some strength, limped to my side, still wary of the man before us.

"So, what's the plan, then?" I said, picking a thorn fragment from my biceps. "We can't just waltz into the immortal realm."

"She's not going to the immortal realm. Over the last twenty years, she's manipulated the Elders into allying with her. She's turned their island into a fortress, surrounded by an army thousands strong. If we're going to even get close, we're going to need the other immortals' help. The minute we leave here, she'll know I turned on her and she'll use my father to bait me back. She's going to expect us. I think we start with Procyon. He's always been loyal to Polaris. If you take claim as her heir, he'll provide aid without question. Altair might need a little more convincing. After the Great War, he proclaimed neutrality for his realm. We'll have to make a pretty good argument, but with the heir of darkness and the son of spring together, it might just be enough to tip him over the edge."

"And what of the mortal leaders? They won't just sit idly by while we plot to slaughter their Elders."

"I think you'd be surprised. The mortals will follow their patrons- they always do."

I scratched Arcturas's head as the half-god paced the hall, his long, graceful strides capturing my full attention. His plan just might work. The journey through each realm would be long, and with arachnae on our trail, it might even be a death wish.

"What's stopping Tethys from executing your father the moment she discovers our plans?" I asked.

Aryx scuffed his leather boot against the carpet, disturbing a layer of dust into the air.

"That's simple. She still loves him." He chuckled coldly at the thought. "She didn't murder him the day she discovered his affair like it's told in the legend. At the last minute, she couldn't do it. I was only a boy when it happened, but I saw her struggle. She dropped the blade last minute."

"Maybe," I said, "but if her own son betrays her, you don't think that'd push her over that edge?"

"Like I said, she'll use him as a strategy to lure me back. My mother is quite skilled at using love to her advantage. She knows I'd do anything to free him." Aryx sighed and brushed his hand against a canvas portrait hanging on the wall next to me.

It was of a handsome, middle-aged man with the same amber eyes. He was holding the hand of a grinning toddler with slightly blurred features, as if the artist struggled to capture the child's likeness because he couldn't keep still.

"If I help you. Promise me that when this is all over, I'll never see you again. I've had enough treachery and deceit for a million lifetimes, and I don't need anymore. I want the life I deserve. And I want nothing to do with you." Aryx's back straightened, and although I couldn't see his face, I knew he grimaced against my words.

The sound of my voice pierced the air in the room until it faded away, leaving a heavy, impenetrable silence between us. Finally, he turned back to me, his eyes fierce and emotionless as they had been when he first entered the chamber.

"If that's what you wish, then I promise it."

"Good." I paused, swallowing the lump in my throat. "So, when do we go?"

Chapter 22

We agreed to stay the night at the manor, keeping watch over Arcturas as she regained her strength. I kept my dagger close, avoiding Aryx's wandering gaze from across the study. He remained in a rocker by the window, scanning the outer grounds for arachnae throughout the night.

I shrugged off his attempts to make conversation, raising my blade in his direction any time he opened his mouth to speak. My mind raced through everything I'd learned tonight, thinking of my parents and my mother's subtle cruelty. As children, my sister and I would sneak into her chambers and watch as she brushed the long locks of midnight hair that fell just below her waist. Wonder danced in our eyes as she'd hum tunes to herself, applying blush to her already rosy cheeks. I never questioned why I was left to play alone in our nursery while Adria and our mother explored the gardens together. While I dressed my dolls with makeshift clothes made from old kitchen rags, the pair would twist flower crowns into each other's hair.

My childhood admiration put her on a pedestal, shrouding the obvious difference between my sister and me. As I grew into adulthood, I simply accepted the inequality between us. It had always been there, so why think it out of the ordinary?

I grew up to believe my father loved my mother, but the more I lost myself in memories, the more I questioned. The subtleties of their strained relationship were there; however, they were nearly undetectable unless looking for them. My mother reaching for her husband's hand as he pulled it away. The empty expressions they shared. The silent tears shed in the late morning hours as my mother sat, unaware of her two daughters hidden behind a closed armoire door.

My father loved me until his dying breath, always embracing me a second or two longer than he did Adria. Maybe that's why she despised me so much. The jealousy. The truth of my birth. Maybe it was fear? Had she known of the power I possessed? Did she punish me and lock me away in order to save her family and her city from the demons that lurked beneath my surface?

These questions ricocheted against my mind as I watched the half-god pace across the chamber. Faint moonlight filtered through thin, floor length curtains, casting shadows across his furrowed brow. Allowing myself to dive into my past was easier than dealing with the pain of my present.

Eventually, I'd have to come to terms with it. I'd exposed myself entirely to a man that lied and manipulated to achieve a goal. A part of me still noticed the broadness of his shoulders, the way his lower lip pouted slightly when he was lost in thought, the blonde, smooth locks of hair that framed a powerful jaw. I shook my head and focused on my anger. Better to feel rage than to the sickening attraction I still held. He wasn't Rune, I reminded myself. He was a killer. A liar. A cold-blooded soldier, willing to hurt anyone or destroy anything that stood in his way.

Flicking the dirt from under my fingernails with the blade, I sunk lower into my chair. Once Tethys was gone, I'd truly be free. I snorted. How many times had I said that to myself before?

Once I escaped the tower, I'd be free.

Once I got to Ursae, I'd be free.

Once I accepted my demons and shadows, I'd be free.

At what point did it end? Was my life bound to be this constant battle for freedom?

I sighed and tried to silence those thoughts. Outside the arched windows, a petal floated in the springtime breeze of the manor's garden. It bounced in the air, spiraling towards the hedges below. Landing in a pond of lily pads, it sunk beneath the surface, disappearing into the murky jade depths.

"You should get some sleep," Aryx said, his voice clipped.

"If you think I'd even close one eye in your presence, you're gravely mistaken. I'm not falling for any more of your tricks."

"Suit yourself. We have a long journey tomorrow. Now's your chance to rest." He shrugged, indifference bitter on his lips.

Arcturas growled low in her throat as he started toward me. Rather than stopping beside my chair, he brushed past, heading for the chamber door.

"Where are you going?" I asked, turning to face him.

Without looking back, he said, "To go get some sleep. There are beds far more comfortable than those shitty old chairs."

#

At dawn, we escaped into the city, blending into the crowds of early risers off to work. Arcturas trailed behind us under the cover of landscaped shrubbery. With the diminishing darkness of night, the city bloomed. We passed through the markets with merchants bustling from customer to customer, selling plump fresh produce. We filled our satchels with rations of hard cheese, fruit, and cured meats. Although the journey to Canissa wasn't long, the roads were treacherous, and the hills were steep. On foot, it'd take double the time as it would on horseback.

Aryx stopped at a fruit stand on the outskirts of the market. Turning to face us, the farmer dropped his armful of apples in surprise at the Spring Prince, inquiring about the price of his plums.

"O-On the house, your highness," the merchant said, bowing deeply.

Aryx bent to collect the bruised apples, now rolling down the street.

"No, I insist. We'll pay." Handing the man his stray produce, Aryx slid a gold coin across the fruit-stand and tossed me a plum.

Scowling, I caught the deep purple fruit and tucked it into my cloak.

"Bless you," the man called after us as we crossed the street.

"Plums? Really?" I glared at him as he bit into the skin of his fruit, the juice rolling down his lips. Heat pooled in the pit of my stomach as I thought of those lips against mine. I clenched my jaw, disgusted by the physical reaction I had in his presence.

"What can I say? They're my favorite." He wiped his mouth with his sleeve and chuckled at my now crimson cheeks.

"Say another word and you die," I spat. My fingers twitched against the sheathed dagger on my thigh. Aryx snorted and took another bite.

"We have one more stop to make before we leave the city," he said, leading me down a narrow alley. Strings of honeysuckle hung from the trellis above us. Their odor was a pungent reminder of Tethys and her venomous beauty. Arcturas trotted behind us with lowered ears. She, too, must have recognized the scent.

The alleyway opened into a vast courtyard inlaid with clean, bleached brick. White stable doors lined the exterior walls. A young stable boy, no older than ten, swung open the center door and ran toward us.

"Ryx!" The boy shrieked happily, leaning into Aryx's tight embrace. Lifting him into the air, he twirled the boy around gleefully.

"Judas, it's good to see you!" Grinning, Aryx placed him back on his feet. "You've grown since I saw you last. You're nearly a man."

"I've missed you! Mother didn't tell me you were coming to see us today, otherwise I'd have Kratos ready for you." Judas's face lit up as he beamed at us.

I shuffled against the brick, tucking my hands in my pockets, rubbing the smooth skin of the plum delicately between my fingertips.

"I brought you something from the North." Aryx dug through his satchel, pulling out a small metal tin. "These are the best cakes you'll ever taste. I had to track them down before I left. They're usually only made for Festival."

Judas grasped for the tin, lifting its lid with wide eyes. The two butter cakes glistened as he scooped a taste of cinnamon icing.

"Thank you, Ryx!" He plucked one into his mouth, grinning with stuffed cheeks.

Between bites of the second, he said, "I'll bring Kratos around for you. He'll be so excited to see you."

The small boy hurried back into the stable, loose red curls bouncing across his petite shoulders with every step. Moments later he returned, pulling a stallion by the reins.

The horse, with its sleek, white coat, stood 20 hands high. It was a giant next to the others in the stables, and it made Judas look even smaller than he already was. Snorting joyously, the stallion nuzzled against Aryx's forehead.

"Alright, alright." Aryx stroked down its long snout. "I missed you too."

Kratos trotted toward me and sniffed at the long braid draped down my shoulder. I brushed my fingers across his nose. A black spot of fur shrouded his left eye.

"Elpis, this is Kratos," Aryx said as the horse nudged me again. "I guess he likes you. I'm not entirely certain why."

I threw him a sharp look.

"He's been with me since he was a foal. You won't find a faster steed anywhere across the realms."

Judas approached me uncertainly, his tiny hands clasped behind his back.

"It's okay, Judas, this is Elpis. She's from Ursae."

His eyes lit up, and a grin stretched from his lips.

"Really? What's it like there? Is it true you only live off butter cakes there? You don't look like you live off of cakes alone?" He erupted with questions. Aryx chuckled beside us as he left me to the wrath of the ten-year-old.

"Well, um, I guess I just exercise a lot," I murmured.

I don't think Judas heard my response, though, because he continued to spew questions about Ursae, not pausing to take a single breath. When he was nearly blue in the face, Aryx cut him off.

"I'm sure she'll be happy to answer your questions later, but I need to speak to your father. Is he around?"

"Aw, okay… He's in the back barn." Judas knelt beside Arcturas and held out a careful hand.

"Easy, Arcturas," I commanded.

The wolf sniffed the boy's hand and licked the remnants of sugar crusted on his fingertips. Judas shrieked with joy and stroked his other hand down her chest. If he had any more sugared cubes with him, I knew they'd instantly be best friends.

I followed Aryx to the back barn, passing through pristine white stables harboring horses with coats of the same bleached color.

"Venia breeds only white horses. It's a symbol of status and wealth for our people. When Kratos was born, his black spot made him a monstrosity. I was lucky to find him when I did. The previous stableman planned to put him down the next day to assure that he wouldn't muddy their bloodline."

I glanced back at the towering horse. He was nuzzling Judas affectionately, causing the boy to break out into uncontrollable giggles.

"What kind of person could slaughter an innocent animal just based on a discoloration of their fur?"

"The heartless kind." A man stepped into the stable, joining us. With velvety, dark skin, he looked slightly older than I was. He pulled each finger of his riding gloves off and tossed them on a shelf of leather work boots.

"Hyppolytos, my friend, it's been too long." Aryx threw his arms around the man in a full, wholehearted embrace.

Hyppolytos smiled, wrinkles creasing at the corners of his jade-colored eyes.

Aryx turned to me and introduced us, "Elpis, this is my oldest friend."

The man nodded toward me.

"I see your travels were worth it, then." He shot Aryx a look and crossed his arms against his chest.

"To my misfortune, they were." I scowled, clenching my fist.

"I'm sorry to hear that. However, as much as it pains me to agree with Aryx, you're the person who can take out Tethys and bring the city peace."

"Trust me, Lytos, she won't buy it." Aryx's smile faded, looking at me with deep disdain.

Hyppolytos grew quiet, watching his old friend watch me.

"Well, I don't know what happened, although I'm sure

Ryx here probably messed up big time. He's not all that well versed in conversation with women. Please accept my apology for whatever idiocy performed." Hyppolytos held out his hand for me to take.

"It was definitely a performance," I hissed, shoving my hands in my pockets.

I thought of our travels to Venia, the quiet words we shared, the connection we had felt. It had all been a lie, a manipulation to get me here. The betrayal was still as bitter as rust on my tongue.

"Well, Lytos, I need a favor. We're headed to Canissa this morning. I was hoping to take Kratos," Ryx said.

"Sure, I bet he'd like the chance to stretch his legs." Lytos looked at me again, eyeing my dirty trousers and stained tunic. "I think my wife has a box of old clothes she was planning on donating. You're about her size. I'll ask her to grab it for you."

"I would appreciate that," I said, suddenly very aware of the stench that clung to my skin.

"Come up to the main house. You can clean up. Have you two eaten yet? We have a couple slices of quiche leftover from breakfast."

"You know I can't turn down Margerie's baking." Aryx threw his arm around Lytos and the two started out the back stable doors and up the hill to their home.

The farmhouse was equally beautiful as the downtown city townhomes. Its painted blue shudders matched the sea of poppies that stretched across the front yard. Trailing Judas, Arcturas met us at the front gates. The two both panted heavily, as if an intense game of tag had just ensued. I scratched behind the wolf's ear, seeking a familiar face in the group of strangers I'd found myself a part of.

"Margie, guess who came by to see us," Lytos called, swinging the glass-paneled door open.

"Oh, I saw through the window, come on in, Ryx! It's so good you're here. I'm just finishing up some dishes. I'll be out in a minute," a soft female voice hollered from down the front hall.

Dishes clanked and cluttered as she finished putting them away. I shifted my weight in my boots, growing uncomfortable from the intimacy of their home. Portraits of family and friends covered the walls, leaving no white paint visible. Their lives were splayed out on the walls. It felt wrong for me to gaze upon them. I was an intrusive force, an outsider, getting a glimpse of their intimate family details.

A petite woman stepped down the hallway. Wiping her small hands against her apron and tucking a strand of blonde hair behind her ear, she beamed. Before Aryx could introduce me, she stepped forward and threw herself around me. Stunned, my arms remained paralyzed at my side, unable to return the friendly gesture.

"Oh, I'm so glad you're here. I'm so glad," she cried as she squeezed tighter.

I was a giant next to her petite frame. I worried I'd snap her in two if I squeezed back.

"Margie, don't scare her," Lytos chuckled, tapping his wife on her shoulder.

Margerie pulled away, her round eyes twinkling with admiration as she looked at me.

"Oh, I'm sorry. We've just been waiting for you for a very long time." She trailed off, looking at her son, who was now stroking Arcturas gingerly across the back.

"I'm not sure what I can do for you, but thank you for allowing me into your home." I smiled softly, but my fists were still clenched in my trouser pockets.

"I told Elpis that you had some old clothes lying around she could borrow," Lytos prompted his wife. She threw her hands up excitedly, her smile stretching across the entirety of her slender face.

"Oh, yes! I'm sure we can find something! Follow me."

She reached for my hand and pulled me down the hallway.

Turning into one bedroom, she motioned for me to sit on a royal red chaise that rested by the window. The bedroom was exquisite. A large window overlooked the pastures down the hill and a four poster bed with delicately carved florals centered the room. Margerie disappeared into her closet, throwing various tunics and trousers into a pile at my feet. By the time she returned, I was buried in pinks and yellows.

"Alright! So there's plenty to choose from. Take what you need. You're nearly a foot taller than me, so I apologize if the trousers are too short. The bathing chamber is down the hallway on your left. Take your time. I'm sure it was a long road from Ursae and, well, Ryx can be hard company." She smiled warmly at me, resting her palms on her cheeks.

Nearly speechless, I whispered a thank you as she closed the door behind her. Undressing was difficult. Large, swollen welts had appeared on my thighs and abdomen. Deep, scabbed over cuts littered my arms from where the thorns had pierced my skin. Every inch of my body was battered and torn.

Wrapping a towel around myself, I hurriedly tiptoed to the bathing chamber and washed. The sharp shower of water was excruciating against my bruised body. Wincing, I scraped away the thick layer of grime.

When finally I was clean, I stepped out of the shower and dried off. Tightly tucking the towel back around myself, I opened the door and stepped directly into Aryx. The hard muscle of his chest pressed into my damp skin.

"Wh-What the hell are you doing?" I stammered, jerking away. His cheeks burned a deep purple as he scanned down my exposed flesh. The towel was a mere scrap, not nearly covering enough.

"I'm sorry. I thought you were done." He held a similarly colored towel in one hand and a change of clothes in the other. Suddenly very interested in his bare feet, he lowered his gaze and stepped aside, letting me pass.

"Yes, well, I wasn't. I'd appreciate it if you didn't barge in on me," I snapped, brushing past him. Nostrils flaring, I glanced back at him. The strands of his tunic were untied, and the material hung low on his chest, revealing the sharp curve of his pectorals. Twin tattoos traced each collarbone with straight, thick lines.

Aryx opened his mouth to speak, but before he could, I whipped my head away and hurried down the hallway back to Margerie's bedchamber, and slammed the door behind me.

Wiping droplets of water from across my brow, I dropped my towel and wrapped it around my head. I breathed deeply and fanned myself, trying to cool the hot flash across the nape of my neck. Aryx was beautiful, classically so. He was a killer, a ruthless liar. Every instinct told me to run. But the woman I'd kept locked in a box deep inside burst into flames with every accidental touch between us.

Pull yourself together, Elpis. I scowled and reached for a black tunic draped across the chaise. After searching for a pair of trousers that fell even close to my ankles, I quickly combed through my hair and started for the kitchen.

Lytos and Margerie sat at an antique round table. The scent of roasted coffee lingered with beams of late morning light. The steam from their mugs billowed into the air as Lytos motioned for me to sit. Margerie rose from her seat to pour coffee and pass me a slice of quiche.

"I'm happy to make you something if you'd like anything else." She rested the plate in front of me and waited for me to dig in. I smiled and took a bite.

"This is delicious, thank you," I said through a large mouthful.

"Oh, wonderful! I'm glad you like it." She pushed her blonde hair over her shoulder and returned to her seat.

The couple stared at me as I continued eating.

"You two will scare her away if you keep eyeing her like that," Aryx said, appearing in the corridor.

His golden hair, now damp, hung at his shoulders and the heat from the shower left his skin glowing in the soft light. I avoided his eye contact, focusing intently on my quiche. My cheeks grew hot at the thought of that tan chest against mine and I found it hard to swallow, my throat suddenly dry. Margerie placed a plate at the empty seat across the table as he sat down. I stared into my mug, avoiding those piercing, golden eyes.

"So, you're headed to Canissa?" Lytos asked, sipping his coffee.

"I think that's the best place to start. You know Altair's reaction when he sees me will be...interesting." Aryx picked at the crumbs remaining on his plate.

"Yes, but if you explain the plan, I think he'll be convinced. He's an understanding God. Just tell him the truth." Lytos glanced at me, then back at Aryx.

"We'll see. I think Elpis has a better chance than I do."

"Why?" I interjected, my ears perked at the mention of my name.

"Let's just say he and I have a rocky past." The trio grew silent.

I scanned each of their expressions.

"It's probably time for us to get on the road if we want to get to the Western City before dark," Aryx said, sliding out his chair and placing his plate in the sink.

The couple chaperoned us back down the hill, where Judas and Arcturas chased each other throughout the stables. Like two old friends, they wrestled and played until each was panting. It amazed me they hadn't tired each other out yet. Kratos, surveying the two from a safe distance, grazed through a feed trough.

"Judas, quit terrorizing that wolf!" Margerie scolded, pulling the boy close to her. "Sorry about him, he just gets

185

excited whenever he makes a new friend."

"It's alright," I chuckled. Arcturas's tongue hung against the side of her mouth. "She loves a good game of chase."

"Ryx, are you going to come back tomorrow too?" the boy asked, breaking free from his mother and throwing himself against Aryx's leg.

"Sorry bud, not tomorrow. But I'll be back real soon, okay? I'll bring you something from Canissa. How does that sound?"

Judas nodded enthusiastically.

"Be safe, Ryx. There's a lot of us here who are depending on you," Lytos said. His expression was sincere as he pulled Judas into an embrace. The man's hands were nearly triple the size of his son's.

Margerie wiped a tear from rolling down her cheek.

"It will be okay. I promise." Aryx hugged his friend tightly and whispered something in her ear.

"Elpis, thank you for being here. Good luck dealing with this one on your trip," Margerie laughed, and leaned into a timid hug. I smiled and allowed her to embrace me. I suddenly realized the gravity of this family's situation. Lytos, and in a few years, Judas, would be called to fight for the Venian army. Not only was Margerie at risk of losing a husband, but also a child. How many other families would be torn apart from this war?

Judas reminded me so much of Vikar before everything happened. They both had an air of fascination around them, believing the world to be a wondrous place. It broke my heart to think how this impending war might change him, just as Vikar had. Another child thrown into the boots of a grownup, robbed of the playful innocence of youth.

We strung our packs across Kratos's saddle and began down the gravel road leading back to the city. It wasn't until we turned the corner street that the trio started back up the hill to their home.

Feeling more at ease with Arcturas by my side, we marched up the street in silence, taking in the bustling city's beauty. People gawked at the midnight-colored wolf as she trotted up the sidewalks, stopping in their tracks and jumping away in fear. When we reached the western gate, Aryx led Kratos to my side.

"Do you need help with the saddle? It can be difficult for inexperienced riders," he asked, offering a hand.

I swatted it away, clicking my tongue as I kicked my foot in the stirrup and jumped into the seat.

"Who said I was an inexperienced rider?" I smirked.

He shrugged and stepped into the stirrup behind me, placing his hands on either side of my waist

"What are you doing?" My back straightened.

"You didn't expect me to walk while you rode, did you?" He asked, foot still resting in the leather hold. I swallowed hard, tightening my grip around the reins. Aryx climbed into the seat behind me, swinging his powerful leg over the horse. His body was warm against mine as he reached around my waist to grasp the reins from me. The fresh, citrusy smell was intoxicating, and I forced myself to not breathe it in. He flicked the reins and Kratos started into a trot.

Chapter 23

Kratos carried us west for what felt like hours. The solid muscle of his legs rocked the saddle forward and back with each powerful step. Color in the trees faded into bright yellows, then oranges, then reds, as we left Venia behind. I stayed quiet, only responding to Aryx in short, clipped sentences.

Ignoring my hints, he continued on with casual conversation. My patience wore thin as the sun slowly crept across the sky. Finally, when it reached its apex, I snapped. Pulling up on Kratos's reins, we skidded to a halt. I jumped to the ground, the imprint of my boots pressing deep into the dirt path.

"If you don't stop talking, I will slice out your tongue," I hissed, throwing my hands into the air.

"Don't bite my head off. I'm just trying to make the trip a little less mundane," he replied, dismounting Kratos to stand next to me.

"I don't want to make the trip less mundane. I just want to travel in silence, arrive in Canissa, and accomplish what we need to do. Just because we are allies at this moment doesn't make up for what you did. And it doesn't mean that I am your friend," I screamed, stomping my foot like a tempered child.

Aryx sucked in a breath. He clenched, then unclenched his fists, glaring at me with smoldering eyes, the gold blazing brightly around his pupils.

"I'm sorry," he said. His tone was as sharp as the blade sheathed across his back. Reaching into my pouch, I pulled out my water-skin and drained it.

"We're out of water. I'm going to go look for a spring to refill."

Before he could argue, I turned on my heels and trudged into the neighboring trees. With Arcturas at my side, we stepped over roots and ducked under branches. Following a faint rush of water, we made our way to a narrow creek that gargled peacefully through the forest.

Bright, young fiddleheads had poked their way through the earth and tall, thin trees stretched toward the blue sky above us. Kneeling beside the creek, I dunked my hand into the water and allowed it to bubble into the mouth of the skin. The woodland air was smooth as I breathed deeply and sunk into my heels, sitting against the cool riverbank. I leaned back, letting my neck relax and my chin tip up to the sky. Sparrows chirped their amicable tunes as a grey squirrel, munching on a nut, sat perched in the branch above me.

This is what I was fighting for.

I had to endure just a little longer until this was all over. The freedom of the forest was sweet on my lips. I Inhaled, then exhaled until my frustration subsided.

"Elpis, I'm sorry," Aryx said from behind me. "What I did was unforgivable. I know that. I-"

"I let you in, let you see everything. I was vulnerable with you, and it was all a lie. You saw how broken I am and you played that to your advantage."

"I know. I'm sorry, truly, I am. I hated having to do that to you." He sat on the bank next to me, tossing a pebble into the babbling water below.

"There was no blade against your throat, you chose to manipulate me. You chose to lie to my face."

"It wasn't all a lie, Elpis. What I said, the things we shared. Those weren't lies." Aryx turned to me.

"That's horseshit, and you know it." I snapped, "I told you things I hadn't even admitted to myself yet, Aryx, and you used it against me."

We sat in silence, watching the stream trickle by. Hatred burned in my throat as I looked at my shaking hands. Funny how in a matter of seconds, everything I thought to be true became a lie. Someone I trusted, cared for, even loved, became my enemy. I couldn't bear to look upon the man who once touched my skin, whispered words of kindness to me, comforted me. He was gone. In his place, a manipulator. An abuser. Someone so selfish they'd use the fragility of a broken mind to their advantage. He disgusted me. Nauseated me.

"I led the invasion into Aquilae. I commanded my men to slaughter those innocent people and burn their homes to the ground. When I said Altair and I have a rocky past, it's because I was the one that held the blade to his chest during the last battle. I fully intended to kill him that day. It would have been easy to plunge my sword through his heart. My mother threatened that if I didn't lead that attack, she would kill my father. If he knew what I'd become, the killer she had molded me into, I think he'd rather have died." His voice trembled as he spoke. "I'm the monster, not you."

I inhaled deeply, staring at the killer sitting beside me. Regret shadowed his eyes, and I watched as his lower lip shook between breaths. The tattoo down the side of his face stretched and creased against the sadness washing over him.

"It's not the blood on your hands that makes you a monster Aryx. Everyone in war causes bloodshed. It's the ease with which you toy with people that does." I sprung to my feet and left the half-god sitting on the riverbank.

Arcturas nipped at his hand as she passed, following me back to the trail. We rode in silence until reaching the gates of Canissa. The shiver of Autumn bit my fingers as I led Kratos through the large, wooden gates. Everything else inside was already frozen to the bone.

Chapter 24

Farmers pulling their horse-drawn wagons rushed past us, hurrying to their fields. The nutty scent of crackling hearths and roasting meats hung low in the air as we carefully weaved through endless stretches of farmsteads and outdoor markets abundant with Autumn squash and cold weather harvests. Children, grimy with soil, pushed through us, giggling with joy. The rolling hills in the distance blazed with scarlet, terracotta, and gold.

"Let's find an inn to stay the night. We'll travel to Procyon's temple in the morning," Aryx said. There was a sharpness in his voice as he led Kratos down the trail.

Procyon was known as the jolly, immortal king. His mortal court was highly revered across the realms. The city flourished under his reign as the pillar of agriculture. Although loyal to Ursae, whispers of rumors spread that he yearned for new Northern leadership. Adria cut off major trade routes between the two cities, and I imagined it took an enormous chunk of wealth from this quaint farming city.

We traveled through narrow dirt roads, looping across red covered bridges and towering silos.

The quartz light of dusk soon settled across the land as we approached an A-frame tavern with painted black shutters and frosted glass windows. Smoke lingered from its chimney and the faint murmur of laughter and soft conversation could be heard from within.

Kratos and Arcturas happily settled into the inn's wooden post enclosure, guzzling down the fresh troughs of spring water and playfully chasing each other around the tapered pasture.

Candlelight illuminated the inn's interior, throwing amber warmth across pink-faced men and women, sipping ale and spooning pot pie from their plates.

"We'd like two rooms, please," Aryx said to the inn-keeper.

The small man, standing maybe four feet tall, threw back his neck to see the half-god's golden face.

Through a thick grey beard that hung to his knees, he said, "Sorry sir, only got one available. We can bring up a cot, though, if you need."

"Whatever's available is fine, thanks." Grumbling, I met Aryx's sheepish smirk.

The innkeeper motioned to the iron staircase behind him and passed Aryx the key.

"The loft is on the top floor, taverns to your left. I think Cook's serving mutton pies tonight. Make yourself at home."

I followed Aryx up the steps, passed the second floor with rows of occupied rooms, and to the third floor loft. Candles, dripping wax down the stained paneled wall, lined the slender doorframe. Ducking through the door, he tossed his pack on a yellow corduroy rocking chair that swayed in the corner and sat at the end of the bed to pull off his boots.

"I'll take the cot," he said, rubbing his aching feet.

"Fine." I swallowed, the room feeling too small, too intimate to share with the man in front of me.

"I'm going to go eat dinner, if you'd like to join me. We should be safe here. I doubt any of the patrons downstairs will recognize you- it seems they've drunk enough to not even recognize themselves," he said.

I began untying my own boots, glancing out the window to watch Arcturas leap over a patch of yellow mums, surprising Kratos, who was grazing peacefully.

"I'll join you. Tomorrow is going to be a big day. We should probably rest while we can," I said.

The two of us descended the creaking stairs and took a seat in the inn's tavern. A jolly, older woman greeted us with two ceramic ramekins filled precariously with steaming pot pie. A flakey biscuit sunk into its thick broth. My mouth watered as the savory steam wrapped around my face, warming my cheeks.

"I'll be back with some ale," she said, her voice creaking from wrinkled lips.

The woman's very essence reminded me so much of the barkeep I'd left behind. Had the city guards come sniffing yet? I suddenly wasn't hungry for dinner anymore.

"I'm sure she's okay," Aryx said through spoonfuls. "You should eat. It's been a long day."

"You don't know that. They could've taken her prisoner or had her executed for all we know." I poked at the dish in front of me, spooning broth over the biscuit.

"They have no evidence to take her in. Besides, the old barkeep's tough. You know that. She's probably kicking some drunk patron to the curb as we speak." He smiled slightly at me, and for the first time, the familiar gold in his eyes warmed.

Aryx was right. Frya was tough. She'd taught me how

194

to survive. How to protect those you care for.

"I just hope she's okay," I said and dug in. Suddenly, I craved my old life in the tavern's back rooms. I missed the way her knees cracked as she hobbled into the room, or the way she jabbed a bony finger at Arcturas when she was up to no good.

"I know. You probably won't believe me, but I do, too. She had an unmeasurable kindness I'd never experienced before," Aryx said. Focusing on me, he set his spoon down.

"Yes, she did. Which made it easy to use her to your advantage, right?" I snapped.

Cook returned with two pints. Thanking her, I drained mine and asked for another. If I was to get through a night in that cramped space with Aryx, I'd need some help. After three rounds of drinks and two servings of pie, I was thoroughly satisfied. Once the hazy cloud of exhaustion set in and I could chase away the thoughts of my old barkeep, I retired back up to the loft.

Glancing out the window to check on my wolf, I didn't notice the soft click of the door behind me. Arcturas and Kratos slept peacefully under the western stars. Their limbs were tucked together, and snouts nuzzled against each other.

"Elpis. I'm sorry." Aryx stepped to the window beside me. "You were right. I used your pain. It was wrong of me. I wish I could take it all back."

"Well, you can't. What's done has been done." I brushed past him, his scent tickling my nose as I trudged for the door.

Aryx blurred past me, blocking my exit. He grasped my hand in his, tracing his thumb across my knuckle.

"Step aside," I hissed, staring at our interlaced fingers.

Electricity buzzed between us. The air thickened between us. Aryx's eyes were vivid in the warm flicker of candlelight.

"No, not until we work this out." He lowered his voice,

the knob of his throat bumped up and down as he swallowed. My mouth went dry, watching his lips close, then part again. I hated that even now, after everything between us, I still craved those lips against mine.

The warmth of his touch raised goosebumps across my forearms as he traced the curve of my neck up to my jaw, lacing his calloused fingers through my hair.

"The things I said, what we shared, parts of it were real. I know, deep down, you know that," he whispered. I closed my eyes, desperately wishing for the man standing before me to be Rune again. His eyes were vivid in the warm flicker of candlelight.

"I'll never lie to you again." He smoothed a loose strand behind my ear.

The veins in his hands throbbed as he brushed his fingertips across my lips. My skin felt as if it would burst into flames, and I leaned into his touch. I wanted his words to be true, for it to be simple between us. Just him. Just me. I yearned for that connection between us, the physical closeness we once shared.

"From now on, it's just me, the real me. I promise." His voice was soft as he lowered his lips to my neck, trailing kisses up my jaw, across my cheek, stopping just next to my lips. Every muscle in my body ignited against him as his hands wrapped themselves around my waist, pulling me closer. Heat pooled low within me, and I clung to every movement of his lips against mine.

"I promise, Elpis, I promise." Aryx's kisses grew frantic as he slipped his hands beneath my shirt, tracing the scars of my past across my back. His cotton tunic was so thin between us, I could feel each arc and swell of his muscular chest pressed into me. A hunger unlike anything before erupted throughout my body and I swayed into him, groaning softly against his powerful legs between mine.

Every piece of my being wanted to lose myself in him, to pour out the darkest parts and lay it all out for him to see, but betrayal was still heavy in the air and it couldn't be ignored. My blood turned to ice as I thought of his broad stance next to his mother, smirking cruelly as the thorns cut into my flesh.

Aryx flinched as I brought the point of my dagger to his throat.

"Step aside." I cleared my throat, regaining composure. "This will never happen again. We will be allies, we will work together towards our common goal and nothing more. I hate you, Aryx."

His jaw dropped, and a painful fury welled in my chest.

"Step aside or I'll slit your throat." I gripped the hilt of my dagger tighter.

Silently, he stepped away from the door. Before he could turn back toward me, I rushed through, slamming it behind me.

Flying down the stairs and out the front door, I hurdled to the pasture, threw myself across Kratos's back and urged him to go.

He broke into a fast gallop, Arcturas sprinting behind us.

Tears blurred my vision as we traveled down quiet dirt roads. When we reached a shallow lake, Kratos whirled to a stop, the muscles beneath his powerful legs flexing against the earth. I dismounted and kneeled beside the shoreline, looking upon the stars reflected in the lake's stillness.

Finally alone, I let myself out.

Sobs disrupted the stillness in the air as all the progress I had made collapsed around me.

I was close, so sure of finding myself.

I'd seen glimpses of the woman I once was.

I'd felt her course through my veins.

Now, only emptiness remained. Emptiness and a hurt so deep, it dug its claws into my very core.

I'd let a man get under my skin, let him see the shadows that lurked there, and he deceived me. None of it was real. How could I have been so stupid? Now here I was, alone. I'd left behind my only true ally. I wished Frya could see me, to hold me in those ancient arms. She'd pat me on the back and brush my hair through her hands, and when all the tears dried up and nothing was left, she'd pull me up from the ground. And she'd probably've told me I was a stupid girl. I chuckled under my breath. Gods, I missed her. Strength was feeling grief. Not becoming consumed by it.

The harvest moon cast golden light across the lakeside. I whispered a quiet prayer to the goddess above. My mother, the omniscient force of night.

Arcturas padded over, nuzzling me gently with her snout. Her yellow eyes gleamed as she pointed her nose towards the moon and let out a long, winding howl.

A battle cry.

"Elpis, watch out!" A male voice struck out from behind me as I whirled around to meet it. Towering above me, a beast with glowing, silver eyes outstretched its claws and was ready to strike.

Chapter 25

A broad, sinewy chest loomed over me, and the tendons and muscles of two hairless hind legs crushed the surrounding earth beneath massive paws. Its claws were as sharp as daggers outstretched above my head. I froze, my blood putrefying in my veins as it opened its wolfish mouth to growl. Oily brown fur pricked up along its spine. Then it pounced.

I squeezed my eyes, waiting for the impact that never came.

An arrow whizzed past me, brushing my cheek, then striking through the beast's chest. It roared in agony, howling and clawing at its wound. I kicked at its hind legs, pressing into the cool soil beneath me.

Arcturas lunged for the creature, her claws scratching at its brown skin. Distracted with my wolf's attack, the beast fell to its knees, swiping its long, muscular arms at her as she bit into its fleshy neck. A vicious roar poured from its open mouth. Hot, sour breath thawed the frosted night air like a dense smoke.

It gripped Arcturas by the abdomen and flung her into the lake. She sunk below the surface. I watched as the beast pounced onto the shallow shoreline after her. Arcturas struggled to stay afloat in the depths further from shore. Each press of her paws hit the surface with a plunk. Whining and yelping, she sunk back beneath the depths, only to burst back into the air, wriggling frantically.

My feet barely touched the ground as I sprinted into the shallows and dove to her aid. A trail of murky silver leaked from the beast's wound, like an oil sheen on the water's surface. I leapt for its back. With my full weight wrapped around its neck, we disappeared into the liquid darkness beneath us.

My grip around its monstrous frame slipped with each desperate lurch for air. I hoped that my attack had bought my wolf some time. My hold wouldn't last much longer. Splinters of wiry fur scraped the tender skin of my cheek as I lost my grip and slid down his back.

No light transmitted beneath the water. The sounds of struggle were muffled, as if there was cotton stuffed into my ears. I took a leap of faith into zero visibility and sped away from the black mass. Arms outstretched I searched for Arcturas, pleading to the gods that she was unharmed. The tether between us still pulsed. It emulated from my core like a second heartbeat.

Just as my lungs reached their bursting point, I hit the surface, gasping for air. All was quiet. The lake, once violently rippling, was silent and still. There was nothing as I scanned the shoreline for the beast or my wolf. I was utterly alone. Or so it felt.

I started for the lakeside, confused and frantic. Maybe higher ground would give me a better vantage point to locate Arcturas. My ankle pricked against splintered fur as I continued to swim, pumping my legs as fast as my muscles would allow.

Before I realized what was happening, claws pierced the bony flesh of my foot. I was thrown into the air. The beast resurfaced, dangling me like a rag doll.

"Elpis!" Aryx called, flying to the water's edge. His arrow was knocked and ready to fly. Before he could find his aim, the beast stretched his arm and hurled me into the air. I skimmed across the surface and crumpled onto the shoreline. The sheer force of the impact stole breath from my lungs. Aryx sprinted to my side, the point of his arrowhead never leaving the beast's chest.

"Find Arcturas. She's still in the water," I wheezed, cradling my right side. Bullets of pain shot through my body and red stained the edges of my vision.

He dropped his bow and dove into the lake, paddling faster than a shark chasing its prey. My vision blurred. The pain was taking over.

I was dying. This was the slow sink into oblivion, I was sure of it.

My eyelids were heavy, too heavy. I fought to keep them open as I stabilized myself against the sandy ground. Roars of battle, both man and beast, echoed in the night air. Get up, Elpis. Get up, Polaris whispered in my ear.

"I can't," I cried, my voice a mere murmur in the moonlight.

Get up, Elpis. You need to get up.

I tried again, once more pushing against the sand. My elbows gave out under the crackle of agony on my ribcage. I'd broken a rib, maybe two. Maybe all of them. My abdomen felt swollen, too full of fluid that I prayed wasn't blood.

She needs you. He needs you. Get up.

A wolf whined in the distance, yipping at the crunch of bone. My body fought against me with every attempt to move. Another whine, a man's cry, two splashes.

I took a deep breath, focusing inwards. She needed me.

He needed me, too.

The tingles were faint. I took another long inhale. One more time, lungs expanded, that's it. As the tingles grew stronger, the pain subsided. Bubbling up from my toes, to my knees, to my chest. Shards of bone mended themselves back together, blood receded back into veins.

With fists clenched, I rose on shaky feet. Long strands of hair hung over my face as I straightened my spine and let my demons take over.

With dagger in hand, I stepped into the lake. Rather than toes touching the rocky bottom, they floated on the surface. With each step, the glow of the borealis rippled across the lake. Starlight fizzled out, leaving an unending stretch of night.

I charged for the beast, tearing into its flesh with my blade. A guttural scream escaped my lips as I sunk through its muscle tissue, straight into its bone.

Snap.

It flailed beneath me, but my grip was too strong to escape this time. Retracting the dagger, I dove on to its back, wrapping my thighs around its neck to block its airway. It flung me back and forth, blinded by the black night I created.

Squeezing my knees further together, I plunged the blade through its skull, piercing grey brain matter until the tip protruded from the beast's opposite temple.

With one final jerk, it exhaled its last breath and sank into the disturbed water below.

A small, black mass of fur floated limply beside me, its thick tail rocking with the motion of the waves. Throwing my wolf over my shoulder, we made our way to shore.

A faint heartbeat knocked against my palm. She was alive. I placed her back on solid ground and smoothed back her ruffled fur. A tear streamed down my face, landing silently on the crown of her head.

"Elpis! Are you hurt?" Aryx sprinted from the shallows,

his bow knocked and loaded for another attack.

"I don't think so, but she is." I stroked Arcturas's head, watching as warmth returned to her fragile body. Her muscles twitched and contracted, as if healing their internal wounds.

She let out a soft grumble, stretching her mended legs.

"Shh, you're safe. Don't move now. You need to heal," I whispered, running my palm down the length of her spine. She whimpered against my touch and opened an eye. The knot in my stomach unwinded as I watched life return to her body.

Aryx dropped his bow and rushed to embrace me, wrapping himself around my shaking body. The tingles receded with his touch, and twinkles of light returned to the sky.

"I'm sorry, Elpis. I'm so sorry," he whispered.

The carcass of the creature lapped against the shore, still warm and steaming. Its silver blood muddied the surrounding waters.

"I thought she was dead." Letting down those fortress walls I'd built up, I clung to him, safe in the warmth of his broad frame. He wiped the tears from my cheek and clasped my jaw between his hands. Our eyes met as he tipped my chin up.

The electricity between us hummed from somewhere deep within our souls.

"You- you saved us. We were dead, had you not followed," I sobbed.

"No," he whispered, brushing his thumb against my lips. "It was I who was saved."

His damp cotton tunic sculpted the deadly curves of his chest. Droplets dripped from his soaked head, creating streamlines across the black tattoos.

I didn't want to be strong anymore, to be silent and cavalier. The dams holding back all the fear and sadness and pain I'd built cracked and crumbled. His eyes were somber as he watched me fall apart.

Those weren't the eyes of the god who betrayed me, the cruel prince who I despised.

They were the eyes of a man who feared. A man who loved with every piece of himself. The man who accepted every shadow, every broken part of me.

Those were Rune's eyes.

All traces of my resentment faded away in this moment. The candid, glorious man standing before me only brought peace to my warring head. My lips found his in a fever of need.

I craved the feel of his skin against mine, the burning pulse between us. We tangled ourselves in one another. His fingers laced themselves into my hair. My hands trembled as I unbuttoned his tunic. He pulled the cotton over his head and threw it to the ground beside us. Amber moonlight washed against the tattoos that traced his collarbone down across the center of his chest.

I ran my fingers down each ink line. What stories did they hold? What pieces of Aryx's past did they represent? I wanted everything, all of it. The gruesome details of his battles, the darkness that lurked behind those light eyes, the pain he inflicted and the pain he tried to heal.

Lost in the feel of my skin, Aryx pulled the corner of my tunic down across my shoulder, gentle kisses trailing behind the scrape of the fabric as it fell to my elbow.

"What you do to me..." Aryx whispered, through ragged breaths, "you strange, perfect creature."

He watched, eyes glazed with lust, as I shrugged out of my tunic,exposing pale skin to the chill autumn air. Standing before him, fully bare, fully vulnerable, I didn't hesitate this time.

We wrapped ourselves together, his hands cold against the perk of my breast as he led us to the earthen floor. As he pressed into me, I ignited and the flame of pleasure intensified until I felt as if I'd explode right there beneath him.

"Aryx," I whispered, feeling my body stretch around him, "promise me that this is real."

Through a breathy groan, he lowered his lips to my ear, my muscles contracting as he drove himself further into me.

"It always was," he growled, shattering me into waves of bliss. The cries of my spiral sent him, too, over that edge, our bodies and minds connecting in the deepest, most fundamental way.

Chapter 26

There was nothing but water. Air bubbled from my lungs as I swam for the surface, stretching my neck as far as it'd reach. I closed in on the ripples of light reflecting the waves above. My lungs burned, begging for relief I couldn't give them.

Just as my cheeks hit the bright, cool air, weeds slithered around my ankles, pulling me back down through the depths. I clawed at my feet, trying to break free. The slimy green binds only tightened. A rush of bubbles escaped with the screams pouring from me. The surface grew fainter and fainter as I plunged into the deep green darkness.

A behemoth creature prowled toward me at the rocky bottom. Its large fins curled as it glided with predatory stealth across the sand. Shimmering fins of velvet purple and black glinted as its long eel-like body curled around me. I needed to act fast before my bones were crushed and the soul inside me was squeezed out.

I kicked at the monster's tightening grip. The scales across its long, winding body pierced my skin. The murky water around me became clouded with brown tendrils of blood.

I needed to fight, to slip out of its hold. My lungs now blazed for air, but the only way out was down. I pushed my arms up above me and sank beneath its coiled body. A fog of disturbed sediment skewed my vision as I struggled to swim across the bottom, tendrils of my hair skimming its pale underbelly.

Something glinted beneath the sand. As I reached for it, the creature jerked its head in my direction. Horns of armor-like skin rushed toward me in a blur. Just as I pulled the rusted halberd from its murky grave, the gargantuan eel struck its fangs into my side.

Agony seared up my abdomen as the eel ripped through flesh, cracking open my rib cage and piercing my organs. Desperately, I swung the spike into its fleshy temple. The creature shrieked and shriveled. Its writhing and wriggling sent shockwaves across my face.

I propelled myself upward, vision tunneling with every stroke. The trail of blood behind me dispersed into the oily blackness beneath. The eel, with ragged strokes of its fins, nipped at my feet as I rose higher and higher.

Finally, gasping for frantic breaths, I breached the surface. The waves stretched across the horizon, no land in sight. Struggling to see the creature I'd left below, I took a deep breath and plunged back under. Suspended in the water column, its soft underbelly rose toward me. As it grew closer, its fins and scales faded away, leaving the form of a man behind. I noticed his golden flowing locks. His bright amber eyes were now a pale yellow. Long, powerful limbs hung spinelessly below him.

I shrieked. Through the clouded, brown water, I saw Aryx, the rusted halberd embedded into the flesh of his lifeless, mutilated face.

Chapter 27

I bolted upright, scratching against the soil of the lakeside. Silent sobs ran down my face as I reached for the man beside me. He stretched and stirred awake.

"Elpis? What's wrong?" he asked, voice rough with sleep.

"N-Nothing, I just had a bad dream," I stammered through frantic breaths.

He yawned and sat up beside me. Wiping my sweaty brow with the back of my hand, I tried to regain my composure.

"It must have been some dream," he said, running his hand up my back. My skin was cold against his touch. Visions of Aryx's lifeless, waterlogged body pitched through me.

"It's nothing," I said, entwining my fingers to keep my hands from shaking.

"Doesn't seem like nothing-" he started.

I stood up abruptly, avoiding the conversation about to happen. My nightmares were mine alone. I'd been through this before. I just needed to breathe. Aryx's bloodied face flashed across my mind once more and I hunched over, my legs crumpling beneath me.

"I just need a... need a minute," I said, retching into the lake beside me.

I vomited until my stomach was empty, tears streaming down my face. The waves of nausea were overwhelming. I hadn't noticed his gentle hands holding my hair in place behind my back. Red faced and breathless, I looked up at him. Concern wrinkled across his brow. He smoothed back my hair and smiled softly.

"Did you dream of the tower?" he asked, his voice a soothing caress over my trembling body.

"Not this time, no." I heaved again, releasing the venom that poisoned my thoughts.

"Let's get you back to the tavern. Maybe some ginger tea will help you calm down," he said, scooping my weak frame into his arms.

Arcturas, now fully recovered, nipped at my feet, an affectionate gesture used to pull me back to reality. Tomorrow I'd need to figure out exactly how she healed, but for tonight I was grateful that she did.

With Kratos in tow, we trudged through the back roads to the now dark inn. I focused on the steady rise and fall of Aryx's breathing, holding an inhale until my own was in sync. His arms, no longer suspended lifelessly in the open water, were tight around me. Stroking my thigh with his thumb, he carried me up the spiraling steps to the loft.

"Let's get you under the covers," he said, his lips mere inches from my ear.

His voice rippled through me. He lowered me into bed, pulling the wool blankets above my shoulders and sat beside me, stroking my cheek until the shivers stopped and my eyelids drifted shut.

"It's okay. I'm here," he said, placing a kiss on my brow.

I cleared my mind, letting the feel of his lips linger on

my skin.

"I'll always be here, Elpis."

Arcturas jumped into the space beside me, curling her body around mine and resting her large, furry head across my abdomen. Its weight kept me grounded. It felt like only yesterday that we curled up beneath the pines, safe from our first storm under their cover.

"You're safe. She'll make sure of that." He chuckled as Arcturas nuzzled into me. "I'm going to see if I can find some tea in the kitchen downstairs. I'll be right back."

He kissed the back of my hand and headed downstairs. Stroking my wolf, I watched as she sank into sleep. The dream still lurked in the dark corners of my mind, but Aryx's smell, still fresh on my skin, chased it further away. A paralyzing exhaustion washed over me and just as my eyes resolved into sleep, he crept back in with a piping hot mug in one hand.

Placing it quietly on the bedside table, he settled into the rocking chair by the window. I grunted, tapping the cold pillow beside me. Smiling softly, he rolled into bed, wrapping his arm around my waist. I scooted into him, meeting the curl of his body with mine.

This was safe.

Embracing the electricity at every point of contact, I slipped into a mindless, exhausted sleep.

"It's rude to watch someone sleep, you know," Aryx whispered. The sun gleamed brilliantly through the inn's dusty window. His eyes, peacefully closed, reminded me of a child having settled into a long nap.

"Well, good thing you're awake, then," I smirked. Beads of light bounced across the morning air.

"Are you feeling better?" he asked, drawing out his

words with a lazy yawn.

Arcturas, now stirring from her own sleep, rolled to her back and straightened her legs into the air.

"Yes, thank you for last night." I trailed off, my cheeks burning. "I'm sorry you had to see that."

"I'm not." He smiled, brushing his fingers down the curve of my hip. "I'm glad I could be there for you."

I bit my lip, trying to settle the ache now throbbing through me.

"What was that beast?" I asked, swallowing hard at my dry throat.

"I'm not sure, but Tethys definitely sent it. It stank of her magic." His nose crinkled at the thought. "It's probably best if we stick together from now on. No running off in a fury."

I punched his arm, my lips curling into a smile that matched his. "Rather than running away, next time I'll just knife you where you stand."

His eyes flickered with darkness and a mischievous grin wrinkled across his face.

"What a violent creature you are. Careful with that mouth or I may hold you captive in this bed all day." His voice was raw as his fingers squeezed the muscle of my thigh.

"You act as if that wasn't my plan already," I whispered, leaning into his touch.

Aryx pulled me against him, lowering his lips to mine. As his fingers began their exploration beneath the covers, Arcturas grunted beside me, jabbing her hind leg into my back.

"I think this will have to wait," I sighed, elbowing the wolf off the bed. Snarling, she trotted to the door and sat facing us, the yellow of her eyes burning holes into me. I rolled out of bed, dressing quickly before she became too restless.

"I'll grab us some breakfast and meet you out front.

Procyon usually meets with his council in the early mornings. If we hurry, we might catch him," Aryx said, throwing the covers off himself.

I stopped in my tracks to watch as the naked half-god stretched away the stiffness in his arms. Tendons and muscles shifted across his back as he reached over his head. My fingers trembled as he turned to face me, sun beams highlighting the fullness of his physique. He was a warrior through and through. Hardened from battlefields and wars of the past.

"I'd appreciate it if you didn't look at me like a piece of meat." He raised his brow at my fingers, now stroking the bottom of my lip.

I snapped my jaw shut and threw my hand in the pocket of my trousers. Clearing my throat, I looked at the floor and swiped at the beads of sweat running down the nape of my neck.

"I'll be outside," I hissed, swinging the door open and rushing down the stairs.

Arcturas sprinted for the pasture, startling Kratos with her yips. The two leapt at one another, a blur of midnight tangled with a gleaming white mass. I breathed in. The crisp autumn scent tickled my nose and mourning doves cooed their lonely tunes.

The Autumn Realm was said to be beautiful, but the flames of color that painted the rolling horizon stole my breath entirely. With smoke meandering from quaint stone cottages, the city felt like an invitation to sip mulled cider beneath a warm flannel blanket and tell ghost stories around a roaring fire. I pictured a quiet future here filled with chilled, misty mornings, and walks through harvest fields.

"Cook gave me the strangest look when I asked if she had any raw chicken livers," Aryx said behind me, interrupting my daydream. He tossed a scrap to Arcturas. Jumping to catch it, she tore into the meat voraciously.

"Here, eat. You'll need your strength today." Aryx handed me a cranberry scone.

My empty stomach grumbled with delight as I broke the pastry in half and nibbled on the corner.

"You ready for this?" I asked, crumbs falling from my mouth.

"As ready as I'll ever be," he said, latching our saddle bags to Kratos.

The road to Procyon's temple was rocky and unkempt. Ankle high piles of withered, brown leaves crunched beneath Kratos's powerful hooves as we traveled into the heart of the realm. Canissa bustled with farmers tending their livestock. My mouth watered as we passed wooden cottages, fresh with the scent of baking bread.

Beyond vast fields of golden wheat, the stone temple nestled into its hillside. Only a round stone door marked its entrance.

"If you're noticed before we reach Procyon himself, things might get interesting. Be ready for a fight," Aryx said, clicking his reins to lead Kratos over a narrow brook. Minnows nibbled at the green murk pooling around its smooth grey stones.

He trotted to the temple's entrance, slowing to a halt before a young guard dressed in uniform grey. As we jumped off our horse, I pulled the hood of my cloak over my face, hoping the boy wouldn't recognize me.

"We're here to see Procyon," Aryx said to him, "We have an urgent message from Ursae."

"King Procyon isn't taking visitors today. The royal court is meeting and they are not to be disturbed," he squeaked, straightening his wooden spear across his chest.

"Please, this cannot wait. It's of the utmost importance," I demanded, lowering my voice slightly as I stepped toward the young guard. He eyed me suspiciously, squinting to make out the outline of my face beneath the thick drapes of wool.

"King Procyon isn't taking visitors today," he proclaimed, sliding in front of the door.

"If you don't let us pass, we'll have to force our way through, and it won't end well for you," Aryx hissed, his eyes darkening.

The boy's throat bobbed, but he stood his ground, tightening his grip around his spear.

"I'm afraid I cannot, sir. And if you try anything, I'll have to call for the city guards to arrest you." His voice cracked as he spoke.

I inspected the boy. He stood at least a half foot shorter than me and couldn't have been over fourteen. His mousy brown hair, shaved and neat, and his pin straight uniform suggested he was fresh from his training.

"Let us pass, boy." Aryx stepped toward him, gripping the sword sheathed at his side.

"Sir, I cannot." The guard marched forward, pointing the spear at the half-god who towered over him.

Placing my hand over Aryx's fist clenched around the hilt of his blade, I said, "Please, we don't want any trouble. It will be brief."

The boy shook his head, swinging the tip of his weapon toward me.

"One more step, and I'll call for the city guards," he cried, his hands shaking beneath the heavy weapon.

Taking a breath, I lowered my hood to my shoulders.

"Tell him the Heir of Polaris must speak with him urgently." I looked into the boy's eyes. They brightened as he realized who stood before him.

"Qu-Queen Slayer," he whispered with buckling knees. He dropped the spear at his feet and sprinted down the street, crying for reinforcements.

"We have seconds until we're surrounded," Aryx growled, shaking his head. "I had it under control. You shouldn't have revealed yourself."

"Well, I did, so let's get this over with and get out of here before they send me back to that tower." I threw the stone door open, diving into the shadows of the temple.

We raced down the narrow corridors, passing flaming sconces. Shouts and stomps of the city guards bounced off mossy, damp walls as we rushed deeper into the hillside. The passage opened into a cavernous hall. At its center, a long table of men and women sat deep in conversation. Their voices cut off at our intrusion.

"So sorry to interrupt," Aryx panted, "but we must speak with King Procyon."

"Who are you?" A crippled, ancient man rose from his head seat.

"Elpis- since you're ripe to tell half the kingdom who you are..." Aryx scowled at me, his voice an angry whisper.

The council jerked their heads toward me, expressions turning frantically as they realized who had interrupted.

"Lords, Ladies..." I started, swallowing hard at their terrified eyes, "I mean you no harm. I have an urgent message from Polaris and, as her heir, I feel it is my duty to deliver it."

Their mouths plummeted to the floor. Panicked whispers and murmurs filled the chamber.

"Silence." The ancient man commanded through a floor length grey beard. He raised his palm to the council, letting the fabric of his periwinkle robes fold below his outstretched arm. "Did you say you are the heir of Polaris?" He pointed his long, beak-like nose at me.

"Y-yes sir. I am." I shifted in my boots.

Aryx stepped in front of me, shielding me from the sharp tip of the man's carved wooden staff now aimed at my chest. Tense silence hung over the chamber, stifling my breaths as the man's eyes scanned me with a serious scrutiny.

"Prove it," he commanded.

A city guard stumbled into the hall, carrying a broadsword at his side.

I closed my eyes, breathing deeply. Focusing into myself, I grasped for the shadows. The familiar tingles rose from the arches of my feet and traveled through my veins, up over my arms to the tips of my fingers.

The man sucked in a breath as I flicked my wrist toward the city guard. His sword glowed and pulsed with my borealis until it disintegrated into flecks of dust. Aryx, grinning wildly by my side, clasped his hands together in awe. The shadows at my fingertips begged to be unleashed, filling my head with violent whispers. With clenched fists and gritted teeth, I dragged them back into their cage and locked them away.

The man bowed to me, his beard pooling on the dirty stone floor.

"King Zecharius, my goddess," he whispered to me.

The council, wide eyed and silent, followed his lead and lowered their heads in my direction. A flurry of guards poured into the chamber, their swords pointing at me in ambush.

"Stop!" Zecharius ordered, raising his hands up to halt the swarm. In a symphony of clanking armor, they stopped in their tracks and awaited their King's orders. He stalked forward, the grey fibers of his beard collecting dust in his path.

"Goddess, what message do you have for our patron God?" he asked.

"We need his support. As we speak, Tethys is prepping her army for an invasion of the mortal realms. We mean to stop her before she has the chance, but we can't do it alone," Aryx said, sheathing his sword. Nodding, the mortal king laced his fingers behind his back.

He leaned beside the white-haired Lord seated to the

right of his vacant head chair. The Lord nodded promptly at the king's unheard command and hurried into the shadows of the dark passageway across from us. Steps echoed down the cavern, stopping short as the creak of an unseen door opened, then slammed shut.

Arcturas growled deep in her chest, her eyes low and back arched. Something didn't feel right. Tingles curled my toes and rushed up my legs, flexing the muscles of my thighs. My stomach tightened as the King turned back around to face us.

"Unfortunately for you, Goddess, the Elders have already notified me of your treasonous plans. You think your treachery can fool Canissa and its king?" He snapped his fingers, and the guards marched a step forward, tightening their circle around us.

"No, the Elders are under Tethys's manipulation! They cannot be trusted," I cried, reaching for the hilt of my dagger.

Aryx slid toward me, his fists knuckle-white at his sides.

"Why should I believe the Queen Slayer over my most trusted emissary?" Zecharius snapped his fingers again.

The synchronized stomp of 12 leather boots echoed through the great hall as the guards closed in on us.

"You are a fool if you don't listen to us," Aryx hissed.

The king snapped his fingers again. "Seize them."

The guards lunged forward, plunging their blades at us.

A blur of black zipped across the room. Snapping armor and the crunch of bones filled the silent hall as blood sprayed across its grey stone walls. A guard leapt for me, sword raised above his head. I dodged the blow just as the iron blade swung across my cheek. Sparks flicked from its contact with the stone floor.

"Elpis. Behind you," Aryx called.

Swirling around, I slit the throat of the guard towering over me, his ruby blood spurting across my brow. A tug on my braid jerked my head back.

The guard pulled me into a headlock, forcing the dagger from my hand. Tingles ignited across my arms as my shadows wrapped themselves between his shoulders, squeezing tightly until arteries collapsed and blood vessels popped from his neck.

Aryx pulled his bow from his shoulder, jabbing the grip into the face of an unsuspecting guard. The lords and ladies of the court shrieked and cowered in a corner, watching the fight play out with horrified expressions.

Leaping into action with newfound strength, the King whipped his staff through the air. Its sharp point cracked against my kneecap, forcing me to my knees. Agony erupted through my bones as I shielded my face from the King's impending attack. An arrow whizzed by my ear, slicing my skin in its path. The point pierced the king's shoulder, just above his heart.

"You touch her again. Next time, my arrow won't miss," Aryx growled. Grit laced with the threat on his tongue.

The guards retreated, rushing to the aid of their wounded king. I struggled to my feet, careful to shift my weight off the crippled joint. Long locks of hair fell across my face as I tipped my chin up to face the court.

What was once a kernel of power within me now roared with the flames of a thousand pyres. The tingles rushed to my broken kneecap. The muscle fibers stitched themselves back together beneath the skin. Serpents of shadows wriggled through my veins, slithering through my chest. Dust fell from the ceiling as the ground vibrated around us, sending pebbles bouncing across the stone tiles. My heart pounded like a battering ram. Invisible strands of energy pulled up on my feet as I prowled toward the King. His sunken eyes were now wide in his skull. His throat bobbed. He was going to regret this. Red flooded my vision as I imagined my hands gripped around his throat, his life spurting out of him with each gurgling choke.

"Touch me again, and an arrow is the least of your concern."

The voice was not my own. While mine was quiet and cold, this voice was malicious and hot. My wolf strutted to my side with a smoldering ferocity. The King retreated, his limp steps slow and terrified.

I could feel his heart fluttering like a hummingbird enclosed in his brittle bone. I wanted to rip the organ from his ribs and claw it to shreds. My nostrils flared at the thought of the blood that would pour from his wounds.

"Goddess, please, please spare me. Think of my people," he pleaded, tripping over the train of his robes and falling to his knees.

I took another step. The taste of his death licked across my lips.

He would die beneath my blade.

I raised my dagger, its razor edge webbed with violet magic.

"Goddess, I beg of you. Canissa needs their King," he cried, crawling away from me.

The dagger was ice in my fist. It whispered in my ear, urging me to plunge it into the king's chest. I pounced at the whimpering, fragile man. Before its gleaming point met flesh, however, a calloused hand caught my wrist.

"Elpis. Stop," Aryx whispered.

The warmth of his body radiated to mine.

"It's okay. Put the knife down." His thumb stroked the soft underside of my wrist. "Come back to me."

The tingling receded, pulling those violent thoughts with them.

"That's it, come back." He stepped into me and stroked my cheek.

The crimson tunneling in my vision faded, and the puppet strings of magic let go of their hold. I felt the fullness of his lips meet mine. He breathed me in, interlocking his fingers with my jaw. My grip around the hilt relaxed. The dagger clattered to the floor.

Everyone and everything vanished. Only the two of us occupied this second in time. He pulled away, tucking a loose strand of hair behind my ear. His eyes smoldered, warming my cheeks. I swallowed the dryness in my throat.

"Good girl." His voice was full of desire.

Before I could wrap myself in his lingering kiss, everything rushed back. What was I doing? I couldn't kill Zecharius. He was just doing his duty. He was right; the people needed him. I sucked in a breath, looking down at the old man cowering before me.

"Oh, thank you Goddess. Thank you," the King cried, a bead of snot dripping from his long nose.

"I-I'm sorry," I stammered, relaxing into Aryx's outstretched arms.

Someone clapped behind us.

"Well, well, well, making a scene like that. You sure are your mother's daughter," a male voice thundered through the hall.

Chapter 28

We turned to see the God of Autumn himself with arms crossed, leaning against the frame of the dark corridor's entrance. I dropped to my knees, bowing deeply before him. Like Polaris, he hovered above the floor as he started towards us, a long, red robe trailing behind him.

The god was glorious in every sense of the word. Tattoos clawed across the olive skin of his bare chest, wrapping over his shoulders and down his spine. He had long brown hair neatly pulled into a braid that hung to his hips and a full beard that enveloped his hardened chin. A crown of gold-dipped antlers wrapped around his broad forehead with a regal weight that only a god could withstand.

"King Procyon, please, listen to us." Aryx rose from his bow.

"You dare command me, Spring Prince?" Procyon's husky voice boomed over us with a transcendent force that could crumble even the strongest of citadels.

He knelt before me, running his thumb across my lower lip.

"Stand tall, my Queen, embrace the power you've inherited with grace."

Aryx watched as Procyon guided me to the table, his mouth now a thin line across his face.

"Sit. We will speak like civilized folk." Procyon pulled out a chair with one long arm and motioned for me to sit.

Collecting myself, I lowered to the chair and clasped my trembling hands tightly. The god sat across from me, motioning for Aryx and Zecharius to join us.

"Lords and Ladies of the court, you are dismissed for the day. Tell no one of what happened here." The council flooded through the exit, figures fading into shadow as their steps receded.

"Now, what is it you wish to discuss? What's so urgent it cost six of my best guards their lives?" he asked.

Procyon raised his hand to Aryx as he opened his mouth to speak. His palms were larger than my face. With one quick grip, he could crush my skull to dust. Procyon looked at me, the deep orange of his eyes sparkling with curiosity and a faint trace of amusement as the half-god beside him grew red in the face.

"It's Tethys. She's gathering an army to unleash on to the mortal realms. We plan to stop it by bringing the attack to her, but we need your help," I explained, stammering through the words.

Aryx nodded silently, encouraging me to continue.

"We think she's manipulated the Elders. She's fortified their island and is using it as base camp. We plan to lead an attack there and hopefully take her down on her own home front," I said.

Procyon fiddled with a large golden signet ring on his little finger. An intricate image of a stag, his emblem, was carved into the solid gold metal.

"I figured she'd get her talons into those fools eventually," he said, flexing the muscle of his square jaw. "We will provide aid on the terms that when you defeat her, Ursae resumes their trade agreements with my people. The city isn't what it used to be. We need those supply routes to thrive."

"I'll try my best, but I'm in no position over the city. The entire royal guard is looking for me on charges of murder and treason." I lowered my eyes, nervously wiping my sweaty palms across my trousers.

Procyon raised a brow.

"They don't know who you are?" he asked, leaning back in his chair. The wooden pegs beneath him groaned under his dense weight, as if they'd succumb to it any second.

"Until a few days ago, I didn't know either," I said, my cheeks hot under his flaming, tangerine eyes.

"I see." He stroked his beard, twisting the golden beads laced through its coarse, brown hair.

"Well, I must alter my conditions then. I will give you command of my army if, when this is over, you reclaim your throne and re-establish our trade agreements your-self."

I gawked at him. I didn't want to be queen or the crushing pressure of the monarchy. I'd seen firsthand how poisonous power truly was.

"Procyon, I-I can't be queen."

"Yes, you can, and if you want my aid, you will." He rose to his feet. "When you've agreed to my terms, send a westward arrow and my army will be yours to command."

I choked on the words now stuck in my throat.

The god turned to take his leave, patting Zecharius on the shoulder.

"Zecharius, old man, if you've learned anything today, I hope it's this: don't get in the way of an angry woman; she won't hesitate to destroy you."

He chuckled as Zecharius's cheeks swelled with humiliation.

"Oh and um, maybe it's time to find a new Elder, eh? One that isn't a conniving snake."

In the threshold hallway, Procyon glanced back at us and blew me a kiss. Before I could plead for him to reconsider, he evaporated into the air, leaving only a trail of mist in his place.

"Well, that was... interesting," Aryx said, relaxing in his seat. "My King, we're sorry for the violence and pain we caused here today. Like Procyon said, an angry woman is the most dangerous force in nature."

"Oh shut it, boy," the king snapped, digging his nails into the grain of the mahogany tabletop.

I snorted, scratching Arcturas's chest as she wagged her tail beside me.

"You will have our support, Queen Elpis. We'll await your signal." The King nodded to me and hobbled across the chamber. "Now if you'll excuse me, I have a few petrified lords I must tend to and new widows I have to notify."

He motioned for us to leave.

We traversed the narrow passageway and exited the temple, leaving the King blue-faced.

"That was easy," I said, laughing away the tightness in my chest.

"You never fail to leave me both utterly amazed and utterly terrified." Aryx grinned, wiping the grime from his leather breastplate.

"Now, I guess we trek to Aquilae. I don't think that meeting will be as, um, easy as this one." Aryx hooked his bow into Kratos's saddle and climbed on to the horse.

"My Queen." He extended his hand to me with a dramatic bow.

"You know, maybe we should ask Procyon to come

back. I like how quiet you get when your masculinity feels threatened." I slapped his hand away and climbed into the saddle.

Chapter 29

The road to Aquilae was long. As we continued south, the air turned gritty with sea salt and ocean waves. Gulls squawked in the afternoon light, following the sun to its zenith.

"What happened with Zecharius this morning?" Aryx asked, glancing over his shoulder to face me. His shoulder blades stretched beneath the back of his sweat glazed, white tunic.

"I'm not sure." My mouth went dry, and I sucked in a shallow breath. "All I could see were my hands around his throat. I wanted to kill him. If you hadn't of intervened, I would've done it, too."

Aryx was quiet. The only sound between us was the clop of Kratos's hooves against the stone laid path. Rolling hills of the Western Realm morphed into steep, jagged cliffs. Dry sprits of grass and coastline flora scattered across the rocky landscape.

"Are you afraid?" he asked. Kratos jerked us forward as he leapt over a stone protruding from the sun-cracked trail.

"Of myself? Yes." I wrapped my arms around him as Kratos trotted forward. The curves of his body beneath my touch sent electric jolts through me. I was desperate for a distraction from the dread bubbling up in my throat.

"Well, I'm not," he said, flicking Kratos' reins.

He should be.

Everyone should be.

That demon I kept locked away was an unstoppable force. If I freed it again, would I be able to keep hold of its leash?

"As half-gods, our power is a weight we'll live with forever. Tipping us closer and closer to the edge. When I was a boy, I nearly lost myself to it." His throat bobbed. "Eventually you learn to settle yourself and control it."

"And what if I can't?" I steadied my gaze on the horizon. The blue coastline of the Southern Sea blurred with the hillside like rough brush strokes on canvas.

"You must. Otherwise, the world will burn. It's the price we pay for our immortal blood. Our mortal minds feel too deeply to keep it locked away," he said, placing a free hand over the back of mine.

I gripped the cotton of his tunic. My blood burned hot. The scratch of power coursing through my veins was an uncomfortable reminder of the lives I'd already taken.

"I was still a boy when my mother killed all of her court. Barely trained and barely old enough to even understand the permanence of death. Whispers of magic kept telling me to kill her. To take revenge for the lives she'd stolen. When I stood above her one night while she slept, I nearly did it."

"And why didn't you? If our power is so all-consuming, how did you stop?" I asked.

"My father once said that love is the strongest fuel for violence. I still loved her. Every day, I regret not plunging that knife into her throat." I could feel the steady throb of his heart against my cheek as I leaned my head on him.

"You were a child with too heavy a weight to bear. It's not your fault," I said. He laced his fingers through mine, pulling our intertwined hands over his chest.

"So were you. I guess that makes us the same."

My heart, matching the rhythm of his, slowed as I let out the air I'd been holding in my lungs.

"I guess so."

I realized suddenly that this warrior, this half-god, this man who I'd grown to fear, then hate, then befriend, was just as lonely, just as broken as I was. He'd called himself a monster once.

I knew then that he truly believed it. It hadn't been a ploy or manipulation. We fought the same battles, the same heartache, the same guilt.

He had betrayed me, and that pain might never heal completely, but his candid words were a stitch in the wound.

The rest of the ride was quiet, save for the click of hooves against stone.

\#

The Southern Realm was known for its glorious gilded gate. Colossal pearl statues of their patron god gleamed in the sunlight. Kratos trotted through the city walls, carved from looming cliffs standing hundreds of feet high. Electricity pulsed within the salted air while the sharp, oceanic breeze pricked at my nose.

"Something's wrong," Aryx whispered, slowing Kratos to a halt. His eyes narrowed, scanning the street before us.

Shadows of massive palms stretched across the vacant building exteriors. Not a murmur of life echoed around us.

"Where is everyone?" I asked, leaping from the saddle.

My boots scrunched against the sandy ground as I, too, surveyed the stone-carved homes. The midday sun reflected off of bleached white dwellings carved into the hillside. The nearly identical, rambling structures took up every bit of flat surface in the cliff side terrain.

"I don't know, but I don't like the looks of this." Aryx continued down the street and disappeared from view.

Arcturas pawed at the ground, her ears sharp and alert. I followed behind, my hand hovering above the sheathed dagger strapped to my thigh. With every rolling wave in the distant ocean, the quiet grew more and more sinister.

Aryx stiffened as he knelt over something ahead.

As I came in close, his reflection peered back at me in the crimson puddle oozing from the mass. I stopped in my tracks with boiling blood as Aryx rolled the corpse over. It was a child, his deep brown skin caked in sand, a carved wooden doll clenched tightly in his stiff hand. I threw my hand over my mouth, stifling the scream now raging through me.

"Something is very wrong. We need to find Altair. Now," Aryx said, closing the child's lids over his terrified, grey eyes.

I dropped to my knees, brushing my finger across his cold, swollen cheek. Aryx rose and continued down the street. After tearing a scrap of my cloak and draping it over the boy's face, I followed him, my knees weak. I'd return for the boy's body and ensure a proper burial.

The scene down the hillside was even more jarring. The bodies that littered the ground threw me to my knees. Men, women, and children, all with frozen eyes and open mouths as if the wake of death snuffed out their screams.

Careful to avoid an outstretched limb or bloody face, we snaked our way through. This massacre hit me like an unrelenting shockwave. My body trembled with a fury I'd never imagined was possible. I kept my eyes level with the horizon, afraid of losing control if my gaze wandered too far towards my boots.

With the stench of death ripe on my nose, we finally reached Altair's temple. On the city shoreline, the waves lapped at the temple's stone steps. Blood muddied the water. The once pristine white marble was now stained a shade of red with the rising tide. The temple's dome-like ceiling flashed in the remaining afternoon daylight.

"Shouldn't we try to find survivors? What if they need help?" I paused, my feet frozen at the bottom ledge.

"Elpis..." Aryx turned to me, a thick, dark fog hung low over his glossy eyes. "There aren't any survivors. I can't feel any life here, only death. Can you?"

I swallowed hard. The stench of hot flesh was too much to handle. The sight of blood dripping down the walls was overwhelming. My head spun. Aryx was right. The only thing I felt here was a void. A thick, chilling vacancy.

"We need to find Altair," he said, holding his hand out for me to grasp. I placed my trembling fingers in his and let him guide us through the temple's entrance.

A falcon squawked in the distance. Its somber cry sent shivers down my spine.

The temple's interior was just as brilliant as its exterior. Rows of glyphs covered the walls from ceiling to floor in ancient murals. The sound of our steps bounced off the walls, causing the flaming gold light fixtures to ripple and waver. The ear-splitting silence of the heart of the temple pushed thoughts of the slaughtered city forward in my mind. All I could see were their lifeless bodies. All I could hear was the squelching of congealed blood beneath the leather sole of my boot.

War was violent, bloody, ruthless. Brutal battles taking the lives of thousands spattered our history like blood stains. I'd seen death first hand, but this... nothing could've prepared me for this.

The child clenching his doll for comfort. His last scream for his mother permanently set across his face. The innocence lost, the lives taken, they were holes punctured in my chest. Heartache pulled my feet backward. Back towards the life spilled on pristine tropic streets.

"I know how you're feeling. Right now, we have to

focus on the plan. We need to be strong. You're at risk of losing control. You're reeling. Pull it back in," Aryx whispered, stopping before a grand, golden archway.

The fists clenched at his sides suggested he wasn't talking about me.

I nodded, fighting the tears that now pooled in my eyes. Aryx pulled me in, wrapping his hand around my head. Planting his lips softly on my brow, he breathed me in. Inhaling my pain, my sorrow.

"This is why we need to stop her. This is what she does. She takes and takes and takes until there's nothing left."

"I'll try." My voice trembled as it whispered from my lips.

"That's all we can do," he said.

Sucking in a hesitant breath, I reached for his palm and led us through the archway.

Pools of turquoise water trickled into a round council chamber. Splitting at the entrance, it flowed around the room, entangled in ornate patterns of cerulean across the aureate floor. In any other circumstance, the great hall would take my breath away, but now it only kindled the inferno blazing through my chest. A round gilded table rested on the center platform of the hall. All of its matching chairs were vacant except one.

Chapter 30

A god, draped in gossamer blue robes, sat with his head in his hands. The curl of his spine was sharp across the rich umber shade of his flawless skin. Lapis lazuli beads laced through the ends of his long black braids. They scraped across the table as he turned to face us. His eyes were piercing, royal blue gems protruding from a clean oval face. Adjusting the gleaming crown atop his head, he rose to meet us.

"I suppose you're here to kill me along with my city," he growled, the veins in his exposed biceps pulsing with each step.

Panic-stricken, I bowed, throwing my hands above my head.

"No, King Altair we-" A snap of his fingers cut off my words as my throat tightened, choking the remaining air from my lungs. The immortal faced me, his toes curled with fury.

"Do not speak, Queen Slayer. I know who you are." He

snapped his hands again. The grip around my neck relaxed.

Gasping for breath, I sputtered and coughed.

"And you." Altair's eyes blazed as he locked eyes with Aryx. "Did the Great War teach you nothing?"

The salty air thickened with a current so fierce the minuscule hairs on my arms pricked straight up. Arcturas cowered beside me.

"Altair, please, I beg you to listen. We've come to warn you," Aryx pleaded, his hands outstretched before him.

"Well, your warning is too late. Tethys's army razed my city this morning. Not a single soul spared." Altair returned to his seat. "Without my people, there is nothing. I am nothing. Do what you came here to do, half-mortal. Be your mother's puppet. Just as you're destined to be." His voice cracked, and the blue of his eyes faded. He exposed the soft flesh of his neck.

"King Altair, please. We came to ask for your help," I said, treading lightly to the round table.

"I have no aid to give you," he whispered. His voice was a defeated, broken man. Not an all-powerful god.

I pulled out the chair across from him and took a seat.

"We're leading an attack on Elder's Island. That's where she's established her army. If we penetrate the outer walls, we take Tethys out before she causes any more mortal death," I said, stretching my palms across the gold surface between us.

The table top was cool to the touch, but the heat radiating from his fingertips singed my skin.

"Like I said, there is no aid. They were all slaughtered in the raid this morning," he said.

"I'm so sorry," I whispered, picturing the lifeless boy, limp and cold, in the sand.

"How can you sit here and wallow in self-pity as the city burns around you?" Aryx interjected, taking the seat to my right, "Tethys is still out there. Don't you want vengeance for the lives lost today?"

Altair turned slowly to look at him.

"You stupid child. Vengeance only brings death. There is no satisfaction, no redemption. Nothing but cruel, silent death. When you've lived as long as I have, think about these words. Think about my people," he hissed, adjusting the feathered golden band across his bicep.

"When I've lived as long as you, I won't care about life or death. I won't have a city to avenge. Help us take down Tethys before she kills thousands more." Aryx straightened in his seat, his voice rough.

"There is nothing I can do. My armies were destroyed. My resources are depleted." Altair slammed his fists across the table, its legs jumping on impact.

"You control the seas and the creatures that live in them. Help us cross the Southern Sea. Fight with us. They deserve at least that much. The children out there who will never grow up, never have husbands or wives or children of their own. Fight for them. Fuck, if all of this is for nothing and we wind up dead, at least somewhere they'll know. We tried. For them," I cried, rising abruptly to my feet. Altair lowered his head.

"Or you can sit here and lose yourself in grief. Wallow in your self-pity. Either way, we're going to Elders' Island. Our success lies in your hands. Procyon has already agreed to send his armies. We have enough men. We need your guidance and your ships if we're going to survive the passage," I pleaded.

"And what of Polaris? Has she also agreed to support this suicide mission?" His eyes scanned me as I paced the chamber.

"I'm sure if needed, my mother will provide as much aid as she can," I said, glancing over my shoulder at the seated men. "But we don't need it. Her power courses

234

through my veins."

"You are Darkness's Heir?" he asked, a brow raised.

"Yes. It's my destiny to destroy the Spring Queen, but I can't do it alone."

"Elpis is more powerful than you could ever imagine. She's fully capable of bringing my mother down, but we need to get her close enough," Aryx said, crossing his arms.

Altair was silent, his furrowed brow racing with thoughts as he stroked his chin.

"You said you have Procyon's army." Finally, Altair spoke.

"What was he promised in return?"

"What?" Aryx asked, shifting in his chair.

"That greedy fool does nothing for free. What did you offer him?"

"Trade routes," I snapped. "We assured him that Ursae re-invokes the trade agreements the late king set."

"How can an escaped prisoner make any political change? Ursae guards have been hounding my citizens for weeks searching for you. There's something else to his bargain you're not telling me. I can see it behind your eyes," Altair said.

I swallowed the rising bile in my throat. Aryx shook his head toward me, eyes dark in shadow.

"Well? What is it, Daughter of Polaris?"

"I agreed to overtake the mortal throne."

A wide smirk curled over Altair's full lips.

"I see...I knew Procyon had another motive. He doesn't just lend out his armies to any half-goddess. He's bargained for a puppet."

"I will be no puppet," I spat. The tingles began their familiar trail up my legs. Breathing deeply, I closed my eyes and focused on locking my emotions down.

"I believe you truly think you won't be, but you're dealing with gods, after all. Manipulation is our specialty."

He chuckled coldly and returned to his seat.

The room fell silent aside from the flow of a peaceful turquoise sea. Sighing, I slumped back to my seat, tracing the veins of my hands. Altair scanned my face, watching the inner battle between my demons splayed out in the wrinkles of my brow.

This broken God had just lost everything. His city, his people, his home. In an instant, there was nothing left. He was right. Vengeance was never the answer. Violence against those that have wronged you is a road not worth taking. Surface satisfaction with deeply rooted darkness. Vengeance consumes you. It blazes around you, eating away all the goodness and brightness of your world. I knew that.

He tangled my freedom in the palm of his hand. Without his ships, this was hopeless.

"We came here today, ready to fight." I sucked in a breath as the blue of his eyes sizzled with power.

"I won't beg or plead. You're set in your ways and your beliefs on revenge. I understand that. All of my life I've fought through hatred, cruelty, abuse. This war isn't about vengeance. This war is about freedom. I've been through hell to sit here before you. I've made sacrifices, pushed away those that I care for. I've nearly lost my life. I've taken lives."

Aryx reached for my hand, stroking his thumb against my palm.

"Those people outside, the ones whose blood now seeps into the cracks of this city, they deserve better than me. Better than Aryx. Maybe they even deserve better than you. But we're all they have. When the city heals, and eventually it will, what side of history do you want to be on? Lend us your ships. Stay on the winning side of this war."

Altair raised a brow. Through pursed lips, he watched

as I rose from my seat.

"Elpis, it's hopeless. We'll find another way." Aryx shook his head, sliding the legs of his chair across the rough temple floor.

I sighed, starting for the golden archway.

"I will get you across the Raging Seas, but I have conditions."

"Of course you do." Turning, my heart stopped.

"When you plunge your dagger into Tethys's heart, you think of my people. Think of every life that was taken today. Every single one. Then twist your blade until all essence of life fades from her entirely." Altair's voice deepened with black tarry, hatred. A kernel of sadness glinted in his brilliant eyes.

"I promise I will," I said, reaching my hand out to meet his. His palm brushed delicately across mine as he bowed slightly.

"Good, now, one other thing. You'll need my falcon. Only he can guide you safely through the rough seas."

"Okay fine. Where is he?" Aryx asked.

"After Tethys's soldiers receded to the sea, he escaped up the mountainside. You'll have to catch him, which is no simple task. The bird's as slippery as an eel," Altair said. He nodded once more to me and, with the snap of his fingers, vanished, leaving a salty mist in his wake.

"What's with immortals and their abrupt exits?" I cried, throwing my hands on my hips.

Chapter 31

"He can't be serious?" Aryx snapped, his breath heavy as we hiked the narrow trail up the jutting mountain cliff side.

My calves cramped in protest as I wiped the sweat rolling down my brow. Moisture pooled beneath my armpits, and if it weren't for the coastal breeze whipping through my cotton tunic, I'm sure I'd be able to smell my stench.

"He said it wouldn't be a simple task," I replied, scaling the jagged rock behind him.

"No, he said catching the bird wouldn't be easy. He said nothing about finding it." Aryx's palm swiped at the hold above him.

The rock chipped and broke from the hillside. I swung sideways, closely avoiding the fist-size stone as it tumbled down the trail and disappeared into mist. We'd been climbing for what felt like hours with nothing but black night sky and grey rock to keep us company. The trail was far too steep for Kratos, so we left him and Arcturas to graze in the dry, grassy valley below.

"Next time I see that god, I swear..." Aryx trailed, his voice straining with each step.

"At least I get to enjoy the view from down here," I said, arching my brow as Aryx chuckled and flexed his glutes.

"Wanna trade places?" he asked.

With my free hand, I slapped his foot. We were closing in on the summit; only a bit more climbing and we'd reach its sharp peak.

"What's the plan when we find the bird? I doubt it'll let us just grab it with our bare hands," I asked.

Since leaving the temple, all I could think of was scaling the mountainside, and it now occurred to me we were exceedingly under prepared.

"I haven't gotten that far, Elpis. Right now, I'm focused on not falling to my death." Aryx threw himself up onto the rock, clinging to the next hold for dear life. "Is it a horrible time to mention that I'm terrified of heights?"

I snorted, following his path until I gripped the rock beside him.

"The brave and powerful war general who led legendary armies and conducted epic sieges, afraid of heights?"

"Yes. And it isn't funny. It's taking all my willpower not to piss myself right now." He scowled, reaching for another loose rock that rolled down the cliff to meet its pair.

"We're almost there. Just keep going." I pushed him forward.

When we finally reached the summit, the skin of my palms was raw and every muscle ached with exhaustion. Panting, I stood next to Aryx, who looked just as disheveled as I. The peak of the mountain reached high above the cloud cover, and a sea of mist rolled around us. The stars above spattered the night sky with millions of twinkling lights illuminating the rocky landscape in shades of silver.

"Funny how, no matter the elevation, the stars feel just

as far away." Aryx looked up at the painting of white light scattered from horizon to horizon.

"They're never far from me. I feel them buzzing around inside me like little fireflies, fluttering in my stomach," I said, leaning against a boulder. "I guess it's my mother. When it's a clear night, I can practically taste her magic on my tongue. It's like the warmest spiced wine."

I lowered my back to the smooth surface, feeling its coolness against my sweat-drenched tunic.

"She's the only one who can quiet all these horrible, broken thoughts screaming inside my head. The only one besides you."

Aryx sat beside me, his shoulder touching mine.

"When I first met you, Elpis, I didn't know just how amazing you are." He brushed his hand across my cheek. Something new flickered across his face.

It was his usual warmth, but it sparkled with an intensity I'd never experienced before tonight. I traced the black ink across his sharp cheekbone, down his jaw, his neck, to the bone of his collar peeking out from the layer of cotton fabric.

"What does this mean?" I asked, stroking the thick, elaborate patterns stretched across his chest.

"It's the mark of Tethys's army. All of her officers have it. It signifies my allegiance to the city and to my queen. It's the brand of war." He wrapped his hand over mine and placed it against his chest.

"Every line reminds me of the people I've killed for her, the innocent lives I've taken."

"When I learned who you were, I hated you. The lies, the manipulation, all of it disgusted me," I started.

"I know. I'm sorry." He let go of my hand and stared up at the sky. Regret glistened in the corner of his eye.

"But now, I know why you did it. I guess you're not as terrible as I thought." I cracked a smile, chuckling breathlessly at the man lying next to me.

"You don't know what that means to me, Elpis." His voice was low as he leaned into me.

I closed my eyes, enjoying the electricity jolting through me as he brushed my lips with his.

"We should probably go find that bird," I said through shallow breaths. He combed his fingers through the loose strands of hair framing my jawline. The slight touch of his skin against mine ignited the blood racing through my veins.

"Fuck the bird," he said, his voice ragged.

Wrapping his arms around me, we melted into each other. Trembling hands explored one another as he lifted me on to his hips. The growing ache I felt pressed against him consumed me entirely as I untied the strands of his tunic. I needed his skin against mine, his heat against mine. The scratch of callouses set fire to my flesh as he ran his hands down my thighs. I didn't care that the night air exposed us. I was numb to the chilled breeze licking my goose-fleshed skin.

All I could taste, all I could smell, all I could feel was him. The familiar prick of rosemary and citrus consumed me as everything burned around us. I ripped the leather lacing off his trousers as he popped the buttons from my tunic. The world hummed with voltaic tremors.

"Do you feel it too?" he asked, sliding the coarse fabric over my shoulder blades. "The energy we create together?"

"Yes," I whispered, my voice heavy in my throat.

"Gods, the way it feels..." he said, circling the peak of my breast with his thumb. My back arched at the coolness of his touch.

"It feels ancient. Nearly savage."

His palm followed the line of my abdomen, leaving fragments of power in its path. My breath was uneven as the surrounding gravel bounced off the earth.

"It feels like fate." His words brushed against my ear,

raising the hairs on the nape of my neck.

His fingers found my center and the ache I felt intensified, like an avalanche rolling down its mountainside, gaining momentum until it became a destructive, unstoppable force.

Just on the precipice, he slid into me, sending shockwaves of joy through my body until my toes curled against the sole of my boot. Tingles scratched at my chest. Lost in the feel of him, I couldn't hold them back. They pumped through my veins, extending to my fingertips with a fury of power.

When I threw my head back, crying out, they unleashed from me, sending a circle of green flames across the rocky mountainside. The mountain groaned beneath us as Aryx reached his edge and spiraled along with me. Panting, I opened my eyes. Tendrils of smoke floated to the sky, rising from the singed earth around us.

"Elpis...your eyes," Aryx said, wiping the sweat from his brow.

"What?"

"They're... they're glowing." Shades of amethyst reflected off his cheekbones, illuminating the sharp curve of his face.

I leapt to my feet, rubbing my eyes until the demon within me receded back into her cage.

"I'm sorry..." I said, pulling my tunic back over my head and buttoning my trousers.

"Hey," he said, grabbing my wrist. "It's okay. I'm not afraid of you."

I pulled my arm away, backing away from him.

"Look around us. Look at the destruction I created. I could've hurt you."

The black singe extended until it faded into the dark horizon. His throat bobbed as he took in our surroundings. Scorched, brittle shrubs rustled in the wind.

"Elpis, look at me." He jumped to his feet, clenching

my jaw in his hands. "You don't scare me."

"Well, I should," I snapped, jerking away from his hold.

Before he could protest, a deep squawk echoed across the cliff side.

"The bird," I cried, taking off toward the sound. Aryx shook his head and sprinted after me, barely keeping up with strained legs. We raced up the peak until the ground beneath us steepened into a smooth, jagged point. At the highest ledge, resting in a nest of dead twigs and grass, sat the falcon.

Chapter 32

The bird cocked its cerulean head and stretched its wings, about to take flight. Its wingspan, like drips of the blue ocean beneath us, stretched as I continued to climb for its nest. Long, slender talons gripped the cliff's edge.

"Easy.... It's alright, I'm not here to hurt you. I just need your help," I said, my voice strained from the climb.

The falcon snapped its black beak, staring at me with luminous yellow eyes.

"Elpis, are you crazy?" Aryx called from the flat below.

Wind whipped across my forehead, throwing strands of hair into my face. My fingers begged for relief as I reached the bird's nest.

"It's okay..." I said, sliding my hand slowly toward its talon.

It flapped its wings again, snapping at my nose nearly inches from its large, ruffled feathers.

"Elpis. Come down, we'll find another way!" Aryx cried, pacing below me with panicked eyes.

"Hush, that's it, it's okay," I said, wrapping my fingers

around its foot.

The bird screeched as I reached for the other leg. He snapped, pecking against my arm, pricking the skin until it bled. I smoothed the feathers across its back, tucking its wings back in. The falcon cried once more, pleading for me to let go.

"Please, we need your help. I know you're probably terrified, I am too. It's okay," I whispered, pulling the falcon into my chest.

Mortal girl. No, not quite mortal. Your scent is powerful. Intriguing.

It looked at me, its wings straining against my hold.

"Please falcon, we need you," I whispered, frozen at the sight of the ground below.

I am Rah. What is it you seek by taking me from my home?

"Rah? That's your name?" I asked, slowly descending the smooth rock.

Why have you come?

"We need safe passage across the Raging Seas," I said, my foot slipping from the loose hold below.

My boot slid down the cliff side, and my stomach leapt into my throat. Feeling for anything to latch on to, I stretched one arm above me. The other still wrapped around the falcon's body. Hooking my fingers into a crack in the rock, I gripped for dear life, my legs dangling frantically above the dark, solid ground.

If you don't release me, you'll fall to your death.

The bird squawked, pushing his wings against my sternum.

"I can't do that. We need you." The skin on my fingertips ripped away as Aryx's cries from below trailed the salty wind around me.

You would dare risk meeting your end for my guidance? What lies beyond the seas that's worth your life?

"My freedom," I sobbed. Blood from my flayed fingertips streaked down my arm. Muscles in each joint of my hand quivered on the brink of failure.

The bird peered into my eyes. Its blue feathers rippled in the night air.

Hmm, so you will steal my freedom to gain your own?

He cocked his head.

"Please. Consider it a temporary theft," I begged, my lungs frantic for air.

Aryx howled below, pleading for me to let go of the bird.

Release me.

"I promise you'll be free again," I groaned. "You'll be in a better world, one full of life rather than death. Altair guided us here. He needs you too."

That old fool? Has he sent you to trick me back into that cage he holds me in?

"Help us and you'll never see the inside of a cage again," I begged, feeling the final two fingers of my grip sliding.

I couldn't hold on much longer. This was it. Gritting my teeth, I dug my nails into the fractured rock. I'd come this far. I wouldn't give up now.

"Help us, and I promise I'll return the favor," I cried.

Rah cocked his head toward the stars. Clicking his beak, his yellow eyes returned to my face.

You are of the night, half-god. Something burns within you I've never felt before. Intriguing.

"Rah, I'd love to discuss this more with you, but in any second I'm going to fall to my death and this journey will be for nothing."

Fine. I will grant you the safe passage you seek. But our deal is sealed. I help you gain your freedom, you will return mine.

"Yes, I promise I will. I promise," I said, the sting of

sweat blurring my vision.

Now release me before you fall to your untimely death.

"How can I be sure you won't just fly away?"

You have my oath.

A golden tear rolled down the falcon's beak and dripped onto my cheek. The warmth of the splattered drop rejuvenated my now-numb hand and the pain of my broken fingers faded away. I took a breath, trusting Rah's booming voice inside my head.

My grip around the bird's wings relaxed, and I scratched my free hand into the crack. Rah stretched his wings and ascended into the air with a rush of gold and azure feathers.

"Elpis, come down. Please!" Aryx roared from below.

With shallow breaths, I slowly descended the wall, wincing with each touch of my mangled hand.

Rah soared around the peak, a beacon of shining blue across the vast darkness of the sky. When finally my feet hit the rough mountain floor, I kneeled on the ground. Heaving with rasping lungs, my bloodied arms went limp with the onset of soreness.

"Are you insane?" Aryx shouted, throwing himself before me.

He ripped the hem of his tunic and loosely wrapped the material around my raw fingers.

"Yes," I panted, eyes still wild with adrenaline pounding through my veins.

"You could've killed yourself! Do nothing like that again, please. I can't finish this without you." He cupped my head in his hands, the golden flecks of his eyes smoldering.

Rah landed, his talons digging into the solid sediment, and fluttered his wings.

Bravery easily becomes foolishness, child. Do not forget that.

"Thank you," I whispered, my eyes heavy as the thrill

of the climb faded from my body.

Aryx glanced between us, confusion wrinkled across his pursed lips.

"So, you'll help us?" he asked.

Yes, Spring Prince, I made a promise to your companion while she so stupidly clung to me above her death.

Specks of black blurred my vision as I relaxed into the warmth of Aryx's arms. He combed the hair back from my sweaty brow as exhaustion took over and I faded into quiet darkness.

Chapter 33

I jerked upright, the remnants of sleep still fogging my mind.

"It's alright, you're safe." Aryx's quiet voice was soothing. A fresh citrus smell wrapped around me as he stepped through bright beams of morning light, pouring through a wall of glass to my left. Sweat drenched the gauzy sheets resting over me. I stroked the clean bandages now wrapped around my arm. My throat was dry and chafed, making it hard to swallow the lump in my throat.

"Where are we?" I asked, peering down at the satin shift draping low over my pale skin.

"We're in Altair's palace, above the city. You've been sleeping for three days now. Try not to move. I don't think your hands are fully recovered yet." He sat on the bed next to me.

"Three days?! What happened to Rah? We have to make preparations." I leaned forward, pausing as a bullet of pain pierced through my skull.

"Easy, easy. Everything's okay. Altair is handling our

transport. There are a hundred ships to take us and our armies across the sea. You need to rest and focus on recovery." He tucked a loose strand of hair behind my ear.

"I've had three days of rest. We need to end this. Now." I swung my feet to the ground, ignoring the cramp in my right hand.

"Elpis. Please, just take a breath." He stood over me, holding out his hand.

I took it and stumbled to my feet. The muscles in my calves felt brittle, as if they'd shriveled while I slept. I flexed my toes and took a dizzy step.

"We need to alert Procyon. It will take weeks for his men to travel from the Western City. We're running out of time. Every breath wasted is an opportunity for Tethys to get one step ahead," I snapped, leaning against the wall for support.

"Fine, fine. Send the arrow. And Rah's here. He returned to Altair's side when the god appeared after you passed out. That old snake just snapped his fingers and materialized out of thin air. If it's that easy for him, I'm not sure why he sent us on a death mission to retrieve his bird." Aryx scowled, brushing his fingers through his hair.

"And Arcturas? Where is she? I need my wolf."

"Arcturas is outside with Kratos. The two have been inseparable since we've arrived. Altair claims he isn't a savage who lets beasts dine at the dinner table beside him. She's waiting for you, don't worry," he said.

"Fine." I wrapped a loose white robe around my night dress, tying the golden rope tightly across my waist.

Twisting my hair into a low knot at the nape of my neck, I smoothed the sleep from my skin. "Let's go send that arrow."

"Aren't you forgetting something?" Aryx asked. He held up a delicate silver chain that held my key.

I swiped it from his hand and quickly fastened it back

into place.

"The key to your heart," he sighed, raising an eyebrow at me.

"Say another word and this key very well might unlock some place else.," I hissed, glaring at his perfect ass in those leather pants.

He chuckled and laced his fingers through mine. "You're just a ball of sunshine in the morning."

"Oh, shut it. Let's go. We've wasted enough time already." Before hearing his response, I rushed through the bedchamber door.

Altair's palace was as every bit adorned as the jewels that dripped from his smooth, brown skin. Unlit golden candelabras, mounted in pairs, lined the narrow walls of glass. Woven rugs stretched across gilded tile, reflecting the early coastal sunlight. Peaceful crystalline waves stretched as far as the eye could see in either direction.

I continued down the hallway, stopping only when I realized I had no clue where to go.

"The stairs on your right lead up to the terrace." Aryx pointed to a set of stairs carved from white sediment.

I hobbled breathlessly up the flight, clinging to the golden railing for support. After three days in bed, my muscles groaned and cramped against the movement.

Potted agapanthus and lavender rustled in the gentle breeze. Their sweet, delicate scent, contrasting the sharp salt of the ocean below, wafted through the small terrace. A trellis of wild jasmine hung overhead. Its small, white blooms speckled around each wooden beam. I leaned over the stone railing, breathing deeply as the tropical sun rays warmed my face.

"It's beautiful here, isn't it?" Aryx wrapped his arms around my waist, his body pressed into my back.

"I've experienced nothing like it before," I said, tracing the veins of his hands. "When I was a child, we'd vacation here in the Southern City for a month or two, probably to escape the harsh cold of the North. Building sandcastles and swimming was all I looked forward to for the rest of the year. One of the few memories of my father I have left is sitting on his shoulders as he waded out into the water, pretending we were explorers on a noble quest. But this view, the scent of the air? It truly is breathtaking."

I smiled, feeling the warm caress of the sun across my face.

Brushing the loose strand of hair aside, Aryx kissed my cheek. "Maybe one day we'll make memories here together."

I straightened against him. Until this moment, every minute brought a new mountain to climb- both literally and figuratively. I hadn't thought about the future. The after. There was only now. Something snapped in my throat.

I couldn't do this. I couldn't let myself envision a future with the man who embraced me. As deeply as I cared for him, and as profound an impact he had on my life, my freedom was mine alone. I'd grown to depend on Aryx. That realization terrified me more than anything else I'd faced. I turned to him, swallowing hard. A speckle of lightness bounced from his eyes, content wrinkling at each corner of his mouth. What I had to do was going to hurt.

"Our agreement hasn't changed, Aryx. I'm fighting beside you, but for a different end goal," I said, my voice shaking.

"What?" he said, taking a step back.

"Don't misunderstand. I care about you, maybe a little too much, but I care about my freedom more. My future is mine alone. I'm sorry." I stopped breathing as darkness flooded across his eyes.

"Aryx please. You have to understand," I pleaded, reaching for his hand. He ripped it away from my grasp.

"Trust me, I understand entirely." He turned away. "The bow's over there with a full quiver in case you miss the first shot."

"Where are you going?" I asked, reaching out again for his wrist.

His heartbeat pounded through his veins as he flicked my hand away and started for the stairs.

"A walk," he said in a voice clipped and sinister. He disappeared into the palace.

Sighing, I picked up the bow.

Maybe this had been a mistake. I'd blinded myself with these feelings I didn't quite comprehend.

I knocked an arrow.

Toying with his emotions, had I created a narrative that our lives would intertwine when everything was all over? What did that make me?

I pulled the string.

The lies I'd told him, the lies I told myself, they were just that. Lies.

The arrow whizzed through the air as I released it, stopping short and plummeting to the waves below.

At the end of this all, only one thing mattered: my freedom. My choice to live quietly somewhere far away where no one could find me, where no ghosts of my past lurked in the shadows. Where I could just be.

I knocked another arrow.

My feelings toward the half-god were strong, yes, but were they powerful enough to drown out the life I'd be forced into? The prophecy connected us together. The chains of fate bound me to him. If I stayed, if I built a life with him, it wouldn't be my own. It'd be decided for me. Just as everything else had been in this world.

I let the next arrow fly. Like the first, it arced into the ocean.

Did this make me just as much of a manipulator as he had been? I sighed, lowering the bow. Only one arrow remained. Knocking it, I sucked in a breath, clearing my head. My eyes closed, letting the caress of the sea enwrap me in its hypnotic tendrils. Breathe, Elpis. Think of your life, you and your wolf. Somewhere deep in the forest, somewhere like the clearing. The ocean sounds faded into a staccato of woodland birds. The warmth of the sun transformed into a blazing campfire with meats, fresh from a hunt, roasting on skewers.

That was what I fought for. I had allowed myself a distraction. I lost sight of the future I yearned for. It wouldn't happen again. Even if it meant breaking the heart of the strongest warrior I'd ever known, then so be it. Under no circumstance would I concede to a future controlled by someone else.

When I finally felt ready, I opened my eyes and released.

The arrow spurted through the sky, flying true until vanishing into the westward horizon entirely.

Chapter 34

"My Queen," a voice behind me boomed, "it seems you're as skilled at breaking hearts as you are shooting that bow." Procyon placed his large hand on my shoulder and chuckled. His electricity radiated against me, drawing beads of sweat from my brow.

"I need to change our bargain," I said, shoving away from him.

"You've shot the arrow. Our agreement cannot be altered, sweet cheeks." His tanned brow creased as he smirked at me.

Altair was right; this God was a snake.

"I'll request a meeting with my nephew and make an introduction. You can discuss whatever you want with him. He is the rightful king, after all. The true patriarch being of mortal royal blood."

"You are also mortal, or did you forget that with all this scaling cliff sides and earth singeing?" He took a seat on the rattan bench beneath the trellis.

"Yes, but I'm also immortal. Only one of mortal blood

can take that role in the high court. Besides, Vikar is a far better rule than I'd ever be." I sat in the matching chair across from him.

"Hmm." He stroked his long beard, twirling the black beads between his forefinger and thumb. "No."

"What's so special about me, anyway? Why is it so important that I take the crown?"

He raised his hand in the air. Before he could snap away, I jumped for his fist.

"Wait! Please, I'll promise you anything else. Just not that," I pleaded.

He raised a thick, bushy eyebrow. "Anything?"

"Yes, whatever you want. Please."

"Fine. I'll break the rule of bargain this one time." The brown in his eyes ignited into an inferno as he grinned widely at me.

"Tell me, what is it you want?" I asked.

"Aside from the obvious," his eyes glanced down at the flesh of my chest, peeking out from the gossamer folds of the robe.

I grunted in disgust, wrapping the fabric tightly around myself.

"Worth a shot." He shrugged, "I want the Spring Prince then. Trade his freedom for yours. My armies could benefit from a ruthless killer like him."

Time seemed to stop. Pacing to the ledge, I looked down at the half-god now trailing the beach, his fists clenched at his sides. Was I so cruel I'd give his life for the sake of mine? I thought of his lips, his touch, the tenderness in his eyes when he looked into mine.

I'd trade one puppeteer for another. Everything he'd fought for was waiting at the cliff side, waiting for me to make the final push as it dropped into the abyss.

"Hurry, my queen, time's ticking."

"There's nothing else I can bargain?" I asked, watching Aryx stand in the shallows with rolled-up trousers and boots in hand. Deep in contemplation, the sunlight spread thin across his cheekbones, blazing against his blonde hair.

"Afraid not." He leaned back onto the settee and crossed his leg.

How casual immortals were when dealing in life. In freedom. In choice. It truly was disgusting how easily they toyed with the lives of their mortals.

The weight of his words nearly broke my spine. Closing my eyes, I thought of the clearing. I thought of my wolf. I thought of myself. Wild, free, at peace in nature. So far from where I was now. Then I thought of the crown upon Vikar's little head- how it pressed into his skull, forcing its heaviness upon the shoulders of a child. He handled the burden with poise, but in its wake, he lost all of himself.

I couldn't, wouldn't, sacrifice the future I had chosen.

Nothing would come between me and my freedom.

If I had to bargain in cold blood, so be it.

No more distractions.

I pocketed my trembling hands and turned to face the god.

Procyon stretched his arms across the bench and un-crossed his leg. The powerful muscles of his thighs pulsed in anticipation. His tattoos ebbed and flowed across his neck, as if alive with secrets. With bargains.

"Fine. Now, send for your army," I said, staring at the floor, my cheeks red with shame.

"You sure about that, Goddess?" Procyon stood from his seat and met me against the ledge, his brow wrinkled into a satisfied smirk.

"Yes," I swallowed, "I'm sure."

"Well... I wasn't expecting this. You sure know how to keep me on my toes." He chuckled. "But so be it."

With a snap of his fingers, the bones of the palace shook. A vigorous tremor whipped through the earth, pro-ducing ripples in the beaches below. Thousands of men in gleaming bronze armor clawed from the sand until only a sea of helmets was visible across the horizon. The sounds of an army setting up their tents and sharpening their blades floated in the salty breeze. No longer was the beach a peaceful haven. It was a war camp.

"Now, a kiss to seal the deal," Procyon said, leaning over me until his face was inches from mine.

"You said the bargain had already been set as soon as I sent the arrow- so no chance," I snapped.

"Ugh, fair enough." He flicked his long brown braid back over a shoulder.

"Well, have fun storming the castle." With one more snap of his fingers, he vanished.

Chapter 35

In the weeks it took to prepare our sixty-thousand men for the impending war, Aryx grew more and more distant. Our meetings with Procyon's generals, Xenophron and Balakros, were succinct and uncomfortable. He'd taken a bedchamber down the hall from me, avoiding my gaze as we passed each other in the narrow hall.

When we sat for dinner, the table stacked with platters of roasted fish and an endless array of fruits and nuts, he would make his plate and retire upstairs for the evening. With each accidental brush of our hands and silent stares, my guilt over Procyon's bargain strengthened until it stole both my thoughts and my dreams.

On our last week of preparation, Altair waved his hand toward the horizon, pulling from the depths a fleet of two hundred warships. The harbors grew restless and overcrowded with sailors and soldiers, itching for the vast open horizons of the sea.

I needed some time away from the bustle of soldiers, with their boisterous laughter and crude jokes. It was a world I had little experience in, and with Aryx's growing heartache, I was certainly not welcome in it. Taking a walk down the empty city streets, far from the harbor, I searched for city folk who'd survived the massacre. Every day, I'd look down back alleys and shadowy underpasses. Every day, I'd find nothing. Once the bodies were buried and the blood scrubbed away, it was as if the city itself had been empty forever.

On a harsh, sunny morning, I took my usual walk. Rah soared above the silent streets, his wings glinting in the sunlight. We passed the Temple of Altair, crossed the city's empty market, and made our way up the sloped street. Finally, at the top of the hill, it was quiet. Not even a murmur of the encampment on the beach whispered through the warm breeze. I stopped to draw in a breath. Up here, where no one was listening, I let myself crack. I felt everything. All of it, once bottled up, now rushed out of me in overwhelming fury.

I wasn't a good person. I never claimed to be, but my bargain with Procyon was lower than I'd ever been before. I'd given up someone else's choice, someone else's future, for my own. What did that make me? There were more similarities between Tethys and me than differences these days. What made me the hero, and she the villain?

Good and evil aren't black and white. There's a spectrum of grey morality that intertwines the moral and immoral. Heroes make selfish sacrifices. They take lives; they cause destruction just as the villain does. In war, bloody, gruesome, deadly war, there is no good side or bad. There are just two with opposing goals. To Tethys, I was the villain, and maybe she was right.

I'd lied, manipulated, and broken a man who cared so deeply for me he'd risk his life if necessary to keep me safe. Yet, he lied, manipulated, and broke me. He had taken advantage of the pain I'd endured, using it for his own vices. There was a time I hated him for it, despised even the sight of his perfect face.

Now the only face I despised was my own. We all made decisions, and we had to live with the everlasting impact of them. Aryx would haunt me forever. When this was all over, would I truly be at peace? Would I truly be able to live my life in carefree freedom? I wasn't so sure anymore.

This war had changed me, and maybe not for the better.

I sobbed, choking on the realization now burning in the back of my throat. Maybe I deserved to be in that tower. I may not have committed the accused crimes, but I caused plenty of pain and destruction. I was a monster through and through. No one was safe in my path.

"Elpis?"

Wiping the sadness from my eyes, I turned to face Lytos seated atop a bleached white horse. His broad chest was bare aside from the silver claymore sheathed across his back. Glistening beads of sweat trailed down his temples.

"What are you doing here?" I asked, keeping my gaze low to hide the swell of my reddened cheeks and nose- evidence of my weakness.

"I came to fight. Margerie threw a fit when I told her, but eventually she understood. I can't just sit by and wait for Aryx to return home." He dropped from his saddle, soothing his horse with long, gentle strokes across its snout.

"Well, Aryx will be pleased to see you, but I can't say he'll be happy you're here to join our army."

"I figured as much." He chuckled, but his eyes burned with a strong will. Nothing would convince this man to return to home. By his firm stance, I knew he'd made up his mind.

"You must be tired from the ride," I said. "I'll walk with you to the palace."

Guiding his horse by the reins, we started back down

the hill, leaving the small spatters of tear marks to evaporate on the stone in the blazing afternoon sun.

"So, how are things going? It seemed tense when you left the city," Lytos asked, smoothing his short brown hair back.

"Things are... okay." I trailed off, scuffing my boot against the gravel.

"So things are terrible," Lytos snorted. "What did my brother do now?"

I opened my mouth to speak, unsure of what to say. He wasn't the root cause. I was.

"What did you do?" Lytos raised a brow.

"We just... weren't on the same page, I guess," I murmured, lowering my eyes to the ground.

"I see."

We walked in silence down the hill, the clop of his horse's hooves loud in the thick summer heat.

"You know, Elpis, I've known Aryx for a long time, since we were practically boys. He holds so much guilt, so much pain. It's like a shadow just looming over him all the time. When you two came to the stable, he seemed...lighter, more himself." Lytos stopped, halting his horse behind him.

Taking my hand, he placed his palm over mine. "It's because of you. He's different when you're around."

Pulling away, trying to hide the tears now welling in my lower lids, I started for the palace. Taking the hint, Lytos followed my trail. The salt of the air stung at the raw skin beneath my eyes.

I couldn't breathe.

It was easy to push Aryx away when he was simply the man who'd lied, but now he was the man who was lighter because of me.

A few days from now, we'd be loading our ships and starting the last stretch of our journey. We couldn't be divided. There were men relying on the strength of their leaders, and right now, I was as fragile as glass. At any moment I was on the brink of shattering, on the losing side of the battle against my demons.

I hated every fiber of my being, every strand of black hair that fell from my head. A part of me, buried beneath muscle tissue and bone, hoped that I'd die on the battlefield. At least that way, I'd spare those around me from my destruction.

Reaching the palace, Lytos said a quick farewell with a light kiss on my cheek. Concern clouded his eyes, scanning my puffy pink face for any glimmer of an explanation. I forced a smile, although soft and sad, and directed him where to find his old friend.

As soon as I clicked my bedchamber's lock, I collapsed. The walls caved in, pushing on my chest until I took up as little space as I could. I didn't want to feel anymore, didn't want to be anymore. I'm not sure how long I stayed glued to the floor, but when I finally gained the strength to climb into bed, ignoring my empty stomach, a wolf outside howled, a pleading cry for the moon.

Chapter 36

Aryx and Lytos were inseparable in the days after his arrival, constantly speaking in serious, hushed voices. I barely left my room, barely ate, barely slept. The only comfort I found was with Arcturas in the palace gardens. In preparing for war, I'd upgraded to a weapon larger than my trusty dagger. In the evenings, when the heat of the day had finally burnt off, we'd sneak to the gardens.

While Arcturas chased squirrels and dragonflies, I practiced my sword skills- swinging and hacking at shrubs and tree trunks until the muscles in my arms were exhausted and refused to raise the weapon. The violent motions eased my aching mind, providing distraction from the hateful thoughts that cascaded through me every waking moment.

My father taught me the basics of swordsmanship, but it had been years since I wielded a blade. My balance was off and my footwork was never quite correct. On the eve before our last, Arcturas and I returned to the garden for one final session.

"When you step into your attack, move a little more to the right. It'll hold your defensive position from any counter attacks better," Lytos said from behind me as I swung at my imaginary opponent. Startled, I slid through the gravel, losing control of my blade's momentum and tumbling to the ground. My hands slipped from the hilt as the weapon spiraled through the air and clattered against a nearby trunk.

"It's not wise to sneak up on me, especially when I'm armed," I scowled, wiping the dust from my knees.

"My apologies, My Lady," he said, offering a hand to help me to my feet. "But if you'd like, I could help you with your footwork. Your blows are powerful. If you tweaked a step here and there, you could be an unstoppable swordsman."

"I usually train on my own," I said, smoothing my tunic. The tip of my tailbone ached from the tumble, but I had to continue. If I stopped, even for a moment, the dark thoughts would return.

"Well, I shall be a silent instructor, then. Only observing. I trained beside Aryx for many years. He taught me everything I know. If you'd like my advice, I'm happy to offer it," he said, nodding and taking a step back.

I took a breath and tried to shut out the extra presence. Lytos watched, leaning against a large willow tree, for the rest of my session. With every clumsy misstep, he'd whisper a correction under his breath.

Swing.

"Shift your weight more as you follow through."

Swing.

"Good, now remember to step to the right as you attack."

Swing.

"Yes, perfect. Try it again."

It had grown dark by the time my body succumbed to

exhaustion. Hobbling and sore, I started for my bedchamber. Lytos, with his fingers interlaced behind his back, followed, as silent as he'd promised to be.

"Goodnight, Lytos," I said, pushing the door open.

"Goodnight, Lady Elpis. Nice adjustments today. You are a fine soldier." He smiled, turning for the hallway that led to his room.

The door hadn't even clicked shut when I slumped into bed. Overwhelmed with a wave of fatigue, sleep found me quickly. Not a flash of an image or an ember of a thought crossed my mind as I tumbled into a near-death state of unconsciousness.

The morning came abruptly, as if I'd just closed my eyes. Our soldiers met the sunrise, loading cargo onto our war fleet to prepare for tomorrow's departure. Once the ships were loaded and the stocks full, Altair summoned us into his council chambers for one final debrief.

"If we split the fleet to the eastern and western seas, we can attack from each gate of the Elders' fortress," Xenophron stated, sliding wooden model ships across the table before us.

The dark brown hair beneath his golden helmet, tufted with horsehair, was short and neat, the sign of a prestigious soldier.

"Yes, but they'll be expecting us from both gates. Why not use the total force of our army to penetrate one entrance, then fight the rest within the keep itself?" Balakros countered, standing beside his twin.

"No, no, no." Xenophron threw his large, scarred hands up, his bushy brows furrowed with frustration. "We've discussed this, brother, it's better to divide and conquer. You act as if this is your first siege."

Balakros scowled, sliding the wooden fleet back together and pushing them to the model island's eastern side. "We're going in blind, brother. We shouldn't take the risk of splitting our strength between two armies!"

The two men continued to bicker, their wooden boats sliding back and forth across the table. I pinched my forehead. If I had to sit through another meeting that ended in one of the twins flipping the table again, I thought I might implode.

"Enough," I commanded, stifling the two men's argument with the slam of my fist against the tabletop. "We will divide the fleets. It makes sense to hit them at both gates. Aryx will command the Western fleet and I'll command the Eastern."

"Great idea, My Queen," Xenophron said, sitting in the vacant seat to my right. Until a few weeks ago, that seat was reserved for one man, and it sure as hell wasn't Xenophron.

"Rah will lead us through the rough areas of the sea. After that, we'll split off. Altair, we'll need your help hiding the fleet. We can't let their forces see our numbers right off the bat," I said, looking at the god leaning casually across the table.

He flicked a speck of dust off his gilded breastplate and gave me a bored nod.

"Aryx, once you get a clear shot, give the signal for your archers to take out the fortress's sentries. Without them, hopefully we'll maintain some element of surprise." I glanced at the half-god who stared at his feet in the corner.

"After the sentries are taken care of, we'll send in our footmen. Balakros, make sure the battering rams are ready to move quickly. We'll have limited time before they alert Tethys."

"It will be done, My Queen," Balakros said, bowing stiffly before returning to his seat.

"Procyon, we'll need to keep Tethys from teleporting out of there. Altair will be busy with the fog, so I'll need you to cast the locking ward."

The god smirked at me and nodded, "It will be done, My Queen."

I curled my lip in disgust and continued to brief our council on each of their roles. When finally all plans were set in place, a silence fell over the group.

"Let's pray that this works," Aryx said, his head still low.

"It will," I snapped, "There is no other option but succeeding."

"Well, there's death," Xenaphron chimed, swallowing hard at the daggers I glared toward him.

"We'll set sail at dawn, then." I rose to my feet, concluding the meeting.

As our council trickled out of the chambers, Procyon knelt down to my ear, his breath hot and damp against my flesh.

"You're not so bad at this whole leading thing. It's a shame. Ursae would have thrived under your command," he whispered.

I threw my hands against his solid chest and pushed him through the entryway. He turned down the hallway with a final wink. When finally the room was empty, I shut the door and let out my breath.

I couldn't think about the death we'd be sailing into in the morning. I knew they would take some lives from us. Even if we were successful and escaped with our army intact, one life would be taken from me.

"Authority looks good on you, Elpis," Aryx said behind me. He paced across the hall with heavy boots. "You'll make a great Northern Queen."

"I'm just trying my best," I said, collecting the toy ships in my arms. "In reality, I have no idea what I'm doing."

"No leader truly knows what they're doing. They command with enough confidence to not be questioned," he said, picking the final wooden ship off the table. He stroked the fabric sail between his fingers, his expression blank and unreadable.

"Aryx," I said, stepping toward him, "I'm sorry for what I said. I didn't think it would affect you this much."

"Affect me this much?" He shook his head, crushing the toothpick mast in his fist. "Elpis, you broke my heart. My feelings were quite clear. You knew how this would affect me. You just didn't care."

"I'm sorry…" Loose strands of hair hung off my head as I glanced at my feet. "I just needed to make my intentions clear."

"Well, you did. They're as clear as day." He began for the door.

"Wait," I called, reaching for his hand.

"What? You want to hurt me even more?" he hissed, the shadows around his sunken eyes thickening.

"I can't lead thousands of men into battle without knowing that we're okay. I can't risk your life and mine. I need you. Please."

His throat bobbed as he stared at our hands hanging between us. "You'll always have me. That's the problem."

He pulled away and rushed out the door.

Chapter 37

The light of dawn announced our time to go. Its soft pink sunbeams brought a cold sweat across my brow and a tightness in my chest. The sailors loaded the last stores onto our ships in wooden crates and barrels. Finally, with a dry throat and restless feet, I commanded the rowers to lower their oars and we exited the harbor.

A few hundred warships, with their oarsmen in sync, followed suit. The beating of drums, keeping time for the rowers below decks, echoed like a heartbeat across the still, crystalline water. The rhythm of my men quivered the wooden decking. Their grunts and groans were a ragged melody of the coming war.

The breeze picked up as we gained speed, licking away the sweat that rolled down the nape of my neck. We exited the safety of the harbor. The frequency of swells increased, rocking the aft deck with voracious anticipation of the looming battle to come.

Leaning against the railing, I watched Aryx from across the bow of his commanding ship. He paced sternly, barking orders with sweat-glistened palms. The golden locks of his hair rustled in the salty air. It was breathtaking to watch this seasoned general command his men, to hold his confident strides, even amid self-doubt.

Catching my gaze, his jaw tightened. The soldiers and ships and oarsmen faded away, leaving only the wire of electricity between us. I sucked in a breath. The hold his eyes had over me was all-consuming. Standing before me, his mental shield was transparent as the wing of a dragonfly. His lips softened with the drawn out seconds that ticked by.

The guilt of my decision ignited once more, and in this secret moment we shared, I knew I'd done something unforgivable.

He's different when you're around.

Just words. A string of syllables forming a sentence with little to no meaning. Now, watching Aryx watch me as we sailed toward a blood-drenched future, they were everything. I could take the pain, the anger, even the rage with a head held high. I was immune to the lashings and the cruelty.

But this?

This feeling warming my iced-over heart. This feeling of lightness in an ever-growing solitary darkness. This, I couldn't handle.

Breaking the current rushing between us, I dropped my eyes to the deck.

Isolation, emptiness, coldness. Those were easy. I'd grown to thrive in the presence of sadness. It was an old friend. Its near companion- self-loathing, I welcomed with open arms.

But something new tore its way in, shredding me from the inside out. What was it that pulled me to the man I'd grown to care for? To the man who broke away the barriers and filled me with warmth? This feeling pushed its way up, rising in the back of my throat, refusing to be ignored any longer.

It over-passed everything else. Every scratch of the others that took property in my mind. In its presence, even my demons were silent.

All I could think, all I could breathe, all I could be was reflected in the golden eyes of my once-enemy, twice-ally, now stranger.

I was terrified to call it what it was, to acknowledge it by name, because if I did, I wasn't so sure what may come of me. I turned to face away, still feeling that channel of energy pulsing through me, connecting us in an unmistakable force stronger than nature herself.

My Queen. Rah glanced from his perch in the spars. His whisper pulled me back to reality. Shoving thoughts of Aryx aside, I watched as the falcon took flight, gliding through the air to land on the railing beside me.

We're nearing the Narrows. Things are about to get interesting.

The Narrows marked the entrance of the Raging Seas, dividing the safe, coastal waters from the powerful, ship-eating swells of the far South. Until a few weeks ago, I thought the Narrows were merely legend.

At the bottom of an empty pint, seasoned sailors with drunken voices and bloodshot eyes told tales of the monsters that lurked just beneath the surface. Swinging their glasses around a dusty old tavern, they told tales of scarcely escaping certain death in the form of titanic, tentacled beasts. I'd laugh along at their foolish tales, dismissing their words with skepticism. Frya, swatting them with the tip of her dishrag, brushed aside the stories of old. The fairy tales of monsters far more ancient than the gods. If only she were here to see the uncertainty in my eyes.

Two dark cliffs loomed over our fleet. Maybe their legends were true.

The jagged rocks were barren and lifeless. Salt composites from millennia of violent storms and spray killed all life that once dared to emerge between the cracks of their sediment.

As we sailed in line through the tight passage, the skies above grumbled and darkened. The Narrows knew of our intentions and forbade us to pass. I clung to the railing of the aft deck, holding my breath as the oarsman barked orders at his men and delicately steered us between the piercing structures jutting from beneath the black, murky water.

The ridge lines pressed closer and closer together until it forced our fleet to sail one ship after another, the beam of our hulls just barely squeezing through.

I turned to face the warship behind us, focusing in on Aryx standing rigid on the command deck. He fixed his eyes on me. The white of his knuckles were clenched into fists. He nodded and whispered an order to the grey, leathery oarsman beside him. Only the sound of oars skimming across the surface echoed between the cliff sides as we pushed on.

Just as the golden cat eye painted on our bow crept through the cliffs into the open horizon, a deep rumbling erupted from the water, shaking the halyards and lines from their coils across the mast.

I turned back to Aryx. His eyes burned holes into me from across the length of his ship. Swallowing hard, I said a prayer to my mother and faced the impending attack.

She has awakened. With a frantic flap of his wings, Rah took flight, soaring high above us.

"Who?" I called, my hands trembling against the cool metal railing.

She is called Scylla, the Guardian of the Narrows.

Chapter 38

Fragments of sediment and rock broke loose, plunking into the surrounding depths. Arcturas paced beside me, her fur pin straight against her back.

"Pickup pace!" my oarsman barked, swinging his tiller across the deck, narrowly avoiding a falling boulder. The floorboards groaned under the abrupt change in direction and my pulse skyrocketed. I heard the crack of splintering wood behind us. I didn't dare look back.

Our fleet raced through the treacherous passage, leaving behind a sunken hull, the screams of her men on the ocean breeze.

An ear-piercing shriek halted our rowers mid stroke. The air thickened. A beast, larger than the cliff itself, breached the surface in front of us. Twelve clawed feet rose from the depths, sending showers of seawater across our bow. It wedged itself between the twin cliffs of the strait, crushing sediment between each spiked toe. The beast roared to life. She blocked our exit to safe waters with scaled, monstrous limbs.

"Reverse!" oarsmen of the ships behind us called. The frantic lapping of oars against water pushed through the violently rising tide.

Scylla shrieked. Her six serpentine heads reared and bucked at the warships. Rows of shark-like teeth nipped at the panic-stricken sailors heaving on halyards to stow their white flax sails.

"Xenophron, Balakros! Prepare your archers! Stow those sails! Faster!" I commanded across ships.

They jumped to action, booming orders and knocking their arrows.

"On my word. Hold. Hold. Fire!" I called, releasing a flurry of black-tipped arrows into the sky. They whizzed over the air like a flock of birds ready to unleash on their prey.

The points of the arrowheads bounced off Scylla's armor-like skin. She howled with rage, swiping her heads across the deck. Soldiers knocked into her scaly necks, launching into the air and wailing as they plunged beneath the rapid, dark surface.

"Hold. Hold. Fire!" I called again. Arrows arced into the sky. Most merely bounced off of her skin, but one sank into the gelatinous flesh of her middle eye. Scylla roared, lashing her wounded head against the bow, sending splinters of pine decking into the air.

"Elpis!" Aryx's voice boomed across the strait, "Arrows won't work! We need the rams!" He plunged his sword into Scylla's thick, armored head, now slithering across his warship, slicing through the iron scales and severing the dragon skull straight through the tendons.

"The ram's not long enough! We'd have to send our ship beneath her feet. She'd surely sink it! It's a suicide mission!" I called.

Another head lurched for the oarsmen, sending me sliding across the deck. Her fangs sank deep into his chest, bones crunching and breaking through skin. With a final gasp, his bloodied body fell limp against his oar, causing our ship to spiral out of control. I leaned against the deck boards as the hull swung around, tilting until the left rail was flush with the waterline.

The ship groaned beneath us. Sailors who hadn't clung to the mast slid into the depths, flailing and screaming for help. Arcturas clawed at the wooden surface, her nails splintered the wood as she, too, slid toward the water. Rowers leapt from their posts, swimming for the safety of the other retreating ships. Scylla plucked bodies from the water using her taloned feet and flung them across the cliffs until only mangled, unrecognizable carcasses remained distending in the raging waters.

I had to do something, or we risked capsizing. Digging into the raised decking, I pulled myself up to the dead oarsman and pushed his lifeless body off the oar. Muscles straining against me, I reeled the oar back to centerline and the keel, creaking in protest, slowly evened out.

There was no time to take a breath, however, because as I regained control of the ship, three of Scylla's heads swung for me. She knocked five of my men off their feet, leaving them unconscious. Unsheathing my dagger, I dove beneath her, jerking the blade into her chin. The sharp edge of my blade shredded the squishy flesh along the length of her under-neck, washing me in her steaming blood as I slid across the deck. The wooden floor boards splintered the tender flesh of my elbow and my body screeched to a halt.

Scylla's neck, now split in half, fell on the ship with a loud thud and the creature bellowed in agony. That was two of six heads defeated. The other four continued to wreak havoc on our fleet as bodies soared through the air, spattering blood across the twin cliffs until the rock stained red.

"Elpis! The ram! Now!" Aryx shouted, his black breastplate glinting red. He shoved a sailor into the rower's berthing. The man cried in agony as his mangled leg, spurting blood from its arteries, bounced down the gangway steps.

My warship floated dangerously close to Scylla. With her remaining heads distracted by the panicked cries of my men, we could make the final blow. Holding the oar centerline, I shouted for my remaining sailors to man the oars. With each rower's stroke, our ship picked up speed and heaved toward the creature.

"Protect that ship!" Balakros called to his brother.

The two ordered their crew to flank each side of us as we continued to press forwards. Noticing the trio of ships speeding toward her, Scylla lifted three of her feet, shifting her weight to one cliff to crack down on Xenophron's deck.

The wood practically disintegrated on impact as the ship split into pieces. Amid the groans of its hull as it sank into the sea, Balakros wailed for his brother, begging him to leap from its deck and swim to safety. Before Xenophron could abandon the wreck, Scylla lunged for him, crushing his body beneath the weight of her foot. The remnants of his crew drifted into the depths, leaving only a trail of bubbles as they let out their final breaths.

With one last stroke of our oars, the curved bronze ram plunged through Scylla's scaly stomach.

"Reverse!" I commanded.

Arcturas, soaked and frightened, pounced toward me. Wrapping her body around me, she cowered behind my feet.

The sailors redacted their strokes, and we glided backwards away from the writhing beast. Her entrails poured out of the ship-sized hole in her abdomen. She shrieked and shrieked in agony, losing her grip against the rock wall and falling into the raging whirlpool below. As she let out a final roar, her body disappeared into the blood-stained waves, joining the graveyard of my men.

I fell to my knees, exhausted from the chaos. Balakros's sobs were heard across the Narrows, filling the silence with grief that only death creates. Hobbling to the aft deck, I grasped at the oar, guiding what remained of our fleet out of the Narrows.

My Queen, what have you done? Rah's voice filled my head as he soared safely above the wreckage.

"I saved my men," I sighed, wiping the sweat and blood off my brow.

You've killed a most ancient creature. There will be consequences for your actions. Be prepared.

"The consequences are worth our lives," I said, leaning heavily against the railing.

"I'll face whatever I need to. These men are worth it."

I wouldn't be so sure. The falcon swooped down to the deck.

Tucking his wings into his chest, he stared at me with worrisome eyes.

"What do you mean?"

Scylla is not the only creature that guards these waters. Her blood will draw them out, sensing a threat.

"We'll face whatever comes," I said, examining my petrified wolf for any injuries or wounds. Aside from her fur being drenched, she was okay. I kissed her forehead in relief and rose to survey the rest of the damage.

We'd lost fifty ships, and with them, hundreds of men. The remaining ships had taken on damage, but nothing too major. Thank the gods. I scanned the fleet for Aryx. He hunched over his oarsman, doused in thick blood and exhausted from the battle. Raising his head, our eyes met and relief pooled beneath the golden flecks of his irises.

"I'm glad you're okay, El," he called, waving across the waters. I smiled softly back.

We were okay.

For now.

Chapter 39

The waters calmed as we sailed on into nightfall. The rowers took shifts, propelling the fleet forward. When the moon was at its zenith, the three remaining command ships rafted together and I summoned our council to the chartroom.

"We need to choose a ship to take Xenophron's command," I said, sitting at a small, dusty table. The air was damp and musty with the stench of seawater and open wounds. A bead of sweat dripped from my nose as I sat, taking in the reported damage from my council. Our glasses of whiskey clinked back and forth against the ballast tabletop, sliding side to side with each soft rocking of swells.

"My men can fill the position. Most are sharp with their bows," Lytos said from across the chartroom.

Aryx's eyes sharpened and he rose in dispute.

"Lytos, you can't be serious. You have a wife and child at home. I only agreed to bring you aboard in the promise that you'd remain in the second wave of our fleet. Now you're suggesting you join the front lines?! Absolutely

279

not," he growled.

"It's not up for debate." Lytos, too, rose from his seat. "My unit has the highest marks in archery. I trained them myself. There's no one else."

"Do not make me say it again." The aura around the half-god grew as dark as the chill in his voice was cold.

Lytos's throat bobbed, unsure if he should push his brother further. "It's the right thing to do, brother. You know it is. There's no one better suited to lead a crew of archers."

"That's enough," I demanded, slamming my fist on the table to break the thickening tension. "Lytos, I can't ask that of you. Think of Margerie and Judas. If you were to be hurt, or worse, killed, how could Aryx or I face them again? Don't take a father away from his son. He needs you. I think we all can agree on that."

Aryx nodded at my resolution. Inhaling deeply, he returned to his seat, his palms twitching as the meeting carried on. For the rest of the meeting, Lytos paced the narrow hall between the chartroom and gangway, his mouth in a silent, thin line.

"My Queen, my unit has plenty of seasoned soldiers handy with a bow. We will take Xenophron's place," an aging general chimed in, her long greying braid trailed down the length of her spine.

"Thank you Hermia. Balakros can debrief you before you retire to your ship," I said, glancing at the silently weeping general.

"Yes, My Queen," he whispered through sobs. I looked into his eyes. They were dark and glazed from the hours of grieving since his brother's death.

An all too familiar pang of guilt struck at my chest, but I shoved it aside. I couldn't afford to fall apart in front of my people. They were expecting resilience. They needed stern, emotionless strength.

I stroked Arcturas's pelt as she slept beneath me. Her

fur was cool against the sweltering, damp draft below decks.

"Now, Rah has told me we're about three days out from Elder's Island. I'm hoping it will be an easy passage, but we can't become complacent. Everyone has to be on high alert constantly. I don't trust the calmness of these waters."

"I'll collect a headcount of wounded or dead within our fleet," Aryx said from his seat beside me. "We'll have a better idea of what we're going into this with."

"Thank you. Send the report back to me when you're done." I stood from my seat, nearly toppling over as a large swell rocked the hull leeward.

We continued planning until the late hours of the morning. My council, yawning and exhausted, finally retired to their ships. The morning would arrive too soon, and with it, another day exposed to whatever lurked in these open waters.

The air was too hot, too sticky down below. I needed the fresh breeze to soothe my pounding head.

Quietly climbing topside, I stretched my sore muscles on the aft deck and threw the oarsman a quick greeting.

The stars above us speckled across the sky, and in the utter darkness of the open ocean, their light burned brightly upon my face.

I took a deep breath, inhaling the midnight air laced with salt. I thought about my father, and the secret love he fought so hard for. It must have been excruciating acting as king in the mortal realm, while your mind frequently drifted to the gossamer realm of the gods. He played his role so well, so carefully, I'd never even suspected he had been unfaithful to his queen. How I wished he could be here now, advising me in the games of war. I leaned against the railing, holding my head in my hands.

And what of my mother? Or should I say mothers? I knew Queen Signe wouldn't approve of my fight for freedom. She followed the rules, stuck to the protocol. Justice, for her, was plain as day. Putting full trust into the palm of the politician, she'd demand I return to my prison. Although, my home in the Northern City was equally a prison as that hundred story tower. It had been the chains that bound me. I hoped that maybe one day it would be the key that freed me.

And what of Polaris, with her wild black hair and ever flowing robes? She, the embodiment of night, accepted the freedom of the galaxies, the darkness of space, the lack thereof of light. She tamed the beasts that howled at a silvery moon, while not keeping them leashed.

I wished we had more time. I wanted to know her, to learn about myself. Something had always been missing, and I hadn't realized until now, standing beneath the stretch of endless stars, that it was her. Everything fit together in a puzzle of clarity when I accepted who I was.

Although a complete stranger, I wanted to make her proud. I wasn't so sure, given my recent choices, that she would be.

I threw my hands over the railing and stared at the dark navy swells gently rising and falling as we skimmed across the sea-surface. Overcome with nausea, I watched crashes of sea foam recede into the next wave, trying to soothe my tired mind.

"Are you okay?" Aryx asked from the shadows behind me.

"Oh...I thought you went back to your ship." I turned to face him.

Moonlight refracted in those golden eyes and washed over his face, illuminating the arches of his cheekbones. His hair, draped at his shoulders, was nearly iridescent in the star beams. This, I decided, was my favorite version of him.

"I wanted to see if you were alright after what happened today." He leaned beside me, watching the small swells lap against the waterline.

"I'm fine," I said, although, truly, I wasn't. I couldn't think of a time I was more not fine than now.

"It's okay if you're not around me. I know the others are looking to follow your lead, but you don't have to keep your walls up. Not with me."

"Aryx, I..." I brushed my pinky finger against his, craving the warmth of his skin. "I'm sorry."

"I know," he said.

"I thought I lost you today."

"You didn't. That's all that matters." His pinky returned the touch.

"I'm sorry... for everything," I croaked, suddenly overwhelmed by guilt. By pain. By hurt. The isolation was too much to bear. Its weight felt as if my ribs would fold in on themselves.

I couldn't stay afloat in the ever rising tide of this reality. If I held myself together for one more second, I would combust- imploding into the one thing I feared more than myself. The demon ran her claws down the back of my spine, begging for release.

"Me too. It was too much to expect from you. All your life you've been imprisoned. You've had your choices made for you. I just thought that maybe, in the end, you'd choose me." His voice trailed off.

We were quiet for a while, letting the ripple of water fill the silent void between us.

"I have to choose myself."

"I understand," he said, pulling his pinky away. "Well, it's late. You should get your rest. Gods know what tomorrow might bring." He started toward the wooden gangway between our ships.

The place where his hand had been grew cold. I didn't want him to go. More than that, I didn't want to be alone.

"Wait," I said, catching him before he took another

step. "Stay."

His back straightened.

"Please don't go," I whispered, reaching for his hand.

"Ell…" He turned to face me with an expression like a blade through my chest.

Before he could argue, I lunged for him, my lips meeting his with a frantic need. Of everything in the world, all I wanted, all I needed, was to fall into him and escape for a while.

Even if only for a second.

Throwing my arms around his neck, I pressed myself closer. The space between us faded away. For a moment, I believed maybe we were okay. Maybe nothing had changed.

He responded with equal voracity, running his trembling hands up my arms, across my collarbones, tracing the curve of my body with his fingertips. The taste of salt was bitter on my tongue. Tears streamed from my eyes. For a glimpse, I let go.

With shaking hands, he unbuttoned my tunic, letting the fabric slide down my arms, raising the hair on the back of my neck.

"I missed you," he said, his words scattered between a trail of kisses. "I missed this."

"Please, stay. Stay with me." My voice wasn't my own, breathless and ragged.

He watched me watching him. I wanted to be the fabric against his body, draped over every inch of him. The thin material licked up his skin as he pulled it from his shoulders. In the night's paleness, his body was electric. Shadows painted around solid muscle, highlighting each solid crease and curve.

The second his tunic hit the deck, I pounced. My lips burned against his as the jolt of energy hummed between us. Our bodies buzzed with the power now flooding in. Aryx's hands made their way down the curve of my hips, leaving agonizing anticipation on their trail.

"Elpis, I need you to hear me," he whispered, his breath warm and sweet against my ear.

"Don't talk. Just be here with me," I murmured.

"Please, I-"

My touch cut him off. I knew what he was about to say, and I refused to unleash it into the world. It would change everything. This feeling, once a simple spark between two strangers in a tavern, had roared to life within me. I couldn't, and wouldn't, let it breathe the night air.

My hands trembled as I unlaced his trousers. Closing the space between us, he combed his hands through my hair, smoothing back the disheveled strands.

"Hear this. Please," he whispered, his eyes now smoldering infernos in the night.

"I don't want to," I cried, continuing with the leather lacing.

He reached for my hands, closing his palms around mine.

"Elpis. Look at me."

I couldn't. I knew that if I did, I'd surrender entirely to him.

"Elpis. Look at me," he said again, tipping my chin up.

Slowly, I raised my gaze, praying to the gods for strength. In this moment of total vulnerability, I'd need more than self will. He clenched his jaw and struggled to form the syllables on the back of his tongue. His internal battleground sketched vividly in each perfect line across his brow. I sucked in a breath, watching as the hardened facade of war faded from his features.

"I love you," he whispered, the words a delicate sound on the ocean breeze.

I froze. His words felt like tendrils of night wrapping around me, cracking my chest wide open. He'd acknowledged it, brought it into existence without my consent. How could he give me his heart? I would surely destroy- if

I hadn't already.

"Say something," he begged.

"I-" I trailed off.

I couldn't admit what I'd known all along. When the time finally came for the truth of my bargain to surface, I hoped to the gods that I wouldn't be alive to see his heartbreak. He trusted me with everything, with love. I couldn't face that. I wouldn't. How could he do this to me?

Anger reared its ugly head. I couldn't contain the rage now boiling over. Feeling my fingernails dig into the tender flesh of my palms, I stepped back.

Aryx followed my step, pleading for a response. A cold sweat of panic glistened his brow as he watched me transform into the demon I tried so hard to subdue.

"Don't," I snipped, pushing him away.

"Elpis. You needed to know. At any second, either of us could be killed. I needed to tell you before I-" His voice cracked. A sharp contrast from the unwavering soldier he'd been merely hours earlier.

"Don't do that, Aryx. Please. I'm begging you," I cried, feeling the heat of my tears trickle off my chin.

"I love you. I know you love me too. We're fated to be together. I could feel it the moment I met you."

"No, we're not. We're not lovers, we're not friends. We are allies, working toward a common goal. Fighting a common enemy. That is all," I hissed, throwing his hands away from mine.

The softness in his eyes froze, leaving a shadowy darkness I'd seen only once before. I sucked in a breath. Maybe I'd let my rage get the better of me.

"Do you fuck all of your allies, then?" His voice was bitter, like a frigid whip through my chest.

"Forget it," he said, turning on his heels.

I watched him, my vision red with rage, as he unlatched the gangway. The shrieks of the pullies sent violent chills down my spine. The planks lowered, joining our two ships.

"I've done some terrible things in my life, Elpis. I've lied, betrayed, manipulated even, but nothing compares to what you've done. Maybe I was wrong about you." His voice was harsh, each consonant a bite from a vicious tongue.

"You are a monster, and there's nothing that will ever change that."

With those final words, he disappeared into the night, returning to his sleeping crew.

My legs felt as if they were bags of sand spilling their grains across the bleached pine decking. Aryx's words still echoed in my head, like a swarm of wasps stinging the gray matter of my brain over and over and over again.

Chapter 40

Stained glass windows painted the rising morning light with shades of orange and pink. Gemstone chandeliers lined the high courtroom, illuminating the panel of judges that watched with disgusted smirks in their wing backed velvet thrones. The king and queen sat center in the line of unrecognizable faces. I'd never seen them before, but an aura of royalty radiated about them like translucent beams of power washing over their smooth, perfect skin.

The queen, with her neck straightened in elegant nobility, eyed me- her brutal lips pursed. The king, his crown delicate atop his marble-carved brow, burned holes in my chest with his censorious blue eyes.

"Lords and Ladies of the High Court," a small, measly man squeaked, "we've called upon you today to discuss these revoltingly treasonous actions."

I swallowed hard as hundreds of pairs of eyes turned to face me. The crowd murmured disapprovals as the man carried on.

"You have not only brought shame on yourself, but also on your family. Because of your actions, the mortal realms have lost trust in the stability of their immortal rulers. These actions cannot go unpunished."

"Please, I've done nothing!" I pleaded. The weight of iron chains dug into my wrists. After scanning the room, searching for any hint of a friendly face, all I found were furrowed brows and disgusted eyes.

"Silence!" the king boomed, his voice causing tremors throughout the cavernous marble walls. "You had your chance to speak. To explain yourself. But that's passed and now it's time to face judgment."

I swallowed hard, entirely frozen by the sheer force of his all-commanding presence. His terrifyingly fierce eyes snipped my vocal cords, leaving me entirely speechless.

"Bring in the testimonials!" the king's aide squeaked. A door behind the panel of judges swung open. Procyon, with his head held high, entered the courtroom. A short, fragile-looking woman trailed behind him, her head hanging low. I watched as the god stepped into the rays undulating from the ornate window panes. His long, braided beard swung across his chin as he took long, powerful strides. I stared at him, hoping he'd recognize me and come to my aid. I wasn't supposed to be here.

"Procyon, please, help me! I-"

Someone kicked the soft side of my knees, throwing me to the ground. My head cracked against the floor, sending blurs of stars whizzing through my vision.

"You don't speak!" a black-hooded figure growled behind me. I pushed myself to my knees, feeling the joints crack beneath my weight. Long, blonde strands of hair hung over my face and suddenly, I realized I wasn't me. I wasn't Elpis anymore. This wasn't my past or my future.

Procyon spoke, but his words were unintelligible. I watched him, trying to translate the string of syllables and sounds coming from his lips. He was furious, his orange eyes kindled with each strand of sentences.

I'd done something so terrible, so horrific, it caused the court to whisper and gasp. Caused tears to stream down the eyes of the queen and the quiet, brown-haired woman to cower behind Procyon.

A faint glimmer of movement in the room's corner caught my eye. Sitting limply in the shadows was a frail, full bearded man. His wrists were bloody and irritated from the shackles that held him to the wall. His eyes fluttered in and out of consciousness. Procyon scowled and pointed a strong, deadly finger toward him, then back at me. Somehow we were connected, but the only thing I recognized in him was the faded flecks of gold behind his tired, amber eyes.

The king and queen rose, pulling my eyes away from the broken man. The king's voice sent ice down my spine, like the coldest of morning frosts. I swallowed hard, shifting uncomfortably on shrieking knees. The deafening ring in my ears subsided enough to make out his words, "Tethys, I no longer recognize you as a daughter of this court. Given the accusations presented against you today, I banish you to the immortal realms. Take her away."

Cold, rough hands gripped around my biceps, pulling me back into the shadows. The courtroom faded away, leaving nothing but a lingering desperation of my impending sentence.

Chapter 41

The following morning came too early, as if time itself had blinked forward. The nightmare, still thick in my throat, haunted me with the rising sun. Our oars skimmed through the water in a synchronous rhythm, greeting another day closer to our ultimate fates. My connection to the Spring Queen hadn't felt this strong before. She'd come to me in dreams, but never like this. I'd lived out one of her memories.

Was her time in court merely a scene tangled in my subconscious, or was it the harsh reality of a time long gone?

I sighed, running my hands down my biceps, expecting to feel swollen, purple bruises from the guard's tight grip as he pulled me back into those frigid shadows. I wanted to tell Aryx of my night time travels, but with every fleeting look, his eyes hardened. The love that once burned so brightly there had run out of fuel, leaving a cold vacancy that split my insides into pieces.

"My Queen, there's something on the horizon," the

oarsman said, his eyes nervously darting from wave to wave.

I peered over the railing, scanning where water met sky. We weren't close enough to see Elder's Island. There, on the port side of our bow, was a small black blip hiding behind the rise and fall of the distant sea-foam waves. The sun made it next to impossible to distinguish.

"Rah, what is that ahead?" I called.

The falcon, in his heavenly perch on our tallest mast, squawked and took flight. He soared into the sky, feathers rustling as he climbed in altitude until his glorious wings were merely a speck in the great stretch of cerulean. I watched the bird until he disappeared entirely, then my eyes focused back in on the shadow staining the horizon. It was dark, but not black. Judging from the blurs of sea foam crashing around it, it was solid. The hair on my arms pricked. Whatever it was, I seriously doubted it was friendly.

Aryx paced across the aft deck of his ship, watching the blip with arms laced behind his back and a furrowed, sun-soaked brow. Given the embers of determination radiating from his eyes, I knew we would be ready for whatever we were about to face.

I swallowed hard and alerted my sailors of the looming threat. The men jumped into action, moving and working along the deck. The oarsman barked orders forward, a hint of trepidation crackling in his voice.

You will not like my report, Rah whispered through our tether, causing a heavy lump of dread to fall through the pit of my stomach.

"What is it, Rah?" I continued to watch the blip, scanning its motion as it blurred and sharpened with each crashing wave.

It is called Charybdis. Scylla's brother. An ancient, powerful creature. It tracked us using the scent of its sister's death. We need to push on before it catches up.

Otherwise...

I swallowed hard. Otherwise we'd be dead.

An obstacle of ancient, primal descent- far older than the elements themselves. We'd barely escaped Scylla's cliffs with a fleet double in size. How could we possibly weather another attack of the same magnitude?

"Oarsman, we need full speed. If that catches us," I pointed out to the horizon, "we're fucked."

The blip was slightly larger now and much clearer. Dark grey clouds, thick and saturated, gathered on the horizon. The sun shrouded itself behind an all-powerful storm, taking refuge from the looming threat. The sky transitioned to a deep periwinkle. Waves gathered force until their crests crashed over our railing, sending misting my cheeks with salt spray. Seasick rowers below deck groaned and retched with each steep roll of our hull.

My Queen, it's too fast. Prepare our fleet for a fight.

Interlacing my fingers around the hilt of my sword, I glanced toward Aryx's ship. He stood with a strong and stoic facade beside the oarsman. The slight bob in his throat and the clenched muscle of his jaw were subtle, but I sensed them. He was afraid.

Hurtling toward our fleet with a speed I'd never witnessed before was a massive tubular eel. Deep green spines, as sharp as an urchin's, protruded from impenetrable skin littered with battle scars. My hands trembled against the railing I now gripped so strongly, I thought my knuckles might break. Our rowers picked up pace, their blades slicing through the water with panicked strength. We weren't fast enough, however. The dreaded anticipation electrified the heavy storm above. All we could do was wait and pray to the gods that we would survive.

Charybdis was closing in on us now. My voice cracked through the air like the shattering sound of thunderheads as I ordered our archers to take aim. As if one entity, they knocked their bows and raised them into the sky. A few more seconds now and the beast would be in range. Waves slammed into our fleet, causing crew and soldiers alike to cling to the railings.

"Fire!"

My command unleashed a wave of arrows into the air. They arched overhead, disappearing briefly behind the misty storm clouds. The front of pointed arrowheads plummeted into the sea, some striking true, some vanishing into the depths.

The archers knocked their bows again, waiting to release the second wave. Before the words could leave my mouth, however, Charybdis reared its forward end into the open air. It had no head, no eyes, just teeth. A large, rounded mouth opened wide. Rows of forked, yellowing daggers pricked from squishy, grey gums. The roar that reverberated from deep within its belly sent a shockwave through the open sea, briefly stilling the storming wavelets, and knocking me to my knees.

Yeah, we were fucked.

A black, wriggling mass of eels poured from its mouth. Plunking into the sea, they raced toward our ships. Sending Arcturas below decks where she'd be safe from the rolling swells, I drew the sword strapped to my back. Watching me, Aryx pulled his gleaming, golden weapon from its sheath.

The world seemed to stop turning, and the air grew stagnant. Time froze. Clouds overhead were so saturated, so heavy, they practically begged for release, pleaded for relief. I swallowed hard and tightened the straps of my leather breastplate.

One moment, everything stopped.

The next, all hell broke loose.

Charybdis flung its massive body across the hull of the closest warship, splintering the wooden chime until the timbers themselves disintegrated into the salty sea. Bodies littered the water, frantically thrashing for help as the army of smaller eels feasted upon their flesh. I could barely watch as my men were eaten alive, screams burrowing through my ears, scarring the inner walls of my mind permanently.

Our arrows penetrated its thick outer skin, but they only angered the creature more. If our ships got too close, the fleet would be swallowed up and doomed to spend eternity trapped in the pit of its voracious stomach.

Crack! Another warship was in pieces, bodies wriggling and writhing beneath the waves, their blood clouding the ocean with a thick maroon haze.

Crack! Another. We'd lost so many already. We couldn't afford much more. I stifled the scream now, plucking my vocal cords like an instrument. The eels continued to shred skin and muscle tissue from my drowning men.

Crack! Another. Everything was moving too fast, too fluid. I couldn't think, couldn't move from where I stood. The oarsman behind me shouted forward, begging me for an order. His voice was a mere muffled string of sounds. All I could hear were the screams of dying men. The tearing of flesh. Charybdis struck again, its teeth now dripping seawater and blood.

Suddenly, there was a firm hand on my shoulder, pulling me to my knees. As my body collapsed against the timbers, a flurry of arrows rushed through the air where I'd just stood.

"Snap out of it!" Aryx cried, rolling our bodies away from a snapping eel now writhing along the deck. I swallowed hard, numb to the death surrounding us.

"Elpis! Let go! It's our only chance of survival. Please!" His voice was hoarse from yelling. My mouth, gaping open, refused to free the words now racing through me. The gold strands of his wind-blown hair and the sharp curve of his clenched jaw faded away. In their place, shredded, bloated bodies. Every muscle, down to my core, convulsed.

"Look at me." Calloused hands wrapped themselves

around my cheeks. "Your men need you. They're dying. They need your help. Let go." Strong fingers stroked away the tears now gushing from my eyes. "Elpis. Look at me."

For a brief second, the blood, the bone, the death fell away. For just a moment, those golden, shimmering eyes pulled me out of reality.

"I need you. Let it all go," he whispered, pulling me to him. Flames burned through me when our lips met. The salty taste of the sea trickled down my throat. I breathed him in. His touch was the blood that pumped through my veins, the air that inflated my lungs. He was the past, the present, and the future. He was everything.

Heavy beads of rain erupted from the sky, the sound of arrows zoomed around us, the roars of our enemy sent tidal waves across the furious sea. In this moment, the feel of his lips took hold of me entirely, and nothing could part us.

Familiar tingles rushed from my toes through my chest to the crown of my head. My limbs felt light, as if I weighed less than a feather. Loose locks of matted, salty hair licked across my face. I closed my eyes, unlocking the demon from her cage.

The world turned to night.

My vision came and went in glimpses as I let my monsters consume me. One moment, I was floating above the waves, encapsulated in a bright amethyst glow. The next Charybdis breeched the surface and gnashed its razor-like teeth toward me. Tendrils of power, curling around my fingers, shot at the beast, penetrating its thick skin. With each blow Charybdis roared in fury, obsidian blood oozing from its open wounds.

Flashes of light cracked across the sky like the lighting of a raging storm. With each purple flash, the gaping faces of my soldiers came into view. I continued to unleash the true self I'd fought so hard to suppress. It felt easy. Like eating to remedy hunger or drinking to replenish thirst, letting her consume me was instinctual, and I reveled in it. My body felt stronger. My mind sharper. Every detail of the world scratched against my skin. With heightened sense, I didn't need daylight to see.

Charybdis shrieked again, letting thousands more black eels flood from its mouth. Like a river blockaded by a dam, the power inside me built up more and more until the walls fractured. I took a breath, preparing my mind for the flood as the dam finally crumbled and the shadows poured out.

The world was shrouded in darkness.

Until it wasn't.

Ultraviolet hues of color pulsed through me, blinding the world in my light.

The vicious roar bouncing from wave to wave went silent. The water stilled.

Everything stopped and for a second, I thought maybe I'd obliterated it all, leaving only the borealis behind. When the light faded, however, the world came back into view. Men gawked from the remaining warships, their eyes filled with wonder, and maybe terror. Waves lapped softly against the surface, pushing limp black eels away from our fleet. The giant worm bellied up and rolled away with the currents. Its body wrinkled and stretched as it returned to the sea.

All was quiet as I returned to the deck. Arcturas, who had burst through from below, howled and sprinted to my side. Every fiber of my being was relaxed, at peace. The weight of the world had lifted from my back. The demon returned to her cage, but this time, I didn't lock her shackles. Somehow, this war between us ended. We'd come to an agreement.

Terrified whispers raced through the crew as they distanced themselves from me. All of my soldiers trembled in my presence. All except one. Aryx pushed through the crowd.

"My Queen.," he murmured, kneeling before me. I sucked in a breath. He'd never taken a knee before me. Here and now, this legendary half-god acknowledged my power over his so publicly. So vulnerably.

I curled my fingers around his cheek and pulled him to his feet. All the rage that had once pulsed through me flat-lined. We came close to death today, too close. Our lives, maybe fated to intertwine or maybe not, were constantly at risk. We didn't have the privilege of fighting or hating or withholding forgiveness. In this moment, nothing he could say, no matter how cruel, no matter how spiteful, would break the current that linked us together.

Later, when I'd washed the grime of battle from my skin, Aryx and I sat in my quarters, having finished a quiet meal together.

"I thought I'd lost you for a minute there," Aryx said, combing his fingers through my matted hair. Candles scattered around the space emitted a dry, flickering warmth. The steady rise and fall of the ocean above rocked the ship gently, like a mother soothing her infant child.

"This isn't the first time we've said that. Nor will it be the last. I can't help but think about our men. How much more of this can we put them through?"

"Elpis," Aryx stopped, tipping my chin to face him, "They knew what they were risking when they signed on. You can't blame yourself."

I swallowed, lowering my eyes to my hands. "But it is my fault. I made that bargain with Procyon, I brought them to sea, I-."

"Stop," he said, kneeling so our eyes were level. "If you asked any of those men out there," he pointed toward the cabin door, "they'd say it's their honor to fight for you. To fight for us. You saved us against Charybdis. Against Scylla. Gods, we wouldn't have made it out of the fucking harbor without you. Yes, it would be different if you were hiding away in a throne room watching men die, but you're not. You're with us. Fighting alongside us. Risking your life just as much as they are."

His gaze burned so brightly into me, I thought I might combust.

"Look, you're always going to carry the weight of their deaths. But you're not alone. I'm here. Let me take some of it. Let me help you." His voice was a soft caress against my skin.

Closing my eyes, I felt the warmth of his chest against my cheek as he pulled me in. It was safe here, easy. Just as before, fighting beside my demon rather than against her, I felt weightless. I felt free.

Aryx knelt before me, placing his hands on my knees, and stared up at me.

"I know you don't want to hear it…" he said, tucking a loose strand of hair behind my ear.

"And I know you're not ready to say it back…" His thumb stroked my cheek, my bottom lip, my collarbone.

"Don't," I whispered.

My skin melted under his touch. He was intoxicating. The sound of his voice was the only melody I'd ever need to hear. His heated gaze, the only warmth I'd ever need to feel.

"Elpis." He leaned into me, our mouths only a hair width apart. The anticipation of his lips pressing against mine ignited every inch of my skin, raising the hairs on the nape of my neck. The space between us felt too great, the air felt too thick.

"When I'm around you, the world fades away. When you touch me, something sets fire. For the first time in my life, I feel worthy. I feel deserving," he said, brushing his forehead against mine. Time hung frozen around us.

"Aryx, I-" His lips cut off my words, forcing them back into my mouth. My thoughts vanished nearly instantly as his scent tickled my nose. I craved it, yearned for it to wrap around me. I pressed into him, tangling my fingers through his hair. The weeks of silence, the heartbroken glares, all of it washed away with each kiss. In this moment, we were infinite.

We were gods.

"I love you, Elpis. I will never stop loving you," he whispered through panting breaths. "You have every piece of me. You've stolen every thought. Every dream. Every waking moment." I felt his fingers trace down my thighs and squeeze my skin.

"You are everything. Always."

I couldn't breathe. He'd taken the air away, but I yearned to stay here in this suffocating electricity. The taste of freedom trickled down my throat and suddenly I realized he was my escape. He wrapped my legs around his waist and lifted me from my seat, our lips never leaving one another for long enough to grow cold.

Chapter 42

We sailed through the night, and at dawn, the rowers began their strokes with cadence chants that shook the boards of our hull. The gentle rocking of the hull skimming across the waves pulled me from a silent sleep. Tucked safely beneath the embrace of the sleeping half-god, I dreaded leaving this bed.

Taking that first step onto the timber deck above brought an end to this dream. We'd have to face another day, another deadly reality. Sighing, I turned to face him. Aryx's features were so soft, a stark juxtaposition from the hardened creases and lines he normally wore. With his lips slightly parted and a sheet of silky golden hair curtaining his cheek, he was a million miles away. Somewhere peaceful. Somewhere he deserved to be.

With a trembling hand, I tucked the loose strands back behind his ear. My throat tightened when his lips curled into a small smile. I couldn't pull him back to this nightmare. Sliding from beneath his heavy limbs, I reached for the white linen tunic that lay crumpled on the floor.

"Just where do you think you're going?" Aryx asked, his voice still thick with sleep. Smirking over my shoulder, I watched him wipe the night from his eyes and yawn deeply.

"I was going to go check in with the oarsman- ensure there was no panic regarding a missing spring prince who didn't return to his ship last night."

"Ah-" He sat up, leaning his chest against the headboard and tucking his hands behind his head. "Well, I'm sure a few more minutes of panic won't do too much harm."

Sunlight from a porthole washed over the thick black lines engraved into his skin. I couldn't help but trace the block-work patterns, following them across his collarbones, wrapping around his rib cage until they disappeared beneath the sheets. His eyes darkened, sending waves of heat crashing through me. My toes curled against the floorboards.

"What's five more minutes, I suppose," I grinned, sliding back toward him.

Five minutes turned to ten, twenty, forty.

It wasn't until a knock on the cabin door alerted us we were needed on deck that we emerged, pulling us from the blissful shelter we'd built.

Rah soared high above the sea, his outstretched wings blending into the vast blue sky speckled with puffy cumulus clouds. It was hard to believe these seas were such a threat. Dark navy waves collided with serene cobalt skies, stretching as far as the eye could see. Aryx returned to his ship, taking command of the aft deck and every so often stealing lustful glances across the glittering waves.

Leaning against the point of the warship, I took in the sweet smell of the waves. White foam bounced from each side of the waterline as the bow cut through each swell with a uniform rise and fall. Something glistened off our starboard side, catching my eye. It breached the surface, sunlight bouncing off its iridescent tail. With perked ears, I listened for the splash as its long, green body plunged back into the depths, disappearing beneath sea foam.

"Oarsman, there's something on the starboard bow." I called aft, "Everyone be on your guard."

The creature breached again, joined by another, identical in color.

"What is that?" I squinted, trying to make out its blurred features. Long green hair was wetted back across a narrow forehead. As the two breached again, a third joined them. Their delicate skin was a pale shade of blue as they extended long, webbed fingers in front of them and dove back beneath the surface.

With each leap into the fresh morning air they grew closer, their beauty coming into view. I leaned farther over the railing, trying to get a closer look as they bounced from wave crest to wave crest. I needed to see them, to hear their soft clicks, to touch their smooth skin.

One creature skimmed the surface and glided past the bow. His back, strong and muscular, melted into a glorious fishtail of shining scales. Green hair rushed down to his hips as he jerked his powerful tail and leapt from the waterline, arcing over the bronze battering ram and disappearing beneath a foamy white wave crest on the other side.

With glimmering glazed eyes, I stepped over the railing to get closer. His emerald stare sparkled and beckoned me to join him.

Treading next to our ship, he lifted his graceful webbed fingers to me, smiling sweetly. The way his slender fingers urged me forward was enchanting. Like a net, they cast an irresistible charm. I wanted to touch his cool skin, to feel that spidery webbing against my face. I took another step over the railing, balancing against the metal post on the bow.

"ELPIS! NO!" Aryx cried from the bow of his ship, now rafting beside us. Shaken from the creature's beautiful trance, its gentle green glow faded away.

"Wh-a-at...What am I doing?" I gasped, gripping against the railing before I fell into the blue depths beneath me. My toes dangled off the decking. The creature hissed at Aryx and dove beneath the sea, kicking the forked fin of his tail furiously as he flurried towards the other ships.

"Don't follow her! Just stay where you are!" Aryx cried, uncoiling the line to lower the gangway between our two beams.

"Her?" I asked quietly, my eyes scanning the water, hoping to experience the glorious beauty of the creatures below again.

"STAY WHERE YOU ARE!" he called, leaping onto our deck and pushing past my entranced crew, all of their heads nearly touching the surface as they stretched over the rails to catch a glimpse. More of the creatures swarmed us, clicking and cooing at the men.

The male creature had returned, his eyes glowing brighter as he beckoned for me.

It wasn't so bad. He wouldn't hurt me.

What if I just let go?

What if I let myself fall and join him beneath the waves? I could leave all the hurt, all the pain, everything behind. I wouldn't be confined by my guilt anymore. Aryx would find someone else to cherish. He'd be rid of the monstrosity I'd become. It was the perfect escape. I weighed the benefits in my mind, finding no disadvantages present. Those around me would be safe, and all would finally be peaceful in the world. There'd be no more destruction, no more war, no more death. If I let go and disappeared into the great blue abyss, my companions would be free.

So would I.

I let my fingers slide from the railing and leaned forward. The air rushed against my face as I fell into the salty waves.

"NO!" Aryx lunged over the railing, grasping my wrist.

My legs dangled in midair, feet skimming the cool waterline.

"It's okay," I whispered."Just let me go. I'll be fine. You'll be fine. I'll be free."

"Elpis, snap out of it! Stop struggling while I pull you up." His fingers were tight against my wrist, spreading a dull pain through my arm.

He didn't understand. I yearned for this. I needed that glorious creature against my body. More than I'd needed anything ever before. Those emerald eyes ignited something within me that nothing else ever could. I wanted, more than anything, to be free of this hurt. This pain. This guilt. That divine creature, dripping with grace, offered peace in the palm of his hand. Everything screamed at me to grasp it and sink beneath the surface.

"Let me go! Just let me go! Let me go! Let me go!" I shrieked, my free hand clenched into a fist as I punched toward his face.

"Elpis, stop! I'm trying to help you!" Aryx shouted, his grip tightening until it felt like my wrist would snap.

He wasn't saving me. He was damning me to a life full of hatred and sadness and fear above the waves. I needed to escape, to take the plunge into the numb existence that waited for me. I couldn't possibly let him pull me back. My fist connected with his jaw in a swift, frantic uppercut.

"Fuck Elpis, stop!" My wrist slipped from his grip as it loosened from the shock of my punch.

I would take the freedom offered and nothing would stop me. With legs failing and fists swinging, Aryx was forced to release me.

A rush of air exhaled from my lungs as my head sank beneath the surface. Drifting through the water column, all light faded into the murky depths until I was shrouded in complete darkness. My lungs burned, begging for air, but I ignored them.

This was the way to freedom.

This was the way to peace.

I closed my eyes and embraced the panic.

The pressure built in my chest as I sank through the water column. All thoughts faded away until a quiet peace settled in. This was my escape, my freedom. Letting the haze take over, my eyelids drifted closed. The rhythm of my heartbeat slowed as the ache to breathe subsided. I knew I was drowning, but I couldn't force myself to care. Death felt like an old friend when he came, appearing in glimpses of the numbness I sought for my whole life. He wrapped his warm arms around me until we became one entity, suspended in water, suspended in time.

My heels brushed the sandy bottom. It was close now, my release. The binds around my heart loosened. Any second now and I would be free. The tingles, although faint, tickled up my legs in protest. I fought to suppress them. This demon of mine, she refused to dissolve. Feeling the sediment slip between my toes, I pushed her back. After all, this wasn't her decision. She wasn't in control. I was.

I waited to fade to black. Any second now and I would cease to exist. Perfect.

Slimy weeds slithered from the ocean floor and wrapped themselves tightly around my ankles, interrupting my sweet, peaceful death.

My eyes shot open.

I'd been here before.

Although my vision was still blurred, my mind cleared from the fog they had lured me into. Like knives stabbing against the interior walls of my skull, my brain yearned for oxygen. I had to breathe. Panic sunk in as I realized just how close I had come.

Reaching for my dagger, I said my goodbyes to death and slit the weeds from my ankles before they could restrain me further. With each slice, a new weed appeared, holding me in place.

Slice, a vine wrapped around my ankle.

Slice, another around my wrist.

Slice, around my neck.

The slimy weeds wrapped themselves around every inch of exposed skin, forcing the dagger from my hand. I was like a mummy, frantically wailing to escape its dressings.

My muscles pleaded for oxygen. If I didn't act soon, I'd shut down, leaving the last remnants of life to bubble to the surface. The weeds tightened, totally immobilizing me.

I'd made a grave mistake letting those creatures take over my mind. This was how it ended. There would be no clearing to escape to. I wouldn't grow old, I wouldn't love again, I wouldn't exist at all. Even my demon had faded from me when I called for her.

I truly was going to die. This time, when death appeared, I greeted him as my enemy. He took hold of my hand. My vision blurred as black speckles splintered my eyesight. They doubled. Then tripled. My ears rang from the lack of breath in my lungs, the high-pitched tone sending final shivers down my spine.

Just on the verge of collapsing, a body dove into the water above me. Bubbles raced around it like a torpedo shooting for its target. They sped closer and through my blinded haze, I could make out only a glint of blonde hair in the dim rays of light refracting from the surface.

Aryx.

The binds loosened as he clawed them away, freeing my feet, then my ankles, my calves. As each strand of slithering weed fell away and drifted limply on the ocean currents, my muscles regained their strength.

Fully freed from my watery chains, Aryx wrapped his arms around me and paddled for the surface, biceps straining from my added weight. Where the weeds had once been, my skin oozed with blood, searing in the high salinity of the water.

Finally, gaping for air and sputtering up salt water, we broke the surface.

"Hurry. Swim for the ships!" he panted, releasing me from his hold.

I swam as fast as I could until every muscle in my body was on the brink of exhaustion. Strong, calloused hands dragged me back on the deck, leaving me heaving up water on the wooden boards. I turned to my side, letting the air flood into my lungs.

Crew members, draped against the railing, reached for the scaled creatures that beckoned to them. Arcturas lunged down the line of them, sinking her teeth into their calves and ripping them to the deck, knocking them unconscious. Like a line of dolls, they now lay limp on the deck, bite marks sunken into their raggedy limbs. I rolled on to my back and watched as a small, white cloud overhead dissipated.

My drenched clothes stuck to me like glue. Tugging at the tunic collar, I released a few shallow breaths. I was alive. I closed my eyes, letting relief wash through me like the calm waters below. Then my blood grew cold as realization sunk its sharp fangs into me.

Aryx.

He was right behind me. He should be beside me by now, celebrating another narrow escape from death.

"Where is he?" I stumbled to my feet and scanned the confused faces of my men. "Where is Aryx? He was in the water with me."

"I don't see him, My Queen. Are you sure?" a sailor

asked, scanning the rolling swells.

"Yes, I'm sure," I hissed, leaning against the railing to search the dark waters myself. Nothing. Not a single sign of life.

He was right there.

Right behind me.

Without a second thought, I dove off the deck and swam through the turbid water. Stroking further and further into the depths, searching for his golden hair in the muck.

He was right behind me.

Something must have happened. I dove further, passing lifeless scaly creatures floating in a cloud of dark purple blood. Their beauty had faded along with their lives, leaving only grotesque, slimy bodies with rows of razor-sharp teeth and long, pointed claws.

My lungs burned, begging me to go back. Frightened to be again sinking through the water column, my mind raced, praying to the gods I'd survive this. It was stupid to dive back in, but I couldn't leave him.

I paused and drifted against the harsh current, scanning the water beneath me for any sign of him. Golden tendrils of hair rippled in the remaining sunlight.

There.

Swimming as fast as I could, I rushed toward his distended body and wrapped myself around his waist. My frantic kicks propelled us back toward the surface while the all too familiar black spots speckled my vision. Throwing my arm tightly around his waist, I gasped for air as we finally broke through.

"Over here!" I called, gliding across the water with Aryx in arm.

The crew rose to their feet, extending hands over the railing to help pull us to safety. It took all of my strength to lift the half-god up toward the ship. A sailor grabbed his collar and he disappeared over the rail. I knew I was safe when I felt the sailor's calloused hands tuck under my armpits and lift me out of the sea.

Chapter 43

"He isn't breathing!" I cried, leaning over Aryx's
cold, soaked body. I tore at the leather straps of his
breastplate and flung it aside. The heavy thud as it hit
the deck was the only sound in an eerie stillness that had
fallen over our crew.

I tilted his head back, opened his mouth, and breathed
into his lungs. There was a faint rise and fall when I exhaled into him.

"Come on Aryx, wake up," I cried, pressing my lips
against his. Continuing to breathe into him, I watched
the rise and fall, rise and fall, rise and fall. Something felt
different inside me. It felt empty, like a piece of myself was
gone, leaving a vacancy that begged to be filled.

"Wake up!" My throat tightened with the onset of
panic. Pushing our mouths together, I exhaled my life into
him, hoping that some shred of me could bring him back.

"Aryx, please, wake up."

The crew was silent, unsure how to handle my desperate pleading. They all knew what I had decided couldn't be

true.

"Wake up!" I screamed, slapping the half-god across the cheek. Rather than retracting against the force, his neck simply rolled to the side. His cheek sagged against the deck boards.

His skin was so cold, so grey. I barely recognized him. He was someone I'd never met before. The lips that had once been so warm, so soothing and gentle against mine, were now a dull shade of blue. The eyes that had once burned so brightly, like the first rays of morning sun, were now muted and tarnished. His hands were so limp, the muscles like bags of sand molded to the hard flatness of the deck.

"Wake up!" I hit him again, hoping the inflicted pain would snap him out of unconsciousness.

He simply remained there, unmoving, unseeing, entirely lifeless.

"Don't go, Aryx. Don't go, don't go, don't go."

Every piece of me broke as I watched his complexion grey.

"Don't leave me. I need you. Please," I whispered, "Come back to me."

His body was too still. There was no electricity spiking between us when my lips met his. I continued breathing for him anyway, continued praying, continued hoping. He still wouldn't breathe for himself.

The hum I felt in my chest when we were close was no longer there. The man laying before me, who used to be so full of life, so full of fight, was now merely an empty vessel.

Vacant of everything except sea water.

He was gone.

My ribs caved in, crushing every muscle and organ inside my body.

He was gone.

I couldn't breathe, couldn't see, couldn't think. Sobs escaped my lips as I crumpled over his lifeless frame. He couldn't be gone. I couldn't do this without him. This man I shared my bed with. This man I shared my heart with. The holder of my secrets, the keeper of my thoughts.

This man that I loved.

I knew in this moment that's what it was. Love. The heartbreak now poisoning my veins wasn't for mere lust or friendship, it was for love.

I screamed and screamed and screamed and screamed. And screamed.

The man I loved was gone.

I'd never hold him again.

I'd never feel his warmth against me again.

I'd never tell him I loved him.

All the surrounding colors faded to grey. The water that was once so blue and vivid, was now a shade of black. The air in my lungs caught fire and seared my insides.

This was excruciating. I'd been tortured, beaten, broken, betrayed, captured, hated. Nothing would ever compare to this. My body felt as if it was being shredded apart. The world was wiped away, leaving us suspended in this moment.

Leaving me suspended in this moment.

There was no us anymore. He was gone. There would never be an us. That realization plunged itself into me further, tearing through my lungs, slashing my heart into pieces, perforating my stomach.

I screamed until my voice died and all that was left were pathetic gulps as I clenched the fabric of his tunic, afraid to let go.

"My Lady, he's gone." Lytos was kneeling beside me. I hadn't noticed him. He placed his large hand on my shoulder. It was cold and uncomfortable. There was no warmth in his embrace when he wrapped his long arms around me. All the progress I made snapped in one instant.

Funny how something you've worked your whole life for can be taken from you in mere seconds. Sometimes, the only way to fully know how much you cherish another is to have them ripped away. One fleeting moment and they're gone. A mere stitch of infinity causing a lifetime of destruction.

I receded back into the shadows.

My vision tunneled.

He was gone.

I loved him and he was gone.

Everything was numb, diluted. I barely felt the sharp ache in my toes, the tingles racing through me. I barely felt the glow of my power as the demon pounced. I barely felt her explode. I barely felt everyone around me launch into the air at the pulse of energy erupting from my very core.

Arcturas howled as the grey sky shifted to black and the moon peaked from the horizon, zooming to its zenith. Regaining my voice, I screamed again, throwing my head back. Our voices became one as we called to the moon, called to Polaris. An amethyst glow encapsulated my body as the demon took command.

"My Queen! Please! Stop!" one sailor begged.

I lunged for him, digging my fingers into his chest. The shadows plunged through him, melting away his tunic, then his skin, then his muscle until I exposed the racing beat of his heart to the cool air.

One after another, I tore into the crew, exposing their organs to the world. Following my lead, Arcturas pounced from one to the next, shredding the arteries in their necks until the pine decking was permanently stained red.

Only one man remained, trembling beneath a silver shield. I stepped toward him as he pleaded and begged.

"Lady Elpis, this isn't you. Please," Lytos cried as I ripped the shield away from him. The metal melted in my hands.

"Please, Elpis. Please. Don't do this. Please. It won't bring him back."

His words were muffled to my ears, as if all sound had

evaporated from the earth. I took a step toward him, violent whispers licking the walls of my mind.

"Elpis. Listen to me. I understand what you're going through. It's agony. But please, fight. I know you're in there somewhere," he cried, sliding away from me.

I took another step, my fists clenched so hard my nails dug into flesh. Droplets of blood fell from my palms and spattered on the pine.

"Fight this Elpis. Come back to us." Lytos's eyes were wild with terror.

I didn't want to fight. I didn't want to resurface. It was safe here, letting the demon take control. Like a switch had flipped, I shut everything out. All the pain was gone. Numb. I was right where I intended to stay.

"Elpis, please. Think of my son. He needs me, just like you said."

Judas smiled with moon cake crumbs smothered across his little lips. What would his father say when he asked why Aryx hadn't returned? How do you explain death to a child without robbing them of their innocence?

Would Lytos lie and say that Aryx had gone on another journey? Maybe somewhere off the continent, never to return?

Or would he tell him the truth? Would he sit his young son down and explain the laws of mortality?

I sunk further into the darkness.

"Aryx is gone. We need you."

We need you. A small piece of me escaped from the shadows. I turned away from Lytos and glanced at the pale, dead man lying beside us. The dead man I loved. These people were my crew. My soldiers. My friends. I slaughtered them all.

"Your people need you, Elpis. Come back to us. He wouldn't want this." With trembling knees, Lytos rose to face me.The tingles receded slightly, and I fell to my knees. Leaning over Aryx, tears streaming down my face, I dug my fingers into his damp skin. The silver light of the moon washed over him.

I screamed again, the strands of hair falling across my face, sticking to the sobs flooding down my cheeks. Nothing would ever be the same again. I ruined it. How many families had I taken a father, a brother, a son from? How many lives did I change forever with my lack of control?

I was the monster they called me.

Shadows faded into his chest and the web of his veins glowed purple. They intensified until the surrounding darkness washed away, in its place the vibrant colors of the borealis. I pushed my power into him, feeling my energy deplete. I didn't care if I died, expanding the shadows until they swarmed us both. If I could save him, death would be worth it. The world deserved him more than it did me.

Sweat beaded on my brow as I continued pushing. Like the tide receding back to the sea, I felt the demon in my chest slowly fade. The back of my hands bleached pale. The half-god beneath me remained still, his neck still crooked, his eyes still cemented shut.

Arcturas howled behind me, her voice strained and weak. Giving my power to Aryx was draining her, too. She stumbled next to me, her legs giving out beneath her muscular abdomen. Staring up at me, her eyes pleaded for me to stop, begged me to redact my shadows.

"I can't," I whispered, digging my nails further into his cold chest.

Arcturas struggled to stay upright. She wavered heavily with the ocean swells. Finally, her legs couldn't hold her, and she collapsed onto the deck. Whining, she nudged her nose into my thigh, imploring me to stop.

"I'm so sorry," I choked, watching her brilliant yellow eyes fade, like a fire slowly extinguishing into the curtain of night. "I'm sorry."

Arcturas whined again. My body was tired, depleted of all energy, but I pushed on. I ignored the cramp spreading through my arms, stiffening my fingers into stone. My power fought against me as I willed it into Aryx's body. He needed it more than me. Even if it meant sacrificing myself, I would continue to push. His chest twitched against my pulse. I sucked in a breath, watching for another sign of life. His skin, still grey, now webbed with tendrils of glowing light.

My knees gave out, forcing me to fall on to his rigid body. No matter how much of myself I gave him, it was no use. His cheeks were still cold, his body still empty. Arcturas sagged into me, her breathing ragged and shallow. I'd come so close to death so many times. He was a friend, then an enemy, now salvation.

"My child..." a woman's voice whispered behind me. The words were as delicate as a flake of snow, floating down to earth. I felt the world go silent in her presence, emulating starlight within each tired beat of the heart buried in my chest. Polaris.

I continued clutching Aryx's chest, refusing to turn and face her.

"Mother," I whispered, "I can't fix this. He's not healing. I've failed you."

"Elpis, it's time to rise. It's time to continue the fight. It's time to let go," she said, placing a cool, gentle hand against my back.

"I can't. I can't. I can't."

Her slender fingers brushed against my cheek as the goddess knelt beside me.

"You have to. He's gone. You'll drain yourself for nothing. You can't heal a soul that's already left its body," she said.

"No. Mother, help me." I looked at her, pleading for something I knew wasn't possible. "Bring him back."

"You know I can't, my love. I wish I could, but his soul is in the immortal realm now."

"Bring him back. I can't do this without him. Mother, I

love him." I fell to the deck, paralyzed beneath the weight of the world.

"Elpis..." she trailed off, smoothing back my hair.

"Mother, I love him. I can't do this."

"I wish I could," she whispered, reaching for my hand.

"It hurts too much. I can't take it. I can't breathe."

The weight of the sky plundered down my throat, collapsing my lungs, squeezing my heart until it nearly burst. Polaris stroked her palm down Arcturas's spine, brushing back the wiry line of fur, disheveled from battle.

The wolf's abdomen swelled back to life, her muscles inflating with newfound strength. I held my breath, watching the opening and closing of her ribcage as her energy returned.

"Elpis. Look at me." Polaris tilted my chin up to meet her gaze.

The purple in her eyes blazed, and I saw my face staring back at me.

"You are strong. You are a warrior. Don't let this destroy you." She stroked my cheek. "He wouldn't want that."

"I never told him." The words seared against my hoarse vocal cords, exhausted from sadness.

"He knows. He's always known," she said.

"Bring him back."

She pulled me into an embrace, cradling me against her delicate frame. I'd never received such comfort before. Never felt the gentle hug or the safety of a mother's warmth. Leaning into her further, I sobbed until my eyes swelled shut. Everything faded away. The slaughtered crew, the darkness of the night, my lifeless love. I was a child again in her arms.

I'm not sure how long she cradled me, hushing away the pain, running her long fingers down my spine. But finally, when everything eased into a dull ache and the trembling ceased, she pulled me to my feet.

"It's time to fight," she whispered, stroking my cheek.

Blurry-eyed and hiccuping, I wiped the last tears from my eyes.

"It's time to fight."

"My men are gone. Our army is dwindling, exhausted from the seas. I'm not sure that we can," I said, wrapping my fingers in hers.

"You will find a way. I know it, my love." She smiled and faded into the night.

Chapter 44

After everything he saw, Lytos agreed to withhold the actual events of what happened to the remaining warships. Conducting a mass burial at sea, we spread word to the fleet that the creatures we fought had lured them to their deaths. Every inch of me dripped with disgust, but I held it together, putting on a stone face and watching as the northern currents carried their bodies home. We'd lost nearly our entire crew, and most that remained were seriously wounded. Our able soldiers were spread thin.

Each warship struggled to maintain their general upkeep. By extending watch and oar duties to account for missing bodies, discontent spread like a brutal plague. Grumbles of mutiny whispered their way through the dark crevices beneath the waterline as exhausted men rubbed their aching muscles and rested their salt-crusted eyes.

Lytos had placed Aryx's body on the bow, draping a golden cloth over his vacant expression. I couldn't bring myself to go up there or to even look at it from the aft deck.

I refused to let him drift alone at sea. Once this was over, we'd bring him home, lay him to rest beneath the green pastures beside the stables.

That's what he'd want.

And so, we sailed on, a rage in our bellies like a kindling fire. We were sick with vengeful thoughts as the memories of lives lost hung heavy in the ocean air. With every mile closer, my hatred grew, devouring my thoughts, until all I could think of was slicing the Spring Queen's head clean off her pretty, slender neck.

She caused this war. She was the reason we were here. It was easier to hate than it was to grieve, and so I did.

After the sun set on another full day of sailing, Elder's Island came into view. It was time to divide our fleet. Hermia guided her ships west, while we continued east. Lytos remained by my side at every waking moment. Not out of loyalty, I imagined, but out of distrust. He kept a constant, watchful eye, waiting for the moment I broke again.

The demon, with a taste of control, clawed at my mind with a fierceness I'd never felt before. My rage stoked her fire, fueling her power, locked away in brittle chains. All my attention shifted to keeping her buried deep in the pit of my core. Constant reminders of slaughtered men and blank, death-clouded eyes were the only way to keep her at bay. She had injected the toxic taste of bloodshed, like a poison, into my veins, and I found it harder and harder to envision the future I was fighting for. Without Aryx, I was nothing. He'd been the link to a life outside of death. With that link severed, I floated away, lost and isolated in the violence of monstrosity.

When our ships neared the eye line of sentries, Altair appeared on our aft deck.

"Lady Elpis," he said, crossing his arms over his chest, "are your men ready? Once I've summoned these storms, it won't be safe in deep water anymore. You'll need to take refuge below the cliff side."

I nodded against a clenched jaw. Our crew was already struggling. I wasn't so sure we could handle the raging fury of an immense squall. Even so, we had no choice. We'd come this far and our only option was to push on.

Altair closed his eyes, breathing in the steady breeze that filled our sails. Glorious golden beams rippled from his chest as the surrounding waters stilled to a halt. He rose into the air, seeming to float above the deck. As he made his ascent, the orb of light around him brightened and burned like the midday sun. A hush fell over warships as we all watched the immortal hold the strength of the seas in the palm of his hand.

His skin ignited in flames as he stretched his palms into the sky. Shielding my eyes from the intensity of the heat now radiating through his flesh, I watched as the immortal took his true form. He was the embodiment of the sun. Summer heat incarnate.

The world shuddered at the sheer force of him. Wind howled against the spirals of power emitting from his strong, muscular arms. Waves thrashed across our bow, growing in size with each raging swell. The clouds above darkened, suppressing even the most minuscule of light ike a curtain drawn against the sky. Pressure plummeted from the air, in its place came a damp smell of thunder sharp on the nose.

Altair rose higher, encouraging the elements to unleash their fury. A crack of lightning zipped through the sky as the storm built around us. The boom of thunder, as deafening as a wrathful cannon, charged through the sky.

A cry for the impending battle.

The air thickened until it begged for its saturated release. Like a vicious symphony, the sky pleaded to its conductor for the final note of this wild crescendo.

With a snap of his finger, Altair freed the storm. The sky split open. Rain spewed from the heavens, creating a veil over the horizon that stretched infinitely across the sky.

"You must go! Now!" Altair called, his voice bellowed with another jolt of thunder, shaking the bones between muscle tissue.

"Oars! At the ready!" the oarsman commanded.

Like the heartbeat of the ship, the drum below decks pounded in rhythm. The grunts of sailors sent shocks between the ship's timbers as we picked up our speed. Hurtling through the waves, we raced the storm. Wind shrieked through the masts. Rain drops fired like small bullets through the air. Flashes of lightning cracked across the sky.

Chaos broke out as sailors bustled about the deck, uncoiling lines and raising our sails to increase speed. The oarsman barked orders at his crew. Below deck, the rowers heaved their massive wooden blades in a synchronized frenzy that hurtled us forward, closer and closer to our destination. Wave crests met pine in violent outbursts of salty spray, washing away in the rain as fast as they collided with the deck. I clung to the starboard railing, steadying myself against the fierce sway of the hull.

A massive swell sunk the leeward side of the deck to the waterline, sending men sliding down the incline and rolling into the dark waves. Feeling my feet slip out from under me, I dug my nails into the railing, the wash of the sea snapping at my worn, leather boots.

"Take hold!" the oarsman roared, straining against his oar as its handle whipped against the aft deck. The timbers groaned in protest as the warship turned into the oncoming swells. My stomach plummeted into my heels as the rail raised into the air, sending me catapulting to the opposing side. The cliffs grew closer as the squall engulfed us.

Through the eyes of a sentry, our fleet was merely a blur, hidden beneath a thick wall of dark, grey cloud, approaching the shoreline with unearthly speed. Under the blanket of darkness, we moored, stowing our sails with trembling urgency, against the towering cliffs.

Our final preparations for war had begun.

Chapter 45

Arcturas paced through the captain's quarters, her black fur now encased in golden armor. I strapped my black leather breastplate to my chest, pulling its straps tight and triple knotting them. With my mother's hair clip tucked neatly into my bun, I stared in the mirror.

The woman looking back at me was a stranger. She had the same black hair, same violet eyes, but her cheekbones weren't hollow anymore. Her jaw was not as sharp. Eyes that used to be dim, now burned brightly with new found ferocity. Shadows lurked just beneath her skin, creeping and wriggling around her neck every so often. She was a new type of beast. One that both terrified and repulsed me.

Mixing a bowl of black ink, I took my brush and painted thick lines beneath my eyes that trailed down to my collarbones.

The mark of the warrior.

Aryx's marks.

I knew what they meant, how much he resented them.

It was time I gave them a new meaning.

I tucked my key into the folds of my tunic, kneeled on the plush red rugs, and whispered a prayer to the gods. We were going in with a dwindling army and a broken leader. A soft knock on the door pulled me from prayer. It was Lytos, his short, dark hair hidden beneath a golden helmet. A golden breastplate, littered with scars, had replaced his usual flax tunic. He was every bit of a soldier as Aryx had once been. Tucked under his arms was a bronze broadsword, its hilt inlaid with small citrine gems.

"Lady Elpis, the men are ready," Lytos said. His voice was a low, steady pulse amidst the apprehension that buzzed through me.

"Okay, thank you, Lytos. We'll be on deck shortly. I wanted to double check Arcturas's armor and make sure it's secure before battle." I clasped my shaking hands behind my back.

"Are you ready for this?" he asked, watching my lip tremble.

"Yes," I whispered, sucking in a breath. I wanted to scream at him, to throw myself against his solid chest. How could I possibly be ready? I was about to lead my men to their deaths. Our numbers were nearly half what they'd been when we set sail. We were about to march into an undeniable defeat.

"I guess that's not a fair question." His bronze greaves clanked against varnished wood as he took a seat by Arcturas on a velvet-cushioned settee. "What I really should ask is, are you okay with all of this?"

I sat beside him, checking the leather ties between the golden plates of armor across Arcturas's chest. She grunted, lifting her arm. A request for scratches. I gently complied, sliding my fingers beneath her chest plate and stroking her thick, black fur.

"No. Of course not, but I don't have a choice anymore.

326

We've come this far."

Lytos nodded thoughtfully. The ever-silent observer. The quiet teacher.

"I wanted to give this to you," he said, handing me the sheathed broadsword. "It was Aryx's. I know he'd want you to use it today."

I swallowed the lump in my throat, trying to force down the pain that welled in my eyes at the mention of his name. The sword was breath-taking. Its blade, although solid gold, was as light as steel and perfectly balanced. The metal edge gleamed like the rising sun. A trail of citrine gems, laced in intricate engravings, followed the center-line of the blade.

"It was his father's before him. Passed down through their bloodline. See the markings on the hilt? Their family sigil," Lytos pointed to the carved sun, crested by a shield of ivy.

"It's beautiful, but I don't deserve it," I said, running a finger down the blade.

"Of course you do. You were everything to him," he said, smiling sadly.

"Please stop," I said, my words quivering off my tongue. "I can't take this."

Lytos grew quiet, his eyebrows curved with an ever-growing concern. We sat in silence, both examining the sword, unsure of what to say. Two strangers grieving over a mutual friend. It was uncomfortable, unconsolable. I was the reason his brother was dead. I was the reason we didn't stand a chance against Tethys.

"Lytos, can I ask you a question?"

"Of course, anything," he said, turning to face me.

"Why are you so kind? I killed Aryx. I slaughtered our crew. I took you from your family- your wife, your son. I don't understand. After everything you've witnessed, why?"

He stroked his chin and settled into his seat. His ocean

blue eyes, simmering with sincerity.

"You know," he started, his voice serious and quiet. "We've all done things we regret. We've all been the villain in another's story. Aryx didn't tell you much about me, or my past, and I will always be grateful for his discretion. I'm not originally from Venia. My mother is, but I was born in Aquilae. I remember little of my real father. All I know is that I wasn't expected, nor was I wanted. Before my first birthday, he sent us back to the East, left behind. My real father never claimed me as his son, and to this day, although I don't even know his name, I've resented him for it.

"As a child I imagined what I would say to him if I ever had the chance. I envisioned screaming at him, asking why he didn't love me, why he abandoned us. I was so full of anger and uncertainty about my identity, I tried to figure out who I was through other avenues. I was a thief, then a mercenary, then a soldier. I bounced from one thing to the next.

"When my mother married my stepfather, she was happy for a while, but he was a drunk and I never wanted him. It had always been just us, and that was all I needed. I refused to understand why she'd want to share our lives with someone else, and I resented her for it. But I hated him even more.

"The first time he hit my mother, I threatened him with a butter knife. I was six. I remember that day so clearly. How the blood trickled from her nose and her eye swelled shut from where he'd punched her. I was furious with him for hurting her, but I was even more furious with her for choosing a man that would do such a thing." He looked down at his boots. The leather toe glistened from fresh polish.

"It was always a cycle. He'd hit her. Chaos would ensue. Then a few days later he'd apologize profusely, making false claims that he'd stop drinking and be a better husband, a better father. It started with a black eye here and there, which turned into broken ribs, broken arms. The last time he attacked her, he threw her down the stairs, nearly killing her. I didn't even think twice when I lunged for him and stabbed him through the heart.

"Rather than thanking me for saving her life, my mother called me a monster. A cold-blooded killer. She sent me away, shipping me off to the soldier's encampments. I hated her for it, too. I used my anger to train, quickly rising the ranks among us, and because of it, the other boys never fully accepted me. Then I met Aryx. He didn't judge me for the blood on my hands or the crimes I'd committed. He accepted all of it. Eventually, he became family. Probably the only I truly ever had." Lytos paused, his voice wavering against a sob.

I couldn't bear to hear his pain, his sadness. In the hours that passed, I let my rage distract me from the harshness of reality. Not only had I lost the man I loved, Lytos had lost his closest friend, his most trusted confidant, his brother.

"I'm so sorry," I whispered, refusing to meet his gaze.

"To wrap up this long-winded answer to your question before, why am I kind to you? Even after everything you've done? It's because that's what Aryx would do. He was kind to a broken boy who was lost in the darkness. He accepted my demons and was patient, supportive, caring. He is the only person who stayed when everyone else in my life had left."

I hadn't noticed the silent tears streaming down my cheeks as he spoke.

"Thank you," I whispered, unsure of what else to say. "Thank you."

"There's no need to thank me." He smiled, taking my hand in his. "Now, take the sword. You're the only one who can wield it."

I took the sheathe in my hands, feeling the smooth

leather against my fingertips. It hummed against my touch, as if the blade within was alive. Holding his weapon, it was as if Aryx was here beside me. Guiding me through the shadows of heartbreak. Guiding me into the light.

"Now, I'll ask you again. Are you ready for this?"

I stood, strapping the sword across my back.

"Yes," I said, and for the first time in a very long time, I truly was.

Chapter 46

Our archers launched their leads into the cliff side. Hundreds of ropes dangled from the rock as they grasped hold and began their climb. The plan, as discussed, was to sneak up the cliff side, gather our forces, then launch our attack on the fortress gates.

My muscles burned as I climbed my lead. Arcturas rose from the cliff, seated on a rickety wooden platform. The wind ripped through us, tearing strands of hair loose from my bun. An occasional whip of a lead broken from stone whooshed passed me, sending the soldier attached to it plunging into the black depths. I tried not to think of the men as they fell, how terrified they must be, how unready for death they were.

Rain washed the glistening sweat from my brow as we continued our ascent. Aryx would have hated this. The climb up the southern mountain was nothing compared to this height. I smiled, thinking of the half-god clinging to the rock, his powerful legs quivering, frozen in fear. As courageous and stoic as he was, he had his weaknesses.

Vibrations rippled down my spine as the golden blade strapped to my back came alive with his memory. The fear of an impending battle faded away, knowing a remnant of him would be by my side.

My palms were raw with rope burn when I finally reached the top. Throwing my leg over the ledge and rolling across the grass, I caught my breath. Only a few hundred soldiers, hunched over and exhausted from the climb, remained. This definitely wouldn't be enough.

"My Queen, we're ready," Balakros whispered beside me.

I nodded, leading my men toward the white fortress gate in the distance. Arcturas strutted low beside me, her ears on alert for any warning of a threat. There were none. Not a single breath of life around us. Lytos caught my eye from across the field, shaking his head. Suspicion wrinkled at the corners of his mouth.

"Something's not right here," I whispered, crouching behind the large stone carving of the Northern Elder.

"I know. It's too quiet. Too easy," Balakros said, scanning the fortress in front of us. I raised my fist for my men to halt. They too hid low in the grass, awaiting my signal.

Everyone stopped breathing.

Everyone was silent.

Only the soft chirp of crickets and a steady downpour of rain filled the seaside air.

Metal glinted in the moonlight from the keep's turrets. Shit.

"Shields!" I barked behind me. It was too late. The sky lit up with thousands of silver arrows. The clamoring of armor behind me filled the air as most of them struck true.

"GO! NOW!" I roared, lunging forward. We sprinted across the field, dodging wave after wave of arrows. I unsheathed the sword, gripping its hilt as I trudged through the mud. Arcturas weaved around man after man until we arrived at the gate. Stained in dirt, drenched to the core, my men and I flung ourselves at the keep, the adrenaline of battle pumping through our bloodstreams.

"Get the ram ready!" I barked, shielding myself from another wave of arrows.

Time seemed to stand still as soldiers, impaled with arrows, seeped blood into the rain soaked grass. Moving in slow motion, the crowd divided to make way for the heavy, iron ram. I searched through the chaos for Lytos. Muddy faces littered the grass, their eyes burning with gritty barbarity.

This was war.

Bloody, deadly, war.

It stole the air from my lungs. Bodies of men sunk into mud, forever lost to the ones they loved. Blood trickled from wounds, staining the trampled ground permanently red. Lytos dove past an arrow, just barely escaping its deadly point. The silver arrowhead sliced his tricep as he rolled through the muck. With crusted, brown armor, he sprinted forward, roaring with the rage of a lion toward its prey.

Blood pumped through my veins at a million miles a minute. The ram retracted with the grunts of its men. Strained muscles flexed beneath their dirt speckled arms as they struggled to swing it backward.

"Push!" Balakros commanded, sending the ram forward. The heavy stone gates creaked in protest against the force. An arrow shot through the air, piercing the front soldier clean through his skull.

We were lambs brought to slaughter. Another wave of death pelted down on us as the ram continued to pound on the door.

I needed to buy them some time.

Taking a breath, I called for the tingles. I'm in control. The demon scratched against the walls in my mind. I'm in control. She growled in protest, refusing to follow my orders. I sheathed my blade and planted my boots in the mud. Grounding me. Keeping me from the shadows. The tingles spread up my legs, into my chest, out to the tips of my fingers. Arcturas growled beside me, her snout wrinkled into a savage snarl. Sinking her claws into the soft muck, she howled at the sky.

Night spread across the horizon once more, blanketing us in the stealth of darkness. The demon slammed against the bars of her cage, furious that I was siphoning her power. I risked losing to her by dancing so close to the shadows, but it was necessary. With the lack of light, the sentries were shooting blind. Arrows continued to dart towards us, but without their visible target, they were easy to dodge.

Loose strands of hair floated around me as sheer, primordial power pulsed through my veins. The sword across my back hummed, its blade beaming like the glorious rays of an early morning sun. I closed my eyes, picturing Aryx beside me, keeping me in the present.

Filling my lungs with the misty seaside air, I reached out my hands. Beams of magenta shot into the sky. The turrets burst into flames as creatures were launched from their posts, hurtling to the ground below. Their sinewy skin, devoured in flames, lit up the night as they fell to their deaths.

"Get those gates down. NOW!" I commanded, continuing to shoot at the walls.

As the fortress burned, the ram splintered through and the heavy stone doors broke from their hinges. As the gate opened, a swarm of deep green, lizard-like monsters slithered from within. They leapt at my men, crushing their skulls beneath rows of razor teeth. One lunged for me and I rolled across the ground, plunging my sword into its chest behind me. Another jumped forward, but before it could land, Arcturas dove over me, ripping the skin from its neck.

Thick, unwavering darkness muffled the cries of men

and monsters alike. Bodies flung around me, some void of limbs, some smothered in bloody grime. Harsh reality set in. We had broken through, but we'd suffered too much loss to press on against this second wave.

Arcturas pounced from one lizard to another, decapitating them with one clean rip of her fangs. Lytos was beside her, the full skill of his swordsmanship on display. Dodging attacks with nearly inhuman speed, he parried and struck with determined, graceful agility. There wasn't a single misstep in his footwork. He outstretched the sword in his hand as if it were the natural extension of his arm. He was glorious. A noble warrior through and through.

"My Queen! Look out!" Balakros cried.

A lizard fell from above, pinning my chest to the ground. It snapped at my neck with immeasurable strength. I flailed, trying to free myself from the incredible weight. My back sunk into the ground, mud oozing between the crevices of my armor, filling my mouth with vile, bloodied dirt. It forced its way down my throat, blocking my airway as I struggled to break free. The creature dug its claws further into my breastplate, snapping with its rows of jagged teeth.

Suddenly, it froze, impaled by a gleaming silver sword. It fell to the ground, twitching as life severed from its body.

A hand reached out from the darkness. "Lady Elpis, are you okay?"

I took it, feeling Lytos's powerful grasp pull me to my feet. The battle carried on around us, the cries of dying men deafening in the night.

"Y-yes. Thank you," I said, pulling my blade from the muck.

"They've taken down the gate. We have to keep moving!" he cried, plunging his weapon into the heart of an oncoming attacker.

I ducked an oncoming blow, throwing myself at the creature. Its throat slit open against my sword's edge. Sprinting through the horde, we dodged and hacked our way to the crippled gate. Like an unstoppable tsunami, creatures poured out in tumultuous waves.

"There's too many of them!" Balakros cried as he plunged his short sword into a sinewy, green chest.

Retracting the blade, the creature fell to the ground, its body squelching in the muck.

"We have to keep pushing forward!" I called, lunging for the gates.

What men remained pressed on, fighting with tireless determination. Carving a path through the mob of enemies, we slipped through the gates.

Somehow, we'd stormed the keep.

The small success gave us newfound energy as the battle continued. The victory cries were short-lived, however. My soldiers froze in their boots, greeted by the monstrosity that awaited us within the keep's walls.

Chapter 47

Towering before us on two legs as thick as oak trunks was a beast with broad, muscular shoulders and two gleaming red eyes. Veins rippled beneath its swollen, tanned biceps and webbed down the length of its arms into enormous hands. A long iron chain hung from where its neck met the bulbous swell of its shoulders. Two sharp horns protruded from each temple. The beast perked up its small angular ears. The iron ring, pierced in its septum, rose and fell with heavy snorts. My legs turned to dust when its large, rounded eyes met mine.

"Good Gods…" Lytos stopped beside me, watching the beast beat its thundering fists against its chest.

"What the fuck is that thing?" I hissed, clenching the hilt of my sword.

Arcturas nipped at my side, wide eyed and frightened by the monstrous obstacle that faced us. Beads of drool dripped from its fanged mouth as clouds of hot breath exhaled from its nostrils. Its eyes were all too familiar, ones

I'd looked upon in both dreams and reality.

"It's the Minotaur. Another beast of legends, like Charybdis and Scylla, before. How in the gods' names did Tethys unleash it?" Lytos whispered, sweat glistening on his brow.

He raised his sword and stepped into a battle stance, awaiting the inevitable attack.

Lifting its thick head to the sky, it let out a roar that shook even the pebbles of earth beneath our feet. My bones rattled against muscle, its battle cry injecting fear into my organs. I couldn't move. My body refused all commands as the Minotaur raised its massive fists toward us.

"Men! At the ready!" Balakros bellowed, his voice trembling against the earth shattering stomp of the Minotaur's heavy feet charging toward us.

The few archers left knocked their bows, preparing to fire. The Minotaur scuffed its feet in the gravel, sending pebbles scattering across the keep's yard. I swallowed hard, raising my blade toward it. The battle outside the fortress gates had gone quiet. Stillness settled in the air. Anticipation twisted and turned through the minds of our men like a spider's silky web. Icy fear creeped into our bellies.

One moment, all was silent, even the tick of time. Then mayhem exploded throughout the yard. The Minotaur charged, lowering its horns as it hurtled toward us. Horn met flesh, flinging men into the air. Bodies zoomed through the sky, bones crunched on impact with solid ground, blood trickled from fatal wounds. Soldiers swung at the Minotaur, but their blades were nowhere near sharp enough to penetrate its tough layer of skin.

I threw myself at the beast, feeling the rush of tingles through my body. My flesh ignited, adrenaline humming in my chest as my blade met sinewy muscle. With all of my might, I plunged it into the Minotaur's back. The metal radiated with power, illuminating the darkness in a wash of amethyst hues.

The beast, now furious, bucked against me, knocking the wind out of my lungs and throwing me from its back. I landed in the muck, cracking my spine against a jagged rock protruding from the ground. Agony boomed through my core, paralyzing me where I lay. I couldn't breathe, couldn't move. The incessant pain now plunging its fangs into my mid-back drowned out all thoughts.

The Minotaur slid my blade from its skin and threw it across the yard. Full of a new found rage, it plowed into my men. All I could do was watch as it threw them to the ground, tearing limb from limb. Our forces were dwindling. We couldn't withstand much more of this. I needed to do something.

Lytos dove for the beast, his sword raised overhead, fully intending to strike. Before he could, however, the Minotaur rocked backwards, its horn plunging through his abdomen. Everything and everyone around us froze. Lytos dropped his weapon, growing limp as realization kicked in.

"NO!" I cried, watching as the Minotaur lunged for him again.

Lytos fell to his knees, strength draining from him with the blood that seeped from his wound. The gravel beneath his feet was painted red, stained with bloodshed. Struggling to rise, I crawled to him, my hands and knees bloodied from the rough ground.

His eyes were cloudy as I cradled his body in my arms. Blood trickled from his mouth. Placing his hands over the gaping hole, I watched him gurgle and choke on the fluid filling his throat.

"Keep pressure on this. Please. Lytos, stay with me," I cried, dragging him from the center of the battle.

The Minotaur snorted and charged toward us. This was it. This was the end. I was too weak to fight back. Even in full strength, I was no match for this supernatural beast. I clenched my weapon, praying to the gods to spare me.

Begging my mother for help.

As it approached, I held up my blade. My muscles cramped against the weight of the weapon. I was going to die. Lytos stared up at me, placing his hand on my cheek. He had accepted our fate, seeking the comfort of an old friend as we faced death together. The beast hurtled towards us, the muscles beneath its skin flexing with each powerful stride.

"I'm so sorry, Lytos," I whispered, closing my eyes.

Tears rolled down my cheeks, and I thought of Aryx. I thought of his perfect smile and the golden flecks in his eyes. I thought of the little crease in his cheek when he laughed and the way his hair fell smoothly to his shoulders. A small kernel of relief blinked within me as I realized I'd see him again soon. We would be together again, free from the binds of the mortal realm. There would be no more suffering, no more fighting for something unattainable.

The Minotaur roared, shaking dust from the cracks of the fortress walls. I opened my eyes to look at Lytos one last time. His expression had faded, like his soul leaving his body.

"I'm so sorry." I kissed his cheek and dropped my blade.

The beast froze mid stride, its nose ring extended in midair. Sounds of war faded away and the air thinned as time stopped. The man in my arms melted into the darkness.

"Elpis. This isn't over. Don't accept defeat just yet," a voice whispered in my ear.

Rosemary peppered my nose. I breathed it in, letting its sharpness fill my lungs. A warm hand stroked against my cheek, tipping up my chin. Brilliant golden eyes greeted mine as I opened them.

His touch was electric, sending waves of current through my body. His skin, once faded and grey, now glowed with beams of morning light. The tattoos down his collarbones slithered beneath his flesh, as if they were living things. My limbs turned to jelly as I stared at Aryx with wide, bewildered eyes.

"Am I dead?" I whispered, sucking in a shallow breath.

He smiled at me, tucking a strand of escaped hair behind my ear.

"No, my love. Not yet. But I need you to be strong. I need you to fight." His voice was as quiet as the rustle of leaves in a gentle spring breeze.

"I- I don't understand," I said. "How are you here?"

"You needed me, so I came."

"I've needed you since the moment you left me." A sob rose in my chest as the words I'd told myself over and over in my head finally poured into the air.

"Elpis. You need to fight."

"I'm so tired, Aryx. I can't do this without you. I brought my men to their deaths. Please don't make me do this," I cried, tears streaming down my face.

Aryx wrapped his arms around me, pulling me into a warm embrace. It felt like morning dew and early flower buds. The void in my chest filled, if only for a moment. It was safe here. Familiar. He smoothed back my hair and kissed me on the forehead. It had only been a few days, but I realized then that I'd forgotten what his lips felt like against my skin.

"You have to. The realms need you."

"And I need you," I murmured, letting his warmth melt away the frigid loss in my heart.

He chuckled, the gold in his eyes glimmering with tenderness. "You've never needed me."

"What am I supposed to do? I can't kill this beast. It's too strong and my forces are all depleted. I don't know what became of the other army, but most of my soldiers are dead or wounded. Hyppolytos is..." I trailed off, thinking of my silent teacher.

"Lytos will be okay. He will recover, I promise you. The Minotaur has a weakness. Those glowing red eyes aren't used for sight. I have to go now. I love you. Always."

"No. Please. Don't leave me again. Don't go," I clawed at his biceps, frantic at losing him again.

"Elpis, I must. Keep fighting. This is almost over." He brushed his lips against mine as his skin became translucent.

"No. Please. Stay. Stay with me. Don't go."

He smiled one last time, grasping my hand in his. With one final phrase, he faded into the night. "I love you."

Chapter 48

As if with the snap of a finger, the Minotaur came to life. It raced toward me at lightning speed. The pain of losing Aryx a second time was too much to bear. I locked it down and promised I'd find the time to fully grieve it. But for now, for Lytos, for his son, his wife, I'd have to fight. He'd make it off this island alive, even if it meant I didn't. I gathered what little strength remained and sprinted away from his unconscious body, praying the Minotaur would take my bait. It sniffed the air, finding the trail of my scent. With perked ears, it altered its course.

I skidded to a halt and took a deep breath. If the beast couldn't see me, its other senses would be heightened. Diving to the ground, I rolled in the bloody muck, covering every exposed patch of skin until I was entirely coated in grime. The taste of iron seeped between my lips. The blood of my own men. Dizzy with nausea, I thought of their shredded limbs and vacant eyes. Bile rose in my throat. I swallowed it back down, refusing to come apart. There was a life far more significant than my own on the line.

The Minotaur continued raging toward me. I closed my eyes and took a breath, stilling the heartbeat pounding in my chest. When it was nearly within arm's reach, I side-stepped. Barely dodging its pointed horns, my legs gave out beneath me. It charged right past, slamming into the fortress wall with a force that quaked the keep all the way to its core.

Dazed, it collapsed to its knees.

This was my time to strike.

Pushing my legs as fast as they'd take me, I leapt into the air, clinging to the beast's back. It roared in protest as I squeezed my legs around its chest, feeling the sheer strength of its muscles contract with me. Clawing at its nostrils, my fingers laced around the pierced iron ring.

Perfect.

I pulled with all of my strength. Sinewy flesh ripped as the metal severed from its nose. Blood spurted from the gash, inhibiting its sense of smell. One more attack like this, and it'd be rendered defenseless.

The Minotaur thrashed in fury, shaking me from its back like a dog shaking droplets of water from its fur. I whipped through the air, somersaulting to the ground. My already wounded spine splintered again, sending shock-waves of pain through my body. Biting hard on my bottom lip, I had to suppress the scream of agony flooding up my throat. I couldn't afford to make even the slightest of sounds.

As silent as the northern night air, I flew across the yard and again leapt for the Minotaur. This time, though, it heard me coming. At the last second, it tilted its horns in my direction, piercing the tender muscle between my shoulder and heart. It sliced clean through my breastplate. The wound, although shallow, lit my flesh on fire. Pushing away from the beast, I rolled to the ground. Dirt clung to the gushing wound, sticking to my glistening skin. Fragments of rock sunk into the muscle tissue, piercing my flesh like minuscule needles over and over again.

Arcturas dove for the beast, sinking her fangs into its bloody skin. It roared again, flailing and striking at the wolf. She was too quick for its frenzied attacks, ducking and dodging each swing of its powerful fists. Ignoring the pain, I let the tingles surge through me. I am in control.

Unleashing beams of power from my palms, I stepped toward the beast. They bounced off its chest, sending flashes of light into the darkness. Blisters of burnt, black skin littered the Minotaur's chest, and the smell was overwhelming, like burning hair and cooking meat. I gagged, watching the Minotaur claw at its chest to extinguish the embers melting into its core.

With another step, I freed another beam from my fingertips. It struck again, forcing the Minotaur to its knees. The impact of its colossal weight shook the ground, sending tremors up the sturdy fortress walls. Particles of sand and stone rained down and encrusted us with an additional layer of grime.

I pounced once more, raising my blade overhead, preparing for a final blow. The sword's edge, dripping red, glistened in the night. I swung at the beast, landing on my knees. Two pale ivory horns rolled to my feet.

Consumed by its pain, the Minotaur wavered and sunk into the ground. Glowing ruby eyes, frantic with rage, blinked into the night. I took one last step, wiping the blood from my lower lip.

Using both hands and my full body weight, I plunged my weapon through the beast's heart. It shuddered against me, exhaling one final breath before collapsing into the mud. Steam rolled off the freshly slaughtered carcass. Heat from its powerful body trickled into the night as life waned from its unseeing eyes. I dropped my blade and sunk to my knees, entirely exhausted, wholly broken.

This wasn't over yet, though. What few men remained

scanned the keep for signs of another attack. The bustle of footsteps and clanking of armor greeted us as the eastern and western fortress doors swung open, unleashing another flurry of beasts. This time it wasn't lizard-creatures, however; it was men. Each enemy soldier was plated head to toe in silver armor. Plumes of red horse hair struck from each helmeted head. Like a sea of bristling cardinals, the men swarmed us. Long silver spears and sharp metal clubs circled us, forcing us closer as they encroached into our space. I scanned the yard for Lytos. He remained limp and still where I'd left him. Aryx had promised he was healing, but for now, it was best for our enemies to think him dead.

Arcturas growled deeply, her black, blood-soaked fur straightened along her spine. We were surrounded. The unending flood of bodies stifled the yard air. There were too many lungs and not enough oxygen to spare. I looked at Balakros. His expression was of dark defeat. We were simply outnumbered and entirely on the losing side of this battle. This no longer was a fight; it was a massacre.

A horn bellowed in the distance. What I thought was an earthquake shaking through the fortress gates turned out to be a few hundred soldiers outfitted on horseback. On their black armor shone a simple sigil- a single star with four long points. Hermia and her soldiers had arrived, bringing with them the entire Northern Army.

Chapter 49

The cavalry slammed into men, knocking them to their feet with wide-eyed disbelief. Flowing into the keep like a river of rapids, the Northern Army slashed and stabbed and pushed their way through. Dirt flung through the air as the cavalry carved a path around the sea of bodies to the fortress entrance. Trailing behind them, we stormed through the doors with new found vigor from our allies.

War calls and the dying cries of our enemies echoed through the dark chambers, filling the quiet stillness with a raging chaos. We continued further down the cavernous halls, knocking down painted wooden doors to clear each room. With Arcturas by my side, I flew through each doorway, scanning the empty spaces for the Spring Queen. Dirt and muck flung through the air as the battle outside pressed on.

A flood of northern men, shoving and trampling against the wall of our enemies, slammed into Balakros and me as we struggled to stay together. Spears lunged into abdomens, swords sliced across limbs, arrows pierced hearts. The strength of our reinforcements entirely over-whelmed the enemy, leaving them scattered and panicked as defeat closed in around them. It was utter turmoil.

Fighting monsters was one thing, but to take the life of another mortal was something else entirely. My mental log of names and faces grew exponentially. Glimpses of darkness flashed through me with each room we cleared. I pushed my rising guilt and grief back down my throat, telling myself that they were on the wrong side of history. They were the villains. My father once told me that death was inevitable in war. It was a necessary sacrifice to main-tain peace and morality over the realms. But these men, these enemies, were fathers, brothers, sons, lovers.

They were just like Lytos.

Just like Aryx.

And so, with the rising guilt, the rising grief, I allowed myself to slip away. To retreat into the safety of shad-ow. To become the monster everyone feared. The demon shrieked with violent delight as I watched man after man fall to my blade. I was losing myself to her power. I held on to reality by a delicate thread, stretching it further and further, waiting for it to snap.

Everything fell apart when my vision went dark and I sank into the depths, only to resurface when my blade plunged into the heart of a northern soldier. The blood stain on his purple tunic expanded as he gurgled and fell limp against me.

"Oh, my Gods. I- I didn't mean to." The hilt of my blade slipped through my fingers, and the golden weapon clanked against the tiled floor as the battle erupted around us. He looked up at me with shocked eyes, his mouth gulping like a fish from water as fluids filled his lungs. I steadied him in my arms, placing pressure on his wounded abdomen.

"Stay with me. I'm so sorry. I'm so sorry." My hands

348

trembled as I watched his expression fade away.

"Please," he choked. "Tell my mother I love her."

My legs turned to liquid as I held him. He was a son. Soon to be taken from his mother. Tears welled in my eyes as we lowered to the floor. He gasped and gargled, struggling to maintain consciousness.

"Please. Tell her," he whispered, his eyes rolling away.

"I'm so sorry. Stay with me. You'll get to tell her yourself."

I pushed harder against his swollen belly, hoping that if I applied more pressure, the blood now spewing from his wound would stay in his veins. His skin, although still warm, sagged against my touch and I knew it was too late. I pulled the helmet from his head, sobbing as I saw the boyish features.

He was blonde, like Aryx, with royal blue eyes now a muted shade of grey. He couldn't have been over fourteen. Forever a boy. He'd never live into adulthood, and it was all my fault. All of this was my fault. How many men would still be alive if I'd accepted my fate and stayed in that tower? If I'd just done what I was told and followed the rules? Yes, I'd rot away up there, but how many would still be here, still be breathing?

Every action has a consequence. Even the smallest, most insignificant of reaction can snowball into something far more overwhelming and destructive. I was the pebble that created this landslide. Now everything swept out from beneath me and I plunged into the darkness, unsure if I'd ever be able to claw myself back out.

I threw my head back, unable to hold in the deafening scream that now poured out of me. The sound echoed through the great hall, hurling soldiers into the air. The fighting stopped. Silence thickened the air as all the light extinguished inside me. I needed to end this. I needed to find Tethys.

Sheathing my sword, I rose to my feet. Avoiding the

bodies scattered across the floor, knocked unconscious from the sheer force of my pain, Arcturas and I sprinted through the large marble arches. A grand spiral staircase twisted and turned above me. I found it fitting that this journey's end began with a staircase. Just as it started.

The stench of plumeria burned my nostrils as I climbed the spiraling tower steps. Cracked marble walls, crumbling beneath thick, green roots, stretched above, blurring at the tower's peak. I continued climbing, taking steps two at a time, until my lungs were heavy and my legs seared with fatigue. Spinning around and around and around, I pulled myself up by the staircase bannister.

The chamber in the distance didn't grow closer with each step. No matter how many times I circled the diameter of the tower walls, it remained a speck on the horizon. I felt as if I'd been climbing for hours, having traveled no distance. Something was wrong, entirely wrong. Sweat dampened my armpits, and I pushed my legs to keep going until I was on the brink of collapse.

Stopping to catch my breath, my knees gave out, and I slipped up a step, chin cracking against the hard stone. The taste of blood oozed from my mouth as I continued to pant, rubbing my aching jaw. Just as I suspected, the chamber wasn't any closer.

I inhaled deeply, trying to calm the rising panic in my chest. Maybe this was a trap? The demon drew a long, sharp claw against my mind. Begging to be set free. I closed my eyes and pressed on, limbing rapidly around and around and around. When her roars receded back into my belly, I stopped to catch my breath. This was useless. I was wasting strength and time. The longer I risked climbing, the longer I allowed Tethys to break the wards around the island.

I paused, taking a moment to think. There had to be something here. Some sign of how to reach the top. I pressed my hand against the stone and closed my eyes, breathing in the sickly floral scent. A faint pulse pushed against my outstretched palm, like a heartbeat. The tower seemed to come to life from my touch. I quieted my mind and continued to listen. It swayed beneath me, rocking with the steady inhale and exhale of my lungs.

Opening my eyes, I watched as a faint shimmer rippled across the wall beneath my palm. Running my fingers across it, my thumb caught a latch. I pulled it and the wall crumbled away, leaving an ornate white door in its place.

Its lock clicked. Of course it'd be locked. Suddenly, I was back in my prison. The splintered door at the bottom of the steps. I pulled my key from its chain and inserted it into the door handle. The metal molded around it, filling the space between its bits. The door groaned against me as I twisted the key, feeling the lock click again. It swung open.

Closing it behind me and tucking the key back into my tunic, I ran down the endless hallway, listening for any sign of life within the musty corridor. Candles flickered to life as I passed them by, ignited by my presence.

The narrow hallway eventually opened up into a blindingly bright throne room. Shielding my eyes from the early morning sun pouring in from the long, stained glass windows, my vision adjusted. Seated atop a golden throne in the shape of a clam shell was Tethys. One slender hand rested across the ornate, bejeweled arm rest. The other held a fine-tipped dagger. The edge of its blade pressed against the trembling, long neck of my nephew.

Chapter 50

"Elpis, my dear. You made it! Good. Good. What a wonderful little family reunion." She leaned her head in her hand and kicked her foot casually across her knee.

"Aunt Elpis?" Vikar's eyes widened. "You're supposed to be in the tower."

His throat bobbed against the deadly edge of the blade. I hadn't noticed before, but blood dripped from the rigid, black vines wrapped tightly around his ankles.

"Let him go Tethys, or I-"

"Or you'll what? Kill me? I'm immortal, or have you forgotten? Stupid, insolent girl." Her lips spread into a dark smirk. Each perfectly placed dimple glared at me with poised cruelty. I clenched my fists, trying to keep the stitches of reality from reeling apart. I had to stay in control, even if it took every drop of self will not to unleash the demon and let her rip Tethys apart limb by limb.

The goddess pressed her blade further into Vikar's throat. A small droplet of blood leaked from the incision, streaming down his neck and staining his perfectly pristine amethyst tunic. "Take another step, and I'll slaughter him where he stands."

Vikar sobbed, his eyes pleading to be spared. Although a foot taller than the last time I saw him, he had the same boyish features. His voice was deeper, more mature than I'd remembered, but the familiar sweet undertone of childhood still lined his words.

Arcturas growled deeply beside me, her deadly eyes like arrows aimed at their target. One word and she'd pounce. Fury blossomed in the pit of my stomach, like a virus infecting my bloodstream until it devoured me entirely. I didn't notice that I'd stopped breathing amidst the shaking rage now coursing through my veins. Stay in control.

"Let him go. He's not a part of this," I hissed, watching the immortal rise to her feet.

"Oh, Elpis. He's as much a part of this as you are. You think I didn't know the moment I left Venia that you and my son had conspired against me?" With a snap of her fingers, the vines slithered up Vikar's legs and tightened around his chest, pinching the exposed skin of his arms until they drew blood.

"It's me you want. Not him. Let him go," I said, leaping forward the second her weapon left his throat.

She snapped her fingers again and a wave of power jolted through me, sending me spiraling through the air. The all-too-sweet smell of honeysuckle was heavy in the air, sucking up the oxygen until my lungs struggled to breathe.

"Haven't we done this before?" she laughed. "You can't touch me. Don't waste your breath even trying."

"LET HIM GO!" I roared, rising to my feet and unsheathing my sword.

Tethys froze at the sight of the golden blade. Her eyes followed the citrine gems that lined its center. "Why do you have that?"

I remained silent, charging at her again. Another snap of her fingers and the goddess evaporated, only to reappear on the opposing side of the throne room.

"Why do you wield that blade?" she asked. There was a tinge of desperation in her voice.

She snapped her finger again, freeing an invisible force that shoved me into the unforgiving metal armrest of the throne.

"It was a gift," I said, wiping blood from my lower lip.

"From whom?"

Arcturas pounced for her with bared fangs, only to skid across the floor once Tethys disappeared again.

A single out-of-place ringlet of golden hair hung down her cheek. Tucking it back behind her ear and smoothing the wrinkles in her blush colored dress, she asked, "Where is my son? Where is Aryx?"

I swallowed the lump in my throat, frozen in place at the mention of his name.

"Well?" she asked.

I halted in my tracks, the sword suddenly heavy at my side.

"Where is he?"

I looked into her eyes, rage burning through me until I felt like I might combust. "He's gone."

She stopped short, eyes widening. "What do you mean, gone?"

"He's dead. Your son is dead. Gone. In the immortal realm," I cried, swinging my blade toward her. She snapped again and vanished, only to reappear behind me.

"I see." A pang of sadness flicked across her perfect face, only for an instant.

I lunged for her again, and again she snapped and reappeared behind me.

"You might as well quit doing that. I wouldn't want you

to tire yourself out."

"He's dead because of you." The words seethed through my gritted teeth.

"No, my dear, he's dead because of you. I've done nothing."

I leapt for her, the demons scratching against my mind. With a wave of her hand, vines erupted from the stone floor, wriggling and slithering toward me. I slashed them away, cutting branch after branch around my ankles. There were too many to escape. The tendrils weaved between my feet, knocking me to the floor. Pain exploded at the base of my spine, leaving me breathless on the throne room tile.

Tethys stepped to the window, watching the violence and bloodshed transpire in the courtyards below. The walls dripped with scarlet death. The clank of blade against blade was deafening, and the roar of wounded men echoed through the keep's interior walls.

"Vikar, it seems your loyal army has sent reinforcements to you," she said, clenching her fists at her side.

"Please, Goddess, please let me go," he cried, struggling against the binds. With each frantic flail, they pressed into him more. Wheezing and gasping for air, my nephew struggled to breathe as they tightened around his chest.

"Vikar, stay still! They'll strangle you if you keep moving like that," I cried, watching as he gulped for breath.

"How sweet it is, how much you care for your nephew." With her hands laced behind her back, she stepped in close to Vikar. He shrugged away from her as she stroked a long, vicious finger down his cheek.

"Don't touch him," I growled, attempting to stand. My back protested, sending agonizing springs up my spinal column.

"It's only fair, Elpis. You took the life of someone I hold dear, now it's my turn." She snapped her fingers, and the vines pressed further into his skin.

Vikar coughed and groaned, his complexion turning blue from lack of oxygen. The vines continued to close around his abdomen, squeezing the muscle until it shredded beneath his skin.

"No!" I wailed, watching my nephew crumple into a heap of broken, bloody bone.

My heart stopped as I entered a world where Vikar ceased to exist. The taste of desperate grief was like iron on my tongue. Tethys smirked, watching me drown.

They say vengeance is never the answer. Retribution was more harmful than healing. In this moment, I didn't give a fuck. I needed to feel Tethys's life slip away between my hands. I needed to watch her body sink into the ground beneath my feet.

For Aryx.

For Vikar.

For all of my men that lay still on the battlefield outside.

For all the innocent mortals slaughtered on the streets of Aquilae.

For my sister, whose death was my prison sentence.

For the woman I could have been.

"You aren't leaving this island alive," I growled, unclasping the dagger at my side. Concealing the weapon behind my back, I took a deep breath, inviting the tingles that rushed from my feet, through my chest, and into the crown of my head. Arcturas hunched low and ready for my command.

I unleashed the demon from her chains. Muscle fibers reattached, bones splintered back into place. The pain was dulled enough for me to rise to my feet. My eyes glowed with moonlight. Wisps of loose black hair floated around me, a current rippling through each strand. Shadows burned in my palms. Time slowed to a stop.

Beams of starlight bounced off Aryx's blade, casting

speckles of stars across the room. For a moment, we were floating in the infinite of space, isolated from all else in the world. My wolf's howl raised the hairs on my arms.

Tethys lifted her hand to swipe me away. Before she could, however, I hurled my dagger from behind my back, its silver point glowing brightly with amethyst. In slow motion, the dagger spiraled through the air, piercing the center of her palm until the entire length of its blade embedded into flesh.

Screaming, I threw myself at the now-horrified goddess, swinging the sword down furiously across her slender bicep. The severed limb fell to the floor with a thud as her shrieks boomed in my ears. My heart pounded against my chest as the demon clawed against my mind, roaring with violent delight. Tethys fell to her knees, cradling her vacant shoulder. Blood spurted from the gaping wound.

"What did you do?" she hissed. Her soft pink gown, now stained a bright red, pooled around her delicate body. I stood over her, realizing how frail she truly looked when her facade of power was ripped away.

"Like I said." I knelt over her, the tip of my nose nearly touching hers. "You're not leaving this island alive."

She brushed her hand across my cheek. The sensation of her spidery fingers against my skin was cold, leaving the vile taste of disgust heavy on my tongue.

"Oh Elpis, my dear. You won't kill me," she laughed.

"And what makes you think that?" I raised the sharp edge of my sword to her neck, applying just enough pressure against her perfectly tanned skin to draw blood.

"Because I can help you bring back my son."

I sucked in a breath. "I don't believe you. His soul is at rest in the immortal realm. There's no way of bringing him back. He's gone."

I pressed the blade further into her skin.

"You're only half correct. His mortality is gone. He shares my blood. His immortal soul is still very much alive."

"This is just another one of your vicious lies, Tethys. I will not let you slip through my fingers," I hissed.

"Fine. Kill me. Live a life without him. Or take a risk, listen to me, save him."

With my blade still pressed against her throat, I considered the options. Did I dare trust her? Did I let her live after everything she'd done, all the blood she spilled? And what of Aryx's father? I wasn't sure where he was or how to find him without her. I searched her eyes for any hint of sincerity, any flicker of honesty.

"Where is Aryx's father?"

"Araes? He's not here."

"Tell me where he is and how to find Aryx. Maybe I'll consider letting you live a bit longer," I said, my fingers itching against the cool hilt of my weapon.

"Oh, sweet girl. Araes is locked away with all the idiotic mortals that dared to question me. Along with those pathetic old men you call your elders."

"What do you mean? I thought the Elders were loyal to you."

"They were once, but over the years, it seems they developed a sense of morality. It was exhausting," she said, wincing as she reached for her grey, limp arm oozing a pool of blood beside her.

"Tell me how to get to Aryx." I kicked the limb out of her reach.

"You have to go to the immortal realm. Past the kingdom, there's a river and a ferryman, Chiron. Make him an offering and he'll take you to him. Now please give me my arm back before I bleed out even more? This is my favorite dress, and it's ruined already."

I reached for a rusted chain beside us and wrapped it around her waist, making sure the bind was uncomfortable. Pulling Tethys to her feet, I gripped the chain and tied her amputated arm against my back. "First you're going to take me to Araes, then you'll show me the way to your son," I said, tugging on the chains. She grimaced and stepped in line behind me as we began down to the fortress yards, passing wide-eyed soldiers, bloody from battle.

Chapter 51

"My Queen, what is this?" Balakros jumped to his feet as we emerged through the gates, leaning heavily on his right leg. Seated beside him was Lytos, nursing a black and blue cheek.

"It's a long story. The Elders aren't here. Load up the army and let's prepare for the return home," I said, as he eyed the mangled arm strapped across my back.

"We lost a lot of men." He swallowed.

"I know, but the mission was a success," I said, yanking at Tethys's chains.

"We were doomed without the Northern Army. They couldn't have arrived at a better time. Although, no one sent for them. I'm not sure how they knew we were here."

"They were here to rescue their king." I swallowed. "He didn't make it."

Balakros looked at his hands, avoiding my eyes swollen with hurt.

"Elpis, I'm so sorry," Lytos said, rising to his feet.

"I can't talk about that right now," I said, my voice

clipped. "We won this battle, but there's still more to be done. For starters, we need to return home."

"Yes, My Queen. We'll take note of how many we have left. At first light, we'll load up and begin the journey home," Balakros nodded.

"Good, and start preparing for Tethys's loyalists to plan a counterattack."

"I thought the plan was to murder her." Lytos pointed to Tethys, now holding her head high.

"Don't point at me, mortal," she hissed, lifting her nose at him. "It reeks of death out here. Can we go, please?"

I turned to glare at her, giving the chain one last tug and knocking her to her knees. "You don't speak unless spoken to."

"My Queen, the men need to rest and recover before we set sail. I'm not sure we have even enough uninjured for a single crew. We need at least one night of recovery, maybe two." Balakros rubbed his swollen, broken knee.

"Setup camp for the night, but no longer. I'm going to continue on to the find the Elders and Araes myself. Rah will guide you through the seas and back home," I said.

"But what about your command? Who will lead us?" he pleaded.

"Balakros, don't be silly. You and Lytos will lead our men home. Make sure they return to their families. To their children. To their wives." I eyed Lytos.

"Wh-what? Me?" Balakros asked, his eyes wider than I ever thought possible.

"Yes. Set up aid tents, get our men rested and healed up. The fortress is empty and full of supplies. I trust you to make the right choices. Everything will be fine, I promise."

"Stay with us," he begged. "How will we make it home without your guidance?"

I shifted under my weight, slowly growing uncomfortable by his desperation. The leather breastplate I wore felt too small, and the salted sweat across my brow stung.

"Balakros. I need to do this. Stay with our men, take charge, be the leader I know you to be. That's an order."

He straightened against my command and nodded reluctantly.

"Yes, My Queen."

"I'll send notice to Procyon and Altair of your arrival," I said, scratching Arcturas behind the ear as she sat beside me, keeping her predatory eye on the quiet goddess.

Balakros limped off, spreading word through the groups of wounded men scattered around the battlefield. Lytos motioned for me to come closer. Nodding to Arcturas, I left the immortal under her watchful eye.

"Try anything and you'll never get this back," I hissed, pointing to her twitching arm strapped to my back.

She rolled her eyes, sighing dramatically and picking at a hangnail forming on a perfectly manicured finger.

"Why do I feel like there is something you're keeping from me?" Lytos asked, his voice merely a murmur.

"There's a chance to bring Aryx back. He's trapped in the immortal realm. I need to go get him," I whispered, watching Tethys wince as she poked at her shredded shoulder.

"How is that possible?" Lytos took in a breath, leaning against a blood-stained boulder.

"When he drowned, his mortal half died. But his immortal half returned to the realm of the gods. If there's a chance to bring him back, I have to take it," I said.

"And you trust her?" Lytos nodded toward Tethys.

"Of course not, but I can handle her. So long as I have this, she'll do as I say. She's desperate to maintain her beauty. She's not going to risk looking like a monstrosity missing a limb forever."

"I guess you have a point," he snorted, watching Tethys smooth back her perfect waves of blonde hair.

"She may be my only chance to get him back. I have to

362

do this." My voice shook.

"I know. Just...be careful. Please," Lytos said, pulling me into a hug.

His embrace was the gentle warmth of an old friend. All fear and uncertainty faded away in his arms. I sighed, letting his scent wash over me.

"Thank you for everything. We couldn't have won this war without you..." I trailed off, forcing the sobs back down my throat. "I wouldn't be here without you."

He placed his hands on my shoulders and smiled, the corners of his bright blue eyes dimpled. "Promise me you'll return, even if Aryx isn't able to."

"I promise," I whispered, pulling him in for another hug. "Get home safe."

Lytos nodded, kissing me gently on the forehead. I watched as he turned to rejoin our men, boisterous and beaming with victory. I may have lost the last remnants of my bloodline today, but these people were my family. Lytos, Balakros, every soldier that marched behind me.

"Now, how do we get to the immortal realm?" I asked Tethys, snarling at the disgust glistening in her eye.

Tethys, leaning against a boulder, struggled to her feet. "Finally. The smell is nauseating. I don't think I can stand to be here one more second. When each of us constructed our temples, we created gateways into the immortal realm. Luckily for you, when I built this fortress, I created one in the dungeons for easy passage off this gods-forsaken island."

"Alright, let's go then," I said, marching back to the castle.

"Unluckily for you, only a full immortal has assured safe passage through. No half-mortal has ever tried, so I'm not sure what will come of you."

"That's a risk I'm willing to take," I said, yanking on the chain that connected us.

"Then you are more of a fool than I thought," she

hissed, tripping behind me.

We plunged into the shadowy depths of the castle, passing frightened rats munching on the leftover bones of Tethys's enemies. We went lower and lower into the cool, damp earth. The dungeons felt as if they'd go on forever. Droplets of seawater fell from the stone-carved ceiling, their impact with the broken tiled floor echoing through the vast loneliness.

The earthen labyrinth mimicked its above ground sister structure with sharp twists and turns. By the time we reached the dungeon's core, day must have faded into night.

A splintered wooden door marked the entrance to the immortal realms. I had expected ornate carvings or glamorous golden door handles, not this rickety old thing that looked as if it was one kick away from disintegrating into splinters. The hinges, rusted from years of salty air, creaked and groaned as I pulled the door open. Nothing but swirling darkness and shadow greeted me behind its ancient frame.

"We go together," I said, pulling Tethys's chains so she stood next to me.

"Stupid girl," she spat. "You're going to get yourself killed."

"One. Two. Thr-" The goddess threw her shoulder against me, propelling us both across the threshold and into the black abyss that waited. Arcturas dove after me, her golden armor reflecting the last shadows of candlelight as we plunged into the immortal realm.

About the Author

As a mom of two littles, D.L. Houpt is used to the daily chaos. From a young age, she found herself escaping in the pages of fantasy novels. She loves writing stories, dreaming up magical worlds, and learning about mythology. When she isn't found typing up her new idea (most likely ignoring her husband to write), she's in the garden with her daughter or enjoying a book with her son.

Engineer by day, she uses her writing as an outlet to uplift powerful women whether they be behind a computer monitor in an office or a shield on the battlefield

If you enjoyed The Shadow of Polaris, please consider sharing with friends, reviewing online, and following on social media for announcements and updates regarding the next two books.

Instagram: @authordlhoupt

Milton Keynes UK
Ingram Content Group UK Ltd.
UKHW032121260824
447474UK00015B/229/J